THE WINTER SOLDIERS

Other novels by Garry Douglas Kilworth

Fancy Jack Crossman Novels:

The Devil's Own

The Valley of Death

Soldiers in the Mist

Other fiction:

Highlander

Witchwater Country

In The Hollow of The Deep-Sea Wave

Spiral Winds

House of Tribes

A Midsummer's Nightmare

The Navigator Kings trilogy

THE WINTER SOLDIERS

Garry Douglas Kilworth

CARROLL & GRAF PUBLISHERS
New York

Carroll & Graf Publishers
An imprint of Avalon Publishing Group, Inc.
161 William Street
NY 10038-2607
www.carrollandgraf.com

First published in the UK by Constable, 2002
an imprint of Constable & Robinson Ltd

First Carroll & Graf edition 2003

ISBN 0–7867–1111–6

Printed and bound in the EU

To John Ball, airman, sailor, boxer, jailer –
oh, and a pretty good marathon runner too.

Acknowledgements

My usual thanks go to David Cliff of the Crimean War Research Society and Major John Spiers, now a curator at the Light Infantry Museum, Winchester, for research, advice and encouragement.

1

The faces of the men were like stone. They looked bleakly across the heights above Sebastopol. Some of them were indeed only boys, a few as young as ten years. Their eyes appeared to have retreated deep inside their heads, and were empty of any expression but the nursing of a nagging, relentless misery. Those in trenches lay in thick mud, their brittle hands clamped to rifles wrapped around with stiff rags. Those in the lines behind, awaiting duty, were only marginally drier and warmer.

The soldiers stared keenly at the party of six saboteurs returning from a mission in Sebastopol. This small group had just passed through the outer picquets. They looked well-clothed in fur coats, fur hats and good thick leather boots. On the surface of things, they seemed men to be envied. They appeared to have the freedom to roam at will. In the middle of a Russian winter, in the middle of a foreign war, they did indeed seem kings compared with their fellow soldiers.

'Keep up, Yorwarth,' growled the tall leader of this group. 'You've been lagging all morning.'

Fancy Jack Crossman, seconded sergeant from the 88th Connaught Rangers, was the first to cross the line of British trenches, followed in single file by Lance-Corporals Peterson and Wynter, Private Yorwarth from the Australia colonies, a civilian barber named Gwilliams, and finally, taking up the rear as always, a Turkish irregular, Yusuf Ali. Every man kept his head low as there were always Russian sharpshooters ready to take it off his shoulders.

'Yes, keep up, Yorwarth,' said Lance-Corporal Wynter, 'don't dawdle!'

Wynter's tone was sarcastic. The words were aimed at his sergeant and not the named man. Wynter was exhausted and he felt everyone in the group had the right to lag behind if they felt so inclined. Wynter was belligerent and nasty but, when it came to comfort and survival, often ingenious. Most recently he had cut a hole in a large thick woollen sock and pulled it over his head. The hole revealed only a small circle of face, allowing the wearer to see and breathe freely. What remained of the sock kept the rest of his head and neck warm. Others, seeing this invention, had followed his example with great alacrity. Now what he had begun in Balaclava was all the fashion in the Heights.

As they passed a group of rag-bag soldiers, a young subaltern jumped in front of Crossman and made noises like a duck.

'Quack, quack, quack, quack.'

Crossman glared at the officer, who continued to grin into his face and make farmyard noises. A corporal came up and put his arm around the subaltern's shoulders, gently steering him out of Crossman's path, as a mother might do a bothersome child. He then turned to Crossman and tapped his own temple with his forefinger in explanation.

'Sorry, chum,' he said. 'Touched. Lost most of his men in a night raid. Came back like that.'

Crossman nodded, realizing. 'That's all right, corporal.'

A tower was chiming a recognizable tune nearby. Guns were booming along the allied lines and from the distant fortifications of the besieged Sebastopol came dull thumps blanketed by the winter mist. The temperature today was not the sword-sharp cold of some mornings, when the freezing winds came down from the steppes and sliced through shivering under-protected bodies. It was a damp stony cold which crept deep into men's bones, awakened painful agues and aches, and was unbearably persistent.

Crossman was not without feelings, even though this war, run it seemed by incompetent commanders, had done its best to drive them out of him. As he passed one regiment he saw that many of the soldiers had cut the sleeves from the greatcoats of dead men and had stuffed them with straw to use as leggings. He pitied their poverty. They had hay and straw bolstering their now brick-coloured tunics, which time had worn thin and filled with holes. With the cold and the shortage of water no one washed any more. Everyone had lice and fungus complaints.

Officers were almost indistinguishable from rank and file. Lace and gold trimming had completely vanished from one officer's uniform as he stood with arms folded, shivering under a ragged turban he had obviously bartered from a Tartar or a Turk. Most of the boots were cracked and split. Cavalry troopers had missing spurs, or none at all. Facings were unrecognizable: their former hues had been bleached, drained from them, dirtied, until they were either colourless or some brownish shade with no meaning or purpose any longer.

Crossman's thoughts were on this subject many an hour. Something had to be done about the unforgivable lack of warm clothing. Supply ships had been lost in storms, the Commissariat was unyielding in its passion for paperwork which delayed further shipments, the opening of stores already in the Crimea, and the distribution of badly-needed replacement uniforms, most of which had been worn constantly since leaving Britain over a year ago.

How can we continue in this manner, he thought, allowing men to die for want of a pair of socks? It was almost as bad as that. These terrible conditions were exacerbated by the total absence of wood for fires. Not only was the army underclothed, it could not keep itself dry and warm. With command of the Black Sea the British Navy could have shipped in cordwood from the Mediterranean. Two or three shiploads could have kept the army in fires for the whole winter! Yet nothing was done, despite the protestations of junior officers, and some senior ones.

To cap it all, there was the lack of shelter. Worn, torn and leaking tents from another era were in most cases the only cover for most of the British troops. There were supposed to be replacements around, but where were they? And would they ever be released?

None of this applied to the French, who had erected huts, had good supply lines and who ate hot food. It was a pity Lord Raglan disliked his French allies so much, or he could have taken something from their example. The French might well have been on a Riviera holiday, compared with the British, who were in Hell.

Most British officers, as well as their men, would have agreed that the war was being managed by fools. Yet battles were being fought and won, against massive odds, and possibly for the first time junior officers, NCOs and private soldiers were taking the initiative. They had had to, for it was missing from headquarters. More than one soldier grieved the passing of a commander-in-chief like Lord Wellington. Happily it seems to be a fact of army life that whenever there is gross incompetence at the top ingenuity rises up from the bottom to counter it.

The six returning saboteurs were billeted in a hovel in Kadikoi, a small village just north of Balaclava. This area had now been populated by sutlers. They were in the main itinerant merchants, traders, riffraff, gentlemen travellers and sightseers (though not so many of those since the weather had turned bad), oxen handlers, camel owners, several prostitutes and their masters, entertainers, anyone in fact hoping to make a penny out of a war in stalemate. Along with these there were the usual camp followers – wives and others – who trailed after an army on campaign. The collection of makeshift stalls and huts set up by Greeks, Egyptians, Bulgars, Tartars, and a score of other nationalities was known amongst the troops as Vanity Fair – or Donnybrook to the Irish – and if there was any small coin left out of one's meagre army pay, and that soldier was prepared to trudge along the trammelled and troughed track over the Col, it could be spent here on food and drink, whatever. Prices were high though, and money was scarce. It was a long way to go to be screwed out of hard-earned tuppences for the sake of a weak beer and unleavened bread.

Some of the stall owners greeted the six, especially Wynter, who was well known to several of the young and old whores prepared to freeze their nether regions for a ha'penny.

'Hey, Harry-boy, you come see Mary tonight, yes?'

'I'll be there, sweetheart,' answered Wynter. 'You keep the blanket warm for me.'

Lance-Corporal Peterson spat on the ground in front of Wynter.

'I wonder it don't break off, like an icicle,' she observed, nodding down.

Wynter rose to the bait. 'At least I've got one to break off,' he snorted. 'That's your trouble. You wanted to be a man and you ain't. If you was, you'd know it's worth a bit of cold.'

'At least I'm not wasting away, like you men.'

Most the six had lost weight over the last several months: Peterson alone had filled out. When she had first joined Crossman's *peloton* she had been a skinny young maiden disguised as a youth, a brilliant sharpshooter but with little else to offer. Most of those close to her now knew her secret, but two of her superiors, Crossman and Major Lovelace, were prepared to overlook it, she having proved her worth. The third, a Lieutenant Pirce-Smith, was new to the world of the spy and saboteur. He was so far ignorant, and kept this way.

Now Peterson had become a burly woman, her beardless chin and cheeks standing out among the hirsute faces of her companions, her small bosom, squashed almost flat by a now extra-tight coatee, normally hidden by the voluminous fur coat she had acquired. Why she put on weight was a mystery to herself and others, since she ate the same fare and underwent the same exercise. It was one of those quirks of nature. Wynter put it down to the selfishness of the female gender. He said she grew large by drawing on the fat of her fellow soldiers, somehow, by the use of Eastern magic.

'You're workin' us!' he accused her. 'You bought somethin' from some Afghani faker. I bet you've got a monkey's paw stuck in your haversack. I'm watching you, Peterson.'

Peterson was no longer overawed by soldiers like Wynter, a conniving, cunning and essentially lazy man who had to be spurred into action, but once there was a crafty and useful tool for Crossman. Once upon a time she had hated men, having tried to make her living as a female carpenter in civilian life, but driven out by the prejudices and stupidity of males who saw their livelihood threatened and their territory being invaded by a wench. Now she simply despised most of them. Major Lovelace she treated as a god, but with the distant reverence of a polite member of a religious group, someone who was not so much a believer as a person willing to go along with others for the sake of being a member. In Fancy Jack Crossman she recognized a man who was prepared to accept her for what she could do rather than for what she was. She admired his sense of fairness, expediency and his powers of leadership.

But for the most part she considered herself better than most men, tougher in spirit, stronger in endurance and stamina, more able to withstand hardships and cold, certainly more able with a weapon, and only on occasion lacking slightly in the physical strength needed to lift a cannon out of a rut, or overcome an enemy with her bare hands alone. At such times she would rather die than look to a man for assistance. So far she had managed to escape having to haul cannons and she was never without a knife to hand.

'It's not a monkey's paw,' she told Wynter this time, as they entered the hovel. 'It's the Hand of Fatima. I've got it hidden. Soon you'll be nothing but a walking skeleton, rattling along, all loose bones. It's the power of the curse, Wynter, you poor fool.'

Wynter stopped short, so that Yorwarth ran into the back of him. They clashed heads. Yorwarth growled, 'Watch it, you sorry arse,' but, pushed on by the man behind, tramped to his cot in the corner of the room.

The reason Wynter was disturbed was because he had only been joking, or half-joking, but Peterson's words had a ring of authenticity about them. Wynter had heard the phrase before, from the lips of Egyptian stall owners who sold slim pancakes they called 'Fatima's Fingers'. The Hand of Fatima and the Evil Eye had been imported to the Crimea by Moslem immigrants. The phrases were not understood by the British soldiers, and subsequently remained boxed in mystery and dusted with menace. Peterson's words were enough to send an icy streak down the back of the sock-headed Wynter, who was superstitious and believed in ghosts, magic and all other mysteries of life and death.

'That ain't legal,' whined Wynter at Peterson, pulling off his tight headgear with difficulty. 'I'll see the general. You can't use gypsy curses in the army.'

'You'll see no one,' said Crossman. He sniffed. 'When are you going to take a wash, Wynter? Look, you're dropping fleas.'

'We all stink, why does everyone pick on me? Everyone picks

on me. You can't use curses like that. It ain't legal. I'll . . .' He changed his mind on meeting Crossman's eye. 'I'll do somethin' of my own. I'll use my pet rat on you. You wait, Peterson. You won't be able to go to sleep peaceful in your cot.'

'That's right, get a rat to do a rat's work,' said Gwilliams, coming in last but one. 'That's right. Anyway, we ate your rat before we went out – remember?'

Wynter remembered. They had run short of meat and Gwilliams had cut the head off the rat Wynter had tamed and roasted it. Fury rose in his breast, for the indifference shown to himself and the lack of mercy shown his rat.

'An' you can shut up, too. That rat was my property. You stole my property, you did. Bloody Yankee-doodles. Bloody civilians. Everyone picks on me. Who's next, eh? Who's next?'

The last to come through the doorway was Yusuf Ali, a man so formidable in physical appearance, being large, rotund, but without an ounce of fat on his powerful frame, further moist words dried to dust in Wynter's mouth. He had once seen a seemingly unarmed Ali slit a man's throat in a split second, the killing stroke visible only by the flash of the knife which had appeared from nowhere, and subsequently disappeared after being wiped on the dying man's chest, before he hit the ground. In some lights Ali might be mistaken for a jolly uncle in colourful waistcoats, pantaloons and floppy boots. In others for the heartless demon of the lamp. Wynter was terrified of him and turned without another word, to throw himself onto the cot he now shared with Gwilliams, they both being spare, wiry men and beds being short in the hovel.

Jack Crossman went straight away up the uneven stone stairs to the room above, where he knew he would find Major Lovelace. The major was sitting on the edge of his timber-frame bed trimming his beard. In contrast to some of the less fortunate officers at the Crimea, the major was clean, smart and well-fed. He was not, however, one of the princely group who had more money than was good for them. He was not one of those whom Crossman despised for their thoughtlessness and arrogance.

Those were officers who had hampers sent from England, taking up hold space on ships which should have been carrying the much needed supplies. Those with chests full of dress uniforms, civilian shooting suits, Runciman boots, black dancing pumps. Those who stepped out of a Sunday morning in tweeds, going for a brisk walk over the Russian landscape with hardly a care in the world, almost as if they were on their family estate back in Britain.

Some of them even imported their eccentricities. One habitually wore a fez and carried a walking stick.

Major Lovelace, though possessing a normal young man's vanity, was not a popinjay. He was dedicated to the gathering of information and the surreptitious destruction of the enemy's property. In order to carry out such work he often had to resemble a Tartar workman or farm hand. Off duty, he liked to be clean and reasonably smart.

Lovelace looked up from admiring himself in his mirror.

'Well, how did it go?'

'We destroyed a small arsenal in Star Fort. You must have heard it go up?' The two men were on familiar terms for a lowly sergeant and a field officer. It was not due to the fact that they had both attended Harrow which was responsible for this, but because the intimate, devious and insidious nature of their work made a detached and formal relationship impossible.

Lovelace smiled. 'I think we heard something, amongst the boom and blast of cannon and mortar.'

'Sorry, I forgot there was a bombardment today. Yes, you're right, the explosion would have been just another bang from here. Well, we did it all right. No one left behind, either. Look,' for a moment he almost called Lovelace by his Christian name, but then stopped short of this leap towards unthinkable familiarity, 'can I speak to you about a problem?'

'Of course,' Lovelace put down his scissors, 'that's what I'm here for.'

'I don't like having this man Gwilliams in the *peloton*.'

'What's wrong with him?'

'Where do I start? He's an American . . .'

'He says he's Canadian. Says he's spent a lot of time below the border, in the west, but he has Canadian citizenship. That makes him loyal to the queen. Anyway, you're not prejudiced against Americans, are you? You seem to like that correspondent for the *New York Banner*. Jarrard.'

'I know an American accent when I hear one. He didn't just pick that up while he was travelling. He's American. He's a civilian. I'm not prejudiced against any man's nation. And Rupert Jarrard's different: I don't have to take him out into the field.'

'Gwilliams was a corporal in the Canadian marines. He's got his discharge papers to prove it. Now he's one of the official army barbers. You know Colonel Hawke proposed him for our merry band of saboteurs? He said a barber must be good with a razor,' he drew the blunt edge of the one in his hand across his throat, 'and that will make him invaluable on assassination missions, now that our Irish-Indian Thug, Clancy, has unhappily drowned himself and taken his skill with the knotted cord to his watery grave with him.'

Crossman realised this man Gwilliams told different stories to different people.

'That may be so, sir,' Crossman was growing frustrated, 'but Gwilliams is not in the marines now. I have no control over him. Oh, he hasn't done anything terrible yet, but I don't want to find myself in a position in an emergency where I need instant and immediate response to an order only to have him blow a wet raspberry at me. The man's positively menacing. And he upsets the others with his continual bragging about the famous characters he's supposed to have shaved – Kit Carson, Henry Wells and Bat Robertson.'

Lovelace's eyes opened wide. 'Never heard of any of them, myself. Who on earth is Bat? Does he play cricket? Or does he clear belfries of flying vermin?'

'Neither. He was a criminal and is now what they term a lawman – and, I understand, well known to citizens of several isolated settlements of the American hinterland. Kit Carson was an army scout whose exploits caught the imagination of the ordinary populace. Henry Wells is the main founder of a new and rapidly growing stagecoach line which links the continental towns of North America. You would have to read some of these pamphlets Gwilliams waves under everyone's noses. They have titles like *The Cowardly Killers of Sheriff Dan Skerrit* and *Who Shot Black Jake of Cutler's Creek?* Jarrard used to write them at one time, before he landed a newspaper job. He said he made most of them up.'

'They sound a little lurid for my taste. And this fellow Robertson – one can be both criminal and a policeman?'

'According to Jarrard, one rarely becomes a lawman in the American west without first becoming an outlaw. The latter seems to be a prerequisite for the job of thief-taking and peace-keeping. Something about being one to know one. Apparently the lines are fuzzy between the areas of employment in any case. Ordinary decent American citizens, like Jarrard, distrust both outlaws and lawmen. And politicians, of course, but I think we share that bias with them. Jarrard also has grave misgivings about Gwilliams by the way. He speaks of him as "a low reprobate" and untrustworthy.'

'I think there's a little bit of the green-eyed monster in Jarrard. He'd like to be in this war too, but he has to remain an observer, looking in from the outside. I think he's jealous that we've taken on Gwilliams. Now look, sergeant, none of the people in your *peloton* are entirely palatable creatures. They're all in there because there's something unsavoury about them, all except Peterson, and we know why the regiment wanted to get rid of her.'

'Her small stature,' replied Crossman, diplomatically.

'Precisely.'

Lovelace began to put on his uniform, while Crossman, actually exhausted after his mission into Sebastopol, lay on his commander's bed and locked his hands behind his head for a pillow.

'Don't get too comfortable. You're coming to see the general.'

Sergeant Crossman was just expostulating when Lieutenant Pirce-Smith, the second-in-command, walked through the door. Both the men in the room could see by his face that he was dreadfully shocked. The sight of an unkempt sergeant lying on a bed, while a major stood beside it, had stunned him, robbed him of speech.

Lieutenant Pirce-Smith had recently replaced the late Lieutenant Dalton-James, but only physically. In all other respects, from their hyphenated names to their immaculate dress, they were twins. Not soulmates, for they appeared to share the same soul, though one was now dead and the other walking God's earth exactly in the other's footprints.

'I was just telling the sergeant that Colonel Hawke wished to see all three of us at our convenience.' He turned to Crossman. 'Which as you know, sergeant, means *now*. So get your dirty feet off my blankets and if I were you I'd change those stinking socks before we go.'

'These stinking socks, sir, are all I have.'

'Then borrow a pair of mine, man, but wash them before return, or you'll get a laundry bill.'

The colonel was as usual buried beneath a pile of paperwork. Hawke – known by many as Calcutta Hawke due to the fact that his mother was an Indian lady and wife of an East India Company man, though in fact he had been born in a small country cottage in Surrey – had taken over from General Buller. 'A hawk for a bull,' Jarrard had said. 'It's extraordinary how many men take on the attributes of their names. Buller was short-sighted, Hawke is keen-sighted. Or reputed to be.' Hawke was lean, with iron-grey hair at the temples. Men termed him a handsome devil and women were known to be afraid of him. His office, and bed, were in a Tartar barn at the bottom of a pleasant slope, beyond which was a peach tree orchard. He greeted the two officers first and then turned to Crossman.

'Been out on a fox hunt, eh? Remind me.'

'Star Fort, colonel,' said Crossman, knowing the colonel was perfectly aware of his mission. 'One of their arsenals.'

The colonel's eyes crinkled at the edges as he narrowed them in approval. 'Well done.' He then turned to Pirce-Smith. 'Invaluable soldier, the sergeant. Speaks Russian now, eh? And pretty good at French and German, I understand. Comes of a fine education, somewhere, which he won't tell me about.' He paused to stare at Crossman, before adding, 'In the meantime, I want to get rid of a general.'

Crossman's heart sank. He had a strong suspicion that he was going to be ordered to do something quite unpalatable. It was not so long ago he had been ordered to shoot a traitor, someone from their own side, a British officer. It had not been a pleasant mission by anyone's judgement. Crossman was not as cold and ruthless as at least two other men in the room. Pirce-Smith he did not know at all, but he guessed that the lieutenant was a kitten compared with Lovelace. The major had not been available for the mission, or Crossman would never had had to commit murder, that being the proper name for an assassination. Lovelace would have done it without a qualm, in the name of duty and patriotism. There was, Crossman supposed, nothing wrong with being a patriot. What worried him were the precedents they were setting for the future.

'A general?' he repeated, bleakly. 'I hope you are not asking me to shoot one of *our* generals, sir?'

Pirce-Smith said, 'You forget yourself, sergeant.'

Hawke waved a hand at the lieutenant. Then to Crossman, he said, 'He is one of our generals, but he's a thorn in my side. I almost didn't need you. He was hit by a Russian sharpshooter while out riding the other day, but the damned fool only struck him in the hand.' The colonel continued. 'They took off two fingers with a bread knife, but he managed to avoid infection, and there's no gangrene, so he's walking around again.' The colonel paused, as if all present should contemplate the vagaries of life. How could fate be so cruel as to let his enemy get away with a clean flesh wound? 'Yes, bread knife, eh?' The regimental surgeons were down to using whatever tools were available for their amputations and various sorts of kitchen knives were being used in the *butchers' tents* where the operations took place. 'No, what I want you to do is to spy on the beggar. General Enticknap. Just keep me informed as to what he's up to, what he's saying to people, that sort of thing.'

'Is this – well, I mean, for the general good of the war?'

Hawke stared at him again, this time the narrowed eyes were not commendatory. He knew exactly what Crossman was saying. He had been told that there had been the same sort of disapproving tone and manner when General Buller, the previous head of Espionage and Sabotage, had ordered Sergeant Crossman to assassinate a traitor. The problem was the sergeant was always seeking moral justification for his actions. He failed to see what the colonel saw – that this was war. Lord Raglan was much the same, possibly worse. Always seeking to keep things gentlemanly and honourable, instead of looking to expediency.

Lovelace broke the silence. 'In a sense,' he said to Crossman, 'it is for the general good. General Enticknap is a blocker and a fusser. He blocks plans just for the sake of it. He fusses over details. Forgive me, sir,' he said to Hawke, 'but to speak freely, if I may, General Enticknap has the mind of a bank clerk. Give him ts to cross and is to dot and he is a happy man. Given a plan of attack with a reasonable chance of success and an acceptable percentage loss of men, he worries, and frets, and eventually decides to veto it when Lord Raglan asks for a vote in that peculiar democratic way he has of shrugging off responsibility.' Lovelace paused, before adding, 'In short, General Enticknap is lengthening the war and costing the lives of soldiers who die in the trenches of disease, enemy shelling and the cold. The sooner we force an all-out attack the better, and then we can all go home.'

'You've got that barber fellow,' said Colonel Hawke, turning from Crossman and assuming that Lovelace's speech was enough for any man to nod his head in agreement. 'Use him. Get him into the staff officers' dwellings, cutting hair, shaving, that sort of thing. Men say things with a barber around that they wouldn't tell their mothers. A barber is like a valet, invisible after a while. You don't notice him. Get Gwilliams in there, in Enticknap's little circle, and see if we can get something on him. That's all, sergeant. Well done, on the fox hunt. I expect you're looking forward to the next one, eh? That's the stuff.'

Crossman saluted and left the room, as the colonel was saying, 'Now, lieutenant, I've been meaning to have a chat with you. You can stay, Lovelace. Nothing you can't hear . . .'

Crossman walked the long mile back to Kadikoi feeling grim. He was certain that an animosity, a vendetta possibly, existed between Colonel Hawke and General Enticknap, and that he, Crossman, was being used as a secret weapon in this personal war. Lovelace had not helped by intervening. Crossman was sure the major had only done so as a diplomatic move to keep the peace, for there was no doubt who would have lost such an encounter. Crossman knew that Lovelace valued him, did not want to lose him, and would rather he swallowed his principles. He could of course neglect to tell Gwilliams to spy on Enticknap, but the efficient Lovelace would smoke that out in a very short time.

Since there was little he could do about it now, Crossman tried to put the whole thing out of his mind. It was one of those unusually bright days that appear as if by magic in the middle of January. For some reason the guns had stopped firing. It gave the scene a false air of tranquillity and hopefulness, for there would be men dying in the trenches: if not by a sharpshooter's bullet, a victim of the elements, melancholy or some dread infection of the body. Yet Jack Crossman could not help but feel lifted, despite his dissatisfaction with those who ran the army. Columns of smoke were curling up from the hills behind the battle area: crofts perhaps, or even hovels. It didn't matter. They were signs of normal life. They were not the black choking smoke of cannons, but white smoke from farmhouses lucky enough to have stockpiled wood for the winter.

A girl, a young woman, came down the track on his left, heading for the edge of Balaclava harbour. In front of her she ushered a flock of complaining geese. Crossman knew the goose girl by sight. He had seen her several times, passing through Kadikoi with her charges. He stopped to let her pass, knowing that if he tried to walk through the middle of her flock the geese would peck at his thighs. As a young boy he had been terrified of such birds. They had been as tall as he had been in those days, and in the past he would have run a mile rather than challenge their territory.

'Hello,' he said. 'A bright morning.'

He spoke in the local tongue and she looked up quickly, surprised, before blushing and dipping her head. Crossman saw that her hair was hennaed a coarse red, making it look stiff and brittle, and that her face was filthy, yet underneath there was a comeliness he had not seen in many Tartar girls. She had round features, with large dark eyes. Some young Tartar swain would fall deeply in love with those eyes and, thought Crossman, would tell her how beautiful she was. When that happened she would blossom from this green girl into a glowing woman. There was nothing like compliments to bring out radiance in females; or perhaps it was simply knowing that they were loved that wrought the change. He watched her back as she swayed along the difficult icy path, wondering if she would look back at him. She did not.

There was a good deal of traffic going down the main Kadikoi street, to and from the harbour. He was not exactly the model soldier in his ratty furs and filth. Yet most other soldiers were in much the same state, and many officers too.

When he reached the hovel he found a horse tied up outside. That was ominous. They had an unexpected visitor. He hoped whoever it was would not keep him long, because now he was thoroughly fatigued and wanted above all things to fall into his cot and sleep away the rest of the day. There was however the welcome smell of hot stew coming from within: probably one of Peterson's concoctions.

Crossman entered the dwelling to find an officer from his own regiment, the 88th Connaught Rangers up on the Heights. He was pacing impatiently up and down the small space taken up by the hard-earth floor. Peterson was, predictably, at the stove. Most of the others were already asleep in their fur coats, or under the odd blanket. The officer, a rather elderly subaltern, stared at Crossman as he came through the door. Neither knew the other, except by sight. Crossman vaguely recalled that the man's name was Thorax or Borax. Something like that.

'Sergeant Crossman.'

'Sir?'

'Colonel Shirley asked me to come and see you. He wants a favour – for the 88th – for your own regiment, sergeant.' The last few words were in the tone of *in case you had forgotten*.

Peterson looked up from her cooking but said nothing. Crossman showed due surprise. 'The colonel wants a favour from *me*?'

The officer seemed embarrassed, and turned away as he said, 'It's those damned bells, you see.'

Crossman did not see. He had no idea what the lieutenant was talking about. Bells? What bells? He was exhausted. His mind was buzzing and he needed to rest. This shortened a temper which had got him into trouble with authority in the past. 'I'm afraid I'm not with you, sir. I would be grateful for an explanation. I'm rather tired so I would appreciate your getting to the point – sir.' His tone was deferential and his delivery polite, but Crossman's manner and the way this came out revealed his confidence in himself as the son of an aristocrat. It might have been a curt demand, prior to a dismissal of the visitor.

Another officer might have exploded. This one simply raised his eyebrows and half-closed one eye. Perhaps it was because he had seen a good few army years, without any hope of promotion since he was incredibly poor and field promotions were thin on the ground. Perhaps he was just war-weary, or life-weary, and nothing really mattered any more. Whatever the reason, he remained calm. Crossman felt the stirrings of a growing respect for the man.

'The bells I refer to,' he said, patiently, 'are in a clock tower close to the position the battalion holds in the line. They are a constant annoyance, disturbing in the extreme. They keep us awake, and mock our very existence. Perhaps that seems a little strong, but you haven't had to put up with this monstrous chiming the way the rest of your regiment has, you and your men, sergeant, being billeted in this cosy little house some six miles behind the lines.'

'With due respect, sir, we spend very little time in this cosy little house. We are more often sleeping in a ditch. I take it the colonel wants us to do something clandestine in order to rid him of these meddlesome clock tower bells?'

'Quite.'

'Why don't you simply knock out the tower with a gun? A round shot in the right place will end its career as a disturber of the peace, surely?'

'The tower is behind Russian lines. It's part of a school for naval cadets. A strange-looking structure, tall, but covered with projections and ledges. It's a rather ugly piece of architecture if you ask me, but then that's neither here nor there. What is relevant is that a very old and revered church stands in its way. We can see the top of the tower in all its Gothic glory, but it would be a supreme gunner who could destroy that tower without hitting one of Sebastopol's ancient holy monuments. The colonel rather baulks at destroying a sacred historical building, as you will understand, simply to remove what is, in the end, only an annoyance. We felt you could perhaps slip over one night from the Heights, with your merry band of men, and blow the thing up.'

Crossman, weary beyond relief now, sat down heavily on the edge of Peterson's cot. 'This,' he said, 'sounds a rather dangerous favour. It would be putting men's lives at risk for what you yourself have described as a mere annoyance . . .'

'There's nothing *mere* about it. It's a huge annoyance.'

'But an irritation, none the less.'

'I'm understating the effect it has on us, because I know that underneath all that muck you're actually a gentleman. As one gentleman to another, I rather dislike having to beg favours, so I make light of what is in fact a very serious matter. This chiming is undermining morale. It eats away at our spirits. It stops us from sleeping properly, damn it, sergeant.'

Peterson interrupted. 'Let's do it, sergeant. We owe the battalion something. It's *our* regiment.'

'All right, all right.' Sleep. He just wanted sleep. 'Sir, tell the colonel I'll do my best.'

The lieutenant allowed himself a smile. 'Thank you, sergeant. It won't be forgotten. Now I must get that nag back to Captain Rushbrooke, he'll be fretting. It's his darling. Personally, I think it's got a weak mouth, but since I'm not a field officer, nor ever will be, nor do I have the wherewithal as Rushbrooke does, to purchase a private mount, I must make do with loans and borrows. I'll be seeing you, sergeant.'

'Yes sir,' said Crossman, and fell instantly asleep on Peterson's cot.

Peterson stared at her sergeant and shook her head. These men. They were her companions, but they had so little stamina. She ate some of her soup, left the rest on a warm stove, and then climbed the stairs to occupy the bed of Fancy Jack, the sergeant whom the rankers in the 88th suspected of being an officers' spy (for why would gentry be in the ranks in the first place?) and the officers suspected of having been disgraced by some scandal and hiding in the ranks under an assumed name.

It was true that 'Crossman' was a pseudonym, but it had not been necessary because of any scandal on the sergeant's part, more that of his hated father, a libertine and whoremonger, who had impregnated Crossman's mother and let her die in a workhouse, later removing the love-child and giving it to his wife to raise. Crossman had always believed his father's wife to be his real mother, and continued to treat her as such, but his father was dead to him, though physically only a short distance away, a major in the 93rd Sutherland Highlanders. Until recently his half-brother, James, of whom he was very fond, had also been with the 93rd, but a sick James had recently returned to Scotland.

When Crossman woke refreshed, much later in the day, he realized what he had done. It had been stupid of him, to make such a promise, but there was no going back on it now. A gentleman's word and all that. Crossman gathered his *peloton* around him and told them what he had pledged to the lieutenant. 'You can refuse to go, of course,' he added. 'I'll leave that option open to you. Peterson and I will go. We've already said we would. But I can't force the rest of you. Especially you, Ali, and Gwilliams. You're not 88th. You have no obligation. This is not an official mission.'

'I go,' grunted the Turkish Bashi-Bazouk. 'You go, I go.'

'Thank you, Ali. I appreciate it.'

Predictably Wynter said, 'Well I ain't goin'. An' that's flat. What do I owe them buggers on the Heights?'

'Loyalty,' suggested Peterson, cleaning her rifle. 'Comradeship.'

'Bugger those.'

'I'll go in this coward's place,' growled Gwilliams, a large stocky man with a magnificent auburn beard that looked as if it belonged on the chin of an Assyrian king. It was, like his hair, long and curly, and it shone like burnished copper in the sunlight. It jutted from his chin like an oblong wavy block and was cut square at the end. 'As you say, it don't mean nothin' if you ain't in a regiment, but I'm not one to shy away from a bit of excitement. Not like this mealy-mouthed lizard.'

'You watch who you're callin' a lizard!' cried Wynter, stung more by the word *coward* than the reptile epithet. 'One of these days you're goin' to get my boot in your back.'

'Any time, lizard.'

Wynter turned away, his mouth sour-looking. There was still Yorwarth left. Private Dan Yorwarth was an unpredictable seventeen-year-old. Along with his family he had been transported to Botany Bay as a very young child, for the theft of a calf. His mother had died on the voyage to the antipodes, his father later, under the whip of an overseer on an Australian farm. Yorwarth had served his time and returned to Britain, where he found it impossible, as it always had been for one without a trade, to make a living, and so joined the army. God knew, if Sergeant Crossman didn't, what resentment and hatred Yorwarth harboured for authority and the establishment. He showed nothing, gave nothing away and if anyone tried to probe, as Peterson had done, they were given short shrift. On the surface he seemed placid enough. Perhaps he had forgiven and forgotten, but Crossman doubted it.

'How about you, Yorwarth?' asked Crossman.

'It's my regiment too,' he replied with sweet naivety. 'The 88th. An Irish regiment. I ain't never been to Ireland, but I'd like to go, some day. They say it's very green.'

'Like you,' muttered Wynter.

'Good.' Crossman was pleased. 'That's enough of us. We can do it without Wynter.'

'We can do anything without Wynter,' said Gwilliams. 'Fact is, things is done better without him.'

But Wynter was not to be goaded into joining the party, if that was the intention. He remained determined to stay behind. When Lovelace returned, Crossman put the proposal to him. Lovelace shook his head. 'I don't know anything about this,' he said. 'I'm due to go up country today, so I'm leaving without knowledge of this unofficial fox hunt.'

'Understood,' murmured Crossman.

The following morning Crossman and his *peloton* set out for the walk over the Col to the section in the British line held by the 88th. Ali was carrying the haversack with the explosives. The sturdy Turk's head had almost disappeared down between his shoulders. He had a turtle-like ability to hunch inside himself when the wind was keen. The sun had disappeared again and it was a bitterly cold day. Clouds seemed to hang in the sky above the hills as if their hearts had stopped. There was no animation in the faces of the men: to smile or frown meant to crack the stiff skin on one's face. Feet and hands were like blocks of stone, encumbrances to the walker. It would have been better had it been just a touch colder, thus numbing their body parts, for there was real pain at this temperature.

The same lieutenant who had visited them at the hovel was waiting in the trenches. He indicated they should keep low as they came near. 'Sharpshooter!' he said. 'Already killed one of the Flank Company early this morning, returning from piquet duty.'

They did as they were bid. Once in the trench, ridged with hardened mud and frozen slops, Crossman asked to be shown the tower. Even as the lieutenant was standing on the banquette pointing it out, the bells chimed. In the stillness of the morning it sounded extraordinarily loud. However, so did the guns, from both sides of the siege, when they opened up after a few tolls of the bells, drowning them out.

'I know what you're going to say,' said the lieutenant. 'The guns are louder. But the guns do not go on night and day, without respite. The chimes of that bell do.' At that moment the guns ceased their barrage. The clock tower was still sounding. Crossman realized it was playing a tune.

'There,' said the lieutenant. 'You hear that?'

Crossman did indeed recognize the melody, as did Peterson, though Ali and Gwilliams remained ignorant. '"Widdicombe Fair",' Crossman said.

'Old Uncle Tom Cobbleigh and all. It used to play a Russian tune, but they've adjusted the striking mechanism. They're mocking us. This might be an Irish regiment, but there're still many in the 88th who hail from England. I don't know about you, sergeant, but I cannot stand being ridiculed. It makes me burn. None of us can bear it. Not the colonel, not the sergeant-major, not even the Irish – they know that if the Russians were aware of the regiment's origins those clock tower bells would be playing "Tipperary".'

Crossman nodded. 'Well, we'll do our best. We'll wait here until dark and then go over there.'

'Right. Some of the men have managed to forage some boxwood from the edge of the French camp. Would you like a hot drink, sergeant – and your men, of course? We can't offer coffee, but there's some tea from Major Swetterton's private mull store.'

'Thank you, yes, sir.'

Crossman sipped his tea with relish. It warmed his hands as well as his belly. Two soldiers in front of him were about to go out on forward picquet duty. They were squibbing their rifles: firing small blank charges of powder to dry out the damp barrels. Misfires and hang fires were common when the rifles had been left unused for a time in the misty damp area of the trenches. Gwilliams warned the two men that the *peloton* would be coming past them, and hopefully back, later in the evening. The two Irishmen, one about seventeen, the other in his mid-twenties, promised not to shoot any shadowy figures on sight. Gwilliams, of Irish ancestry himself, chatted to the two men, finding they were uncle and nephew, from Cork, and that they'd joined the army because they were cold and hungry.

'Sure, I'm still hungry,' said the uncle with typical Irish humour, 'and a lot colder, besides.'

They went off after that, into the gloom of the falling twilight, though it was still afternoon.

Once the darkness was complete, Crossman and his men set out too, over the rough ground. Yorwarth and Gwilliams were carrying carbines, slung over their shoulders. Crossman had his private weapon, a five-shot Tranter revolver. Ali carried a variety of pistols and knives. Only the sharpshooting Peterson carried a conventional British infantryman's rifle, a 0.70 calibre long-range Minié which she would not part with, even on such an enterprise. It fired a ball the size of a man's thumb and she had more faith in her rifle than a bishop in his God.

They could see a lit cross out there in the darkness, hanging suspended on the edge of the night. This belonged to the church which stood in front of the clock tower. The cross was cut in the wall, making a window, with votary candles behind it. Normally such crosses were used to guide wayfarers, shepherds and travelling strangers to the church at night, should they be lost in the hills. Now, as Peterson pointed out, it was guiding a motley collection of saboteurs to their target.

They passed through the inner picquets with whispered code words and over rocky and bouldered ground to the outer picquets. The two Irishmen had been talking in Erse to each other, but changed to English when the *peloton* arrived. They waved them cheerfully through, murmuring that they would tell their mothers if they didn't return, but not their fathers in case they got the wrong man. It was meant to be a joke, but Crossman felt a sharpness enter his soul, thinking that in his case it would be the wrong woman. Crossman was pleased that Wynter was not with them, since he could never pass an Irishman or Scotsman without an argument of some kind. Without a doubt Wynter had Celt in him too, but he only needed a small excuse for a fight of some kind and if someone came from another country that was good enough for him.

As they neared the Russian defences, crawling on their bellies, Crossman could see that the enemy was preparing for a night bombardment, moving guns from embrasures to barbettes. The former obviously offered better protection to the weapons and the gunners in daylight hours, but a hole in a wall has a narrow field of fire. Up on the platforms and firing over the wall they could turn their cannons in any direction, their protection being the darkness. Allied guns could return fire at the flash, but the chances of striking their target were greatly reduced.

There was a picquet hole just in front of a low drystone wall, beyond which lay gravestones and wrought iron crosses. The two Russian picquets were talking to one another in growling murmurs. Crossman indicated by sign language that they should slip by the sentries, without disturbing them. It seemed a little harsh to send in Gwilliams with his razor, and Ali with his knife, to slit their throats, when all they were doing was guarding a church and clock tower. If his men were put at risk, of course, Crossman would have little compunction if they had to kill the Russians.

His men slipped amongst the graves like shadows. The picquets were looking outward, still chattering, towards the British lines. Soon two parties went around the two ends of the church. On the far side it was peaceful and still. At this point the Russian line curved, to sweep behind both the church and the clock tower. The saboteurs were able to lever open the wooden door to the tower with the minimum of noise. Ali and Yorwarth drifted inside. It was their job to place and set the charges in and around the chiming mechanism itself. They had thought about blowing up the tower, but this would have been an unsure business.

There were no sappers amongst the six: Ali was the explosives expert. The army in its wisdom had chosen its saboteurs by the cut of their character, rather than any talents and skills they might possess. This was the way the army did things. If you were a cook in civilian life, in the army you became a roughrider responsible for managing horses. If you were the son of a butcher, used to slaughtering livestock, you were put in the artillery. There were those who would have liked to think the army was all for increasing a man's width and breadth of expertise, but their cynicism and actual belief in the recruitment service's indifference to such matters as putting the best man in the right job was not misplaced.

Just as Ali was about to ascend the tower's spiral staircase the Russian barrage opened up. Howitzers, cannons and mortars brought the night crashing down around their ears. Flashes went along the flanks to either side of the group, and Crossman noted that there was a concentration of mortars *behind* the church, protected as it were, by the holy site itself. The Russian fire was of course quickly answered by the artillery from the British side. Shells burst overhead, raining hot pieces of metal over the area. No round shot was used, because of the idea that one did not destroy an ancient holy monument, while shells were essentially weapons which blew men to bits, not property.

'You see that?' said Yorwarth. 'A whole bank of mortars!'

Peterson was infuriated. 'They're not playing fair,' she said. 'We should do something about them.'

'We're here for the clock tower,' Crossman reminded them. 'We'll report them when we get back, but we're sticking to our original objective.' He could see the disappointment in the faces around him in the flashes from the shells. 'I know, I know,' he said, acknowledging their expressions. 'But deviations to laid plans are apt to gang aft a gley. Maybe we'll come back another night.'

Once the barrage had finished, Yorwarth and Ali entered the tower again, striding up the spiral staircase using a thin beam of light from a dark lantern to light their way. Crossman and the others kept watch below. The smell of gunsmoke was in the air and fumes drifted up the stairwell. It was as much as they could do to swallow and remain silent. The minutes went by. Suddenly the clock chimed, sending out its notes across the now black and still landscape.

'Bloody "Widdicombe Fair",' muttered Peterson, as the last notes died away. 'Damn me if they haven't got a cheek.'

'Just think of those two up there,' Crossman reminded her, nodding towards the top of the tower. 'It was loud enough down here.'

Still the minutes continued to pass by, with no sign of Ali or Yorwarth. Crossman began to grow anxious. It was a delicate business, laying a charge, but there was a limit to the time it should take. Just when he was about to go up and see for himself what the matter was, Yorwarth arrived breathless at the foot of the stairs.

'Stuck!' he announced, dramatically. 'Ali. Stuck fast. Plugged in a hole up there.'

'Have you lit the fuse?' whispered Crossman.

'Burning away.'

Crossman ordered, 'You three stay here. If it goes up, get back to the British lines. Don't come looking.'

Crossman snatched the blinkered lamp from Yorwarth's hand and took the stairs three at a time, passing first one side chamber, then a second, to finally come to the belfry itself. There he heard the sounds of a struggle. He opened a shutter on the lamp from a slit to a wider beam and witnessed a backside and a thick pair of legs protruding from the ceiling. The corpulent Ali was wedged firmly, a round body in a square hole. The legs were windmilling as their owner struggled.

'Ali,' said Crossman. 'Can you hear me?'

The boards were thin, with gaps, and Ali could hear him perfectly well.

'Stuck!' grunted the Turk.

'I can see that. Can you reach the fuse?'

'No. Two metres away.

'God in Heaven. Look, I'm going to hang on to your legs and try to dislodge you.'

Crossman, who was taller than Yorwarth and able to get a better hold on the Bashi-Bazouk, gripped him round the knees and pulled. He lifted his own feet off the floor and swung there, like a monkey from a rope, for a few moments. Ali moved about two inches then stuck again. The trouble was, he was not fat in the ordinary sense, he was just large of girth. It was all muscle.

There was nothing to give really, around his waist, it being firm and solid. Crossman knew they had about five minutes left to free the Turk and get out of the tower. The charge they had laid would not bring down the tower but it would go through several floors and ceilings, and both men were likely to be killed.

Ali said, 'Go, sergeant. Leave me.'

'No.'

Ludicrously, the quarter hour struck, and having heard the song so many times in the barracks, the names automatically went through Crossman's head: Bill Brewer, Jan Stewer, Peter Gurney, Peter Davey, Dan'l Whiddon, Harry Hawk, Tom Cobbleigh. Crossman found himself wishing he had Uncle Tom Cobbleigh and all, along with Tom Pearse and his grey mare, to help unplug Ali from the hole. The notes of the tune were deafening. They rang in Crossman's head even after the bells had silenced themselves. He tugged and twisted, pulled and wrenched, and finally heard a tearing sound, as Ali's coat ripped apart and he came loose, crashing down on top of him. The pair jumped to their feet and rolled down the spiral staircase like a pair of manic balls.

At the bottom of the staircase they flung themselves out into the night. A few seconds later the charge went off. A mighty clanging followed the explosion as one of the great bells came hurtling down the staircase in the wake of the two men and shot out of the same doorway, to bounce and clatter over the rocks. Debris from shuttered windows came in like hail. When the pitter-patter of falling chunks of wood and splinters had ceased there came shouts from the cadets' school. Shots were fired, but it was probably panic firing, at no real target, for none came near the *peloton*.

'Follow me back,' ordered Crossman. 'Nobody gets in front of me. Quickly now.'

They had hoped to be past the picquets by the time the explosion took place. Now the Russian sentries would be on the alert, watching fearfully in every direction, but certain that something grave had happened to their clock tower. Crossman whispered to Ali and the pair of them set out together with the others close behind. Near to the picquet hole they fell onto their bellies. Crossman went out on the right flank and Ali on the left.

They now had to kill the two men they had heard talking, just a short while before. It was an unpleasant but necessary task.

Crossman came in from his direction, knowing that Ali would be doing the same. On reaching the fortified hole he drew his hunting knife and threw himself over the soil parapet. Scrabbling around in the darkness he found himself grappling with a strong figure. At first he thought he and Ali had grabbed each other, but the smell of the other man told him he was wrong. He had not the same odour as the Turk: not worse or better, just different.

Hoping that Ali had his man too, Crossman began a life-and-death struggle with his opponent. Earlier clouds had passed over and the stars were now visible above. A weapon in the other man's hand flashed in the light thrown down by these stars. Both combatants had gripped each other's right wrist, almost by instinct, so it was a matter of who managed to free his weapon hand first. Crossman tried to roll his man over, so that he could bear down with his weight on his knife and thus force the blade into the Russian's chest. Before he could do this, the Russian spoke.

'Damn ye, ye bloody bastard. I'll tear yer heid off and piss down yer neck, so ah will!'

Crossman gasped. 'Jock? Is that you?'

'Whut?' He felt his opponent relax a little. 'Who's this?'

'Jack. Jack Crossman.' Feelings of alarm went through Crossman. 'Ali – don't kill anyone,' he called. 'They're friends.'

A dark lantern was thrust into Crossman's face, which had been blacked just like that of his adversary.

'Is that really you, ye bloody idiot?' cried a shocked and apologetic Jock McIntyre. 'Whut are ye doin', attacking a man without warning? I nearly had ye there.'

'Nearly had me,' scoffed Jack. 'I was a second away from putting you in your tomb.'

'Like hell ye were. My *sgian dubh* was all but sticking in yer ribs, Jack Crossman.'

Jack was released and stood up, at the same time he stepped on something soft. An arm. Jock and whoever was with him had obviously already killed the sentries. The next moment more bodies came tumbling into the hole, followed by shouts and shots from the churchyard. The Russians had isolated their problem now. They knew a raiding party had been and was on its way back to the British lines. They would be firing at everything and anything: sights, sounds, even smells.

'Couldn't wait for you, sergeant,' said Yorwarth. 'The buggers are swarming about out there.'

'Whut? More of them? Is it the whole bloody battalion you've brought with ye?'

'Only five of us,' explained Crossman. 'How many of you, sarn-major?'

'Three,' said Jock in a very satisfied tone. 'It only takes three kilties to do the work of five Sassenachs.' Jock was the sergeant-major of the 93rd Sutherland Highlanders, they who had stood in the thin red line tipped with steel and repelled the Russian cavalry at Balaclava. He was an old friend of Crossman's. The pair had shared many a whisky together in the canteen and respected one another. Neither had much admiration for Wellington's 'Secretary to the Master General of Ordnance', their commander-in-chief, Marshal Raglan. There was still rivalry between them, however, when it came to operations in the field.

'What are the Highland Brigade doing out here?' asked Crossman. 'You should be guarding Balaclava.'

'Spiking guns, when we're permitted to do it, and not stopped on the way by the 88th,' explained Jock, with some chagrin. 'It's a raiding party, ye ken. We got bored, back there.' The Highland Brigade was still situated just north of Kadikoi and just occasionally some of them got into high spirits after a few drams of malt liquor and felt they just had to break out. Raiding parties were just the thing to get the heart racing again.

'Is this an official raid?' asked Crossman. 'Or a whisky raid.'

'Och, a bit o' both. Never mind that now. Whut are we goin' to do? We could make a run for it, but then we'll maybe be shot by our own lads. We can't stay here till dawn and that's a fact. If we get caught in the daylight we'll not be able to cross to the Heights without getting picked off by sharpshooters.'

At that moment there was firing coming from another part of the Heights. It sounded as if the French were making a sortie. The British section of the siege line was quite short now, since they were down from 34,000 to 11,000 men, with 23,000 lying sick and wounded. Thus it happened that the French sortie was close by. Shots were whistling around the picquet hole, now that the Russians had guessed their men out on sentry-go were either dead or captured. A grenade exploded with a bright white fizz of light, just in front of the hole. It was time to take their chances and vacate the area.

'We're off,' said Crossman to his men, and to Jock McIntyre, 'are you coming?'

'Lead off, sergeant.'

They scrambled out of the hole and began running across the rough ground, yelling to their own picquets, 'Wellington's boots! British patrol returning – British, British, don't shoot. Wellington's boots!'

Wellington's boots was supposed to be the code to ensure a safe return, but very often officers forget to tell the picquets the words had changed, or the picquets subsequently forgot them. This was not deliberate. When men had been cold and wet, and without sleep for up to seventy-two hours, they tended to become less efficient and more forgetful. Shouting 'British' in a strong British accent was the best way of ensuring that you were not shot by your own side in mistake for an enemy sortie.

Crossman ended up rolling into a trench and scattering a makeshift table on which there was a lamp, a deck of cards, and some drinks.

'What the bloody hell . . .?' cried a young ensign. 'We're trying to pass a peaceful night here.'

Crossman was joined by others tumbling into the trench, Jock McIntyre along with them. 'Sorry,' said Crossman, automatically, and then he became a little miffed. 'Actually, there is a war on. We've just risked our lives to get rid of that damn clock tower for you!'

The ensign cocked an ear. 'You're right! I haven't heard "Widdicombe Fair" for a while now.'

Another officer said, 'You really did it?'

'Blasted it to pieces. One of the bells went whizzing by my ear,' replied Crossman. Gwilliams added, 'It'll take a long Thursday to fix that pile of junk.'

'I say, well done,' said a lieutenant to Crossman, ignoring Gwilliams. 'Listen, I don't know you, do I? Are you 88th?'

Once again, Crossman knew that in the darkness, in the muck and mire, with his uniform in shreds and what was left of his rank and facings hidden beneath his fur coat, he had been mistaken for an officer. It was true a lot of officers had country accents, or regional ones, and not all of them were recognizable as gentry by that alone, but there was something in the range of vocabulary and the delivery which marked one. Clearly the way Crossman spoke gave others the impression that he was an officer. He rarely bothered to put them right.

'We've never met. I'm, er, special duties. One of Lovelace's.'

'Oh, him,' said a third officer, whose epaulettes told Crossman he was an officer, but his rank was not evident. 'Lovelace. Colonel Hawke's pet.'

Resentment flared in Crossman. 'Yes, well, I'm one of Hawke's pets too.'

'No offence, old chap.'

'None taken.' Crossman turned to Sergeant-Major McIntyre. 'Sorry to have spoiled your raid, Jock.'

'Och, we had our excitement. That's what we went looking for in the first place. There'll always be guns to spike. Let's leave these sirs to get on with their game of cards. I'm for mah bed. I'll be seein' ye again, Sergeant Crossman. Ye'll be happy to hear yer father is talking more of going hame. Scotland's aye on his tongue these days, though in truth it's nae warmer there, than here.'

'Goodbye, Jock.'

McIntyre having let the cat out of the bag with his 'sergeant', the card-playing officers were looking at Crossman rather askance. He gathered his men together and set off with them, back towards Kadikoi, pleased with the night's events. As they neared the hovel they saw two women leaving. Wynter had been indulging himself, spending his pay on whores, while the house was empty. The *peloton* all trooped in to find him lying on his back in the shared cot with his head cupped in his hands.

'Enjoy yourselves, did ya?' he said, as they flung themselves wearily into their beds. 'I did.'

Crossman barked, 'You're on firewood duty, Wynter. Get out there and find some.'

The lance-corporal's head came off the bed in a flash. 'What? Why me?'

'Because you've never learned not to crow. You're a blamed fool, Wynter. If you'd have congratulated us on a good fox hunt, or even just asked how we did, I'd still have chosen you, but I'd have felt less satisfied with my choice. You find us some firewood, and some water, or there'll be Hell to pay.'

Wynter remained on the bed.

'NOW!' shouted Crossman.

Grumbling, Wynter rolled off his cot and began to put on his battered, split boots. He caught Gwilliams grinning at him.

'Bloody Yankee-doodle,' snapped Wynter. 'You ain't even got a country to call your own.'

'America's my country,' retorted Gwilliams.

'America ain't a country, it's a continent, like Africa. We've *all* got a continent. Europe's mine. America's yourn. But you ain't got a *country* to speak of. Just a collection of States.'

'The United States is a country!'

'No it ain't at all. It's a bit of the continent of North America, an' the smallest bit at that. We've got the biggest bit, which is Canada.'

With that Wynter marched out of the doorway, before Gwilliams could riposte, leaving the American fuming. Crossman took this opportunity to take Gwilliams upstairs with him, where he could talk to the barber in private. He explained to Gwilliams that Colonel Hawke wanted him to spy on General Enticknap, while he was cutting the latter's hair, or shaving him, or fixing his bones, for Gwilliams maintained he had learned the art of bone and muscle manipulation from the Algonquin Indians in Canada, and often offered to walk on someone's spine, or to massage them with his large, strong hands. There were those who swore by Gwilliams' skill with bones. It was another reason why Hawke had wanted him for the *peloton*, since the colonel believed someone who could fix bones could unfix them just as easily. Indeed Gwilliams could dislocate a man's arm or leg in a moment, with a clever twist. It followed then, that he could break his neck with the same ease.

Once the talk was over, Gwilliams agreed to listen and learn the secrets of General Enticknap. 'It don't bother me none.'

'You don't see it as, well, distasteful? Spying on an officer serving in the same army? One of your own?'

'See, that's where I'm useful, sergeant. This ain't my army. The general, well, he ain't my man, so to speak, he's yours and that blamed idiot Wynter's. Now if you asked me to spy on Wynter, why I'd do it for nothing, without pay or found. If there's any person gets my goat around here, it's him.'

'He goads you on purpose. You shouldn't rise to it.'

'Can't help it. In my blood. I swear I'll swing for him, one of these days.'

'And swing you will,' warned Crossman, 'if you kill a soldier in this man's army. They're very fond of hanging criminals. Murder's the perfect excuse for them. They sort of look upon it as proper poetic justice. You can't steal money from a man who has stolen the same. That doesn't happen. It's not in the book of law. But you can kill a man who has killed. This kind of rounded justice – events turning full circle – seems to satisfy something in the breasts of certain senior officers. They are often those who continually smoulder, like a slow match, nursing grievances of some kind or another. Perhaps they were passed over for admiral, or failed to get a deserved knighthood? Who knows. But they're out there waiting for men like you, so they can soothe the savageness in those superior breasts, if only for a short time.'

'Can I go now, sergeant?' asked Gwilliams, clearly bored.

Crossman indicated he could. Once Gwilliams had descended the stairs, Crossman sighed and shook his head. Perhaps he talked too much, about things of little interest? Was he a driveller? Well, clearly men like Gwilliams thought so.

Crossman felt something crumple in his fur coat pocket as he removed his outer layer. The letter! He took it out, now soiled and dirty along the creases. It was one sheet with some beautiful handwriting, clearly that of a feminine kind, though the loops and twirls were economic in their use. It read:

My Dearest Cousin Alexander – I met a friend of Lavinia Durham at a ball just yesterday fortnight who told me an extraordinary thing. It was said that you are serving as a common soldier in the Crimea under an assumed name. Strangely, I could believe it of you. You were never a conventional person, but I am not sure if I should disapprove of this character trait, or admire it. Since I know that your brother James is also in the Crimea, along with your father, I wonder how you all fare under these circumstances.

He paused in his reading to trim the candle. Jane obviously had not heard that James was now at home. The candle burned brighter. He continued the letter.

Do you have to salute them when you see them and beg their pardon? It really does mystify me. I would so much like a letter from you, Alexander. We were so close as children, in the same house, the same nursery, for six years and sharing the same governess. Do you remember all, or do you select the best memories? I think I rather follow the latter course. I remember, for example, the day you threw a plum at me under the tree house, when I called you a coward for not wishing to remove a fish from your father's fishing line. You missed of course. You never were very good at hurting people. I wonder at you now, having to shoot Russians. Do you shoot Russians, Alex? (There, I've used your pet name at last!) I shall send this letter to Lavinia, in the hope of it reaching you. If anyone knows who you are and where to find you, it is she. She loved you deeply, you know, and she is one person you hurt without compunction.

The letter was signed, 'Your most affectionate cousin, Jane.'

Crossman sighed again. They sought him out! Why couldn't they just leave him to do as he would? Lavinia had brought him the letter in some triumph, also of course hoping that he would open it and read it in front of her, so that she could learn its contents. He did no such thing and she went home to her Bertie, a quartermaster, still in ignorance.

Cousin Jane. Yet, not really a cousin, since the 'uncle' who was her father was actually one of those very good friends of one's parents who were merely termed as uncles. Jane Mulinder, of Derby. Of course he remembered all. He had been five when she had come to live with them in Scotland and eleven when she left. By that time he had been desperately in love with her, as only an eleven-year-old could be with a pretty cousin. Of course he had showed none of this at the time, it being a period of making faces, sticking out one's tongue, and generally showing contempt for the weaker sex. But he had missed her dreadfully, once she had gone, and often dreamt of dark ringlets falling over a heart-shaped face which glared back at him when he sneered.

He didn't know whether he was going to answer the letter. It had been stuffed inside his tunic for a week now. It was unlikely. There was no time. Inclination? No, no time. This was war. Frivolities would have to wait. Lavinia should have known better than to reveal his presence to his cousin. It was very bad of her. Very bad.

2

Freezing sleet had been falling all night long, but by the morning it had gone, replaced by a cold hard wind. All along the lines the cannons were silent: not because the artillery units were apathetic, or because their officers were already drinking, smoking and playing cards with cavalry officers, or even because the more artistic of them were painting or writing poetry. Not even because NCOs and common serving men were sitting, staring into space, recalling the Sunday sermon which spoke of Hell being a torment of fire and brimstone and thinking that under present conditions such a place would be more like Heaven. These could have been put forward as the reasons for the silence, since this was what was happening all along the firing line, but the real reason for the inactivity was that what little water they had, was frozen in the wells, streams and of course the buckets, standing by the cannons where it was used to sponge out the barrels after firing. Without water the cannons could not be used. They had to be cooled before being reloaded, or the next charge down the barrel might explode as it was being rammed home and some luckless soldier would lose his arm, or worse.

Crossman and Lovelace were walking through Vanity Fair after having been up to high ground to view part of the Russian line which stretched from Sebastopol to south of Chorgun village, a wavy six miles which vaguely followed the upstream direction of the River Chernaya.

'Colonel Hawke's not very happy with you, sergeant, putting your *peloton* at risk like that.'

'It was for the regiment – such as it is – I think the 88th's down to about a third of its strength. What's more, I'd like to try another raid on their behalf. On our way back from Star Fort the other day I noticed a huge storehouse just inside the defences of Sebastopol. There'll be coats and blankets in there. I'd like to get them for the battalion.'

Lovelace sighed. 'You've got to stop thinking about your old regiment. In any case, is it fair you should be making these raids for the 88th when half the army is freezing to death?'

'I can't worry about the whole Army of the East. I can only deal with those closest to me. I'm told the Chinese have the idea that because there's so many people in China they can only afford to worry about their own family. Charity begins at home. It makes a certain amount of sense. If every family looks after its own, there is no general problem.'

'Except in the case of orphans and abandoned old people.'

'I knew you were going to bring up something like that,' growled Crossman, thrusting his mittens into his pockets. 'I have no answer for that, except to say that here, in the Crimea, we all belong to one family or another. There are no orphans or solitary old people. If each regiment sees to its own, then no one falls through the net.'

'Look, sergeant, you keep forgetting something. You belong to me now. One day this army will have an intelligence-gathering regiment, a set of men dedicated only to spying and sabotage, but until then we have to make do and mend.'

'You mean we have to keep our activities secret from Lord Raglan, who loathes and detests the type of work we do.'

Lovelace nodded. 'As you will. Lord Raglan, in that cosy farmhouse of his, is living in cloud-cuckoo-land. We cannot fight a war without information. We need to know their strength, their disposition, where their magazines are, where they keep their stores, how they supply themselves, and occasionally make them suffer the discomfort of having to do without their ammunition and supplies by blowing them up.'

'I know all that,' said Crossman, a little more irritably than he intended it to sound. 'But my little group does more than that. We seem to be completely dedicated to destruction – of property and people. This business of spying on General Enticknap leaves a bad taste.'

'I know that upsets you. I don't like it either. But Hawke is our man, like it or not, and we have to keep him happy. In some ways he's right, to try and weed out the cancerous elements in the army. We are soldiers and soldiers are employed for one purpose only, to fight wars for their country. If there were no wars, we would not be needed, but we both know that there will always be tyrants and despots who wish to wage war on their near and far neighbours. However, those wars are best fought efficiently, so as to get them over with as quickly as possible and return to a peace where trade and industry can flourish. Do you agree?'

'Of course, but . . .'

'Well then, generals like Enticknap *prolong* wars, drag them out, cause unnecessary death and suffering.'

Crossman expostulated, 'I have no proof that Brigadier-General Enticknap is prolonging this war.'

'Ah, well, sergeant, *proof* is not a necessary ingredient, since you are in the army to follow, while it is up to others to lead. Colonel Hawke feels he has proof and that should be enough for me, let alone a sergeant. Do you see what I mean? We have to trust our superior officers, or there'd be no time for the actual fighting, it'd be all questions and answers. What has Gwilliams found out so far? I understand he gave the general a haircut just yesterday.'

'I've written it down.' Crossman removed two folded sheets of paper from under his sheepskin and gave them to Lovelace, who put them in his pocket without reading them.

'Now,' said Lovelace, 'we have a new fox hunt for you.'

'Just me?' asked Crossman, stopping to hunch deeper inside his coat, his breath coming out as white vapour. 'Or the *peloton*?'

'All of you. You may be aware that during the last two months the number of deserters has increased dramatically. Some of them go into Sebastopol of course, those who have foreign connections – German, Polish, whatever. But others have gone over the hills, up onto the central plateau and the steppe. There are reports that a group of British deserters has taken over a

Tartar farmhouse in the north and are operating as bandits. You are to take your men and kill or capture these deserters. They're upsetting the local people who are not necessarily on the side of the Czar. Their ringleader is said to be a Corporal Reece, deserter from the 41st Welch. I'd like you to bring him back alive, if you can, so we can set an example.' Major Lovelace's eyes were quite cold and devoid of any expression as he delivered these instructions. Crossman had noticed that his commanding officer could be quite a warm and affectionate human being when speaking with him socially, but when in his role as commander of a group of saboteurs, assassins and spies he was quite ruthless.

'It doesn't sound a very savoury task. I can quite sympathize with a soldier who has run away from a place where he is expected to give all he has, including his life, and yet receives precious little in the way of food, clothing and shelter.'

'Yet you will do it, sergeant.'

'Of course, sir. I will do it.'

The goose girl crossed their path ahead, with her grumbling birds. She looked up, saw it was him, and gave him a secret smile, before hurrying on. Crossman thought about her geese. She would have to guard them every waking, and sleeping, hour to prevent hungry soldiers from stealing them.

'Oh, one other thing, sergeant. I want you to take Lieutenant Pirce-Smith with you. He needs to be initiated into our ways. You will be in charge of course. I'll make that plain to him. He can't expect to lead a *peloton* first time out.'

Crossman stared at Lovelace. A great sense of foreboding fell on him. No officer in the British Army was going to take orders from a sergeant, not once authority had been left behind. He could foresee great quarrels and arguments, threats of court martial on return, at the very least refusal to carry out tasks necessary to protect the lives of the group. Once out there, in the wilderness, amongst the enemy, in the heart of the winter, every soldier had to pull his weight. If one man failed to do that which was required of him, then the whole was endangered. It was bad enough with the sometimes rebellious Wynter. It was worse with the civilian Gwilliams. There would be tenfold any leader's problems with an officer who felt he should be in command, rather than some sergeant.

'This won't work,' stated Crossman. 'You know it won't.'

'It's not my decision. It's felt that where we went wrong with Lieutenant Dalton-James was that we excluded him from any field work. Except for the assassination of course, and he fell into that one by accident. Look,' Lovelace put a hand on Crossman's sleeve, 'I know it won't be easy. I know that. But actually Pirce-Smith is better material than Dalton-James ever was. Dalton-James was from a high-born family. Pirce-Smith is the son of a clergyman. Deep down he's your basic English country squire type. He's not completely out of touch with the common man.'

'I don't know if that's better or worse.'

'Whatever – it's got to be done. I'll wager that after one fox hunt he'll decline any others. You won't lose command, if I have anything to do with it.'

'I hope not. It's my one consolation. That out there I'm in charge of my own destiny.'

Crossman had promised his men a hot meal in one of Vanity Fair's expensive 'restaurants'. They passed Mrs Seacole's British Hotel and went into a shack owned and run by an Armenian-Egyptian, Karman Fussel. Fussel somehow managed to turn unappetizing goat meat into the most exotic food one had ever tasted. It was possibly the sauce he put on the sis-kebabs, or the way he basted them in their own juices, or the herbs and spices he used. Whatever, British soldiers had never tasted anything like Fussel's five course dinner of a small steak, followed by fried liver, then three sticks of kebab meat, melted goat's cheese twisted round a roasting stick and finally frozen sherbet. Crossman had received some money from his stepmother and he used this to pay for the meal.

After the meal, which was superb in everyone's estimation, they all sat back in their chairs for coffee and a good smoke. Crossman had his chibouque, purchased in Constantinople, which he enjoyed to the full. The long curved stem on the pipe helped to cool the smoke before it reached his mouth and even the harshest tobacco, purchased from local Tartars who grew it on the slopes, tasted relatively sweet. Peterson had a short clay pipe, a favourite with most soldiers, which she used to send clouds of smoke up to the dirty ceiling of Fussel's eating place.

'This is the life, eh?' cried Wynter, who then proceeded to burst into song. The others joined in, all except Ali and Gwilliams. Even the Australian Yorwarth knew the words, since the songs were part of his history and heritage too.

'So?' asked Peterson, just before they were to leave, 'what's this all about, sergeant? You taking us into the jaws of death again?'

The place was beginning to get rowdy. Many soldiers had come to drink, not to eat, and some were far gone with the harsh liquor, which was not particularly cheap in price. A fight was brewing in one corner, where voices were raised over the general hubbub. It was likely there would be some floggings in the morning. It was all right to get drunk quietly: it was how you handled the drunkenness afterwards that was important. Crossman had to raise his voice to be heard by his soldiers.

'What's all what about? I just thought you soldiers could do with fattening up.'

'For the slaughter,' she said. 'Come on, sergeant, we know there's a fox hunt. There's always a mission after you've been for a walk with Major Lovelace. What is it this time?'

'I was told that we were to be sent on a holiday,' replied Crossman. The liquor had mellowed him to an unusually jovial and teasing mood. Wynter's eyes were opening wide and began brimming with hope. 'Colonel Hawke, bless his boots, thought we deserved a long rest. He asked if we'd like to go to Yalta, to enjoy the hot Roman baths there. Yalta is a bit like Constantinople, much smaller of course, but with many pleasures. You remember the pleasures of Constantinople, that city of popes and emperors, do you not Wynter?'

'Sergeant, I'll never forget it.'

'Yes, I don't suppose any of us will.' What Crossman remembered was the flea- and rat-infested barracks there, with its stinking drains and rotten interior, which had now become a hospital for the sick and wounded sent from the Crimea. 'Well, Colonel Hawke asked me whether Yalta would be a suitable spa for my weary men.' Crossman took a sip of his drink, knowing that all eyes were on him. 'I of course refused,' he continued in a serious vein. 'I told Colonel Hawke that my men were strong in spirit, strong in body, and patriots to the core. It is not for us, I informed Colonel Hawke with great pride in my voice, to languish in paradise while others toil for the common good of the war. My men, I said, spurn the dissolute life of the wastrel. Duty, duty, duty, is the word that hangs from the lips of every member of my *peloton* . . .' Crossman could see the more intelligent members of the group had already started to twist their mouths, having realized they were being joshed. Wynter, however, had still not got the joke. His mouth hung open in sheer disbelief. Fury was about to erupt from the depths of his simple soul. 'No, I said to Colonel Hawke, what my men would really like to do is go north, up beyond the hills, and look for deserters. Another fox hunt would do their hearts good and turn yet another grey day into Christmas.'

'You said *that*?' cried Wynter, sorely wounded. 'Why can't we go to this Yalta? You never arsked us! You should've arsked us.'

There was general laughter now. Crossman knew he had upset them all a little, with his cruel twist of humour, but Wynter's swallowing the bait had applied a little balm to the hurt. Yorwarth ruffled Wynter's hair and told him not to be so much of a baby.

'You're the bloody baby,' snarled Wynter. 'You ain't even felt a razor on your chin yet.'

'When do we go, sergeant?' asked Ali. 'I have to tell my woman.'

'We start tomorrow. I'm sorry, I don't know how long we're going to be. It's one of those open-ended missions. I'm not even sure how and what we do, when we find these deserters. It seems they're living by raiding local farms and causing a great nuisance of themselves with the Tartars. You know at the moment the Tartars have no great love for the Russians, for this is the Ukraine, not Russia proper. However, if there are British and French who are raping and pillaging, and causing mayhem, then the Tartars just might re-form an old alliance with the Cossacks, and then we'll be for it. The hordes led by Genghis Khan and Tamerlane will ride roughshod over the world again.'

'What is he talkin' about?' cried Wynter, aggrieved. 'Everybody else has got a sergeant what talks sense. We get one that talks drivel.'

It was a true state of affairs, that when Fancy Jack Crossman had one drink too many, his education began to show. The 'Fancy' part of him peeked out from behind his normally rigid mask like a loose woman's lace petticoats under her gown. That harsh wine made him feel rather superior to the company he had to keep. Even now Wynter had brought it out into the open, he was still sadly inclined to parade his knowledge.

'I don't suppose,' he said, 'that anyone would join me in a glass of wine to toast Jason and the Argonauts?'

'See!' cried Wynter, accusingly. 'There he goes again.'

Ali said sourly, 'Who was this Jason?'

Before Crossman could patronize the group further, Gwilliams interrupted quietly. 'Jason was a Greek. An ancient Greek. A sailor, who sailed over the Black Sea, just as we've done, looking for the fleece of a golden sheep. His ship was called the *Argo* and he stopped in a good many places, had a good many adventures. Jason came to the Crimea, just like us. It was called Colchis, then. While he was here he met the witch-princess Medea, who helped him yoke together two fire-breathing bulls with brass hooves so's they could pull a plough. In the furrows, Jason planted dragons' teeth and from these teeth sprang an army of fully-armed soldiers. Soldiers like you, Wynter, and you, Peterson. Warriors. Ready to do their damn duty.'

'Milly McGee the harlot of Liverpool,' groaned Wynter, 'we've got another one. Two of 'em. 'Less he's makin' it all up.'

'No,' replied Crossman, impressed. 'He's not making it all up. We have an American scholar amongst us. You should get together with your countryman Rupert Jarrard,' he suggested to Gwilliams. 'He's a follower of the ancient Greeks too.'

Gwilliams spat on the stove, where it sizzled. 'Jarrard? Him? He's a fraud.'

'You know him? You don't like him?'

'I know his kind and I don't like his kind.'

'I no like. I no like at all,' growled Ali, furiously, shaking his matted curls angrily. 'Always bad for the Turkish people.'

'Rupert Jarrard?' said Crossman, surprised by the Bashi-Bazouk's outburst. 'What have you got against him, Ali?'

'Not the American, the Greek!' cried Ali. 'Turkish people no like Greek people. This Jason. I gut him like a fish if he comes to steal gold from my house. I rip stomach open. I cut off head.'

They all realized at that point that Ali too was getting very drunk and that was a dangerous situation. Ali could change from a tame bull to a wild one in a few seconds, given enough alcohol and once he did that no one, not even Crossman, could control him. His thick hard body would break free of any restraint, would smash through any barrier, would roll down any opposition.

It was time for more food, to soak up the strong wine. Crossman yelled for bread and potato mash, and some hot mugs of coffee. Fussel saw that they were sent over very quickly, having a landlord's eye for trouble over the horizon. Ali had been drunk in his establishment once before and it had taken seven men a week to clean the place up after the fight the Turk had started, plus a good part of the night's takings for broken furniture. Food, however, would take the Turk's mind off anything else. He loved his stomach more than he loved his 'woman'.

On the way back to the hovel, Crossman spoke with Gwilliams.

'Where did you study Greek mythology?' he asked.

'There was a preacher who looked after me once, when I was young. He taught me to read. Once you can read there ain't a piece of knowledge in the world that's out of reach.'

'That's true. Not many people realize that, though, even when they can read. I don't believe my brother and father, for instance, ever opened the pages of a book once they left the school room, save it was a pamphlet on the sale of horses, or sporting guns. Their knowledge of hunting is extensive, but it's a knowledge learned by doing and observing, not from the written word.'

'My learnin' is patchy,' admitted Gwilliams. 'I only know what was in the preacher's bookcase. O' course, there was a good deal there, him being a man who liked history and facts, and was up on the beliefs of others.'

'It's still commendable. No harm ever came from knowledge. Plenty from the lack of it. Say, Gwilliams, how do you feel about this business of spying on General Enticknap? It doesn't bother you?'

'He ain't nothin' to me,' said Gwilliams, kicking at a frozen rut to hide his impatience with the question. 'It's not like I was watching my own family, or even a brother American. Like I say, he's nothin' to me, at all.'

'You don't mind spying on your own side?'

'You heard what I said, sergeant.'

'I did indeed. I suspect you have a good memory, Gwilliams. What happens when all this information becomes redundant, of no use to you. What do you do to get rid of it from your mind? How do you cast it out?'

Gwilliams stopped in mid-stride. The others were well ahead and he stared at their backs, as if gauging whether he could be heard or not. Finally he said what he was going to say.

'Listen, sergeant, I ain't no angel like you. It don't mean a cuss to me what I do when it comes to watchin' and listenin'. That knowledge is gathered up legitimate. If people don't want their business passed on, they should keep it locked inside, not spill it out all over. When this war is over I can sell what I know to my other people. There's those who want to know what's goin' on in other armies, how they fight, deploy, go into battle, what their weapons can do, what their weak points is, that sort of thing. I can sell it on, easy. The US might go to war against Britain some time. It ain't so long since the States and the UK were fighting.'

'Over forty years,' said Crossman, 'and it wasn't a war that the British or the Americans remember with any clarity.'

'Not everybody wanted it, that's true. But it happened.'

'So, while you're spying for us, you're spying against us?'

'Does it taste sour, sergeant?'

'No – just makes me realize how naive I am compared to some – to you and Lovelace. He doesn't do it for money, of course. He just enjoys it for its own sake. But he's as ruthless as Crassus, just like you.'

Gwilliams realized he was being tested again, and he chuckled. 'The Roman general, right? Defeated the leader of the slave army, what was his name? Spartacus. That was him. Spartacus who had his hideout on the slopes of the volcano Vesuvius.'

'No flies on you, Gwilliams.'

'I hope not, sergeant. I hate flies. Dirty, filthy creatures.'

They left their conversation there, both feeling they were a little closer to the real man behind the fur coat.

The following morning the household was roused at dawn. It was a milder day. Up on the Heights someone had managed to thaw some buckets of water for the gunners and one or two early-morning cannons were barking at the enemy. Crossman gathered his armed and kitted band ready for the march into the hills. Ali, who had slept elsewhere, was waiting on the doorstep. They went on foot, since horses needed fodder in the winter and it was hard to come by in the hinterland. Most gloomy in their thoughts, they trooped along the Kadikoi track between the houses and stalls, towards the grey line of hills to the north. A woman came to one of the windows in her slip, not expecting to see anyone out so early, only to find Wynter gawking up at with a leer on his face. She pulled some ragged curtains closed with a petulant look.

'Let's hope we don't run into any Cossacks, sergeant,' said Peterson.

'Bloody Cossacks,' said Crossman, who had a price on his head amongst the Russian cavalry. 'They'll be the death of me.'

At the top end of the village they found Lieutenant Pirce-Smith waiting. He stood like a soldier, rigid as a tent pole, waiting for them to reach him. An attempt had been made to muddy him up a little, make him look less like a parading officer and more like a renegade, but it was surface stuff. Crossman could see the man was uncomfortable, like someone not used to acting wearing greasepaint. When they drew alongside him, Crossman said, 'If you'd like to join the file sir, behind me.'

'Behind you?' It was simply a repetition of his words. The officer did as he was told, going between Crossman and Gwilliams. Ali was leading of course. Although Crossman and Peterson were familiar with the landscape, Ali had spent half a lifetime in and around the Crimean region. Wynter was the other man who should have known where he was going but Wynter was one of those soldiers who simply followed his leader, not taking account of where he was going or where he had been. He was usually aware of his immediate surroundings but where those features stood in the world he had no real idea.

They passed cork oaks, laurels and cypress trees, among others, keeping to depressions. In the summer there would be cattle on the upland plains, as well as sheep, but the landscape was devoid of life on this winter day. Smoke was curling from farmhouse chimneys up on the slopes. The faint booms of the guns behind them seemed to belong to a different world, a world of mud and noise. Here on the level uplands, there was the same kind of peace that Goethe found on his mountaintops.

Suddenly, Ali's hand went up. The patrol immediately fell to the ground. Pirce-Smith was just a second behind everyone else when he realized what was expected of him. Ali made a sign with his fingers. 'Cossacks,' whispered Crossman to Pirce-Smith. The officer could see nothing but he knew better than to lift his head to peek. There came the drumming of cantering horses on the turf and the clinking of harness metal. Then silence again. Ali waited for a time then made a motion for them all to rise.

'That was close,' said Pirce-Smith.

'That was ordin'ry, sir,' replied Wynter. 'That weren't even half a mile off.'

Pirce-Smith did not converse with lance-corporals, except through his senior NCOs. He made no reply. He was, however, a man anxious to learn. While he felt that discipline and correctness were necessary to the army at all times, he was no fool and realized that here was a unit in which the rules had to be relaxed a little. This was like a hunt, not a fox hunt – he felt that was a poor analogy – but a boar hunt. A hunt for a wild animal with a group of loosely connected individuals. But even on a boar hunt there were those who led and those who followed.

Pirce-Smith had been given a hard time by his so-called fellow Guards officers when he had joined the army, simply because he was not from a high born family. Mercifully he did not have 'the smell of the shop' about him, his father was not in trade, so he had not undergone the torture that one or two of his colleagues had gone through. One man, Ensign John Morten, son of a cordwainer, had been made to endure such misery at the hands of his fellow officers (backed whole-heartedly by the colonel of the regiment and his aides) he eventually blew out his own brains. However, many clergymen were the younger sons of genteel families, and though Pirce-Smith's father was not one of those, but simply a man with schooling and ability, the lieutenant had only had to endure such things as soaked beds after coming off duty, and dollops of garden mud squeezed into his boots. In the end he saw the wisdom of transferring to a less elite regiment, a regiment of foot, where such things as one's father's status were not quite so important.

With this rite of passage the twenty-four-year-old Pirce-Smith felt he had earned his commission in the army the hard way. He was an officer and he wished to be treated as such, even on unofficial patrols out in the Crimean hinterland, where the law had rougher edges and was not so fine a tool. He did not have to socialize with rank and file, and had no intention of doing so. At the same time he was eager to be a success at the business of spying and sabotage. He greatly admired Major Lovelace, who in turn seemed to think Crossman a worthy soldier. This Sergeant Crossman appeared to know what he was doing and while he was out here Pirce-Smith was determined to absorb what he could, without compromising his status as an officer to any great depth.

Some game birds flew up in front and startled Pirce-Smith out of his thoughts.

'It's all right,' said Crossman. 'No need to be alarmed, sir.'

In spite of his previous thoughts, Pirce-Smith was nettled.

'I'm not alarmed. Just surprised, that's all, sergeant.'

'I don't mean you personally, sir. I mean the Russian cavalry. If they were in the vicinity they might have seen those birds and investigated.'

'Oh.' Pirce-Smith looked about him. 'How can you be sure they didn't?'

'Ali would have smelled them – the Russians. He has a very sensitive nose.'

The *peloton* stopped for the night in a ruined turf-and-stone dwelling, which afforded them some cover. Ali made an earth-oven, invisible from a distance, which allowed them to eat hot food. There was not a great deal to be had, but enough to stave off the hunger pangs. Crossman advised Pirce-Smith to sleep with his water skin in the pit of his stomach, to prevent the water inside from freezing to solid ice.

'If you run out of water,' he told the officer, 'we shall have to abandon you.'

'Why?' It was a controlled question, no hint of rancour. 'Why would you have to leave me, sergeant?'

'Because each man is carrying just enough for himself, sir. If they were to share with you, there'd be two of you at risk, instead of one. With two men at risk, the whole mission would be in danger of foundering. I hope you see what I mean, sir.'

'I think I do.' This time there was an edge to the words, which caused Ali to look up from his task at the oven with narrowed eyes. Later, in the moonlight Pirce-Smith was sitting with Peterson, who seemed a quiet and orderly youth, and not so much the 'soldier scum' that Wynter, Gwilliams and Yorwarth appeared to be. He suddenly became aware of a foul smell close by him and turned to find the Bashi-Bazouk irregular breathing into his face. Ali showed his teeth: not so much a grin as a baring of the fangs.

'Listen, you,' said the Turk softly, poking Pirce-Smith's chest with a stubby finger, 'you no speak bad with the sergeant. The sergeant my friend. You speak bad with him, I kill you. Yes? You go against sergeant, I shoot you goddamn head. I blow brains. Good, you understand.' His heavy hand came down hard on Pirce-Smith's shoulder, a friendly gesture which almost broke the officer's collarbone. 'I like you, officer. I no want shoot you goddamn brains out.' With that he left the stunned Pirce-Smith alone with Peterson.

Peterson was cleaning her rifle. She didn't look up into his face, but she said, 'Don't worry too much, sir. He said that to me once. I expect he says it to most people.'

'So he wasn't serious?' Pirce-Smith was relieved.

'Oh, yes, he was serious all right, sir. You harm his precious sergeant and Ali would cut your throat without a thought. He's murdered a few men in his time, I'm certain of that. Some people seem to take the law into their own hands and get away with it. Ali's one of those. I doubt he'll ever hang, whatever he does. It's one of life's mysteries.'

'Is it indeed?' Pirce-Smith went to sleep on the cold, hard ground with a bitter mind. He was damned if he was going to be bullied. Yet, at the same time, he had to be a little wise, remain cautious, for out here there was no army, no system, to protect him. He might very well end up with a smile on his throat and no retribution to follow.

That night was a terrible one for Pirce-Smith. He spent it mostly awake and shivering, trying to get comfortable, trying to keep warm, with a cold goatskin at his belly, and failing miserably on all counts. It seemed to him he was ill with something, though he did not know what. Cholera? Dysentery? He had a touch of the latter, but it was not that so much as an overall physical problem. A malady of sorts. However, he was sure he would be left behind if he complained of sickness, so he bore it through the night. What sleep he did get was fitful, and he woke with a bad taste in his mouth. However, after stretching and stumbling around in the grey dawn, he felt a little better. Wynter eyed him as he strode up and down. There was malice in that look, but Pirce-Smith had too much else to concern him at that moment, to take notice of insubordination.

The others woke to a grey and dismal morning, though it had to be said the light out on the steppe was good due to the wide open skies and flat rolling landscape. There was nothing to impede it. At the start of the trek they came to a stream which had cut a deep scar into the soil and rock, thus giving itself some protection from the winter. A little water was trickling through the ice. Three men were down at this beck, taking their fill of the freezing water. Ali smelled them from the other side of the rise. Crossman decided to go and investigate, since they could not continue their journey without being seen. 'I'll go down and see who they are,' he said. 'The rest of you stay out of sight – all except Peterson. You follow me up and keep your Minié on the nearest one to me at all times. If you have to fire, shoot the man in your sights, no matter where the threat is coming from. I'll take care of the other two, understand?'

'Yes, sergeant,' said Peterson, and the others nodded.

Crossman removed his mittens and took out his revolver. He cocked it with the cocking-trigger. Pirce-Smith said, automatically, 'That's not standard issue, sergeant.' No one took any notice of this statement. Crossman left the group and with Peterson just behind him, he crested the rise and walked straight down to the men below. One of them saw him coming and shouted at the other two. They picked up their weapons which had been lying on the frosty ground. Watching him approach they spoke between themselves. The language was Russian. Crossman believed them to be deserters from the other side. The shorter of the two standing men was carrying a sword in his hand.

'Good morning!' he called, in Russian. 'Where are you heading?'

The man at the front, big, bearded, with a stiff shock of coarse black hair on his bare head standing up at least four inches above his skull, growled, 'What's it to you?' They were dressed in rough clothing, though all wore the Russian Army grey greatcoats. Like Crossman's band, they were mostly filthy dirty. One had his feet bound in rags. He was still sitting on the ground. There was a makeshift stretcher nearby. Clearly the other two had been carrying their comrade. Something about the man's accent made Crossman ask, 'Are you Poles?'

'I might be,' said the dark man. 'But I say again, what's it to you?'

'To me? I don't want trouble, that's what it is to me. I have a sharpshooter up on that slope. You can see him. He'll cut down the first man that moves against me. So, I ask again, who are you? In which direction do you go?'

The big man squinted at Peterson, who was lying flat, looking down the barrel of her Minié rifle, some fifty yards away.

'Perhaps we could shoot you both,' said the man, 'before you get us?'

'Unlikely,' replied Crossman, calmly. 'Are you deserters?'

Another man, the one sitting on the ground, his back arched into a hunch, replied to this question.

'Are you?'

'No.' Flat denial. Crossman saw no sense in getting chummy with these men, who might wish to tag along with them. 'But we're not interested in taking prisoners. Are you going upstream?' That direction was away from the Russian lines. What Crossman could not afford was an ambush when he returned by the same route, once the fox hunt was over. These men, most likely deserters, might try to buy their way back into the favour of their commander, if they returned with good information. Having obviously spent one bad night out on the steppe, where all nights were bad, they might be disillusioned with the idea of escape and wish to get back to the warmth of fires and the smell of cooked food.

'We go where we please,' said the big man. 'Who the Hell are you to be asking questions, anyway?'

'Over that hill,' said Crossman, 'I have a company of men. They give me the right.'

The man on the ground said, 'Don't pay him any heed. He's a good man. He carried me all day yesterday. Yes, we've deserted from the Russian Army. They treat us like curs. I was beaten so badly my spine cracked. I can't use my legs. We're going up into the Ukraine. We won't be any bother to you.'

'I'd rather see you on your way.'

'You go to Hell,' snapped the third deserter, a small bulky fellow. He seemed to have a brainstorm and suddenly lunged at Crossman's midriff with his sword, a worried look on his face. The big man was at that moment standing shoulder to shoulder with Crossman. Padded thwunking sounds came from his great-coat, as a rifle ball went through it, entering the back and coming out through the chest. Then the sound of the shot drifted down from above. Crossman kicked the sword from the bulky soldier's hand, sending it somersaulting through the air. It landed in the stream, skidding from the fringe ice. The fellow with the injured spine groaned as the big man's body hit the ground like a felled tree near to where he was sitting.

'Idiot!' snapped Crossman, at the sword wielder. 'What did I tell you? Your comrade's been shot now.' Crossman glanced at the giant at his feet and saw that he was indeed dead.

The swordsman stared bleakly down at the supine body. Covering the two remaining deserters with his pistol, Crossman yelled to Peterson, 'Get the others down here.'

Soon Ali and the rest of the *peloton* were with him, the two Russian deserters staring hollow-eyed at the group.

'Christ!' said Wynter, prodding the dead man. 'Got a big enough hole in his chest. You do that, Peterson?'

'Leave the corpse alone, Wynter,' ordered Crossman.

Gwilliams said, 'Grisly bastard, ain't ya? A dead man's entitled to some respect.'

'Not bloody deserters,' replied Wynter. 'Can we go home now, sergeant? We've done the job, ain't we?'

'Are you blind, Wynter? These are not our deserters,' snapped Yorwarth. 'In any case, the sergeant said we're looking for upwards of thirty men.'

Pirce-Smith asked, 'What are we waiting for, sergeant? Why are those men looking so frightened? A mistake occurred. Regrettable, but shouldn't we be on our way? We do have a mission to complete.'

Ali shook his head. 'We should do it, sergeant, I think so.' He was staring at the two deserters. Wynter caught the drift and moved away. So did Yorwarth and Peterson. Gwilliams said, 'I don't mind doing it.'

'Do what?' cried the lieutenant. 'What, Peterson?'

'We can't leave them here,' she replied. 'They know we're out here now. If they're caught by their own people . . .'

Some light came through the greyness in Pirce-Smith's mind. A chill went through him. 'You're not suggesting we kill them, sergeant? That would be cold-blooded murder. Is that why they're looking so scared? Assure them now, Ali, that we're not going to kill them. It's unthinkable.'

Wynter said, 'The sergeant's in charge. He could make you do it – sir.'

Crossman broke his silence. 'Enough of that, Wynter. You enjoy these situations too much. Sir, if we leave these men behind they endanger all of us. We might find a company of Cossacks waiting for us, when we come back. I can't hazard the mission or my men for the sake of two deserters.'

'One of them crippled by the look of it!' cried Pirce-Smith. 'I was going to suggest we leave a man to assist with the litter.'

'The officer's crazy,' muttered Gwilliams. 'I think we should do away with him too, before he does for us all.' He was not serious, but Pirce-Smith was shocked enough to stumble backwards and reach for his pistol.

'Put it away, sir,' Crossman ordered. 'Unless you're going to use it on these two.'

Lieutenant Pirce-Smith seemed to gather himself up all of a sudden. A confrontational expression took the place of a confused and bewildered one. He stared grimly at the group around him. His pistol was now in his hand and pointing directly at Crossman.

'Sergeant,' he said. 'I am the senior rank here. This has gone far enough. I am assuming command by right of the queen's commission. You will now follow my orders.'

'Yorwarth,' said Crossman, wearily, 'disarm Lieutenant Pirce-Smith, if you please.'

'Yes, sergeant.' A swift crack on the lieutenant's forearm with a carbine stock removed the weapon from his grasp.

Pirce-Smith gripped his bruised arm. He staggered back. 'This is mutiny,' he said. 'I'll have you all hung for this.'

'This is not mutiny, sir. You are talking of Buller's Bastards. Oh yes, that's what the general used to call us. His bastards. It's not meant as an insult, it is in fact a fairly accurate description. This *peloton* is not manned by your common legitimate soldier. We are outcasts from our regiment – illegitimate if you like. Just as kings used their bastards, their out-of-wedlock but often beloved sons, to do their dirty work, so General Buller formed his bastards to carry out his underhand activities.'

'What's all that supposed to mean?' growled Pirce-Smith, glowering.

'It means this is not a legitimate unit on a lawful mission. It means that command goes to whoever Colonel Hawke wishes it to go to. Behind the British lines you are a lieutenant and I am a sergeant. Out here I am a brevet general and you are a private soldier. That's what it means. Now when you decide you can behave yourself, I'll return your pistol. Until then you will do as you are bid. You wouldn't be the first British officer I've shot out of expediency.'

Pirce-Smith grumbled something about it being 'monstrous' and turned away.

Now Crossman turned his mind to the problem in hand. The two deserters from the Russian Army were gawking at the exchange between the two British, not understanding what on earth was going on. Since there were no visible signs of rank about any of the group they could not know it was a battle between a sergeant and an officer. Had they known they would have been utterly astonished. In their army the common soldiery was so much muck on the boot of the officer and to have a ranker argue with an officer would have meant a severe flogging at best, but probably a death sentence.

Crossman stared at the poor pathetic creatures attempting to escape from the army which had conscripted them.

'Are you Poles?' he asked again in Russian. They nodded dumbly. The trouble was, time had passed and though the two men expected to be shot they were not so resigned to the fact that it had driven out all their terror. He could see how scared they were by the way they held hands, like two women at the funeral of a loved one. Unlike Pirce-Smith they actually understood that it was necessary for them to die. So they waited for the inevitable, one sitting, the other standing by his side, staring with frightened eyes at their captors and executioners.

Crossman sighed. 'We've left it too long,' he said.

The others knew what he meant. Prolonging the shooting made it that much harder. The victims had suffered the torment of waiting for the guillotine to fall. It was a crime against humanity to torture condemned men with the agony of waiting. If it was to be done, the execution should have been carried out within minutes. Now there was familiarity between executioners and victims. It would not do, now. They had come to know their victims as human beings in need.

'I do it, sergeant,' said Ali, cocking his own pistol. 'You go on.'

'No, no. It's too late.' He spoke to the standing prisoner. 'You will be pursued, probably caught, since your friend cannot walk. If we let you live now, will you promise not to inform on us? You will not be asked for the information, so I ask you not to volunteer it.'

Of course, they promised. They promised on their lives, their mothers' graves, on the heads of their babies, on their own souls. They would not breathe a word of the British group's whereabouts. Who are you? they asked. Deserters like us, from your own army? Yes, well, deserters did not inform on each other.

They helped each other. They were after all in the same boat together, were they not? They were like brothers. Brothers did not hand in brothers. They protected them. And so on.

Crossman nodded and made a motion for his *peloton* to follow him up the next slope.

'They will tell, sergeant,' said Gwilliams. 'They'll do what they can to save their own hides.'

'I know, I know. But it was too late. We'll have to return by a different route.'

'They'll probably freeze to death before any Russian party catches up with them,' Peterson offered. 'Look, they can't move from there, can they? Not both of them, anyway. It's all of a piece.'

'You're probably right,' Crossman replied.

'If they're going to die, we might as well shoot them now,' Gwilliams said. 'Ali said he'd be the one.'

'I've made my decision. We're on our way.' Crossman strode out in front. Pirce-Smith caught him up. At first Crossman thought there was going to be an apology and reconciliation. Nothing of the sort.

Pirce-Smith said with a sneer on his face, 'Don't think because you finally agreed with my decision that it's going to help you at your court martial.'

'Oh, stuff it, sir,' called Wynter. 'It won't wash, you know. Not out here in the field. What the sergeant says, goes. There, you don't often get that out of me, but there it is, for all to swallow.'

Pirce-Smith said nothing more. He was clearly fermenting inside. He dropped back, to walk in his regular place, looking like the whipped dog who will one day tear the throat out of his beater.

Over the next few days and nights the group crawled over the frozen wasteland. This was an ancient landscape, whereon tribes and peoples had fought over the millennia. Here there had been Venetian colonies. There was the palace of the Tartar Khans in Bakhchiserai, between Sebastopol and Simferpol. The Byzantines and Genoese had been here, fought here, died here. Crossman was by no means invested with a sense of the paranormal, but he felt the presence of ghosts on the uplands, of warriors like himself. And, although the terrain had a rolling untroubled surface, there was no swift means of travel in such weather. It was a case of plodding on. At night they stopped in gullies, mere creases in the undulating grasslands, finding what shelter they could in this open world.

On the fifth day they entered a valley where the local climate was somewhat milder than that up on the dull-green grasses of the trapezoid downs. From the top they could see the narrow isthmus joining the Crimean peninsula to mainland Ukraine. To the east was the Sea of Azov, to the west, the Black Sea. Descending to the valley from the undulating plateau steppe they discovered three yurts and a herd of goats near a force of water cascading from the side of a cliff.

'Who are they?' Crossman asked of Ali.

'Khazars, maybe. I think so.'

Crossman nodded. Lovelace and he had talked about the history and geography of the region in which they operated. These talks had made Crossman more aware of his environment. Lovelace was a wholly professional intelligence officer. He deemed it necessary to arm himself with as much knowledge as possible about a wide variety of subjects, but all to do with the work in hand. Were he in India he could tell you all about its history and its peoples, their religions and cultures and what they ate for breakfast and what they did in their beds at night. The same if he had been in some region of Africa. As it was, Lovelace knew the Black Sea and its surrounds and very little about India or Africa.

Crossman had likewise learned about the area. He had learned about various groups of pastoral nomadic people on the Caucasus. One of these was an ancient Turkic-speaking people called the Khazars, who at one time ruled an empire which in the south had extended along the northern shore of the Black Sea from the lower Volga and the Caspian Sea in the east to the Dnieper River in the west. Although it had begun as a commercial empire, with merchant traders gathering new regions and minor kingdoms, it ended with the Khazars exacting tribute far and wide, from Alani and other northern peoples, to Magyars around the Donets River, from the Goths and Greeks, and from various other Bulgar and Slavic tribes. However, by the twelfth century their power had dwindled and died and they ceased to be mentioned in the records.

Crossman knew that, although such races and cultures disappeared from the written record, they were often kept alive by the locally spoken word. These 'Khazars' he had come across were probably the last remnants of the descendants of the original tribes. No doubt like most other European peoples – Celts, Saxons, Goths, Vandals, whatever – the Khazars were now only there in spirit, the tribal blood like their language and much of their culture having long since been altered.

'Are they likely to be hostile?' he asked Ali.

The Bashi-Bazouk spat on the ground. 'Goat people,' he said. 'Not fighters any more. Of course, if you steal their goats, they will kill you. Or,' he added, on reflection, 'if you take their daughters. Yes, then they will kill you. But for now we can speak with them. Take tea. Eat bread. Come, we go to see their headman.'

They went to the tents and the nomads invited them in. Indeed, they were most hospitable. The tea was nothing like Crossman had ever tasted, but it was palatable. There were also some immensely sticky cakes, hard and layered, like Greek baclava. Wynter enjoyed himself with the cakes. So did Peterson. The others found them too cloying and needed vast amounts of tea to wash them down. Crossman asked his hosts, through Ali, whether they had seen any more people like him, foreigners. On being told they had seen an 'English' by the headman, Crossman became a little excited. The deserter bandits were supposed to be operating in the area to the north-east of the Crimean uplands, which was where the group were at that moment.

'Ask him when he saw this man,' said Crossman.

Ali had a few short words, which as always sounded aggressive to Crossman, though the headman took no offence.

Ali turned to Crossman. 'Two years ago,' he said, grimacing.

'Two years ago?'

'Yes. He see him at Chufut Kale.'

'Way down there? Oh, wait a minute,' Crossman recalled

something. 'There was a Scot who climbed Chufut Kale, in 1852. Laurence – Laurence Oliphant. He was looking for the Karaim.'

'Ah, Jew peoples tribe. Not at Chufut Kale, or Mangup. Not lately. All gone down to coast, to Evpatoria and Yalta.'

'Yes, that's what Oliphant found. All that remained were the ruins of the ancient synagogue. So, they haven't seen our deserters? But it must have been Oliphant they saw two years ago. When did they arrive here?'

'Yesterday.'

Crossman realized they had no more up-to-date information than he had himself. He thanked the headman for his time and for the hospitality. Then he ordered his men out of the tent.

'Ah, can't we stay here an' sleep?' asked Wynter, staring at one of the headman's daughters.

'Out.'

They found a rock overhang where they could light a fire. Gwilliams and Yorwarth went off to look for fuel. Peterson was put on sentry duty. Ali remained with the descendants of the Khazars a while longer. Wynter was sent for water. Lieutenant Pirce-Smith took himself to one side, away from the group, while Crossman studied the maps given him by Lovelace (who had torn them out of a book written by an English traveller in the region) in order to make a decision as to where they should start looking for the deserters. Of course, if they stayed long enough in the area, the bandits would make themselves evident, but Crossman wanted to surprise them, rather than have them descend without warning upon his encampment in the early hours of one morning.

One map had details of local farms marked. Crossman saw that the nearest of these was some four or five miles up the valley. That was where he would start. He folded the maps carefully and wrapped them in goatskin, before putting them in his haversack. By that time Wynter was back with the water. 'Bloody heavy that. Why do I always do the heavy stuff?' Pirce-Smith came across as if looking for an argument. 'I should like some of that to wash in.'

'Help yourself, sir,' said Crossman. 'Wynter can always go for another load.'

''Ere!'

Pirce-Smith took a pan full of water and walked back to the spot he had chosen for himself, away from the others. He washed his hands and face and wet his hair before smoothing it down and combing it. Wynter watched the officer with an expression which was a mixture of indignation and amusement, not an easy look to acquire. Firstly, he considered it a waste of good cooking water. Secondly, why wash away a good warm layer of dirt, which would be needed in the middle of the night.

Once the officer's ablutions were over, Crossman walked over to him.

'Would you like me to explain my plans?' Crossman asked.

'If you feel you must, but please, not on my account.'

'I was asked to keep you informed of everything, so that when the time came for you to take out your own *peloton*, you would have some experience in these matters.'

Pirce-Smith stared, before saying, 'Do not presume too much, sergeant. I'm a hunter myself, at home. Stag as well as fox. One learns one's own tracking techniques. If I can follow a stag's spoor through the Cumberland hills and the Scottish Highlands, I think I can do as well here.'

Crossman kept his temper even. 'Hunting animals is a good deal different from hunting men. I've been on the Crimean peninsula for over six months. That's five months longer than you, sir. You may believe you know everything there is to know about finding an animal that can think as readily and as keenly as yourself but you would be wrong. There is nothing to replace experience in such matters.'

'I would hardly compare the intellect of a deserter with my own – I was educated at Eton and Cambridge.'

'It has nothing to do with education and everything to do with cunning and resourcefulness. What makes you think that because a man is a deserter he's simple? For all we know this Corporal Reece is your, or my, intellectual equal. Perhaps he's brighter than both of us. Just because a man is born into poverty it doesn't mean to say he can't think. I have known some very smart men who dug peat for a living. I have known even cleverer ones in household service. There's a few aristocrats I could name who rely on servants to think for them.'

'I don't need to be patronized by you, sergeant. I am well able to learn by observation. You just keep doing whatever it is you do and I shall stand back and be amazed by it all.'

Crossman saw he was going to get nowhere here. He walked back to where Gwilliams and Yorwarth were lighting a fire. At that moment Ali came up from the yurts. He had one large giggling woman in tow. With his free hand he was waving Crossman to come down to meet him. The sergeant did so, wondering what Ali was up to. The Turk seemed to have wives – or women – all over the place. Surely he had not found another one way out here?

'This woman,' said Ali, presenting the chubby girl, wrapped in goatskins which had not been completely cured, 'is willing to sleep with me. There is one down in tent who want sleep with *you*. I tell her, no, he is too skinny man, no good stamina, but she still want sleep with you.' He gave Crossman a broad grin, then said, 'Go down, sergeant. Go on, go on. Her father not mind. I speak with him. We pay him a little money – not much – just a few coins. He happy to lend his wife to me. I do same for him, sometime, maybe. You go to older daughter. She very ample,' he cupped his hands to his chest. 'She nice round lady.'

'I think not, Ali.'

'Ahhh,' Ali waved a hand as if giving up on Crossman as a good sport. 'You always like the Durham lady, in the camp. I see you sleep with her many time. But she no mind, you want to keep warm one night out in steppe. She no mind. Anyway, you no tell her, eh?'

Crossman looked over his shoulder to make sure Pirce-Smith was not privy to this dangerous conversation.

'Ali, you mustn't keep saying I sleep with Mrs Durham. I don't.'

The Turk looked affronted. 'You *do*. I see you.'

'That was a long time ago. Several weeks ago,' replied Crossman, becoming desperate. 'I was ill. I – I was hardly aware of what I was doing. Besides, Mrs Durham and I are old friends.'

'You be friendly with this girl, down in tent. She be friends with you. Easy.'

'No, I can't. I can't really explain why I can't, but I can't.'

Ali closed one eye and looked thoughtfully at Crossman. Then he nodded slowly. 'Ah, now I see. You having troubles with the pissing, eh? You having troubles with water? Ali get you herb tonight, fix you right. All right, you no go with girl yet. It make you sore to go with her. I fix it up, later. Now, I go back to tent with this one.' He pinched her breast, lightly, and she gave a low throaty laugh. 'Not long, sergeant.'

Ali returned to the camp later to perform his own ritual ablutions and to cook the meal. He preferred to do it himself, knowing that British soldiers were the worst cooks in the world. He was in fact a very good cook, especially when he was dealing with his own type of food: meat dishes like *karniyarik* and *hunkar begendi* with goat's meat in place of beef. Of course, the soldiers did not mind someone doing the cooking, and it was a bonus when the meal was edible let alone delicious.

After eating, Ali licked the fat off the fingers of his right hand, the left being retained for other less mentionable duties, and gave a deep sigh. He had drunk tea with Khazars, slept with a woman, and eaten his fill of his own food at a campfire. This was all that could be expected of life for a warrior such as himself, except for the occasional war, to liven it all up. He was one of those who had followed Xerxes across half a continent to teach the Greeks a lesson. So far as Ali was concerned, the lesson still had to be taught, since they hadn't learned it all the other times. This thought normally irked him, but tonight he felt very good. He felt like a true warrior on the plains.

'Let us have a song,' he said, with the glow of the fire still deep and red. 'Lieutenant. You give us a song?'

'Oh, no, no.' Pirce-Smith looked around at the expectant faces in some embarrassment. 'No, I don't hold a tune very well. In fact, my father used to forbid me to join with his choir. In any case, I know only hymns – Christian songs. You might not like them, being a Muslim.'

'I no mind Christian songs,' cried Ali. 'I like. Here, I sing first.' He immediately opened his wide mouth and a soulful *turku* came forth. Ali's normally forbidding countenance suddenly turned dreamy. He was lost in his own music, the buzzing tune carrying the words on its back. Gwilliams thought he had the knack of it, after two verses, and tried to join in, though he had no idea what he was singing. However, it became plain to him that a Turkish *turku* was not easily grasped and he fell silent again. However, his impatience could not be contained and as soon as Ali had finished his song, Gwilliams took up with one of his own.

'Oh, the corn liquor jug is dry, and the bottle's drained of rye,' he sang, 'and there ain't a whisky in the cask – oh what're we gonna drink I aaaask you? What are we gonna drink, I ask?'

Suddenly everyone wanted to contribute, with Peterson singing '*Widdicombe Fair*' all the way through, to the accompanying groans of all the raiders except of course Wynter, who had not gone that night. Only the lieutenant failed to sing a song. Gwilliams remarked to Crossman later that he could never fully trust a man who had no sense of humour, or a man with no visible music in his soul. 'Clockwork men, that's what they are, if they can't find a bit of mirth in themselves, or a melody.'

'I'm inclined to agree with you,' replied the sergeant. 'However, we may be judging him harshly. Perhaps he's afraid to show us how human he really is, in case we take it for weakness. Some of them are like that – good men – but having to present an impression, a different person to the world – because they're afraid of discovery. Inside, most of us are vulnerable, but men like Pirce-Smith are worried that their underbelly will show if they join with the rank and file.'

That night was a particularly cold one. They all slept in a heap, like bears in a cave, keeping each other warm. All except Pirce-Smith who could not be driven closer to the herd, even by a night of freezing winds and low temperatures. In the morning he was so frozen he could not move and they had to carry him to the fire, to thaw him out. Even when he could bend his legs and arms, he still sat there shivering, staring into the flames. Crossman felt for the lieutenant in his misery, but he wasn't going to attempt to offer sympathy. It was not wanted. Such was the stuff of women and kings, and not required by an officer of foot.

That day they walked to the first farm. After just a few hours observing the farm, they could see it was inhabited by Tartars. Crossman and Ali paid these good people a visit and were rewarded with information about the bandits. The 'English' were two farms along, the house being on the edge of a canyon, and they had caused a great deal of trouble. Farms had been raided, cattle had been stolen, likewise vegetables and even money, though it could not be spent out here. Possessions, such as clocks and lace, had been taken too, presumably required at the captured farmhouse, the occupant of which, the brother of the man Crossman was questioning, had not been seen since. The Tartars did not seem capable of organizing themselves: at least, this was true of the group Crossman visited. They seemed highly relieved that the British soldiers had arrived to sort things out.

With the farmer's instructions in mind, Crossman took his men up to some hills behind the farm occupied by the deserters.

'Here's how we are going to carry this out,' said Crossman to his men. 'I shall go in first, to get the lie of the land. I'm not going to put a time on it, because I might have to be with them for five or six days, perhaps a week. Lieutenant Pirce-Smith will be in charge. It will be up to him to decide if and when to attack. Sir,' he turned to the officer in question, 'I don't have to tell you that we're more than likely outnumbered four or five to one here. Please, no heroics with my men. No frontal attacks which will expose our weakness in numbers. My soldiers are trained for sneak attacks. Send in Ali and Gwilliams first, to cut a throat or two and put the fear of God up the enemy. The idea is to harass them, get them on edge, so that they're not sure whether they can trust their best friend or not. This is not a battle, with honour at stake. It's a dirty little combat in a grubby corner of the earth, and it's about survival of the most cunning. Colonel Hawke wants Reece alive if at all possible. If a few stragglers get away, please don't pursue them. Our duty is to smash this gang of thugs, not go chasing over the globe for every last mother's son of them. Peterson can kill one or two at a distance and retire, then come back and kill one or two more. That's the way we do it, picking them off, until the whole breaks apart. They've all deserted the battleground once, they may do the same again, if they think the fighting is going to get tough. Am I understood, sir?'

Pirce-Smith snarled, 'Of course you're understood, sergeant. I'm not a monkey.'

'Then I'll be off.'

Crossman left them on the ridge, heading towards the curl of smoke he could see in the distance. His Tranter was in his pocket and there was a German hunting knife in the top of his boot. On the way down he amused himself and kept his fear at bay by inventing devices in his mind. He did this in rather a general fashion, so that he could picture his machines, but not in detail. He was no engineering genius, but he did have a love of brass and glass instruments, of railway engines, of gadgets and contraptions. When he and his friend Rupert Jarrard got together, they exchanged all the latest gossip on what was new in the world of machines. It was a passion both shared, along with smoking and good conversation. Crossman had not seen Rupert for some weeks and he missed his company. He wondered about Gwilliams and his friend. They were both Americans, yet they seemed to despise one another. Crossman wondered whether it was the neighbour syndrome. Almost every nationality had a near neighbour they hated, or at least disliked in the extreme. With the Scots it was the English. With the Norwegians it was the Swedes. With the Basques it was the Spanish, with the Bavarians it was the Prussians, and so on, and so on. Perhaps Gwilliams and Jarrard came from different parts of North America, parts which had a distrust of each other. There was the north–south animosity, but so far as Crossman knew, both came from the north-west. It was most intriguing . . .

'Hey! You! Stop there.'

A scraggy-looking individual was leaning over a rock, levelling a rifle at Crossman. Crossman put his hands in the air.

'I'm unarmed,' he called. 'Are you British, sir? Like me? I heard there were British at this farm.'

Crossman's accent had a mixture of Scottish lowland and Northern English counties about it – border country – but anyone with half an ear could tell it was not the accent of a common soldier. He knew this would make the rifleman suspicious and that it would take a little more persuading to get the man to come out from behind the rock. Crossman didn't want to be shot out of hand.

'I'm not an officer,' he called. 'I'm a sergeant. Was. Till I ran off. Fancy Jack's the name. Fancy Jack Crossman. You could've heard of me. 88th Connaught Rangers? A lot of people know me.'

'Oh, is that right? Never heard the name.'

'Well someone might have, at that farm there. Why don't you take me there, so I can talk to someone?'

'Why don't I just shoot you where you stand, Fancy Sergeant Jack? It don't mean much to me. I'll be hung anyways, if I get caught. It won't matter I killed another man.'

'It'll make a difference to you, and you know it. They'll post up a list of your crimes on the parish church notice board for all to read. Do you want your mother to hang her head in shame for having a son who's called a murderer, as well as a deserter? Running away from a fight in panic's one thing. Killing a man in cold blood is another.'

The deserter with the rifle emerged from behind the rock. He strode towards Crossman. At first Crossman thought he was going to receive a rifle butt in the face. But either the man thought better of it, or that had not been his intention in the first place, because all he said was, 'You come with me, Fancy Jack. Morgan'll want to see you.'

3

The man who led Crossman through the frost-covered farmyard was as unkempt and unwashed as himself. It was obvious he had been on guard, exposed to the raw weather, for many hours. A straggly beard and moustache thick with icicles hung heavily from his chapped cheeks. His long matted hair stuck out from beneath his torn forage cap like dirty straw. The clothes on his back were a motley collection of local furs and army uniform. He was a hunched figure, with bandy legs, pinched face and hollow chest. Crossman guessed he was actually from an English town, rather than a village, which made Crossman's former warning about notices posted up in the parish church less potent.

The farmhouse was a ramshackle affair with bowed stone walls and a turf roof which had collapsed at the northern corner. A door with leather hinges hung on its post, its bottom edge resting on the porch floorboards: it would have to be lifted every time it was opened or closed. Such windows as there were looked tiny and mean, like the sunken eyes of some sick, ill-tempered beast. Crossman was led to a barn which looked more substantial than the house itself. The deserter opened the doors to the barn and told Crossman to go inside and wait. Once he was in there, the doors were closed and barred, leaving him in partial darkness.

Crossman was able to see after a few minutes, if only dimly, for barns are seldom made so tight that no light enters. There are always cracks between the boards and in between the walls and the roof. Weak light found its way in. Moving around in the semi-darkness, Crossman tried to get his bearings. At one point he struck his chin on something, right in the middle of the barn. He reached out and, after feeling it, discovered a pair of woollen socks. These socks were occupied by the feet of a hanged man, who dangled from the central rafter by a long hemp rope.

'God save us!' exclaimed Crossman, shocked to discover the body. Now he realized he could smell the corpse, even though the temperature inside the barn was probably as low as it was outside. If anything Crimean buildings tended to lock the winter inside, even when the sun came out again, and thus they became ice houses for the preservation of meat. Here was some sorry piece of flesh, swinging back and forth a little where Crossman had started it off, like a creaking pendulum. He reached out and grasped one of the feet, to stop the cadaver from spinning. It was icy cold to the touch and as hard as stone.

As his eyes became used to the darkness, Crossman studied the clothes of the corpse and decided this was the farmer, the Tartar brother, who had gone missing. He realized now that Morgan Reece and his gang would never surrender to the authorities. There was no hope that they would escape the gallows. Crossman decided he had still done the right thing, for he had to gauge the strength of the farmhouse, both as a fortification and from the point of view of how many defenders it had, where its weaknesses were, and what was the best attack.

Crossman remained in the barn for the better part of three hours, before someone came to fetch him. It was not the man who had originally taken him there, but another, a Derbyshire man from the sound of his accent. Crossman was taken from the barn to the house. Just inside he found a roomful of men, some twenty of them, draped around, eating stew. They stared at him with hard eyes as he passed through, though not one spoke to him. Crossman sensed despair amongst them, almost as a disease like a cancer, spreading and growing. For the most part they were not upright men. They hung on their own bones, like the clothes of a scarecrow hang on sticks, and, although like flints, their eyes were ringed with darkness. They looked nervous and uneasy, like men who have pitched their all into one wager and were hoping for a miracle, knowing that in real life miracles were few and far between. Far, far back in those haunted eyes was the look of doom.

A Tartar woman was cooking for the men. She looked up with moist, bleak eyes as Crossman passed her and he guessed she was the dead farmer's wife or sister: one of the victim's relatives.

Crossman was pushed through another doorway and the door closed behind him. He found himself in a room in which boxes had been arranged like a desk, with a man seated behind them. The man was writing in a ledger of sorts and he motioned for Crossman to sit in a rickety chair, opposite him, but implied that silence was to be observed. It was as if he were some bank manager preparing a mortgage for an important client, while a debtor waited in forced patience for his attention. A wood-burning stove was throwing out a great heat from one corner of the room and Crossman enjoyed the comfortable feeling of home-fire warmth for the first time since he had been in Colonel Hawke's office. For a moment it lulled his senses into believing he was in a croft back home, with one of his father's tenant farmers wishing him well and bidding him sit by the grate where the heat would soften his boots for him.

Crossman did as he was asked. The writer had to be Morgan Reece. Crossman could see a corporal's stripes on the sleeves of a coatee which hung on a hook behind the makeshift desk. The coatee looked surprising well-brushed and the buttons were clean. There was webbing hanging there too, and a Minié rifle was propped against the wall, looking as well cared for as the clothes, with an oiled stock and metal parts.

When Reece finally put down his pencil and stood up, Crossman could see that he was a very large man, hard-muscled, with enormous, powerful-looking hands. Those hands were ingrained, like the brow and the neck, with black grime. Crossman guessed this was coal dust and that most likely Reece had been a miner. In fact he must have been a miner so long that subterranean explosions and daily contact with coal dust had permanently tattooed him.

There was a certain fastidiousness about Reece, at odds with his rough, granite looks, which caused Crossman to think that if those stained parts of his skin could have been cleaned, then

Reece would have ensured this was done. His hair was marble grey and stood up stiffly, about one inch, from his head. Unusually, it hardly grew at all around his neck and ears. The skin there was as creased as a well-used map. Crossman guessed the man's age was about forty, or thereabouts: he had been expecting a younger man.

'So – Fancy Jack, is it?' said Reece in a strong, lilting Welsh accent. 'I've heard of you. In fact I spoke to you, once, before a battle. What was it? Inkerman, I think. In the stockade together, we were.'

Crossman did not remember him. The sergeant had been thrown into a prison cell, accused of murdering a British officer. There had been a number of men already in the cell. It had been dimly lit, a battle was going on outside, and Crossman was understandably at the time in an agitated frame of mind. It was not surprising that he could not recall this man.

'You don't know me, do you?'

'No,' confessed Crossman. 'If you were there, I didn't notice you.'

'I was down for a flogging.' He was wearing only a shirt in this hot room, while Crossman was suffering still inside his furs. 'They weren't going to beat me, not again. I'd had enough of that. When the walls were blown down by that round shot . . .' Crossman did remember this, for it was when he escaped from the cell himself. 'I took to my heels. I ran. And I kept running, you see, and ended up meeting with others on the trail through the hills. Men who had had a bellyful of battle, who'd seen their comrades fall with their guts spilling out, or half a head missing. They'd had enough of officers who had slush for brains, who'd used them like cannon fodder, throwing them into a battle not of their making. Cowardly bastard officers, who kept well out of the way, when it came to it.'

'Many officers fought bravely and died beside their men,' replied Crossman, quietly. 'There were generals who fell in that battle.'

Reece turned and nodded his great head. His large hands gripped the edge of Crossman's chair. They were hands that could crush a man's windpipe with ease, if the owner so wished.

'Yes, you're right, some of them. Not all of them sat and watched. But then it is a war of their making. Men like me – and maybe you, sergeant? All we want to do is earn a shillin'. I'd had enough of the mines, you see. They killed my father and my older brother, who coughed up black sludge from their lungs as they died. That wasn't for me. I wanted to join the navy – all that clean fresh sea air – but it was a long walk to Cardiff and I found myself in the army instead. The regiment came to town, I was drunk, and there you have it. Now I find myself breathing cannon smoke and killing people I don't want to kill. Men like me. Poor men. Working men. Have you seen the way the Russian officers and NCOs take cudgels to the common soldiers, to make them fight harder? Treat them like animals, they do.'

'Russian officers are different. They treat their men differently.'

'Listen, man,' said Reece, leaning over him and breathing into his face, 'British officers have got more in common with Russian officers than they've got with us. The two of them speak the same way – I mean they talk about balls, and hunts, and dining out at clubs – all that kind of thing. They're both gentry, you see, with gentry pastimes. We don't have pastimes, we're too busy working. The British gentleman has nothing in common with us at all. We're like two different creatures: dogs and rats. We're the rats. We scrape about for a bit o' cheese, while they're fed on cream chicken and God knows what, given it like, in a silver bowl, without having to raise a finger. We're the ones who raise the fingers. We work them to the bone for gentlemen, British and Russian alike.'

There was a lot of sense in what Reece was saying. A gentleman did have very little in common with the ordinary working man. They moved in two separate worlds and only came together when the gentleman wanted to be driven somewhere by coach, or wanted some work done, or wished to be waited upon at the table.

'Which brings me,' said Reece, 'to the point I'm chasing after. You're a gentleman, Fancy Jack. Where do you fit in?'

Crossman felt the hairs on his neck prickle. He had thought, after the discussion about the prison cell, that he was home and dry with Reece. But the Welsh miner was a clever man. He had gradually put Crossman at his ease, then come in with a question that made his mind reel. What was he to say?

'I was a gentleman once, but no longer. I'm the victim of my own class. They're just as hard on me – harder in fact – than they have been on you. That's why I'm here.'

'Yes, man, I'm interested to hear why you've come to visit.'

'I'm the leader of a group of deserters, just like yours. We've been holed up in the hills north of Simferopol. Got chased out of there by the cavalry. Now we want to hook up with you. God man, it could benefit us both. Think, if this keeps happening,' he gave a short laugh, 'we'll have our own army.'

'How many?'

'How many men? Twenty-two, when I left them.'

'Why would a man like you desert?'

'You know – I was court martialled for murder. They were going to hang me.' Crossman put on a bitter, hard expression. 'I wasn't given a proper defence. They just wanted me out of the way. It was a conspiracy. They don't like having gentlemen in the ranks.'

Crossman was hoping and praying that Reece had not heard of him walking around the camp after the Battle of Inkerman. If he had, he would know all this was a lie. Crossman's hand went surreptitiously to his pocket. He had still not been disarmed and his revolver was of course loaded. Reece was the kind of leader who expected efficiency of his soldiers and perhaps he thought they had checked their prisoner for weapons. The reasons did not matter. What mattered was that Crossman could shoot Reece and be through the window in a moment, should this suddenly become a necessary option. Whether he would get much further than the yard outside was a question he couldn't answer.

Reece cocked his head to one side. 'I don't recall any talk about the hanging. I've seen many men hanged in my time. And many more shot by firing squad. Even when it's commonplace, there's still talk around it. The gallows is different to the battlefield or the hospital bed. Even when there's soldiers falling in their hundreds, or dyin' of cholera by the dozen, they still talk about a hangin'. Scaffold stories make a fascinating subject, sergeant. Men are interested.'

'No, they kept it pretty quiet, my sentence I mean. The

execution was to be carried out in secret, my father being a major in another regiment.' Crossman forced another quick laugh. 'You know what us gentry are like about scandals. We hate scandals.'

Reece paced round the chair, staring down at Crossman with narrowed eyes, and Crossman felt his life was on a thread at that moment. They had already dispatched the Tartar farmer, perhaps others in their course of terrorizing the district. They would think nothing of slitting the throat of a sergeant they suspected of coming to betray them.

'And this joining up you talk about? Who's to be the chief of that lot?' asked Reece. 'You, with your sergeant's stripes? You outrank a mere corporal, that's what you're thinking, eh? I already have a sergeant here, amongst my men. This is not a line regiment.'

Crossman didn't want to appear to cave in too easily to demands, he adopted a grave expression, as if this was a serious point.

'Well, that would be for you and I to discuss. I didn't come here with any set idea in mind. Maybe we could both still command our separate forces? Perhaps come together only when a combined force was needed? I'm open to suggestions.'

Morgan Reece didn't answer. Instead he went to the window and stared out at the cold world beyond. Crossman had no idea what was going on inside the man's head. He kept his grip on the butt of his revolver, prepared to use it. At a moment Reece could call in his minions to dispatch Crossman, or perhaps even do the deed himself, with those big hands. The sergeant was not going to go without taking some of them with him.

Finally Reece said, 'I'm going to let you live – for now. We'll talk more later. But before you think that this man's a soft touch, I'll tell you a little story. When I deserted, after getting out of that jailhouse, it was with another man, a friend of mine from the valleys. We stole horses and rode off into the hills. After two days my friend's horse went lame. He didn't want me to, but I shot the creature. Just as I would have done a pit pony, or any animal in pain. I shot it through the head, though he pleaded with me to just let it go, to roam the grasslands.

'After that we shared the one horse, taking turns to ride or walk, so's to keep on the move, thinkin' the troops were after us all the time. In one rocky place my friend slipped, broke his ankle. We strapped it up, with a splint and everything, but it wasn't any good, you see. It still bothered him so that he couldn't walk. I was exhausted too. One evening, I could see he was finished. He couldn't go on, not unless I let him ride all the time, and that would mean I would be finished too.

'I looked at his ankle and told him he was done. He looked back up at me and said angrily, "So, what are you going to do, Morgan? Shoot me like you shot the horse, is it?" I told him yes – and I did.'

'You – you shot your friend?'

Morgan Reece touched his furrowed brow with his forefinger.

'Right through the head. He didn't feel a thing. It was him or me, see? Nothing to do with friendship or any of that stuff any more. There was only one horse and he was the one with the injured leg. He was the one holding us back, not me. It had to be done. Look at me, sergeant.' Crossman looked at him. 'I'm an emotional man, see. Most of us Welsh are creatures of the heart. It shows in our poetry, in our singing. But I'm not sentimental. That's a different thing altogether. Sentiment is what destroys a man, cloys his spirit, brings him down in the end.'

'Yes, I can see it would be sentimental of you, to let your friend live and take his chances with the elements and your pursuers.'

'Not funny, sergeant. Not funny at all. I just wanted to illustrate to you what kind of man you're dealing with. You step out of ranks while you're here and I'll have you killed without a further qualm.' He gave Crossman the first smile he'd seen on the other's face. It was like a rock crumbling under a great weight. 'You'll become one of my stories, my illustrations, to use on people like yourself, when they come stumbling in here with their own tall tales.'

Crossman realized he had been dismissed. He walked towards the door and opened it, but before he stepped through he said to Reece, 'And the Tartar in the barn? Was he someone else who was holding you back?'

'That was necessary, sergeant.' He nodded towards the other room. 'You're free to enjoy the rewards of desertion from the British Army, while you're my guest. Warmth, shelter and hot food. It's more than the soldiers on the line get. Much more. No drinking during the day. It's one of my rules. If we're attacked I want sober men about me, not a lot of drunks. In the evening you can partake, if you have a mind, but not to excess.' Reece gave Crossman a cryptic smile. 'See,' he said, 'even their officers could not do that – stop them from getting drunk.'

Crossman could see that no other explanation was going to be forthcoming so he joined the men in the other room. The smell of the stew was overpowering and Crossman suddenly felt that animal called hunger gnawing at his stomach. He went to the woman who was cooking and asked her in the local dialect for a plate of stew. When she ladled some into a tin dish for him, he thanked her in her own language. A ghost of a smile appeared for a moment on her face, then it vanished as one of the men got up and grasped Crossman's wrist.

'What did you say to her, Johnny-boy?' asked the soldier.

Crossman stared into the man's face with hard eyes. 'None of your damn business. Let go of my wrist or I swear I'll break your face.' The words came out with such force and venom the man actually let go of him, then, on realizing how craven and foolish he looked in front of his friends, he said, 'You better watch your back, sergeant.'

A butcher's knife was lying on a wooden block beside the Tartar woman. Crossman snatched it up with his freed hand and said, 'You threaten me, you trash? I think I'll kill you now, then I won't have to watch anything, will I? I've just been told there's no law here, sonny, so what do I have to worry about, killing a cur like you?'

There was stillness in the room. Hardly a man breathed. The Tartar woman moaned softly. Then a quiet voice from the doorway broke the deadlock.

'Sit down, Gunner Randle. Who told you to interfere with my guest? Sergeant, put the knife on the block. Listen, all of you, how many times do I have to tell you if we fight amongst ourselves we won't last a month. You, each and every one of you, are deserters. You're worse than scum in the eyes of every decent man and woman from your homeland. You have not got a friend in the world, except he sits in this room.'

'He spoke to the woman,' said Randle, defensively, 'in Russ.'

'And if he did?'

'They – they might be plannin' something.'

'Ah, I see. Fancy Jack Crossman and a Tartar wench are going to take on thirty men and kill every damn one of 'em?'

'Well, no, but . . .'

'Randle, if you think something's wrong, then you tell me, you don't start one of your artillery brawls in my farmhouse.'

'Yes, corp.'

'Was that a surly "Yes, corp" or an I-see-the-sense-of-this "Yes, corp"?'

'The second.'

'Good.'

Reece went back into his room and conversation started up again, with Randle sitting in one corner a little apart from the others, silently contemplating his knees. He had been humbled by Crossman in front of his friends and he had to spend time coming to terms with this. Crossman did not want to make an enemy who might cut his throat while he slept, so he went to Randle while he was eating his stew and said between mouthfuls, 'No hard feelings.' Randle looked up, slowly. Crossman now saw that beneath the facial hair was a youth of perhaps only eighteen summers. A boy. Crossman suddenly felt sorry for Randle, probably a young man who had been behind a plough in Shropshire until a few months ago, when the recruiting sergeant of some regiment got him drunk and offered him the queen's shilling, along with a lot of drivel about good pay, good food and exciting world travel with his new 'family'. 'You know how it is,' continued Crossman. 'Temper's on a short fuse. It's this damn war. I never should have left home in the first place.'

A light entered the boy's eyes. He nodded, briskly. 'That's how I feel.'

Another man appeared at Crossman's elbow, a man with a sunnier temperament than most in the room. 'Our Billy givin' you trouble, sergeant? He's all right, ain'tcha lad.' The man ruffled the boy's tousled hair with his fingers. 'Just a bit edgy, eh? What's to do, sergeant? You come to join the merry band? Outlaws, we are. Just like that there Robin blagger, back in Merry England times. Rob the rich to feed the poor. That's us,' he laughed. 'We're the poor.'

'Except you're robbing the poor to feed the poor.'

The man's eyebrows went up. 'That's good. That's very good. No flies on you, eh sergeant? What made you run, eh? Me,' he continued jovially, 'I thumped a sergeant – beggin' your pardon. It was the man, not the stripes, what made me do it, you understand. An' he was not much of a sergeant at that. But if it wasn't that, it'd be something else. Davy Kershaw's just not the man to lay down and die of cold or cholera, or wait for his head to be shot off. I was just lookin' for an excuse to run and the sergeant was it. So, what made you start like a rabbit out of a harvest field and run for the hills?'

'Too much cheerful talk. It got me down.'

Kershaw guffawed, earning several frowns from the melancholy men who filled the room. 'I like you, sergeant. You're a dry one, you are. You an' me'll make a team all right. Get this lot out of the doldrums, eh?'

Kershaw was wearing the uniform of the 13th Light Dragoons. There were one or two other troopers there, which surprised Crossman. They were usually fairly dedicated soldiers, men who loved the cavalry and were there entirely by choice. Had Kershaw been in the fateful charge of the Light Brigade? What had made him so disaffected with the army? Crossman put the question to Kershaw, bluntly.

'My Betsy died,' replied Kershaw, his head and shoulders dropping. 'They did it to her.'

Several soldiers' wives, accompanying their husbands, had died in the Crimea. 'I'm sorry. Was it cholera?'

'Cholera? No. They shot her.'

Crossman was still mystified, his expression obviously revealing that fact.

'After the charge,' explained the trooper. 'There weren't nothin' wrong with her, but they shot her anyway. She had blood on her, but it weren't hers. More like mine, or some other beggar's blood. Wilson, probably. He was shot to bits next to me. We was covered in Wilson, pieces of him, Betsy and me. I yelled at 'em, but they took no notice. They went around shooting all the lame and wounded horses and they killed my Betsy by jammy. She was the best mount a man ever had. I punched the staff sergeant that did it.'

'Then you ran.'

'Like the wind, sergeant,' said Kershaw, his face lighting up again, grinning. 'Like the blessed wind.'

All for a horse, thought Crossman, wonderingly. This man was going to hang for a horse. A flash of anger over a mute beast and a man's life was forfeit. And he knew it too! Kershaw knew his sudden fit of rage had put his whole existence in jeopardy. He covered his despair well, with jocular quips and dry humour, but it was all a theatrical show, for underneath the man was festering. The grin was false, the light within artificial. He was a dead man already, and all for the love of Betsy, a mare who cared only for the hand who fed her oats.

Crossman left Randle and Kershaw whispering to each other. He went to another part of the room where he could be alone to finish his stew. The rest of that day and that evening he simply observed what went on around the farmhouse. Strangely enough, or perhaps not, it was run on strictly military lines. There were duty rosters posted up on the wall and each man had his daily tasks to perform. Picquets were posted and relieved at the normal regulation times for a well-run army. Reece was a stickler for discipline and clearly the other men were afraid of him. He was a formidable personality as well as being a large man who was obviously handy with his fists and boots. It seemed the deserters had given up one regimen, one set of masters, for another not so dissimilar. The main difference was they had their physical needs catered for here, whereas back at Sebastopol their welfare was at the bottom of the list.

That night some of the men went out on a raid for stores. It seemed this was becoming more and more dangerous as the local people now expected them and had of course armed themselves accordingly. Their weapons were older and less reliable than those of the deserters, who for the most part still had Miniés or carbines, but still they managed to kill one of the raiders. When they returned, Reece gave a little speech on being told of the loss and reminded them they were still at war and that casualties are part of any war. Reece could have been a general, handing out platitudes to his weary troops. What was more, the troops seemed to accept these words, nodding gravely to one another, forgetting they were not part of a legitimate army and were actually despised bandits who, if they were caught, would be hanged while others sneered in contempt. There was a lot of talk about 'comradeship' for a while, then the dead man was forgotten and the talk went on to dividing up a large wheel of cheese which had been stolen from one of the raided farms.

Later that day Reece sent for Crossman. 'You're going out on the next raid,' he told him. 'It'll give you a chance to prove yourself.'

'I'm used to leading, not following.'

'It won't hurt you to take orders for once, damn you. I've been taking orders all my life from lesser men than myself.' Reece was standing out by the barn in a sharp wind which brought out the rawness in his cheeks. They were mapped by red veins, like tiny cracks in his skin. 'If it came to it, I'd take orders again. You may be a sergeant now, maybe even a deserter, though we'll find the truth of that in due course, but for most of your life, Fancy Jack, you've had it easy. Hunting, shooting, fishing on your da's estate? Silk shirts and breakfast at eleven in the morning, eh? A dog at your feet by the fire while a servant brings in the brandy?'

'And you?'

'Try crawlin' along a black hole a hundred feet down in the earth, just enough room for your shoulders to brush the sides of the tunnel, the blackness hot and airless around you, the whole weight of the world pressin' down on your back. There's a panic in your breast like a wild beast, clawin' to get out, but you can't let it free because you'd go mad before you got to good clean air, and you've got eight to ten hours down there before you see the day or the stars again.' He sighed. 'I've seen 'em dragged out of the mine, screaming fit to wake the dead, their eyes like saucers. It's enough to choke you with fright. And it wouldn't be so bad if your masters – the ones who grow rich on your sweat and fear – actually cared about you. But I've seen 'em seal off a collapsed tunnel, men still alive in there, then go off to some damn lunch at the town hall, to laugh and joke with the mayor and corporation.'

'I can't believe that.'

'I've seen it.'

'You've seen them laugh and joke after a pit disaster? Never. I know there are some heartless men out there, concerned only about profit, but they all put a face on, of concern, be it false or otherwise. If they sealed off a mine shaft with live men still down there, it had to be for good reason.'

'Oh, they talk about the fear of explosion, about losing a greater number of men in the effort to save a few, but when it comes right down to it, they don't really care. We're animals to them. Pit ponies, canaries, men. That's the order. If a man breaks his leg, a support timber falls on it and cracks it in two, say, he's left on his own to mend. By the time he can walk again his family's starving and he's been thrown out of his hovel for not paying his damn rent. His ten-year-old son is in jail for trying to feed the family by poaching hares, his daughter's taken to the streets and his new baby's died of damp of the lungs. I've seen it all, sergeant. It's no good you makin' excuses for your kind. You get your legs shot off in this war and you go home to mamma and a basket chair. Get wheeled around by some lackey. Silk cushions. Tea on the lawn. Miss What's-her-name and her cupid's-bow lips calling to offer sympathy. Me? I end up beggin' on some street corner, sleeping in an alley at night, swingin' my stumps through some crutches made of tree branches that the Quakers have given me . . .'

At that moment one of the deserters taking air in the yard, young Gunner Randle it was, suddenly jerked backwards and fell to his knees with a shocked expression on his face. His action was immediately followed by the sound of a distant shot. The boy stared down at himself then began frantically to tear off his clothes. Crossman had seen this often enough before, on the battlefield. Wounded men were desperate to know whether they had been gut shot. A wound in the belly meant a slow but certain agonizing death. Such a victim might as well shoot himself through the brains, or get a friend to do it, because it would be less lingering and painful. Randle now had his shirt off and found the bullet had gone in just below the ribcage. There was a hole there, seeping blood. He let out a wail of fear.

Reece crossed the ground between them quickly, scooped up the youth as if he were an infant child, and carried him swiftly to the house, at the same time roaring, 'Get out of the open. Find cover. That was gunfire, damn it! The boy's been hit.' Bemused deserters began running this way and that, seeking a hiding place. No more shots followed the first, however. The assassin was not stupid. There was no positive knowledge of where the shot had come from. Further shots, with everyone primed and watching the hills around, might have helped to locate the sharpshooter. After a while men began to drift back to the farmhouse, Crossman among them, to see what was happening there.

Peterson was dejected. 'I didn't manage to kill him properly,' she said. 'He was alive when they carried him into the house. I saw one of his arms move. I think I hit him in the lower chest.' She and Pirce-Smith were making their way back to the *peloton*. For his part Pirce-Smith was astonished that Peterson had hit the target at all. She had been at least a thousand yards away.

'I don't think you have anything to chide yourself for, corporal. It was a magnificent shot.'

'But he wasn't dead.'

'As good as.'

'Oh, he'll die all right.' Her tone was bitter. 'He'll take hours to do it though. Maybe even a day or two. Do you have a horse, lieutenant?'

Pirce-Smith gave her an uncomfortable look. 'Yes, I have a horse.'

'If it broke its leg and you had to shoot it, you'd make sure you killed the beast with one shot, wouldn't you?'

'I suppose.'

'That's the way I feel about my work. If I've got to do it, and I do because I'm a soldier, then I want it to be quick and clean. Pain is the worst thing in the world. I wouldn't want my worst enemy to suffer pain.'

'Oh, I would,' came the cheerful reply. 'I can think of any number of people I'd like to suffer pain. My old schoolmaster, for one. He whipped me raw for the most minor offences. I suffered a great deal under his hand. I should like to see him curled up in agony . . .' The officer broke off there, remembering who he was talking to. One didn't usually converse with a corporal, not on informal terms, giving away one's feelings and emotions like this. Pirce-Smith occasionally slipped in such a way as would have earned him a few sneers from his fellow officers if they had witnessed this scene. It was, he agreed with himself, rather a contemptible show of familiarity.

'You'd like your old schoolmaster to be gut shot, would you, sir?' growled Peterson. 'To die screaming, with a thirst that can't be quenched? Is that the idea?'

Pirce-Smith stopped in his tracks. 'I think you forget yourself, lance-corporal,' he admonished, stiffly.

Peterson should have replied that it was *he* who had forgotten, that they were an informal group and the normal barriers did not apply. Sergeant Crossman had reminded Pirce-Smith of this fact several times while they had been out, but it never penetrated the mind of the clergyman's son. He was so taken with his elevated position in the army, he wanted special duties *and* to retain all the respect and deference that was due to his rank. Well it wouldn't do, but Peterson was not the one to tell him so. Wynter might have done. Crossman would certainly have done so. But neither of those two common soldiers, as different from each other as they could possibly be, was here to correct this pompous ass.

They arrived back at the camp without having spoken another word to one another. Gwilliams asked straight away, 'What happened?'

'I shot one of them,' replied Peterson, 'that's what happened. Didn't get him clean though. The sergeant's there. We saw him.'

'What did I say?' Wynter offered. 'I said he'd be all right, didn't I? He's got more lives than a cat. You shouldn't have moved so quick, sir. Didn't he tell you to wait a few days? He's bin gone less than two, and you go and panic.'

Pirce-Smith went into a fury. 'I've already spoken with Lance-Corporal Peterson about this familiarity. You will not question my orders, do you understand? I'm in charge here. I hold the queen's commission. If I have any more insolence I'll have that man flogged when we return to Balaclava.'

'Oh, right – sir,' said Wynter in a sarcastic tone.

'I mean it!'

'Course you do,' Gwilliams said. 'I can see in your eyes you mean it. But will it happen? We don't think so. Not for no crime like "familiarity". You're a goddamn fool, Mr Smith.'

'Under martial law I can have civilians flogged too.'

'You no flog me,' said Ali, coming over to the group now. 'I break you fuckin' back you try flog me. Listen, sergeant tell you no do nothing for five days. Already you do something and only two days. You got camel shit in here,' Ali tapped the side of his head. 'This no regular army. This sabotage. Rules no good here. Only good thing is stick to plans.'

'This sounds like a mutiny to me,' said Pirce-Smith, backing away from the Bashi-Bazouk.

Yorwarth, who had been cleaning his weapon, spoke up for the first time since the two had returned. 'Mutiny? That's an ugly word, that is. Men can hang for mutiny. If you're going to use that word when we get back to the lines, sir, tell us now, while we've got the chance to do something about it.'

Pirce-Smith frowned. 'What do you mean, do something about it?'

Yorwarth stared at the officer down the oiled barrel of his gun. 'I think you know what I mean, sir.'

Actually, Randle didn't take long to die, considering the type of wound. He was with his maker in four hours. Crossman had watched the poor boy go through all kinds of Hell and torment up to that blessed release. At the last he called for his mother, repeatedly, as dying youths often do, hoping she could stop the pain for him as she had done when he was little – not so many years ago, less than a decade. Had she been there her heart might have died with him. The poor boy was long past the stage where she could rub yarrow leaves on his knee-scrapes and kiss his forehead to make it all better. Pale as a tallow candle he slipped away, the terror locked behind his eyes. Reece had sat beside the wounded youth the whole while. He cursed God for a few moments then turned to Crossman.

'Who was that out there?'

Crossman said, 'Why ask me? It could have been anyone. Most likely a disaffected Tartar. Maybe that woman's husband?' He pointed to the cook who sat in the corner staring bleakly in front of her.

'That woman's husband is swinging from a beam in the barn.'

'I merely make an example. You think it's one of my men? That doesn't make sense. We're out here to join forces. Why would we go shooting each other?'

'I've only got your word for that. But we'll find out what you're about tonight, on the raid. Bury the boy,' said Reece to two of his men.

'Is it safe to go outside?' asked one of them.

'It's dark, for Christ's sake. Do it at the back, then. On the far side from the hills. You want his corpse here all night?'

'I'll help you,' said Crossman. 'Do you have a dark lantern?'

Reece said, 'Do it in the light from the window. Tomorrow we're going to ride out and look around those hills.'

Crossman's heart gave a skip. 'Ride?'

Reece stared at him. 'Why, yes, sergeant – ride. There are half a dozen horses tethered in the vale beyond, with two of my men watching them.' He nodded and gave a kind of smile. 'What, you thought we went on foot all the time? That would be rather foolish, wouldn't it, eh? To have no cavalry? You surely noticed there are troopers amongst us? Guthrie, for example, 17th Lancers. He came with two mounts. And Kershaw, he picked up a horse at a corral north of Mackenzies Farm. We're getting more mounts all the time. Soon we'll have a cavalry between us. We'll be our own Cossacks.'

Crossman was disturbed. Reece had horses. His men had none. That put them at a further disadvantage. Now there was a disparity in speed and striking power, as well as numbers. Nothing he could about it now though. He had to bide his time and keep his plans flexible. He stared down at the body of Randle, a pale pathetic length on the ground. The two conscripted sextons were already busy with adze and spade, chipping away at the hard-frosted earth, as resistant as iron under their hacking. Damn Pirce-Smith. Hadn't Crossman told the officer to wait? They just couldn't do it, these infantry lieutenants. They had to be seeking the path to glory. To stand around and do nothing was anathema to vicars' sons who wanted to be climbing the promotion ladder. Now that officer had endangered the life of his sergeant, the corporals and privates of the *peloton*, and himself. It had turned very messy all of a sudden.

'You on a Sunday stroll or what?'

Crossman broke his reverie and begged the soldier's pardon before taking up a shovel and helping them carve out the grave.

Reece held a short service, during which he quoted Corinthians 13 and the Song of Solomon by heart. He was pure chapel, through and through. The valleys would be proud of him, were he not a murderer and deserter from the army. 'I was a God-fearing man,' he told Crossman, 'though you might not think it. You can't go down amongst ancient forests, walk back through those old darknesses, and not feel the moist fingers of God's hand on the back of your neck.' By ancient forests and old darknesses, he meant the coal mines of course. Reece went on to say how he had been forever finding fossils of fern leaves on pieces of slag, and how they had brought to him the wonder that he was holding in his fist evidence of primal woodlands now vanished from his land. Reece had many of the Welsh traits about him: he was a poet, he had the deep-timbred voice to go with the art, he was melancholy as a matter of pride as well as fact, and chapel religion was etched into his soul. On being told, he acknowledged the poet in himself with some evident pleasure, adding, 'As to melancholy, why man, there are no happy poems at the Eisteddfod.'

Come the next evening it was time for the raid. Crossman was given a horse and he and five others, including Kershaw, went out into the gloaming. The raid was to be completed during twilight, since they did not want to ride in complete darkness, which would be sheer folly. Some distance from the farm they were to attack, they dismounted and proceeded on foot, to prevent warning the occupants with the drumming of hooves. The farmer was alert though and watching for them. This man was a Greek and had the patience of Mediterranean peoples. His family – sons, brothers, uncles, whoever – opened fire on the raiders before they could close with the stock in the stables.

Crossman heard the rounds pinging from the loose stones around him. Most farmers' weapons were old and ineffective at any range, but there was no guarding against the lucky shot, be it only one in two or three hundred that found the target. Crossman fired back, high, so as to be sure of missing. Then he joined Kershaw in a wild attempt at battering down the stable door with a heavy rock. The pair of them managed to smash through a wooden bar and enter the stables without being hit. There were only two mares inside, one a heavy plough horse. Kershaw led them out, back through the fire from both sides, after giving Crossman a flaming brand. He pointed towards the farmhouse with the words, 'Burn it!'

Crossman chose to misunderstand the order and at risk of his life mounted his horse and rode through the flying lead to throw the lighted brand on a hay barn which stood close to the house. Then he spurred his mount and joined the others in the retreat. They had been perfectly happy to leave him behind, but cheered when he caught up. Kershaw looked back and swore under his breath.

'I said the house.'

Crossman feigned astonishment, followed by a staunch denial. 'You did not. You pointed to the barn. I thought we were giving them a warning not to resist next time.' He sounded genuinely annoyed at being questioned, even to himself.

'Bah!' cried the trooper. Then, still looking back, he grinned. 'The wind's blowing their way. The house'll go up too, if we're lucky. Is anybody hit? No casualties?'

No one was wounded. Crossman reflected that it would have been a very unlucky act of God had they been. Twilight is the worst time for shooting people, especially if they're moving swiftly. The shadows play tricks with the eyes. Half-light makes men jumpy too, so they jerk the trigger, rather than squeeze it. It's an eerie business, he thought, defending your home as the sun goes down and the grey shades that are the prelude to night get deeper and deeper in hue. A kind of surreal phantasmal scene superimposes itself on the hard real setting over which the action takes place. The shooter fires blindly at what he thinks is moving, but is often wrong about the composition of his target, especially if there are birds out there to further confuse his dazed state of mind. All this, added to worn and inaccurate weapons, and the fear that accompanies such a situation. To actually hit a target in such circumstances would be remarkable.

They took the two horses back and Kershaw went in to see Reece. When he came out, he nodded at Crossman. 'You next.'

Reece was wearing a sheepskin coat. His fire had died very low in the grate and he did not seem inclined to get up and put another log or two on it. In front of him, at his table, was a battered old chess set, with one or two pieces missing. There was a woodchip in place of a knight and a salt cellar where the white queen should have been.

'Do you play chess?' Reece asked, without looking up.

Crossman shook his head. 'Never bothered to learn.'

Now Reece raised his head. There was a frown on his face. 'You surprise me, sergeant. I thought all gentlemen knew how to play chess.'

'What, instinctively? No. It never interested me to learn. My brother plays, and my mother, but my father and I were always too impatient to learn such a painstaking game. It's not in my nature to sit pondering something for minutes on end. I don't even like practising at something. I like to do it. My brother once tried to show me different strokes with a cricket bat. It all went in one side of my head and out of the other. All I wanted to do was play. I couldn't wait to get the bat in my hand, hit the ball and score some runs.'

'You prefer quick action, do you, boyo? Myself, I think chess is one of the most fascinating pastimes in the world. The royal game! I could play it all day long. You'll never be good at anything unless you practise. Didn't your da ever tell you that?'

'Frequently. Actually, I find I'm middling-good at most sports and games, and that's enough for me. Who wants to set standards for oneself that will eventually be impossible, once infirmity or injury sets in? The scores I achieve I will always be able to reach. I'm not for the high slopes. Now you, you'd probably have made a good general, whereas I have always preferred someone above me, to take the final responsibility.'

Reece continued to stare at him. 'Yes, I'm surprised. Surprised and – disappointed.'

'I'm sorry for that, but you shouldn't generalize when it comes to people. There are good aristocrats, and bad. There are some who like chess and those who loathe it. Everyone is different.'

Reece leaned back in the chair. He cupped his big hands behind his larger head. 'Kershaw told me you set fire to the barn when he ordered you to torch the farmhouse.'

'Kershaw is not accustomed to giving orders. Either he was not plain or I misunderstood.'

'Or perhaps chose to misunderstand?'

'What difference did it make?'

Reece let the chair come forward again and brought his hands down hard on the tabletop with a loud cracking slap.

'The difference it made is that I still don't know whether I can trust you. Well, that'll be discovered one way or another with my next raid. We've found a group in the hills, six or seven men. We're going to wipe them out tomorrow at dawn. You'll be in the vanguard, sergeant.'

Crossman swallowed hard. 'Six or seven men? How do you know it isn't part of my group?'

'Because this one has an officer with it. It's obviously some unit sent out to spy on us. You don't have any officer deserters with your lot, do you? I never heard of an officer deserting. They don't need to, do they, eh? They just pack up and go home when they damn well please, and never a goodbye or a thankee to the troops left behind. They buy their commissions, and sell 'em like they do their horses.'

'You saw an officer?' Crossman knew that Pirce-Smith had no insignia showing. 'What rank? Captain? Major?'

'Who the Hell knows what rank,' growled Reece. 'You could see he was an officer by the way he was struttin' around, throwing out orders like some oriental despot, like some damn potentate from a Chinee kingdom. I know an officer when I see one.' His eyes narrowed. 'I also know 'em by their boots and trouser bottoms.'

Crossman silently cursed Pirce-Smith. It was something Crossman had noticed too, at the outset, then let it slip his mind. The boots! Good riding boots of high-quality brown leather. Not the sort of boots a common soldier would wear.

'He might have taken the boots from a dead Russian officer.'

'These were English boots. I saw them plain enough through my spyglass. I'm not daft, man.'

'No, you're anything but stupid, Reece. Well, so we attack this group at dawn?'

'They won't be expecting us. They're a bunch of slow tops. We saw their fire, first off – smoke curling up, see? They put it out, quick like, but by that time we had their measure. I rode out with two of my men and made it to a vantage point. When

I got them in my spyglass one of them was still trying to stamp out the fire, while the officer strutted up and down, yellin' at them and shaking his fist into their faces.'

Something dawned in Crossman's mind. The only man amongst his *peloton* who would be stupid enough to light a fire in enemy territory would be Lieutenant Pirce-Smith. Yet if he was the one remonstrating over the lit fire then something else was at work here. There was more to this than a clumsy error on the part of the *peloton*. Some deeper motive was responsible. Crossman could do nothing anyway, but go along with Reece's plan of attack, and hope to salvage a victory from it.

'I hope we're going out with enough men,' said Crossman, trying a little reverse psychology. 'They might be stupid at spying, but if a patrol has been sent after us, you can be sure they're sharpshooters.'

'How many would you suggest?'

'For five or six enemy? At least twenty. To be sure of success.'

Reece shook his head. 'Too many. I thought fifteen. This may be some ruse or other, to draw most of us away, so that a larger force can attack our base. Kershaw can lead fifteen men, you amongst them, while we remain on the alert here. This time you'd better prove yourself, sergeant, or I'll be forced to do something with you. And I'll want to know where your own group is hiding when you come back. It's time we sorted things out between us, one way or another.'

'Agreed,' replied Crossman, promptly. 'I can assure you, Reece, that you have my full cooperation on the matter.'

Reece shook his head slowly. 'God, I hate you sniffy-nosed toffs, I really do. But with more men we could really take control of this area. Turn it into a fortress. Then the bastards would just forget about us. They wouldn't want to waste good men on bad.'

Just before Crossman left the room, Kershaw entered with one of those cheerful, triumphant looks on his face.

'Another deserter just come in,' he said. 'You want to see 'im, Reece?'

Crossman's heart sank to his boots. If this was another one of his men, sent in by Pirce-Smith, there might be problems. If not, then he would be from the right or left attack lines back at Sebastopol, which was equally disturbing, for he might conceivably have information about Crossman's group. Not everyone in the army was as tight-lipped as Crossman, or Lovelace, would have wished. Orderlies and batmen were privy to conversations and had been around their masters so long they went unnoticed. It was the barber's shop syndrome. Crossman waited to see who would walk through the doorway.

It was not one of his own men. It was a soldier from the 47th Foot, or so his cap badge said. He stumbled into the room with a recognizable shade of blue about the lips which Kershaw, and others, had somehow missed. Crossman recognized it though. Reece, too, had noticed the man's unsteady walk, and combined with the pallor of his complexion, this was enough to make him jump up from behind his table and yell for Kershaw.

'Get him out of here!' he cried.

Kershaw looked shocked by the reaction from his leader and grabbed the man by the sleeve. 'C'mon, fellah, you're obviously not wanted here.'

'Send him on his way,' growled Reece. 'Give him some food and water, but get him gone.'

Once the man, who had spoken not a word, was out of the room, Crossman said, 'He'll be dead by morning.'

'I think he knows it, too,' Reece replied. 'You could see it in his eyes. Must have been sleeping near a drain or something.' It was a common belief that the main cause of cholera was inhaling bad smells. 'Goddamn, you would think these people would know cholera when they saw it, by this time. I don't want no epidemic runnin' through this farm. We've been free of it, till now. A few bowel problems, but nothin' so serious.' Subconsciously, he wiped his mouth, as if to breathe the very air of a cholera victim was deadly.

Crossman, sensing that tonight was a watershed in their relationship, turned at the door and asked Reece one last question.

'Tell, what *really* made you run?'

Reece looked up. 'From the army? You want to know, don't you? Not just curiosity, is it? You need to know what makes men like me twist and turn. Well, I'll tell you, sergeant. I asked the question that no soldier asks. That no soldier even thinks about. I started asking what this war is all about. When you do that you find precious few answers. So far as I could find out, it wasn't about anything at all, sergeant. Oh, I got a lot a tangled bits about Russia taking over Turkey, and the rest of us being worried about it, but in the end it seemed to be about nothing more than a few princes and political men playing a game . . .' He pointed to the chess board on his desk. 'Then I asked myself the next question a soldier shouldn't ask himself, but which isn't possible to avoid, once you've asked the first. I said, Reece, do you want to die for all this mess? Do you want to freeze to death in a bloody ditch thousands of miles away from the land of your birth, for men like Raglan, men who spend their whole lives grinding you under their heels?' He paused before adding, 'Naturally the answer was no. What other answer could there be?'

What other answer indeed. Reece was quite right. A soldier did not ask questions about why he was fighting. Most had absolutely no idea and were not much interested in knowing. A soldier earned his pay by obeying orders. He got drunk at the canteen, enjoyed the comradeship the army had to offer, went whoring or home to his wife, and complained about his daily fare of salt beef and biscuit. He knew he looked good in uniform, be he the ugliest brute ever to leave a farm. A soldier's pride came from belonging to a regiment, elite or otherwise, with a glorious history. Every regiment had one or was determined to get one. What and who you were fighting for was, for the most part, irrelevant. Welsh, Irish and Scots soldiers were as loyal and fought as ferociously for their officers as did English soldiers. Nationalism was not a question. Regiments were formed of recruits from all four corners of the British Isles, along with a sprinkling of other nationalities. It always seemed remarkable to Crossman that men from these four separate nations, three of them with a long history of being at odds with the fourth, should hold each other and their common will to win so precious.

'I don't know what to say to you,' Crossman told Reece. 'It's not a pot of worms I would like to put my hand inside.'

Reece gave him a resigned smile. 'I don't blame you, sergeant. I did put my hand inside, and now it's stuck.'

Kershaw was impatient to leave.

'There're not enough mounts for all of us. We're on foot, so we got to go now, sergeant.'

They set off over the countryside by the light of the stars. It was slow going. It was not so much the larger boulders which impeded them, as the fist-sized stones that made them stumble and fear for a broken ankle. Still, progress was made. Kershaw let the sergeant into a secret which Crossman had suspected was the case all along.

'Reece, he thinks this is your lot out here. He's not stupid. I think so too. We think you're workin' under army orders, Sergeant Crossman.' Kershaw grinned the whole time he made this speech, as if he were telling a humorous anecdote. 'Oh, and by the by, if you're thinkin' of doing somethin' you might like to know that Cartwright, on back of you, has a carbine pointed at you. He'll let rip if you as much as look like runnin' or doing anythin' else unbecomin' of a deserter from the British Army.'

Crossman did not look behind him, knowing that Cartwright would indeed be there, loaded carbine at the ready.

'I understand. But you're both wrong.'

'I hope we are, 'cause I quite like you, sergeant. If you are one of 'em though, I reckon you must be pretty galled. Fancy them lightin' a fire! No wonder the officer was peeved. We'll save someone from a floggin', that's sure.'

'Save him how?'

'By blowing out his lights,' said Kershaw with another broad grin. 'Not much point in floggin' a dead man, is there?'

At dawn the raiders were creeping along a gully which snaked up and above the place where Crossman had left his men camped. They emerged on a small plateau which overlooked a series of cliffs and caves. Beyond these geographical features, in the very far distance, was the deserters' farm, sparkling in the morning frost. There was no movement around the caves. Kershaw trained a spyglass on the area.

'I can see where they lit the fire,' he told one of his cronies. 'Maybe they're all inside the caves.'

'They must have left a sentry out,' replied the man. 'They can't be that daft.'

Kershaw took a look at the peaks surrounding the caves but could find no sign of a sentry.

'We'll go up there, on that cliff edge. When they come out of the caves, we'll cut 'em down.' It was a reasonable plan.

The deserters found themselves nooks and crannies, with vantage points overlooking the caves in question. Kershaw posted two men at the rear, guarding the exit to the gully, in case they were attacked from that direction. There was no other way up onto the plateau, so Kershaw felt that his men were reasonably secure. Crossman sat leaning against a rock, observing the scene below. Cartwright remained at his back.

The morning crept on. A weak sun came out, slanting directly into their eyes. Kershaw realized he had not taken the light into account and was at first a little upset at his own lack of foresight. However, they were looking downwards and the light was not a big issue. Still no one emerged from the caves, however, and it came to the point where even if their pursuers were all sluggards, they would have needed to leave their beds to relieve themselves or drink something. Noon eventually arrived. Kershaw knew he had come too late. 'They've moved,' he said. 'We need to do a search. We're still fifteen against six, so I don't want you men to get jittery. We'll go down to the caves and see if we can pick up their tracks.'

The file of deserters returned down the gully, then used a goat track to reach the caves. Kershaw went first, peering into the darkness of the caves. His mistake was to assume the caves were empty and to be too easily satisfied of that fact, because in truth he could not see to the very rear of them. All he could actually see were three dark tunnels which wormholed into the soft rockface. Since his was a surprise attack, and there were no sentries posted by the enemy, his firm conviction was that any occupants of the caves would have come out long ago. He had no inkling that the whole thing was a trap and that he and his men had been lured to an exposed position with no cover at their backs.

He called his men forward and as they stood there, contemplating the remains of the camp, a volley of fire came from within the caves. Muzzle-flames flared out of the darkness. The stink of gunpowder was coughed from within the tunnels. Four of the deserters dropped immediately, Kershaw among them. The others either stood stunned and helpless, or ran like game birds this way and that, looking for cover that was not there. One even ran towards the mouth of one of the caves and lost half his head to a bullet which came out to meet him. Then some began shooting, wildly. Two men lay prone on the ground, their training coming to their aid, but after discharging their weapons they had to come up to reload, and exposed themselves to fire again.

One of those who stood shocked and gawking at the carnage was Cartwright. Crossman's revolver was out in a flash and he shot the luckless man through the chest before Cartwright could gather his wits. Another of the deserters saw the incident and fired at Crossman. The round creased Crossman's cheek. He turned to fire two shots at his attacker and missed with both. Ali came flying out of one of the caves at that moment and stabbed the man repeatedly in the back of the neck, until he fell with a groan to the ground. By this time three more deserters, one of them wielding a Highland Brigade broadsword, lay on the frosty ground. With ten of their number gone, within as many seconds, the others threw their weapons to the ground, yelling for quarter.

Pirce-Smith emerged from a cave with smoking pistol in his hand. He was followed by a grim-faced Gwilliams. The others came out of the remaining two caves. 'Corporal,' said Pirce-Smith to Wynter, 'bind the prisoners, one to the other, in a line.'

'What with?' cried Wynter, reasonably, looking round.

'Haven't you got any cord, man?' asked the officer, irritably.

'Me, I have cord,' said Ali, retrieving his knapsack from a cave. 'I make prisoners.'

Once the deserters were secure, sitting in a roped circle, with bowed heads and Peterson guarding them, Crossman spoke with Pirce-Smith.

'Whose idea was this plan?'

'My idea, sergeant,' snapped the lieutenant, defensively. 'You disapprove?'

'No. Not at all. I left you with the problem of drawing them out and avoiding a frontal attack. It was well devised. However,

I thought the first shooting was a stupid act, especially since I'd been amongst the deserters less than twenty-four hours, but this was good. To divide and conquer. Simple but effective. You handled it well, sir.'

'I don't need your approbation, sergeant. And I take exception to being called stupid . . .'

'I didn't call you stupid, I said the incident was stupid. If you like to assume the mantle, do so. Can we leave it there, sir, and stop arguing amongst ourselves? I am still in charge of this fox hunt. You're now back in the role of an observer. There's still the matter of fifteen or sixteen deserters back at that farm. The odds have been considerably reduced now. We might well consider a direct attack.'

'It's still more than two to one.'

'You forget, I know their dispositions now. I know the way their leader thinks. There's one problem. They have mounts.'

Pirce-Smith nodded. 'Cavalry against infantry.'

'I was thinking more that they could escape without our being able to follow.'

At this moment the Bashi-Bazouk came over to shoulder the officer out of the way, saying, 'I fix sergeant.' Ali referred to Crossman's cheek wound, which the Turk treated with a poultice of some healing plant he always carried with him. Crossman was told to press the poultice against the seared groove on his face, but this became tiring after a while and even though Ali remonstrated with him, he found he could not keep it up.

Gwilliams was placed on sentry duty, along with Peterson. Yorwarth asked Crossman, 'Do we go in and cut a throat or two, now?'

'No, Reece'll be on the alert when Kershaw and his men don't return.'

'What about setting fire to the place?'

'They have a hostage. A Tartar woman. I'm certain Reece would let her burn. We shall post ourselves in two and threes around the farm. The source of their water, the well, is at least thirty yards from the farmhouse itself. Reece has ordered a bathtub to be filled with drinking water, but with fifteen men in the house, that won't last long. Sooner or later they'll have to attempt the run to the well. When they do, we'll pick them off.

I'm hoping our first attack will cut them up enough to drain their confidence in their superior numbers.'

He explained his plan to all those who were not on sentry duty.

'We go in first as a complete group tonight.' Crossman drew a plan of the farmhouse on the ground. 'Here,' he pointed with a stick, 'is the room in which they normally congregate. Reece is usually in this one, next to it. We begin by pouring fire into the main room through the windows, hoping to wound as many as possible. We have to hit them hard and quickly, while they're still wondering where their raiding party has got to. After a first furious attack, we split into three smaller groups and post ourselves at three separate points around the farm, but not so far apart that we can't protect each other against a cavalry attack. Thereafter we wait until dawn and pick them off as and when they show themselves.'

'What if they try to use the horses to escape?' asked Pirce-Smith.

'Then we hit as many as we can. There are not enough horses for all of them, so I'm hoping for a rift amongst them. Since they can't all ride off into the night, the argument will at first be that they all stay and fight together. When this breaks down they'll start fighting amongst themselves for the mounts, in order to escape. As I said before, they may decide to attack us using the horses. Some of them can't ride at all. Others not well. They're mostly infantry soldiers, though a few will be farm boys and used to horses of a kind. Any cavalry attack will not be well co-ordinated and our groups will be close enough to produce flank fire. Any questions?'

Ali said, 'Maybe they double ride? Two man to one horse?'

'Maybe. If they think of doing that, many of them will probably get away. We can't cover all possibilities. In which case, we shall continue to hunt them down. My hope is that without enough experienced riders they won't be able to organize such a retreat.'

Wynter was sceptical. 'Sounds messy. We got this lot,' he pointed at the prisoners. 'Why not just take them back and say we did our best?'

Yorwarth snorted. 'Half a job? That'll satisfy the major.'

'Better a dressin' down from Major Lovelace than gettin' your arse shot off,' countered Wynter.

'Might be a good idea to shoot your bloody arse off,' retorted Yorwarth. 'Save you stinking out the place with your damn farting every five minutes. I swear you eat shit on the quiet, Wynter. I never smelled anything so foul in all my life, before I met you.'

'Sleep upwind, is my advice,' replied the unperturbed Wynter, 'then you won't have nothin' to complain about.'

4

Just as it was getting dark Ali, who was on guard at a high point, called down that an attack was coming. Reece had not waited for Crossman to come to him. The leader of the deserters had taken the initiative and had come looking for the sergeant. The enemy were on horseback and on foot, and they still outnumbered the defenders. After the first few shots, the prisoners held in the caves guessed what was happening, and began yelling down to their comrades below, calling for rescue and the destruction of their captors.

Wynter rushed into the cave with his bayonet fixed. 'Anyone makes another sound and I'll run 'em through,' he swore. 'Just try me if you think I'm bluffing. I'm not regular army. It don't matter to us whether we bring in prisoners or not, and we'd just as soon not if we're given any kind of excuse.'

They took him at his word. During the night there were spasmodic exchanges of fire, but nothing serious. Just as dawn crept over the horizon there came the screams of dying men from the deserters' position. Ali and Gwilliams had got a man each with their knives and had slipped away amongst the grey stones, in the grey light, to rejoin Crossman's group. The situation began to unnerve the enemy. If this small band of men had killed and captured the first fifteen of their number, they could surely do the same with the second half of their gang. With the true morning light the firing increased. Victoria carbines and Minié rifles blasted at each other from high and low. Chunks of rock flew as large calibre balls struck boulders and stacks. It was now stalemate of a different kind. Every man had his niche and was well hidden amongst the natural fortifications. Lead would continue to fly back and forth with no definite result, unless something unusual happened.

The unusual came from young Yorwarth. The Australian managed to wriggle along a rock chimney to a position where he could see the enemy's mounts. Taking up a stance in a rock chimney he shot one of the horses through the head. The dying beast let out a horrible unearthly scream before dropping to the ground with a thump. The other horses panicked and started thrashing and kicking.

Most of the deserters' mounts had been hobbled at the ankles but two were tethered to boulders. These two broke away and bolted. One of the deserters shouted, 'They're killing the horses. We'll be trapped!' Now it was the men who panicked. One rushed for a charger, cut its hobble, and jumped on its back. He rode off towards the farmhouse, only to be shot out of the saddle by Peterson. A second one tried, and a third. One of these managed to get away. The rest of the deserters began to fight amongst themselves for the remaining three mounts.

'Down amongst them!' ordered Crossman. 'Shoot to kill!'

The *peloton* then moved swiftly down the slopes, firing at will, the deserters now thoroughly disorganized. Two of them tried to escape on foot. The first was shot in the legs by Ali, with a kind of blunderbuss he carried. The second was felled by the butt of Gwilliams' rifle; the American was fast on his feet and determined not to be outrun.

Lieutenant Pirce-Smith was attacked by a deserter visibly foaming at the mouth. His heated brain had been maddened at the height of the battle, and he came at the lieutenant shrieking. Crouching like a big cat, he sprang, avoiding the swing of Ali's blunderbuss barrel, to slice the air with his sword just a fraction of an inch before Pirce-Smith's throat. No longer human, the face was black with rage, the lips thickened with blood, the eyes wide and rolling. The officer stood his ground and shot his attacker twice in the chest with his pistol. The man dropped, not quite dead and still twitching, at the officer's feet, his head on one of the infamous brown boots.

It was Pirce-Smith's first close-quarter action and he was surprised to see how steady his firearm hand had been. A while later, when the action was over, he was again surprised to find himself shaking violently. His teeth rattled in his head and it was all he could do to stand upright since his legs were almost uncontrollable. He did his best to hide the shock he was going through from the others, being ashamed of his reaction and mistakenly feeling that it was somewhat cowardly to tremble like a frightened child. Ali took him aside, gave him a drink, and murmured his admiration for the calmness Pirce-Smith had shown when faced with death. Pirce-Smith was grateful for both water and words.

In the meantime, Crossman pursued a man into a cluster of rocks, ordered him to drop his weapon and halt, and when this order was ignored the sergeant shot the man through the spine. The soldier, a sergeant sapper, fell to the ground with a groan. He lay there staring bleakly up at Crossman, who kicked his weapon away from him, then went back to the main fray to assist his men. When Crossman returned, the sapper's eyes were glassy. A new wound gaped. Left alone, he had cut his own throat. Crossman could not help but feel it was for the best. Hanging a man was unpalatable enough, but when the victim had to be assisted to the noose, lifted and carried in some form of chair or litter, with public eyes following his progress, it made for a most unbearable execution.

With the new prisoners under guard, Crossman thanked his men and praised their actions. 'Well done. Any wounds? Peterson?'

'My shoulder, sergeant. A bayonet.' Her face was the colour of old bread. Crossman told her to sit on the ground until she could be attended to.

'Any others?'

Yorwarth, it seemed, had a broken jaw, from a rifle butt. Since he could not speak to tell of it, Wynter did it for him.

'Strap his jaw up, Wynter, until we can get him to a surgeon.'

'I'll fix it,' Gwilliams said. 'I've fixed many a jaw, collarbone and broken joint. Is there any liquor, sergeant? He can still scream. His throat's not broken.'

'The Turk has some,' replied Wynter. 'Ask him. But don't

you go cracklin' no bones near me. I can't stand the sound of grinding bones, specially in a man's face. It gives me a funny feelin' in my belly. Just you wait till I've gone for the water.'

Peterson, still on the ground, said, 'What, you volunteering to go for water, Wynter? It's worth a blade wound, to hear that.'

Later, Yorwarth's face was looking like something that had been cobbled together with sticks and straps. He was quietly drunk and beyond pain. Peterson had been attended to by Ali, and began looking much better once she got some soup inside her. Pirce-Smith had been observing her a lot of late and she knew he suspected her of being something other than she claimed. She asked Crossman to have a word with the officer about it. It was Pirce-Smith, however, who came to Crossman.

'The leader, Corporal Reece. He doesn't seem to be amongst the prisoners.' Pirce-Smith nodded towards the sullen group of men huddled in the cave.

'No,' replied Crossman. 'He's one that got away. I think there were four who escaped on horseback. One of the horsemen was the Pestilence we happen to call Morgan Reece.'

The lieutenant's humour was buried too deep beneath his sense of duty and overwhelming current feeling of self-importance.

'I don't follow.'

'The Four Horsemen of the . . . Oh, never mind,' sighed Crossman. 'I don't see the man, he's not here, so one of those who escaped must have been him.'

'You told Colonel Hawke we would bring him in alive.'

'No, Colonel Hawke asked me to do so, and I said I would try. The colonel is not expecting miracles. It's unfortunate, but we don't have mounts ourselves.'

'There are two remaining horses.'

'Peterson can probably walk, but Yorwarth will need to ride. Also two of the prisoners are too badly wounded to go on foot. Would you have me execute them here, without a trial? No. Then the two horses are spoken for. Reece will have to wait until another day.'

Pirce-Smith, surprisingly, remained calm. It seemed he had lost his taste for trying to assert his authority over Crossman. In all attempts he had come off worse, mainly because of the collusion between the sergeant and his men. In fact, he was biding his time. Yes, the colonel had told the lieutenant he was there in the role of an observer, that Sergeant Crossman was the man in charge, but the colonel was not here to see things. Pirce-Smith felt sure that once certain circumstances were explained to the colonel, he, Pirce-Smith, would be vindicated in his attempts to take control of matters. An officer instinctively knew what was the best course to take in any given military situation: that was his vocation. A sergeant, high born or not, was subordinate to that instinct. The colonel must be made to realize that it was impossible for a lieutenant to remain a dispassionate observer, while his sergeant made all sorts of errors of judgement. It could be expected of no officer worth his salt.

'I wish to speak to you of another matter, sir,' said Crossman, interrupting Pirce-Smith's train of thoughts. 'Lance-Corporal Peterson feels you are sitting in judgement over him the whole while.'

'Peterson? Well, I just find the boy strange. There's something peculiar about him. What was he in civilian life?'

'A carpenter. Actually, a cabinet maker.'

'Really?' the officer glanced over at Peterson, who was quietly sipping her soup. She caught the look and turned away. 'I would have taken him for a callow bank clerk, or something of that nature. There's something of a *smoothness* about him.' Pirce-Smith's voice fell to a whisper. 'I don't know whether you've noticed, but he bears all the mannerisms of a sodomite, sergeant. I'm not accusing him of anything, you understand, but I feel there is a latent force at work there. When the other men talk of whores, in the way that common soldiers will do, a look of annoyance, almost *anger* comes over the boy's face. It leads me to believe that not only is he not interested in wenches, as any strong-blooded soldier is, but he actually dislikes them. You should keep a keen eye on that youth and steer him away from any unfortunate tendencies to follow an *unnatural* carnal course.'

It was all Crossman could do not to roar with laughter.

'I shall bear your warning in mind, sir,' he said, with all the gravity he could muster. It was not enough.

'You find the situation funny, sergeant?' Pirce-Smith's prickles were up again.

'No, no – I can understand your concern, sir. Peterson, well, he doesn't like doing his ablutions with the rest of us, but I always put this down to natural shyness. He's a quiet, kind-hearted boy, despite his remarkable ability with a rifle. He was raised in a remote country district by his mother, with no father present, and that probably accounts for his – his *strange* ways. The way he sits, and holds his plate when he eats, and that moist look in his eye when we come across a dead animal. He's a sensitive creature, whose model has been his mother, who I understand was a fine gentle creature with a heart of gold. Why, he hardly needs to shave yet. You must have noticed that?'

'Yes, of course, but there are many boys here in the Crimea whose faces have never felt a razor. It's just that . . .'

'Jesus Christ,' interrupted Crossman.

The lieutenant rocked back on his heels. 'What? You shock me, sergeant. To blaspheme in front of a superior officer?'

'No, no. You misunderstand, sir. I was just drawing a comparison. Christ was a carpenter, was he not? He was not interested in the ladies, not in that way. Perhaps we have the makings of a Messiah in young Peterson?'

'You *are* making fun of me, sergeant,' said Pirce-Smith, stiffly. 'It does not do you justice. I resent it very deeply.'

Crossman realized he had overstepped the mark and was seriously offending his lieutenant. 'Forgive me, sir,' he said, 'I mean no disrespect, but Peterson has been with us a long time. I merely sought to lighten a situation which was also becoming offensive to *me*. I'm sure you have the *peloton*'s best interests at heart, but I fear you are completely on the wrong track in this assumption. Peterson is a fine soldier and I am wholly convinced he is not interested in sodomy – I am absolutely certain of it. So, forgive me, lieutenant, if we dismiss the subject now. I'm sure you understand that I always have the best interests of my soldiers at heart and I'm grateful for your observations, but in this instance you are mistaken.'

Pirce-Smith cleared his throat. Clearly the subject itself was unpleasant and distasteful to him, so there he left it with a, 'Quite. Well, I shall continue to give you the benefit of my observations, whether they be mistaken or not. Good night to you, sergeant.'

'Good night, sir.'

Later, when Pirce-Smith was out of the way, Peterson came to Crossman.

'What did he say? He was talking about me, wasn't he?'

Crossman smiled. 'He thought you were trying to get into bed with Wynter.'

A look of such utter revulsion came over Peterson's face, Crossman had to growl out a laugh this time. Peterson said, 'Wynter? What, he knows about – about me?'

'No, he thinks you are a male homosexual, Peterson.'

'What?' Her face was a picture.

'It's a reasonable assumption to make, given the circumstances. Let's not labour it.'

'A male what? I don't know what one of them is.'

'It's a man who prefers the sexual favours of other men – to those of women.'

'Oh?' Clearly this quirk in life had never entered Peterson's thought patterns before now. She struggled with it for a while, silently, before shrugging. 'Well, that's a turn, isn't it? I don't feel ignorant. It's not something I would get around to knowing, things being as they are.'

'You're surely aware of women who enjoy other women?'

'Yes, but that's different. Women are nice soft creatures, mostly with nice ways. They seek comfort in each other. They let men do things to them, because that's the way things are, but you should hear how much in contempt they hold men, when men aren't around. I can't understand it, the other way around, sergeant. I mean, what's nice about a man? Nothing. Not their ways, not their bodies. That's why men prefer to fall in love with women and to kill each other. That's why men would rather live with women, because they can't stand each other. Isn't that so, sergeant?'

Crossman shook his head to clear it and found it still tangled with her argument. 'I don't follow your reasoning, Peterson, though I'm sure to you it's perfectly sound. Can we leave it there?'

'Does it bother you, sergeant?'

'No, not a great deal anyway. I would just prefer not to delve too deeply into matters of human biology that few of us understand. They lead nowhere. Now, if you would like to talk of Mr

Brunel's latest achievement in the field of engineering, then I should be happy to accommodate you, Peterson. Yes?'

'No,' replied that soldier, and went back to her warm fire to contemplate the fathomless mysteries of mankind.

For most of that evening, both prisoners and captors were licking their lips, trying to get the taste of gunpowder out of their mouths. The loading and firing of weapons involved biting the paper cartridge, which inevitably meant a residue of gunpowder on the tongue. It was an acrid taste which opened up the taste buds and seemed to stay in the mouth for long hours afterwards.

One of the prisoners died of his wounds in the night. There was nothing Crossman or anyone could do to save him. A round from a large calibre firelock, a Brown Bess or a Minié, left a huge hole and often smashed through vital arteries and organs, and shattered bones. Flesh tore away easily under the impact of a chunk of lead which was over two-thirds of an inch in diameter. Crossman reflected that in this war there was around thirty times more chance of being hit than in previous wars, if you were up against the mighty Minié. In the Peninsular wars one round in 460 fired was likely to hit its target, while with the Minié, it was down to one round in sixteen. The modern rifle was a devastating weapon, highly accurate over much greater distances, with great penetrating power. Crossman wondered whether any new rifle could ever become more powerful than this weapon which could shoot through three or four bodies in a closely packed column of men.

Those who had slept woke to a bitterly cold morning, with the wind slicing down from the Ukraine like a scythe. Wynter, who was never seen out of ratty-looking fur hat, head-sock and mittens, rose stiff and blood-eyed to begin arguing with Gwilliams. The barber had started the day by bragging that he had shaved an American frontiersman, a fellow by the name of James Bowie, just before a battle called the Alamo, which he said was in a place called Texas. Wynter, whose first experiences of travel were in this war, and whose knowledge of geography was sparse, considering that before the age of seventeen he had not been more than fifteen miles from the hut in which he was born, hated it when Gwilliams went on like this.

'Boo-ey? Never heard of 'im,' said Wynter. 'Ain't never heard of no place called Texas, neither.'

'You ain't heard of much at all, now have you?' said Gwilliams, wryly. 'The Alamo was where we taught the Mexes something about fighting, my friend. Something about the mettle of us Americans.'

Pirce-Smith, who had been unable to sleep because of the cold, and had sat up through the bleak small hours running the day's events through his mind, over and over again, and wondering at his reactions to the killing of the madman who almost took his life (whether he trembled afterwards because he almost died, or because he had killed another man) felt inclined to join in this conversation for once. It had been a long lonely night for him and he needed human contact, even if it was with these common soldiers that even Wellington had called 'scum'.

'So far as I recall from my military studies,' he said, 'the Battle of the Alamo was a defeat for the American defenders.'

'That's true,' replied Gwilliams, waving a stick he was about to consign to the flames of the fire, 'but a great one. A few good men up against vastly superior forces. They all died – Davy Crockett, Colonel Travis, Jim Bowie himself – which was a shame 'cause I shaved him real good, real close. He said he hadn't had a chin so shiny since he last drunk milk. They was heroes, every one.'

'You survived, though?'

'Me? I weren't in the battle. I was on my way north. Just happened to be passing, is all. I shaved both sides, you could say, 'cause there was an American who fought for the Mexicans, man by the name of Johnson from Illinois way. He was a sharpshooter, just like Peterson here. Shaved him too, on my way through. Edgy fellah. Nicked his chin. Wouldn't keep still, not for one minute.'

Wynter was disparaging. 'An American fought for the Mexicans?'

Pirce-Smith said, 'You should not be so caustic, Wynter. There were Europeans on the side of the Mexican general, Santa Ana, as well as other Americans. Mercenaries. Some of the best troops in the world have fought as mercenaries. I myself think that patriotism and honour are by far the most noble motivations for a soldier, but you must not dismiss the mercenary soldier with such contempt. Look at the Swiss! They provide many foreign armies with well-disciplined troops.'

Gwilliams said, 'I myself don't much like mercenaries.'

'Damn it man,' said Pirce-Smith, 'you're one yourself.'

Gwilliams looked up from poking the fire with astonishment on his face, then he roared with laughter. 'Ain't that a fact, though. I *am*.'

Crossman broke camp just after eight o'clock. With the severely wounded on the horses, they slowly made their way south-west, back down to the frozen trenches of the Sebastopol siege. After a few more nights in the open, they eventually reached their lines, having circumnavigated the place where they had run into the three Russian deserters. Crossman was taking no chances with the Cossacks, who had marked him out for special attention since he had killed several of their number.

Lieutenant Pirce-Smith had reaffirmed his decision to seek a court martial for Crossman. Unfortunately, it was the officer who was ordered to Colonel Hawke's presence first, which put the sergeant at a huge disadvantage. Lovelace was away on one of his own missions. Were he there Crossman could have expected support from him. As it was, he was on his own. He did not know the colonel well. Hawke took over from General Buller some while ago, but Crossman had not had the same contact with his new commander as with the old. Buller was a more open, affable man than Hawke, who tended to be sharp, sometimes abrasive, and whose cold clear thinking organ was a superior mechanism to Buller's old brain. He had been appointed by some dark department of the government back in Britain. He reported to them only, leaving Lord Raglan, that despiser of spies and saboteurs, completely unaware of these undercover activities. Raglan knew of the colonel's presence of course, and that he had something to do with 'gathering information for the purposes of improving the position of the Army of the East and other British armies on campaign abroad' but the commander-in-chief believed Hawke was some kind of administrative engineer, collecting statistics and general facts for the furtherance of technical progress.

Hawke, who in turn despised the general staff, many of them

close friends or relatives of Lord Raglan, fostered this view of himself by dropping such snippets as, 'Did you know that if we increased the diameter of the wheels of our 6-pounder guns by a mere two inches they would travel through this thick Crimean mud with a great deal more ease than they manage at present?' Lord Raglan thought him a bore and had only twice invited him to dine, though the peer was always civil and apparently willing to listen to Hawke's enthusiastic utterings. There were generals who were aware of Hawke's real work and status, but they were not inclined to give him up to Raglan, since they realized that the lives of their men, and perhaps themselves, not to mention the outcome of the war, depended upon the intelligence gathered by Hawke's clandestine methods.

Hawke listened patiently to Lieutenant Pirce-Smith's account of the fox hunt, pursed his lips when told that the main object of the exercise – to capture Corporal Reece – had failed, but brightened his countenance on learning that the gang had been broken, with a number dead and others in chains.

'The main thing is, lieutenant, did you learn anything? Were you able to take advantage of Sergeant Crossman's experience in the field? I hope we can make something of you in this department.'

'I – I learned a great deal,' replied Pirce-Smith, with some hesitation in his voice. 'Although . . .'

Hawke's face, clean-shaven, his hair cropped short and standing in tight clumps on his narrow head, was like granite.

'Although?'

'Well, I have to request a court martial for the sergeant,' replied the lieutenant, coming rigidly to attention. 'I'm afraid he not only disobeyed an order – several orders – was insolent and insubordinate, but he incited his men to mutiny. I was ordered by him to be disarmed and this illegal order was carried out.' Now that he had said it, it sounded right and proper, and he felt entirely justified in what he was doing. This was nothing to do with personalities. It was to do with the rule of law in the army.

Hawke stroked his chin with a strong, lean hand. 'I see. These are serious charges. I feel, lieutenant, that before we proceed any further we ought to send for the sergeant. I wish to enquire more deeply into this affair before making any sort of judgement. Do you agree?'

'You are going to arrest him, sir?'

'No, when I say "send for him" I mean exactly that.'

Crossman was duly sent for and arrived to find the two officers still in an awkward silence. Hawke began by questioning Crossman, who gave his version of the events which took place when the *peloton* came across the three Russian prisoners. Hawke was left nodding, holding his nose between prayer-straight hands.

'So,' said the colonel, 'you did not execute the Russian deserters.'

'Of course we didn't . . .' began Pirce-Smith, but Hawke interrupted him with a sharp, 'Not you, sir, the sergeant.'

'No,' replied Crossman, 'we did not. We – I waited too long, sir. I realize that by leaving them alive we were jeopardizing our mission.'

'But you are human, too, and they were beginning to grow on you as fellow human beings, is that it, sergeant?' finished the colonel in a rather disapproving tone which sent a warning tingle up the spine of Pirce-Smith, who began to wonder about his senior officer's point of view. 'This *humane* streak you have in you has always been rather worrying to Major Lovelace and myself, sergeant, as well as to your former commander. General Buller felt it could be exorcised by more experience in the field, but it seems to me it still lurks within you, ready to betray you sometimes. Well, you know I'm not at all happy with you, over this, but since you had the sense to avoid the area on your return we'll let it pass.'

'Thank you, sir.'

Hawke now turned his grim attention to the lieutenant, whose eyes had been opened just a little wider in the past few moments.

'Lieutenant, are you a locksmith, perhaps? Are you familiar with the cryptic workings of locks? I mean, we all have a little knowledge of locks, and imagine we know what goes on inside them when we turn the key, but when it comes to repairing them, taking them apart, putting them back together again – could you do such work?'

Pirce-Smith was naturally bemused by this sudden change of direction and shook his head. 'No, I don't think I could, sir.'

'If you wished to gain knowledge of levers and ratchets, and whatever other mysteries locks held, who would you go to?'

The lieutenant shrugged. 'A master locksmith?'

'Even though you, as a gentleman, would consider yourself in all other ways to be the superior of a tradesman like a master locksmith?'

Again that warning tingle up the spine. 'Yes, I believe so.'

'I would say so too,' acknowledged the colonel. 'Yes, a master locksmith. Now, when it comes to espionage and sabotage, there are those of us equivalent to master locksmiths, while others are merely apprentices, not even, I fear, journeymen. Do I make myself clear?'

'In a roundabout way, sir.'

The colonel's voice was still calm while his face darkened. 'I think I make myself damned clear, sir. As clear as bloody crystal. If this fox hunt had failed because of any mistaken idea that my orders were to be loosely interpreted, I should be extremely sorry. *Now*, lieutenant, I should like to enquire whether you think it advisable to proceed? It's entirely in your hands of course.' The colonel leaned back in his chair, making it perfectly clear that he was offering the junior officer a gate through which he could run and dance in a flower-covered meadow, while if he stayed where he was, he would surely sink slowly in the mire of a sucking marsh and drown himself.

'Sir,' protested the uncomfortable lieutenant, 'there is an NCO present!'

'Do you or do you not wish to proceed with this court martial?'

Pirce-Smith hesitated only a second. 'No, sir, I do not wish to proceed.'

'Good. Have you any other complaints?'

'No, no sir, I do not.'

'And you, sergeant? What about the lieutenant?'

'The lieutenant was new to the work, sir. He made one or two errors of judgement, which I'm sure he's aware of now. I might add that he fought bravely when things came to a head and at that point was wholly a part of the team.'

'Glad to hear it. Now, overall I think the hunt was a success. You performed well, both of you, and I'm happy that this motley band of deserters has been, in the main, brought to justice. They will be executed of course, after a trial. I should think no more about it, if I were you. As for this Corporal Reece, if he continues to operate as he has done, he too will eventually end up before a firing squad or the hangman. You may both go to your quarters now. Sergeant, I want to hear about our friend, General Entick-nap. Get your barber chap onto it.'

'Yes, sir.'

'And sergeant – thank the men.'

'Yes, sir.'

Crossman left the room first. Pirce-Smith lingered on a flimsy excuse, not wishing to walk with Crossman, either in terrible silence or having to exchange very awkward conversation. Once he was sure the sergeant had gone, the lieutenant too made his way. He felt utterly devastated. It was as if chaos ruled the world at last and the forces of evil had been unleashed on the home-lands. Not only had a gross piece of malfeasance been supported, the colonel had actually asked a sergeant to use his name in thanking common soldiers for doing what was their duty and their privilege, to fight for their country. One did not express gratitude to ordinary soldiers for doing what was expected of them. You could praise them for their courage in battle, you could reward them for acts of valour, but to *thank* them? Why, that was extraordinary!

In spite of his depression and anger at the colonel's decision, in one small corner of himself Pirce-Smith was relieved. Courts martial were grisly, messy affairs, as solemn as a hanging, and one did not always come through without stains on one's character, even as the innocent accuser. One was in the limelight for a while, with the eyes of brother officers on one, while counter accusations were offered by the defence, and outsiders were left wondering whether there could ever be smoke without fire. It would not have been a pleasant business. It could never be a pleasant business. And now that he thought about it, how could Colonel Hawke conduct such a trial in secret? It was impossible. The work of the spies and saboteurs would have to emerge and Lord Raglan would be asking what in blue blazes a group of 88th Connaught Rangers was doing gadding about the Crimean steppe – except that the commander-in-chief never used such language. How foolish that he had not seen the impossibility of such a trial before now. But then his recent experiences had left his thinking rather ragged. What was he to do now? It was bitterly cold, but he felt he ought to go to his tent and write a letter to his father. Yes, it was his duty as a son to keep his father informed, to let his mother know he was still alive, and to be remembered to his cousins and friends. He would light one of his precious candles, warm his hands and the ink in the flame, and lose himself in words. Despite the freezing weather he began to look forward to the exercise. He would wear the kid gloves his father had sent him as a birthday present: useless for outdoor wear in the Crimea of course, but he had cut away the fingers and now they served him for just such activities as this.

While Pirce-Smith was considering his words to his father, Crossman was on his way to visit his regiment at the front. This was his penance for living in relatively comfortable conditions in the hovel in Kadikoi. He had to remind himself how badly his fellow soldiers were faring, before resting from his labours out in the field. It was not pleasant in the trenches. Those of the bedraggled, wet figures who recognized him and felt like greeting him, did so, but with hollow enthusiasm. For the most part those still on their feet were exhausted beyond caring. One of the reasons Reece had given Crossman for deserting was the conditions at the front. 'I'd spent twelve hours on duty in wet clothes and was done in. I couldn't have kept my eyes open a minute longer if my life depended on it. Then I was given more duty . . .' The shortage of manpower in all regiments was a prime cause for overwork and fatigue in the men, and though new recruits were arriving in dribs and drabs, they were not enough to fill the gaps, and in any case they fell sick and succumbed to the freezing, damp conditions in the same way as the veterans of the war were doing.

Crossman might have had some sympathy for Morgan Reece if it had not been for the Tartar farmer hanging from the beam in the barn. It was true that Crossman did not know whether Reece had been directly responsible – perhaps some of his gang had run wild without his knowledge – but now that he was known as the leader no leniency was possible. There was also the story Reece told him, of shooting his crippled friend, but

Crossman had no way of knowing whether it was true. It was possible the corporal had invented or altered the truth to impress Crossman with his ruthlessness. However the sergeant looked at it, Morgan Reece was a doomed man.

Passing an artillery post, Crossman watched a corporal lay an 18-pounder gun. Ordnance had always fascinated him, not because of its power to kill, or even its destructive force, but because of its engineering and the skills involved in a safe firing of the piece. This gun had just been fired and the spongeman was swabbing out the piece while the ventsman was stopping the vent with a leather-coated thumb to prevent an explosion from smouldering residue. Many a spongeman's arm had been lost through air escaping from the vent and residue in the bore going up. Now the loader placed the charge and the round shot into the bore, while the spongeman had reversed his spongestaff to ram both home. After the ventsman had pricked the charge bag and inserted the tube, the firer put the smouldering portfire to the tube. Crossman put his hands over his ears. Nevertheless an ear-splitting bang made his head sing. Not for the first time he was thankful he had never followed through with his idea of joining artillery. To have to suffer that thump in the head every few minutes! It was unthinkable. Addled brains did not come into it.

After visiting the lines, Crossman went back to Kadikoi where he found that Gwilliams had already taken it on himself to visit a house frequented by certain senior British officers, where they drank coffee, had their nails and hair cut, and where they were shaved. Crossman was pleased he could leave this distasteful duty to the American.

The following day Crossman was visited by another American, his friend Rupert Jarrard, who first peered round the doorway and seemed to satisfy himself on some count, before entering.

'What was all that about?' asked Crossman, the room being empty. Ali was with one of his 'wives' and the others were at a Greek shack which sold kebabs and retsina. Since Crossman could not face meat or alcohol this early in the day, he remained alone.

'Just making sure that dolt Gwilliams wasn't around.'

Crossman shook his head. 'What is it with you two? I would have thought two North Americans . . .'

'I don't like the man,' said Jarrard. 'Plain and simple. Him and his tall stories! Who has he shaved recently?'

'A fellow called Bowie?' said Crossman, smiling.

'Jim Bowie? He died at the Alamo twenty years ago.'

'So Gwilliams said. It seems John Gwilliams gave him – and another American fighting on the other side – their last shaves on earth, just before the battle, then went on his merry way northwards, the Mexican army not willing to pay out for shaves or haircuts prior to a battle in which many of them would lose their lives.'

'Can you believe such hogwash?' growled Jarrard. 'It's a wonder he didn't shave Santa Ana himself. I doubt Gwilliams is thirty-five years old. That would have made him a kid at the time of the Alamo. Kit Carson. Jim Bowie. The man is incorrigible. I'm not even sure he's an American. His accent has a Canadian twang to my ear. Some say he is from the other side of the border.'

'Well, *that's* hogwash too, Rupert, and you know it. Your countrymen have a variety of accents. You're a nation of immigrants.'

Jarrard grudgingly conceded this fact. 'Anyway, enough of this character Gwilliams, how are you, my friend? Anything new for me on the invention front?'

'Not seriously,' but Crossman's voice raised a little in excitement, as it always did when speaking of matters mechanical, 'Have you met the photographer Mr Roger Fenton? I've seen some of his photographs. They're excellent. Mark my words, Rupert, the painter is dead. Photographs. They are the art form of the future. Why, think of the military uses for a start. Army officers would no longer be required to sketch and paint as they are now. I imagine there'll be a unit – like an artillery unit – specifically to take pictures of battle grounds and defences.'

'Oh, yes, I can see it now. The ventsman, the man with the portfire, the spongeman – all preparing a camera for a shot at the enemy.'

'No. Be serious. This is a remarkable change. History is being made.'

Jarrard shrugged. 'This Fenton. He seems to be just taking pictures of live officers.'

'No, not necessarily. I've seen him photographing the troops too.'

'What I mean is,' Jarrard continued, 'he should be taking pictures of dead ones too. Think of the impact back in Britain. Pictures of the battlefield after Inkerman. Soldiers with their guts hanging out. Shattered bodies. Limbs lying around. Men with no heads. Pictures of the cavalry walking back after the Balaclava charge.' Jarrard appeared to drift away into a dream-place for a minute or two, before he continued. 'That'd open the eyes of those damned politicians you have sitting on their fat asses in the comfort of their taverns and coffee houses. Maybe if they saw some pictures like that, there'd be no more wars.'

'You have a point there, I concede. Only, better to show the dead and broken horses. That would cause an even greater sensation. Men are expendable, but good horseflesh is worth a lot of money. There would be tutting at Tattersalls. Breeders would be shocked to the core. The public would demand the instant return of the Army of the East, before any more animals were caused distress.'

Jarrard snorted. 'Jack, this war is turning you into a cynic.'

'I was a cynic even before I came to the Crimea, Rupert. More to the point, are you getting anything out of this war? It's gone a little dull on you, hasn't it? Recently. Not much going on except a few howitzers and mortars lobbing their projectiles in the air, and one or two sorties. What are you finding to write about?'

'Well, for a start your Lord Raglan has had a visit from yet another of my countrymen. A Captain George Brinton McClellan of the United States Army came to have a look at your siege. He wanted coverage in my paper, wouldn't you guess it. Ambitious man, McClellan. Wants to be a general – don't they all – and knows the value of publicity back home. I was happy to oblige of course. My editor liked the piece enormously. Folks over the Atlantic are not much interested in foreign wars unless we can tell them that the British have called in an American to give advice on strategy and tactics and all those things warriors need to win a war.'

'Is that what he's here for? To advise?'

'Not at all,' replied the unruffled Jarrard, 'but well Hell, I've got to spice up the story for them. What's the point in saying he's just here for a jaunt?'

'I believe it's you who's incorrigible – not Gwilliams.'

'Don't let's get back on to him again. Oh, and I covered a quaint little wedding, with a soldier and his bride jumping over a broomstick to make the marriage official. No priest. Just a damn broomstick. I take it that's all legal?'

'So far as I know they only need permission from the colonel and to pronounce their intention to be wed and to exchange their vows. Here, in the army, we usually have a "best man" at the wedding too. In case the groom gets killed in battle and the new wife is left destitute. It's the best man's job to marry the widow if this happens. Usually he's a good friend of the groom.'

'He would have to be. And either well-heeled or a handsome son-of-a-bitch, otherwise the new wife might think it better to remain poor. We have it too. But I've often wondered, what happens if both the groom and best man are shot to pieces with the same shell?'

'Then one must assume the lady will either go hunting or fall back on her own resources, but you know, if a widow has children to care for – to clothe, feed and provide shelter for – she must have a certain income or they will starve. What could a woman do here in the Crimea? Work as a sutler perhaps, or for one of the more established sutlers, but that's poor employment – a few pence a day, at the most. I can't think of any answer to it. I just pity the poor creatures who are left destitute and hope they can make their way back to Britain where the parish can take care of them.'

'I've heard,' said Jarrard, 'that you have reached into your own pocket.'

'Most right thinking men would, would they not? Especially for wives of the regiment.'

Crossman spent the best part of an hour with Jarrard, who then said he had to be up and about, looking for copy. 'Got to keep up with fellahs like Russell. Can't have *The Times* getting all the exclusives.'

'Surely *The Times* is no competition for your paper in New York?'

'Word gets around though. William Russell is a winner. Rupert Jarrard comes in second. Can't have that. Oh, and by the way, there're some point-to-point races tomorrow, in the south valley. Will you be there?'

'If I can make myself small. You know it's mostly officers at those meets.'

Jarrard left Crossman, who immediately lit his chibouque. Finding he was creating a fug in the small room cluttered with the cots of his men, he moved to the doorway. The weather had improved and a low, weak sun nestled in the hills to the east. Crimean weather was very changeable, switching from day to day without any sound or apparent reason. Tartars had a saying: *If you don't like the weather, wait a minute.* Some days it seemed as if the Arctic had moved down to replace the peninsula in the Black Sea. On others the sky was dark and sombre, with hardly any light penetrating the clouds. Still others it drizzled, or rained, or sleeted, or snowed. On the odd occasion it was like today, a mild, almost spring-weather day, with a water-colour-blue-wash sky.

So, although it was not warm, it was not unpleasant standing leaning on the doorjamb dressed in an unbuttoned coatee. He puffed away with pleasure on the rough tobacco which had been home-grown out near Yalta and cured at Balaclava. Suddenly a voice bellowed from afar, breaking his reverie. He turned angrily to face the speaker, who was striding towards him. It was an officer from the Highland Brigade, an elderly and rather grizzled major, but not, thank the Lord, Crossman's father.

'You there,' said the venerable major. 'Sergeant, is it?' He peered closely at Crossman's coatee, for the stripes had faded almost out of sight.

'Yes, sir. Sergeant Crossman, of the 88th.' Crossman emphasized the number, so that the major was fully aware that he was not from any Highland regiment. The officer himself was from the 79th Foot, called the Cameron Highlanders. Crossman came to attention as the major strode on and stood before him, hands on hips.

'What are you doing here, sergeant?' asked the officer, staring at him keenly. 'Convalescence?'

There were one or two hospitals in Kadikoi, including Mrs Seacole's British Hotel, and men were sent down there from the front to recover from wounds or illnesses which were not serious enough – or too serious – to ship them to Barrack Hospital at Scutari, where the firm no-nonsense Miss Nightingale was earning the reputation more suited to a powerful dowager, sweeping through with her army of thirty-eight nurses and demanding that the mattresses be washed, the rotting floors repaired, the vermin cleared and the overflowing sewage cleaned up.

'No, sir,' replied Crossman, still at attention. 'Special duties, sir.'

'Special duties?' The major frowned. 'What sort of duties?'

'You have to speak to Major Lovelace of the Rifles, for that information. I'm not at liberty to divulge it, Sir.'

The major's frown deepened and his drooping grey moustache seemed to drop yet another inch. 'Well, look here, sergeant,' he said at last, tapping his boot with a riding crop, 'you don't seem to be doing very much at all at the moment. I need someone to teach school. The Highland Brigade has brought only one schoolmaster-sergeant to the Crimea and he's fallen sick. I've got a chapel full of wild urchins, several soldiers and some of the locals waiting to have their heads stuffed with knowledge. You're the man to do it.'

A chill of fear went through Crossman. 'Major Lovelace . . .' he began, but was interrupted with an impatient, 'Don't know the man. Doesn't seem to be here, does he? Can't be doing with all this. Have a great deal of work on my hands at the moment. Colonel wants a school teacher and, Sergeant Crossman, you're it. Report to the chapel at the top of the rise, where you'll find your eager audience waiting.'

'I'm not a fit person to teach school, sir,' said the panicking Crossman, a last ditch attempt.

'Nonsense. You sound as if you've had some education. Not out of the gutter, are you? Sound like a steward from some provincial noble's estate, or a store clerk aspiring to the gentry if you ask me, sergeant. Couldn't care less which. Haven't the time to bother. Indeed at some other time I might resent a common soldier puffing himself up, trying to escape his station in life, but at the moment I'm desperate for anyone. Now, you *will* go to the chapel, and you *will* take care of this matter. Am I understood? You don't have to teach 'em Greek or Latin. Just adding and subtraction, multiplication and division, reading, writing, stuff like that. Get the youngsters reading the Bible. If they read the Bible they'll learn the difference between good and evil and stop thieving from the tents and sutlers' stalls and we'll have a lot less urchin-crime.'

Crossman's heart sank. He knew he was trapped. The major was watching him like a hawk. He was going to have to do what he was told and there was no help for it. Tapping out his pipe on his boot heel, he went back into the hovel and collected his fur coat, hat and gloves. He joined the major a few moments later and the pair of them walked up the rutted street towards the chapel. At the top of the street the major parted company with him. 'I know you now, Sergeant Crossman of the 88th. I shall send someone to check on you later. Do a good job and I'll recommend you to your colonel. Do a bad one, or try to skip duty, and I'll hang you up by your testicles from the chapel flagpole. Am I clear?'

'Oh, very clear, sir,' replied Crossman, resigned.

Crossman continued trudging towards the chapel, which loomed large at the end of the village. It was a square stone-and-mortar building, one room, with comparatively elaborate-looking internal architecture in parts, due to the fact that it had been built as a Russian Orthodox church for the peasants. It had been abandoned as a place of worship and had become a barn to shelter livestock through the winter. When the Highland Brigade took it over, the roof had collapsed in the middle and the door was off its hinges. A little work from the regiments restored it sufficiently to be of use as a storeroom and school. Down one end there were boxes, crates and canvas bundles filling about half the floor space, down the other were some benches. It was into this area that Crossman dragged his feet. He was thoroughly daunted by what he saw.

Sitting on the benches was every assortment of childhood – except children in fine clothes. Most were dirty-faced and dressed raggedly, though some had rough but serviceable coats. There was one young boy, matted hair like that on a camel's rear, a filthy face with two white eyes staring from it, crooked teeth and ears like large coins stuck to the side of his head, a girl's ragged dress underneath and a cut down frock coat with the tails dragging at his heels over all. In his grubby hands he clutched a fur hat that appeared to have caught the mange.

This child was fairly typical of the whole class. Some of the girls wore boys' trousers. Some of the boys, like this one, wore dresses. It all depended on whether they had an older brother or sister, for hand-me-downs were all that was available to most families. Why waste good money on materials, needle and thread, for something that the child was going to shed within the year? No one would think of making fun of a boy in girl's clothes: it was too common to be unusual. For Crossman it was difficult to tell the difference, since all had long, greasy hair, countenances covered by layers of grime, and big boots.

There were of course not only army brats there, but local urchins too, sent along by their mothers to get them out of the way. That education might improve their lot was an enlightened view which would have been difficult to find. Some of the local children had chosen to be there, rather than clearing fields of stones, or chopping wood. It was a hard world for a youngster and sitting on a bench learning a foreign alphabet by rote was a lot easier than hauling water. At that age they learned very fast and most of them now spoke English and French: they needed to, to sell anything they could get their hands on to the soldiers. They learned their numbers too, for the same reason, and it was a cunning soldier who could cheat a six-year-old Tartar out of a farthing.

So far as the army was concerned, camp followers' children were better off under the watchful eye of a schoolmaster-sergeant than running wild around the camps. They too thieved: anything edible for the most part, but also kit to sell. They would wander out into the spent battlefields to look for weapons and equipment, left by dead and dying soldiers, which they could sell, even to the Russians during a truce. The French would buy Russian and British arms, and the British would purchase French and Russian weapons. There's nothing a soldier likes more than a souvenir of his holiday in the Crimea, to take home and hang on the wall of his house.

Crossman surveyed the rest of the class with a wary eye. At the back of the room sat the soldiers: would-be paymaster-sergeants, orderly room clerks, quartermaster-sergeants, and the like. It was for their benefit that the army had formed these schools. As more and more administrative work was devolved to ordinary soldiers, more education was needed by those soldiers. The children, and anyone else that liked to be present, were an add-on to the original idea. There were even two wives in the room, prepared to listen while they sewed, though education was of little use to such women.

'Aaa-hem,' said the nervous Crossman, clearing his throat.

One ferret-faced child immediately wrote this down on her slate. Two others, seeing this, did the same, laboriously, the chalk squealing and setting teeth on edge. 'Ahem. Can – can anyone tell me where the last lesson left off? What was the content or the subject?'

Blank looks were the reply to this general question. Thirty pairs of eyes stared straight into his face. When he stared back in apprehension, several of those pairs were suddenly diverted, switching to study rafters, floor and walls, equally terrified that they would be asked a question directly. What the students saw was a tall, rather stern-looking figure with a fierce look in his eyes, whose toffee-nosed speech indicated that he was learned beyond any ordinary schoolmaster-sergeant. Clearly this man knew everything there was to know in the world and would come down hard on those who failed to live up to the same standard.

'Come, come,' cried Crossman, unconciously adopting the phrases of his old schoolmasters, 'surely we know what the last lesson was about? Anyone? You, the soldier at the back. Yes, the lance-corporal?'

'Me, sir?'

'I'm not sir, I'm Sergeant Crossman. Perhaps I should have told you that at the outset. My name is Crossman, Sergeant Crossman. It's no good you telling me all your names, I'll never remember them. Now, corporal, what was it that the last tutor was teaching you?'

'Why pick on me, I 'aven't done anythin', sergeant.' He sounded so much like Wynter that Crossman wanted to bark at him straight away, but managed to refrain.

'I'm not picking on you as a punishment, man. I thought you looked intelligent enough to remember what happened yesterday. Clearly I was wrong.' Again, to his discredit, his old schoolmaster's voice came out of his mouth. 'You appear to have the retention span of a cranefly.'

'It was numbers,' said one of the women, without looking up from her sewing. 'Addin' up and takin' away.'

'Good,' said Crossman, sweating a little despite the coldness of the room. 'Numbers. Let's start with you. The child in the front. What is the sum total of five and three?'

The child immediately burst into tears.

'Not that child then, another one,' said Crossman, wildly. 'Anyone? You, the bigger boy.'

'Ate.'

'Very good. Yes, eight. The sum of five and three is eight. Now, what about three and five? Is that the same answer?'

The boy, wearing the hat of a French Zouave, screwed up his face. 'Is that a trick question?'

'It's just a question. An ordinary question. Anyway, you don't have to answer. One of the others. The girl with the runny nose.'

The children all turned to look at each other, to see who had the runny nose. Several of them started to reply at once, after their neighbour had pointed to them, while others ran a well-practised sleeve under the offending organ.

'Oh, God,' groaned Crossman, to himself. 'I knew it would be like this.'

At that moment the lean figure of the elderly adjutant from the Highland Brigade poked his head around the doorway and, seeing Crossman in place, said, 'Well done, sergeant! I knew you'd take to it like a fish to water. You chaps who aspire to higher things! I envy you. I've nowhere to go, being as it were, at the peak of my ambition. Where next for a man of noble blood?' He confessed quietly, 'I never wished for a colonelcy. Too much responsibility.'

With that, the major was gone, out into the sunshine again. If he did but know it, that was Crossman's own sole ambition at the moment. To be out in the sunshine. Nothing more. Instead he was stuck in a classroom full of expectant students. If he could have cried 'Woe is me!' without frightening thirty men, women and children, he would have done so without question. Now they stared at him like an exhibit in a museum. What was he to do? Carry on with this arithmetic, which did not seem to be going well at all, or start some new train of learning? Suddenly he had a bright idea. Why not teach them something he was interested in himself? Surely his enthusiasm would be catching and they would all enjoy the lesson, instead of treating it like some cavalry skirmish, he being the cavalry and they being the Russian gunners at their guns? Inventions and discoveries, that was the thing!

'Talking of numbers, did you know,' he began, and they all leaned forward seeing that his eyes were sparkling, 'did you know that only last year – last year – the English autodidact George Boole created *symbolic logic*? Yes indeed. He published a short treatise, which I have read from cover to cover, entitled *Mathematical Analysis of Logic* in which he maintains that logic must be connected to mathematics – numbers and such – and not to philosophy, which in the past, as you are all probably aware, was the case. This is all laid out in his latest pamphlet, *An Investigation of the Laws of Thought*.'

Eyes had seriously glazed over again. Crossman was not surprised. He too was not all *that* keen on theoretical discoveries: bits of paper laying out various theories and results of investigations of the mind. He liked his discoveries and inventions to be more solid. Bridges. Ships. Railway engines. That sort of thing. Clearly his audience was not greatly taken with George Boole, genius or no. There were no images to grasp when discussing such things. It had been all right as an opening gambit, to sort of link what they had been doing with what they would be doing. Yes, he had definitely made progress, but he did not want to lose them now.

'Four years ago,' he continued, in hushed tones, 'there was a French naval engineer by the name of Stanislas Henri Lureant Dupuy de Lome.' Those scratching on slates with chalk looked up in panic. He hurriedly assured them, 'You don't have to remember his full name. Simply "de Lome" will do. Anyway, this brilliant man developed an armoured frigate,' he dropped his voice almost to a whisper to build up the suspense, '*steam-powered and screw-propelled, no less.*' He waited for this fascinating information to fall on the waiting ears, then continued with, 'An ironclad with great speed! What now for our wooden ships with flimsy sails? Why, warfare at sea has been transformed. And I have it from my friend Rupert Jarrard, an American here in the Crimea, that one of his countrymen – John Ericsson – has developed a revolving gun turret which could be situated on the deck of such a vessel, to sweep the seas 360 degrees.'

A child was clearing its throat. 'My da,' he said, nodding at those around him. 'My da is in the Royal Navy.'

'So's mine,' said a girl. 'Mine's a warrant officer.'

A soldier spoke up. 'Iron ships? Why, they'll sink as soon as you look at 'em.'

'But they don't,' replied Crossman. 'Anything hollow enough will float on water.'

'Yes, but,' said another, 'they'll always be breakin' down. Now sails is reliable. You can't do better than sails. And iron's too heavy for sails to push along.'

'What about the doldrums?' cried Crossman.

'What?' asked the soldier.

'Windless days. Becalmed ships? If you have an engine . . .'

'Always breakin' down,' stated the soldier again, to the approval of his friends on the back row.

Crossman swallowed a retort. Instead he countered with, 'If Crampton's locomotive can do for land, then de Lome's ironclad can do for the sea.' He tried for a more mundane tack. 'What about Isaac Singer's sewing machine, then?'

Now he had the attention of at least two of his audience. The women ceased sewing and stared at him aggressively. Then Crossman recalled the Paris riots, when tailors and seamstresses took to the streets to protest violently against the introduction of Thimonnier's sewing machine, invented a short while before Singer's contraption, which they claimed would put them all out of work. Thimonnier was ruined and had to return to his native town of Amplepuis and resume his own trade as a tailor.

'Well, perhaps not the sewing machine. Ah, ah, I have it. *The electric clock.*'

He did indeed have it. Eyes went round with interest. A brilliant idea came to him. Absolutely brilliant, and absorbing, and full of great shining promise. 'I'll tell you what we shall do,' he said. 'We shall attempt to fashion an electric clock. We'll make one, out of . . .' He looked around him, seeing nothing. 'Well, out of bits of wire and paper and wood. We shall power it with wind and magnets, to create the electricity. Electricity!' His tongue savoured the word. 'Magic, you know. Sheer, undiluted magic. You know what electricity is? Power. Harnessed storm lightning. When you see that jagged forked lightning flash, that is – ' he remembered the major's idea of stuffing religion into the children – 'that is *God* sending electricity to the earth. Oh, yes, we are all a little afraid of lightning – I can see you looking worried – but the sort of electricity we shall make is much milder. Instead of a great flood of electricity, we shall have a tiny trickle, just enough to power our electric clock – invented, by the way, by a Scot like myself, Alexander Bain. An Englishman, Wheatstone, also claims to have made one, but his was a very fancy version to do with electrical distribution of time – yes, you see, I can read in your faces it was much too *fancy* for the likes of us, ordinary folk, who want to see the practical application of such a thing.'

'Let's get this right, sergeant. We're goin' to make a clock,' said one of the soldiers, 'out of electric.'

'Not out of electric, but powered by electric. Look, we need all sorts of bits and pieces to make the clock, then other bits and bobs to make the machine which will provide the electricity. Give me that slate,' he said, taking one of the few slates available from a child in the front row, 'I'll write down what we need. If all of you can go out looking for these parts, we'll have everything we need in no time. Now, first off we want to make a small windmill, so we'll need material for the blades . . .'

They crowded round him in great enthusiasm, even the two women, while he wrote the list. Soon each child, each adult, had memorized the bits they felt they could find without too much trouble, and they dispersed, all talking excitedly. Most of them had never owned a clock. Parents of ordinary families would send their children to the church, or to the market square, to look at the time on the public clocks, if they needed such exactness.

Mostly people relied on the position of the sun in the sky, or the feel of the thing. If you were hungry, why then, it was around noon, surely? If there was no sun to go down in the evening, a cloud-filled day, then you waited until the light drained from the sky. More recently of course there had been these things called *Time Tables* issued by the railways, which told down to the very minute of the times that trains left stations, but most ordinary people were not touched by these.

Crossman sat on the edge of a bench and hummed to himself. The classroom looked more like a chapel, now that it was empty. How strange it was to find himself a school teacher all of a sudden. He wasn't half bad at it, either. Had taken to it like a duck to water. Look how they had suddenly become interested in learning. Everyone out, running around in the pursuit of knowledge! He would tell his mother in his next letter how he had inspired a whole band of men, women and children here in the Crimea, to go out and seek . . .

'What the blue blazes are you about, sergeant?' roared a voice from the doorway. 'Come here you confounded man!'

The silhouette was that of the adjutant.

'I'm sorry, sir?' replied Crossman in wounded tones. 'I thought I was about my business of teaching.'

'Teaching?' fumed the major. 'Teaching? Teaching what? They're all running amuck, stealing everything they lay their hands on. Did I not tell you that the precise reason for having them in the classroom was to stop them thieving? And here you are encouraging this criminal behaviour, sending them out with that exact idea in mind.' The major reached out beside him and hauled a grubby boy into view by the ear. 'Now, tell me again, brat, what the sergeant told you to do.'

'Go – go – forth and plunder, yer worship.'

'Go forth and plunder,' repeated the major with a growl. 'What are you, sir, some kind of Faggin?'

'I think you mean Fagin, major. The "a" is a long vowel. No, no, sir, I'm no corrupter of orphan's morals. Not at all. You see, that phrase "Go out and plunder" was just a sort of figure of speech, to get them enthused, to fill them with eagerness for the hunt. You see,' he smiled at the major, 'we're making an electric clock.'

The major's eyes narrowed. 'You dare to correct me, soldier? I'll have those damn stripes. I'll have you on the cannon. I'll flay the bloody skin off your back. Electric clocks? Damn your eyes, sir. You're here to teach 'em numbers not bloody high physics. Two and two, sir. Two and two. Electric clocks? I tell you this, if any more stores go missing you'll pay for them out of your private's pay, because you ain't going to be drawing a sergeant's pay any longer.'

With that the major stormed off. Gradually, Crossman was able to reel in his charges, all returning excitedly with the bits and pieces he had sent them out to find. However, the clock, once they had finished, failed to work. Somehow they had trouble producing power, though Crossman felt it should be easy enough, since he had pored over drawings and written instructions in magazines when he was back in Britain. The hands – two pieces of coat hanger wire – failed to budge. Even when the class gave the device a nudge and finally a thump, time stood still.

But everyone had had a great deal of fun and the whole exercise, so far as the class was concerned, had been far more interesting than learning arithmetic. A crucifix was removed from a window niche and the stillborn clock placed in its stead. It stood there unbowed and unapologetic. That the so-called 'dynamo-electric machine' had failed to jolt it into life was not its fault. The eyes of the class often wandered to it, when the current lesson was less than interesting, to rest there in pleasant speculation of what might have been.

Crossman later went to the major to apologize and tried to explain again that he was attempting to put some interest into the lessons, so that the poor creatures on the benches did not drift away into a world of apathy. The major did not understand, but he accepted in the end that Crossman's intentions had been pure. He withdrew his threat to 'have Crossman's stripes' and told the sergeant to be more careful in future in the way he conducted his duties. Crossman, knowing that the major could not have demoted him anyway, quietly assured the old gentleman that it would never happen again.

5

'So, what's to do? You're some kind of school-ma'am now, eh sergeant?'

'If you find it funny, Wynter, you might like to join my students at the chapel tomorrow. We're going to learn to read.'

Wynter glowered, first at the sergeant, then at Peterson, Gwilliams and Yorwarth, who were grinning broadly.

'I can read as much as needs be,' he snarled. 'There's nothin' clever to reading.'

'Oh, yes there is,' Peterson said. 'There's everything clever to reading.'

'Gwilliams,' said Crossman, 'upstairs, if you please.'

Gwilliams followed Crossman dutifully up the narrow turning stone stairs into the small room above which served Crossman and Lovelace as a bedroom and an office. There was just enough space to put two mattresses with about six inches between, a Spanish chest owned by Lovelace, a single chair, and a jug and washbasin, also owned by the major. The major's uniforms were hanging from nails on the wall: something he hated but was prepared to accept, since there was no room for a wardrobe in this small hovel's second storey. This did not concern Crossman, who possessed only the uniform on his back.

Lovelace also had a footlocker, which contained his civilian shooting clothes, a pair of shooting boots, and two matching double-pinfire Lefauchaux shotguns, custom made. He had first seen the Lefauchaux in the Paris Exhibition of '51, where the new sporting gun had taken the world by storm, and had fallen instantly in love. Lovelace was a fickle gun man, however, and was apt to stray once the honeymoon was over. Already he was considering an *affaire* with a new shotgun that rumour had it was being developed by James Purdey, in England. If that happened the Lefauchaux would be used less and less, until one day they would find themselves offered as the stake in a wager or, worse still, relegated to a nephew with no real sporting flair.

Cobwebs and dust abounded in the room and down the stairs. This did not bother either of the occupants, since neither was afraid of spiders (unlike Wynter and Peterson, who both went into fits of terror at the sight of one) and dust was an eternal problem solvable only by God, when the time came to salvage what was left on the earth after Judgement Day.

'Sit down on my cot, Gwilliams. I'll take the major's.'

'What's that?' Gwilliams pointed to a splintered hole in the floorboards.

'That? Oh, mousehole I should think,' replied Crossman.

'Wasn't it made by a Cossack's musket ball? I heard about that.' Gwilliams looked around the room. 'Climbed in through that window at midnight, so I'm told. Blasted you in your bed. Only you wasn't in your bed. You got out real quick when you heard a creak, just before the shot was fired and you killed him with a hunting knife, yelling, "Goddamn Don Cossacks, how dare you interrupt my sleep?" It's almost a legend.'

'Is that how legends are made? I always wondered. Actually, I didn't kill him. I pinned him to the floor with the knife and left him. It was either Wynter or Peterson who finally shot him, as he tried to rip his foot from the floor. I think it was about two in the morning, but I agree midnight sounds much better. Things happen at midnight, don't they? The crossover time, when witches and goblins are abroad. I'm not sure I said that bit about being asleep,' but even as he confessed this, Crossman saw the look of disappointment on the face of Gwilliams and he decided that perhaps being the hero of a legend would be helpful to him in the Crimea. 'I think my words were, "Wake me, damn you? I was dreaming of my lover." And it was *bloody* Cossacks. Those blue devils are the toughest fighters on horseback. Oh, we're more disciplined. We're eager and proud, but those Cossacks have been on the backs of horses for several thousand years. They rode with Yermak and Genghis Khan. They've been mostly outlaws and fugitives in their time. Did you know that if for any reason a squadron of Cossacks were just to dismount and abandon their horses, the beasts would form themselves up in rows of six? It's true. I've seen it. The men and their horses are part of each other, inseparable, magnificent together.'

'So that was it? Dreaming of your lover? That's real poetry, sergeant. Real poetry.' Gwilliams picked up Major Lovelace's razor from the top of the Spanish chest, opened it and studied the blade in the light from the small window. 'Nice workmanship,' he murmured. He closed it and looked down at the rest of the major's kit. 'Part of a gentleman's matching set, eh? Hair brush, comb, scissors, strop – all jacketed in silver. God, I would be a gentleman too, if I had the money. Why not? To own a razor with a steel blade that good? Why not?' He opened it again and stared along the edge. 'See how it's honed to perfection? You could cut through to the bone with one draw. I bet the major splits a hair in two before he uses it, eh?'

Crossman laughed. 'I do believe he does.'

The razor was finally replaced and Gwilliams sat down. 'You want to know about Enticknap? Nothing solid, yet. I got my suspicions though. I think he's selling to the sutlers. Stores. Goods belonging to the army of Queen Victoria of England, God bless her little pointy chin . . .'

'The United Kingdom,' interrupted Crossman.

'If you say so. United Kingdom. United States. We all like to be united, don't we? Or maybe just some of us. Anyway, he's selling government property. That's what I've heard. He's not the only one, of course. There are others doing the same. It can be a hobby.'

'He's the only one I'm interested in,' said Crossman, quickly, in case he heard something about his own father. Much as he hated his father he did not want to learn he was a thief. Scandal in the family would touch everyone, not just Major Kirk. And despite everything, he did not want that.

'Why a general? That's what I ask myself. Don't they have enough already, without risking their careers, their reputations?

Then you gotta say no, they don't. They never have enough. They've always got to get more.'

'You have the same jaundiced view of wealthy men as I have, Gwilliams.'

'Well, maybe that's how they get that way.'

'Many of them do absolutely nothing to get it. Don't you have inherited wealth in the States? Many of them just wait until daddy dies and then they slip right into his shoes.'

'I don't blame 'em for that. Give me some, I say.'

'I suppose I don't either. Give me a fortune and I'd probably follow James Brooke, late of Widcombe Crescent, Bath.'

'Who's James Brooke?'

'He was a young lieutenant who was severely wounded in India twenty-odd years ago, whose father died and left him wealthy. When he recovered from his near-death experience he bought a Royal Navy yacht and sailed to the Far East, where he cleared the seas of Dyak pirates and was invited to become the next rajah of Sarawak, in Borneo. There he now resides and rules three races, the Malays, the Chinese and the Dyaks, and is much respected for his impartiality and his thrifty life-style. Brooke offered the country to Queen Victoria, but she refused it.'

'Why'd she do that?'

'I don't know, but I believe it's probably for the better. Rajah Brooke would have become governor, most likely, and as such would have had to report to and take orders from the British Government, who are excellent bunglers when it comes to managing foreign lands. As it is, he has no one to answer to but the people of Sarawak, and if he doesn't like some European carpetbagger who is out to exploit the natives, he wraps him up and sends him off on the next boat leaving Kuching. Instead of being a governor he's a king, and a rare one at that, a king who for the most part has his feet on the ground and his head firmly on his shoulders.'

'By God, I should like an adventure like that. I should like to become king of a foreign land.'

'Maybe you will, one day, Gwilliams,' said Crossman, smiling. 'There's plenty of world left. For the most part I would just like to go there, to a place where the moon and stars are close enough to touch and the people are light of foot and light of heart.'

'I'm glad you told me that story,' said Gwilliams, touched. 'You say it's true?'

'As I live and breathe.'

'Rajah Brooke, eh? I'll think on that one. Some true stories are more colourful than poetry, ain't they? I look on myself as an adventurer, Sergeant Crossman. I see myself seeking things. I don't know what I'm looking for, but by God I'll know when I find it. It's out there somewhere. In the meantime, I've got a sly job to do, and I'll do it to the best of my ability, you can be sure of that.'

'I am sure of that, Gwilliams. I have to tell you that I was unhappy about taking you into the *peloton*. I said as much to Colonel Hawke. But he insisted. Now I'm glad I did. What is it between you and Rupert Jarrard, by the way?'

Gwilliams' expression darkened at the sound of the newspaper man's name. 'That fake?' he said. 'Don't you ask.'

'All right, I won't. I was just curious.'

'Rot him.'

'If you say so.'

Later, Crossman strode into the classroom of the chapel and stopped dead in his tracks. Sitting amongst the urchins in the front row was Mrs Lavinia Durham, wife of a quartermaster and one-time lover of Sergeant Fancy Jack Crossman of the 88th Connaught Rangers. As Alexander Kirk, the youngest son of a Scottish nobleman, Crossman had virtually promised himself to Lavinia when he suddenly learned about who and what he truly was, and what his father had done to his natural mother. He had then, without a by-your-leave to his intended, rushed off and joined the Rangers under an assumed name.

He had left Lavinia to the gossips, who had in their inimitable way torn her apart. This had resulted in her marrying beneath her station, a captain up from the ranks, Bertram Durham, a merchant's son. Crossman knew he had caused her some pain, which he now deeply regretted. Since then she had come to his bed while he was recovering from a wound, something else he regretted, and she had subsequently assisted him in kicking a laudanum habit. Their histories were entwined and seemed fated to continue so, unless one of them should be strangled or smothered by the other.

'Lavinia – I mean, Mrs Durham!' said Crossman in an annoyed tone. 'What are you doing here?'

She had been doing something with a child, helping an unfortunate boy with crossed eyes draw a picture on his slate, and she looked up quickly. Her small round face seemed to shine from within. The shapely nose, the sweet mouth, the humourful eyes were all turned full-force upon him. Not beautiful, but impishly pretty. There was a good deal of Shakespeare's Titania dwelling in Lavinia Durham's breast. A small flint-hearted fairy peered out through soft-looking eyes. He could not help but melt under that gaze or be captivated by her prettiness.

There was no mark of the war on her countenance, though perhaps her soul bore some dark patches. She tilted her chin, the way she used to do before going into battle against him. Inwardly he groaned. He knew he was in for a fight of some kind, though he had no idea what it was all about. With all her flounces and petticoats, she could be a determined antagonist, and he was not looking forward to skirmishing with her in the classroom.

'I heard there were some interesting classes going on at the chapel, sergeant, and decided to end my boredom by coming here.'

To add to his consternation the door opened behind him and yet another person came into the class. It was the goose girl. She gave him a little curtsey before looking round the room.

'Please?' she said. 'Where to sit?'

'You – you may sit where you please,' he replied, awkwardly.

'Yes please, where to sit?' she repeated, compounding the confusion.

Lavinia Durham raised an eyebrow, then patted the seat beside her and said, 'Come, child, sit by me.'

Child? thought Crossman. There couldn't have been more than five years between the pair. Lavinia Durham was sending a message to him, that the girl was too young for him. The goose girl sat on the bench next to Mrs Durham and then looked eagerly at Crossman. It seemed his fame had spread throughout the land. Soon there would be Cossacks and their women coming to hear his word. Perhaps, he thought, I missed my vocation. I should have been a Methodist preacher. He felt he ought to nip things in the bud. The schoolmaster-sergeant was on the mend but he wouldn't be back for a few days. In the meantime Crossman felt the lessons ought to lose their lustre. He ought to try for something boring. Poetry! There was nothing like poetry for putting people off learning. It had certainly worked with him at school. Twice he had received the strap across the backside for falling asleep in a poetry class. What to give them, though? Burns? No, no, he had come to appreciate Robert Burns over the years. Coleridge? Nor him, for his flights of fancy were actually quite alarming in their way and stirred the imagination.

Wordsworth! That was the man. Insipid, in Crossman's opinion. Sugary, dripping with apricot jam. Yes, that was the one.

'Today,' he said, his voice echoing in a most disturbing manner in the hollowness of the chapel, 'we shall be looking at a certain poet. One William Wordsworth, who died last year . . .'

'Five years ago, I believe,' murmured Mrs Durham.

'Yes, precisely. Five years ago. He wrote a poem called "The Lost Love" and it goes something like this, though I obviously can't recall the piece exactly, you can be sure of one or two lines. It seems there was a maid, fair as a star. None of her suitors praised her and very few of them, it has to be said, actually loved her. She was, in the poet's words, a violet by a mossy stone.'

'Oh, stuff!' said Lavinia Durham. 'Is this aimed at the young chit beside me? Are you trying to seduce her by comparing her to Lucy in Mr Wordsworth's poem? *A violet by a mossy stone half-hidden from the eye – fair as a star, when only one is shining in the sky.* That's not a compliment you know. I wouldn't want one of *my* admirers to say that if I was the only woman in the world I should be considered beautiful.'

'Is – is that what he's saying?' asked Crossman. 'I thought he was considering her to be a jewel? And I certainly do not have designs on the young woman,' he added indignantly. 'I merely thought this would be a good rhyme to start things off.' Damn Lavinia Durham. He would pick the one poem she obviously knew well.

'It's a very silly poem. *She lived unknown, and few could know when Lucy ceased to be.* If she was unknown, then no one could know when she ceased to be. Choose another poem. I know, what about . . .' Mrs Durham went on to quote three or four other Wordsworth poems at length, until he had to call a stop to her recitals.

He spoke severely. 'I am trying to run a lesson here, Mrs Durham. If you insist on interrupting I shall have to ask you to leave.'

'You're so masterful, sergeant,' she said, batting her eyelids. 'I'm sure we are all in terror of you.'

Needless to say the soldiers and the children thought this badinage flowing between the lady and the sergeant was great fun. Only the goose girl did not appreciate it. She was looking from one to the other with a curl to her bottom lip. *She* knew there was a special bond between these two, simply by the tones of their voices and the way they looked at each other, and *she* did not like it. The sergeant had looked at her, several times out on the paths and tracks, and she had come to consider him quite beautiful. She had not come here to share him with this old woman next to her, who seemed to have a certain spitefulness on the tip of her tongue. He was to be hers and even goose girls with hennaed hair could be jealous of fine ladies. However, the sergeant was now pointing to the door.

'Leave,' he boomed. 'You are disrupting my lesson. I insist that you leave immediately, Mrs Durham, so that I can teach the soldiers and young civilian scruffs in peace. Go, before I order two of those burly Highlanders at the back to remove you by force.'

Lavinia Durham pouted. 'You wouldn't dare.' The soldiers certainly wouldn't dare and looked about them in alarm, should the sergeant carry through with his threat. After all, this lady was the wife of a captain, and even in the lawful pursuit of an order from an NCO, there could be terrible repercussions. In fact, the soldiers in question were already forming excuses as to why they shouldn't be ordered to remove the lady from the classroom, when she suddenly got to her feet.

'My dear,' she said to the goose girl, 'you must beware of that man. He breaks hearts and scatters the pieces with a sneer and a laugh . . .'

'Lavin . . . Mrs Durham, don't be melodramatic.'

'Be careful, Alexander,' she whispered as he passed him, her nose in the air. 'Be gentle with her. She is not made of bronze, as I am.'

Crossman heaved a sigh of relief once Lavinia had gone. Of course she had only come to disrupt his lesson. He realized that. Once she had made her point she would have left anyway. It was her way, to make him suffer a little. And he had no designs on the goose girl whatsoever. Nor, he felt, should the girl be interested in him. He had done nothing to encourage her, apart from wish her good morning in her own language and to offer a smile. Was that so bad, to pass pleasantries with a human being in this freezing hell? This place of ice and snow, of sleet and hail, which bordered the Black Sea? Even now the girl had cheered a little and was looking at him with clear eyes.

'I am glad to have you in the class,' he said to her in her own language. 'You are welcome.'

She blushed furiously and looked down at her knees. One or two Tartar children giggled, though he had no idea for what reason. Having wasted enough time already with frivolities, he began the morning lesson again, this time choosing to study the alphabet, and finding the response much the same as if he had chosen to continue with poetry.

In the afternoon he was actually free to do as he pleased and now that he had done something mildly useful with his morning, he felt he could go to the point-to-point races without any feelings of guilt. He knew he had to be careful though, in case he ran into his father. There was quite a crowd there. The course was already churned up a little when he arrived, two races having been and gone. A lieutenant from H Battery, Royal Artillery, had won the second one. The first field had been swept aside by someone from the 5th Dragoon Guards. There were spectators from all the divisions, this being prime entertainment, but of course most of the common soldiers were from the Highland Brigade. Point-to-point was primarily an officer's sport, like shooting game, and rank-and-file followed an unspoken rule of staying well back and viewing events from a distance.

Crossman found Rupert Jarrard, who had remained at the rear to wait for his friend, before pushing to the front. He took Crossman with him and the sergeant felt very uncomfortable under the glares of subalterns, captains and the like as he followed in the newspaperman's wake. 'Hey,' said Jarrard, turning when they reached the rope that fenced in the race track, 'do you want to wager? Give me a couple of guineas. We'll put them on that captain from the 68th. See him? Over there, trotting his nag back and forth to keep it in prime. That, my friend, is a nice piece of horse flesh. Bound to win. Stake my reputation on it. Here, let's have the money.'

Crossman reluctantly gave Jarrard two guineas and watched as the American shouldered his way through cherry-trousered cavalry officers who lisped at him to watch who he was pushing. The sergeant then stood awkwardly, surrounded by a sea of commissioned officers, some of whom occasionally stared his way, though none actually told him to be off. Then he felt a tap on his shoulder and expected the worst, only to find Major Lovelace standing there, removing his kid gloves, smiling into his face.

'This is brave of you, sergeant, coming in amongst the enemy.'

'I'm with Jarrard, sir. And I have a lot in common with these men.'

'Oh, I know. Old Harrovian. But I thought you had turned your back on us, sergeant, and now I find you indulging in old habits. Hard to break, eh? Ingrained in the soul, the pursuits of the idle rich.'

'Point-to-point? Even farm hands . . .'

'I'm teasing you, old man. Well, have you wagered yet? I have it on good authority that the lieutenant on the bay shipped the beast from County Cork on a naval yacht only a fortnight ago, so it's fresh from the green grass of Ireland. It looks strong, doesn't it? I shall put ten on it, I think. What about you?'

'I've just given my money to Jarrard. I think we're going with the opposition.'

'My dear chap, there isn't any. But good luck, anyway.'

Now that he was speaking with a major all interest in him had gone from the rest of the officers around him. It was true, he did not regard them as the *enemy*. They could have been his school chums. However, they did regard *him* as something less than worthy. Here was a man from a good background choosing to remain in the ranks. That could at best be suspicious. What had he done that he buried himself amongst the scum of the earth? You had to have a damn good reason to crawl into pig swill. They could think of a dozen reasons why a gentleman should wish to be anonymous. Debts he could not cover. A lady he had scandalized. An affair of honour at which he had failed to appear. These, and many other reasons for his presence amongst the common soldiers, were in the minds of those who guessed his origins and wondered at his sin.

Jarrard arrived back with the wager slips. He rubbed his hands together. 'Right, we're about to make our fortunes. Good day to you, major. You're well I trust?'

Lovelace answered in kind and the three men then fell silent as all Hell broke loose around them. It was nothing but the madness of the race as men cheered their favourites up and down the course to the finish line. It was the bay that won, with a smiling young lieutenant on his back, and Lovelace was not at all surprised.

'Inside information,' he explained to Crossman. 'I was in Somerset two years ago when a cousin of mine won three races on that very same horse. It was only a two-year-old then and I surmised it would not have lost any strength in its limbs since then. In fact last night I paid my respects to the lad who rode it today and asked him if I could trot his nag for him. He obliged me, of course, flattered that a major should be interested in his mount. It did not seem lame or short of wind in any way and I came to the conclusion that it was still the same flyer it had been when in the hands of my dear cousin.'

Crossman smiled. 'You never leave anything to chance, do you, sir?'

'Oh, I don't know,' replied the major, airily. 'Someone else may have had a cousin's horse here which they were equally convinced was a Pegasus waiting to unfold its wings.'

Jarrard, however, was quite cross that his horse had lost.

'I had it on the best authority,' he grumbled.

'We all do – we all do,' replied Lovelace. 'Alas, all authorities cannot be right.'

There were still several more races to go, so the three decided to run a pool and share out at the end. This was more successful, since Lovelace did most of the choosing and he just happened to choose winners. When it was all over they went to one of the sutler stalls, that of a Bulgar who roasted particularly good goat meat over charcoal fires, and had some of his fare in bread. It was good, a feast in fact. There was also cheap wine to be had. Lovelace insisted that they left the wine until they got back to the hovel, where he had six bottles of good French claret in his travelling box, but Jarrard wanted something to wash the meat down, so they purchased a bottle of Spanish red.

'*Vino brutal*,' said Lovelace, showing the roughness of his tongue after he had tasted the drink. 'My steward at home will never speak to me again, if he hears of this.'

Crossman, who was enjoying himself immensely, laughed and went to turn away, when he came up against a body. Unfortunately it was that of another major and he spilt his wine down the front of this person. When he looked up to apologize Crossman found himself staring into the face of his own father. Immediately he came to attention, saluted, and said, 'I am most heartily sorry, sir. I had no intention of – of spilling my drink on you.'

Aware that he was disguised by dirt, beard, long hair and a considerable loss of weight, Crossman felt he might yet get away without being recognized. He had spoken in the rough tones of a common soldier, having heard them enough from Wynter and his kind. His father had not seen him for some years and there was no reason to suppose the elderly major would expect to find his son in the same army, on the same fields of battle, in the war against Russia. He was however staring at Crossman rather strangely, his white moustache quivering, and those piercing blue eyes cutting deeply into Crossman's heart.

'Clumsy damn oaf!' cried the major. 'Blind are you? What is it you are, eh?' He stared at Crossman's sleeve. 'Damned sergeant! Pushing yourself a little too far forward, sergeant.' He brushed the droplets of wine from his uniform with a sour look on his face.

'The sergeant is with me, major,' said Lovelace, coming in. 'It was an accident.'

Crossman winced. He wished at that moment that Lovelace would stay out of it. He wanted his father to walk off, whether in a temper or not. The last thing he wished for was to keep him there, staring into his face, and wondering where he had seen those eyes before.

Major Kirk glared at Major Lovelace. 'Who asked you, sir? The impudent pup has ruined me jacket.'

Jarrard piped up now. 'I'm sure he didn't mean to. If it's a matter of money . . .'

'Money, sir? Who are you? Damned Canadian, by the sound of you. Do I look poor, eh? My batman will get rid of this stain within a minute. It's the *inconvenience*, sir. Keep your money. And keep your mouth shut, if you please.'

Jarrard became bolt upright within a second. He stared at the major. 'What?' he cried. 'I'm an American, not a Canadian, and if it's satisfaction you want, we Americans will give it every time.'

Crossman groaned. 'No, no. Please, this was all my fault. I won't have you duelling over my errors, Rupert. Please stay out of it. If you want to fight someone, fight me. Major, I have apologized. I can't do more.'

His father turned on him and there was a gleeful look of triumph in his eye.

'Voice changed all of a sudden, eh?' His face hardened to stone. 'Think I don't know my own whelp when I see him. Run away from home, damn you? What are you doing in the ranks, boy?'

It was all up. His father knew him. He stared back at the man he hated so much.

'It was of my own choosing. I had no desire to be in the same fold as you, sir.'

'What? Blaming me because your mother was a trollop? You think she was the only wench I bedded? Not by half, boy. Not by half. Don't even know you as my own son. Only my wife, the lady you called mother, persuaded me you was and I've come to think she was wrong. I think you've chosen your mark. You was always intended for the gutter. Now, James, he's twice the man you are, sir. He don't run away from his responsibilities. He don't look at me as if I was some kind of low creature. God damn your eyes boy. I gave you a home, I gave you a name, bastard that you are, and this is how you repay me.'

Lovelace and Jarrard now realized who this major was and they knew it was not a good idea to interfere. They faded into the shade of the Bulgar's stall.

'I'm not *repaying* you for anything, sir. I'm simply following my own path. I prefer the ranks.'

Major Kirk had gone a dark shade of purple. 'So you can make me ashamed? So I have my brother officers bleating about me behind my back, saying poor Kirk, his son's in the ranks you know, a mere sergeant in a foot regiment. That's the idea is it? To cause a scandal? Well I disclaim you, sir. I cast you off. You are no longer my son, never were in fact. Just the whelp of some whore of a maid . . .'

'You are speaking of my natural mother,' said Crossman in a dangerous voice. 'If you say one more word, Father, I'll slap your face here in public. See if you can explain it all away at my court martial. I can prove my real identity, you know, and James would never disown me as a brother, not even to save you from a scandal. James is an honourable man at heart, and I love him as much as I detest you. He knows that. He might be afraid of you, but not enough to deny me.'

Major Kirk looked around him and saw that though there was no one close enough to hear them, several officers and a few men were looking in their direction, aware of a fracas. They were arousing interest and the panic showed in the elderly man's face. He could get away with a great deal but he was too proud to withstand a great scandal. It would pull him down from his pompous heights and leave him without a friend. At least, the kind of friends such a man makes. And without these so-called friends he would be nothing at all and prey to his enemies. Major Kirk had made almost as many enemies as Lord Cardigan in his way and there were many who would have given their eye teeth to get even with him.

'Monstrous!' he muttered. 'I'll see you again, sir, you damned scamp. You slubber! I'll have your skin, believe me.'

With that Major Kirk strode off, leaving Crossman a quivering wreck of a man. He could never come up against his father without feeling drained and weak at the end of the encounter. It was easy at times when his father was not there, to dismiss him, but he was a powerful presence and he always left wounds in his wake. James was absolutely terrified of the old man and would normally go out of his way not to upset him. To stop his hands from shaking Crossman rammed them into his pockets and slunk back to where Jarrard and Lovelace stood.

'My God, man,' said Jarrard, 'that was horrible to witness. You didn't tell me you had Zeus for a father.'

Despite himself, Crossman smiled. 'Yes, Zeus. I wonder what that makes me?'

'A hero, in anyone's view,' remarked Major Lovelace, coming out of the shadows. 'Jarrard is right. My own father is a Tartar, but nothing compared with yours. I would not like to be in your boots.'

'I don't like them much, either,' replied Crossman, 'but unfortunately I've got to wear them. Well, the cat's out of the bag now. I wonder what he'll do about it? He might try to have me sent home.'

'Colonel Hawke would have something to say about that.'

'My father has powerful connections.'

'So has Hawke. I shouldn't worry, sergeant. I think he'll seethe and simmer for a day or two, make a few enquiries, and find himself coming up against forces he can't control. Just keep a low profile for a while. You've got a fox hunt coming up, in any case. I think I'll bring it forward a day or so and get you out of the way. I'll have to inform Colonel Hawke about what's going on, but I don't think he'll be very impressed with Major Kirk. I know this is easy to say and difficult for you to act on, but I should try to forget about it and just sink yourself into your job.'

Crossman went back to Kadikoi in a depressed state of mind. A man's father is a powerful force in his life. With one breath his father had denied him, yet with another he had called him his own. These contradictory statements showed how even Major Kirk was struggling with the idea of his son's illegitimacy. The old man could, of course, have denied him from birth. Major Kirk could have consigned Crossman's mother to the workhouse for good and all and put her claims down to the ramblings of a madwoman. Many gentlemen did just that. They fornicated and forgot. If the mother of their child appeared with a baby in arms, they called the authorities to remove her and the brat. If she persisted she most likely ended up in Bedlam. By that time she was probably ready for the place and spent the rest of her life there. The child either died or went out onto the streets, where it begged or stole, and was often shipped off to a penal colony. Not many illegitimate children of baronets ended up calling themselves gentry and benefiting from the kind of life Crossman had enjoyed as Alexander Kirk.

Crossman believed his stepmother had been the main force behind his father's acceptance of him in the family home. She was a woman who took her responsibilities and duties as a human being very seriously. So far as Major Kirk was concerned, his wife had grave failings: she was too sentimental, too emotional. She had, as soon as she laid eyes on Crossman, seen the resemblance to her husband. Crossman looked even more like the old man than James did. All knew the truth of the matter, even had some of them thought the maid had lied about who was responsible for her condition. Certainly Kirk himself knew he had bedded the woman and the face of the child, as it grew, would have amazed even the most sceptical with its likeness to the major. They might have said James was the changeling, but never Alexander.

Yet, Crossman admitted to himself, this could not be the whole story – that his stepmother had taken him in. The baronet could, at that time, have covered up the child's existence. He was a man of means. Somehow something had brought him to tell his wife of his indiscretion – this particular indiscretion at least – and that began the chain of events which led to the baby being accepted as the second son. It was the thought that his father actually loved him as a son which brought Crossman the most grief. That a man like Major Kirk, whom Crossman considered to be the scum of the earth, should have some finer feelings was quite upsetting. It was difficult for him, with his father, to step outside the role of child, and to children bogey men are *all* bad. They can't be good in some ways and bad in others. They must be evil through and through. It made him thoroughly miserable to imagine that his father was actually capable of loving him. He didn't want to be loved by such a man, not one scrap. He wanted hate from him, so that he could feel justified in hating him back. This halfway-house feeling did not satisfy his need to loathe the man who had destroyed his real mother without a qualm.

That his father was also a courageous man in battle, he could accept. Many unscrupulous men were careless of their personal safety. That he had a code of honour, which did not include the care of women he had ruined, was also not incompatible with physical courage. It was such a man's ability to love that could not be reconciled in Crossman's mind with his behaviour towards his fellow human beings, those who shared the earth with him.

'I hope the man is put to the sword,' he thought, as he lay in bed and wrestled with these demons. 'I hope some Cossack seizes his chance and puts an end to my agony, and his own. He surely cannot be at peace with himself. He would surely be happier to be rid of such a heinous life.'

He fell asleep with these wishes in his head, not believing a single one of them.

Waking in the early hours he found they had not gone away. Lovelace was now in his bed, snoring. The cold dawn rays were slipping through the window. Crossman winced as he remembered yesterday's embarrassing encounter. Both father and son, surely, at that moment could have died of shame. To be bawling at one another in the middle of a ring of soldiers. How humiliating it appeared now! Someone must have reported the incident. Major Kirk at least would be the butt of any conversation amongst the officers of the 93rd, both yesterday, today and tomorrow. Entertainments were few and far between. The tiger of malicious gossip ran riot in such circumstances. As to Crossman, many of them would be wondering who he was, this sergeant, that a major should allow him to walk away after such insolence and insubordination.

Deep down, Crossman knew that what upset him the most was the knowledge that he was his father's son. That man he seemed to hate so much had passed some of himself on to his son. How much of Crossman was Major Kirk? How much of his father's personality and character had been handed down to his youngest son? Perhaps a great deal? Perhaps they were as bad as each other? All this confusion of identity was so hard to bear. Would he indeed end up hating himself as much as he loathed his father now? Perhaps in ripe old age his father would mellow, become beloved of everyone, and leave Crossman as the nasty middle-aged rake who had dowagers clicking their tongues and young men casting scornful glances. Would Crossman become the old fox that his father was now? It was an unpleasant thought. Damned unpleasant.

'Oh my God,' he groaned aloud. 'What am I to do now?'

'Go back to sleep,' murmured the figure in the next cot. 'I strongly advise it. In the morning light it will look differently.'

'It is the morning light and it looks ghastly.'

'I mean breakfast time, sergeant. I'm quite fatigued, so I would appreciate the rest.'

Within a few moments the major was snoring again. Crossman arose quietly, and took pen, ink and paper from one of the drawers in the major's chest. He began a letter, staring every so often out of the window at a cockerel that seemed at every second on the verge of crowing, yet never actually managed to clear its throat and let rip.

My Dearest Cousin Jane, I would have expected to hear of your marriage before now, to some handsome young earl or lord, or even a prince. I would put no man beyond your reach, knowing that you are a non-pareil *and untouchable in the beauty stakes. Even when you were six and had those funny teeth you were still the prettiest young lady for a thousand miles. Yet here you are writing to your wretched cousin sequestered in a foreign land, albeit one where the sun shines brighter, the flowers bloom with more colour and the sea is of the deepest blue. I am well, as you can imagine, for this is but a holiday for the Kirks. Yesterday my father and I had an interesting conversation about biological matters: subjects not fit for the ear of a young unmarried lady. He (my father) still has his old temper and I am afraid we left each other on bad terms. It needs someone like you (he was always sweet with you, was he not, cousin Jane?) to sugar his tea for him and to turn him into a presentable human being. His choler will kill him one of these days. I must take my share of the blame though, for I seem to fuel his rage.*

Now, Jane, why are *you not married? I myself was once engaged to a very beautiful French lady, but I have not heard from her in an age and I fear she has found another. Who could keep such a lady at this distance with all those gallants sweeping around Paris, gathering up such flowers? Some young stalwart has taken her in his arms and has told her he would die if she refused his offer. Who can blame her? I am not the man I was when first we met. Indeed, for all this bountiful land has to offer I seem to have grown a terrible beard (I look like some mad Russian monk fallen from grace) and to have shed my puppy fat. Possibly I look better without the latter, for my face was never better covered up and my bones, which are my most attractive features, have come to the fore to present themselves to the world at large.*

Jane, you would weep for the poor soldiery here in the field. I have been very fortunate in being chosen for special duties and do not have to spend hours in a freezing trench. The sight of our pitiful army is not one I would force upon anyone in Britain. We are indeed a ragged, unhappy bunch, some of us worse off than others. Our leader is fairly comfortable in his farmhouse, but I do not blame him for that. We see very little of him and he surrounds himself with his relations. That I do take issue with, for this war would be ended more quickly if his advisers had more intellectual strength and were less sycophantic.

The candle gutters and looks ready to give up its flame. I must end this letter here. I shall pass it to our mutual friend, Mrs Durham, who will no doubt find some way of getting it to you. She has many admirers amongst the yachting set, who go back and forth. I hope it finds you well in health and happy in heart.

I remain, as always,
your most affectionate,
Alexander

The candle was not 'guttering' of course, for it was now daylight outside, but he needed an excuse to wrap up the letter. He could have rambled on for hours, but it would only be babble and he knew his adopted aunt would be horrified if Jane received a letter some ten pages long from someone who had no intention of courting her. Three pages were fine. That was very cousinly and proper. He put the pages in the same envelope which had borne her own letter to him, having no other. Then he crossed out his own name and wrote hers.

Well, there! He had done the right thing. He had received a missive and had now replied. His duty was done. Yet, it had not been so irksome a duty as he had thought it might be. Jane was a very pleasant girl – a *woman* now of course – and thoughts of her had carried him home and back to times more agreeable than the present. She had allowed him to recall the scent of the blossoms on the greengage trees and the newly-scythed hay at the bottom of the long garden . . .

'Sergeant!' came Wynter's harsh strident tones, yelling up the stairs. 'You're wanted down 'ere.'

The beautiful moment was gone: shattered like a bowl dropped on tiles. Crossman sighed and descended the stairs, still in the fur coat he had put on to keep out the cold while he wrote the letter.

'Keep your voice down, Wynter. The major's asleep.'

'Sorry, I'm sure,' whined Wynter, 'but there's a cove here wants us to help him. I said we was special duties and not on for that kind of thing, but he won't listen. Says that don't matter, 'cause his is a special job.'

A naval gunner stood in the doorway. He was a big man with a dark beard that covered the whole of his weathered face, leaving only two holes for his eyes. It was as if they were staring through a thick hedge. His massive shoulders blocked the light from the doorway almost completely. On his feet he had some Russian boots, which he had obviously taken from a battlefield, but such boots must have been on the feet of a giant. On his head was a fur hat, the kind sold by the sutlers, probably made of the skins of domestic cats.

'You Crossman?' he growled in a deep voice. 'Lieutenant Pirce-Smith said you and your men would help.'

'Help what?' asked Crossman, inwardly cursing his immediate superior, who was obviously looking for ways to get his own back for the last fox hunt.

'We've got a cannon out here, a 24-pounder that's got to be shifted, taken up to the front line. Admiral's orders. Just got it off a ship in the harbour and hauled it this far, but now it's stuck.'

'We'll be right out, sergeant.'

'Grateful.'

'UP, UP!' Crossman yelled at pretenders and genuine sleepers alike. 'Boots on. Oh, I see you haven't taken yours off, Gwilliams. Let's have you up. Take a quick drink of water and grab a piece of salt beef and biscuit. Then out into the cold day, my little doves.'

'Wait,' cried Wynter, as the others began rolling out of their cots, groaning and reaching for their boots. 'You!' he yelled after the retreating gunner. 'Ain't you got oxes to pull the gun?'

'Oxen, you mean. The only animal we had for a while was a camel and he dropped dead on us. We ate him over three days. Still got his tripes. We might give you some, for helpin' us, but I'm not promising mind, since it ain't mine to give away, really.'

Wynter came back. 'I don't want no camel tripe. Liver an' kidneys, yes, but not its guts. They look as tough as old Harry, those beasts and you can bet their innards are not tender.'

Once they were all ready they went outside. The freezing air stopped every man in his tracks for a moment, then they moved forward, slowly, as if wading through a viscous fluid. The seamen were sitting on and around an enormous piece of ordnance, smoking pipes and looking as if they would rather stay there than move. The gun was quite unlike any of the rangers had ever seen. The greened barrel was shaped like an elongated dragon, the muzzle being the dragon's mouth, with snout, nostrils and teeth. Twin ears acted as a foresight on the weapon. There were tucked claws and wings at various points along the barrel, blunted and smoothed against the gun, presumably so they would not catch on anything the cannon brushed against. The whole barrel, longer than a British gun of the same calibre, was covered in green scales.

'Where did this come from?' asked Gwilliams, running a mitten along the weapon. 'Looks oriental.'

'From far Cathay,' replied an artillery man promptly. 'Took from a Chinese battle junk in a river war out that way. Fancy hunk of ordnance, ain't she? Spits fire and death, just like a real piece. Roars like a good 'un. Scares the livin' daylights out of the enemy.'

Wynter stuck his arm in the jaws of the dragon's mouth.

'Ow, sergeant! It's chompin' me arm off.'

'Stop fooling around, Wynter,' said Crossman, but he could not help admiring the piece. It was like a bronze artwork, rather than a machine of war. Some Chinese weapon maker had laboured over it in forge and workshop until it satisfied his yearning to make something beautiful out of something deadly, perhaps in the way medieval sword makers had spent long hours perfecting blades, decorating them, and finally giving each weapon a name like *Excaliber*. Crossman had no doubt this gun had a personal name. *Dragon from Hell* or *Fiery-Mouthed Killer of Men.* Now it was in the hands of staid and starchy British soldiers, who liked their guns straight and simple, looking as if they were there to do a job, not to decorate the battlefield and solicit admiring glances from followers of Asiatic sculpture. They were the sort of men who preferred a sombre minister of the Church in his black suit to a Cantonese mandarin in gold and red robes. Point and shoot, that's what was required of a gun. Not, oh ain't that a dandy piece, let's put it on the mantle so everyone can look at it. It was the kind of gun you might find standing within the gates of some diplomat's country estate, to impress visitors. On the battlements of a Chinese fort, green roof tiles and red gun ports, or a huge junk with ribbons and flags streaming from the masts, it would have fitted in. Here in the mud and muck of the Crimean peninsula it appeared entirely out of place.

A barked order from the hairy gunner had his men knocking out the bowls of glowing tobacco and stamping their feet in readiness.

'Right, sergeant, you and your rangers go round the far side, while my lot take the left. We got to be quick, for as you can see the wheels has sunk in the mud, and if we don't move the bastard soon she'll freeze solid where she stands and we'll never get her on.'

Crossman took one look at the way the cannon was listing and knew that the right side was sinking even further. It was an imperceptible movement, but it was indeed going down. Co-ordinated by the artillery sergeant they made a concerted effort to move the gun, but it remained stuck halfway up to its axle.

'Peterson,' said Crossman, turning to that soldier, 'are you all right?'

Peterson had gone a ghastly grey colour. 'No, sergeant. It's my shoulder.'

'Of course, the wound. You're excused.'

'Thank you, sergeant.' She stumbled back towards the hovel, leaving Wynter looking very pained.

'Some people get out of everythin',' he said.

'Yorwarth,' asked Crossman. 'How about you?'

Yorwarth could hardly speak at all through his broken jaw, which had been splinted in rather a strange fashion by Gwilliams. His face looked as if it had been framed like a picture in order for it to go into an exhibition. Yorwarth rattled something in the back of his throat.

'He says he's all right,' interpreted Wynter.

Crossman stared hard at Wynter.

'Well, he does!' cried the indignant lance-corporal. 'I wun't say he said otherwise, would I? He can hear all right, even if he does look as if his head's bin blocked by a carpenter.'

This was true. Now, to business. Crossman sent Ali away to find some metal angle irons he had seen leaning against a house in Kadikoi a few days previously. They were still there, because Ali returned with them a few moments later, an irate naval rating following him and telling him that bloody Tartars couldn't just steal what took their fancy, without a by-your-leave or excuse me. The Bashi-Bazouk turned and told the rating in broken English that he would cut off his head, arms and legs, very soon, if the rating called him a Tartar just once more. And what was more, he would slice him open and feed his intestines to the dogs if he continued to follow him. The salt got the message and, still grumbling to himself in the kind of voice Wynter often used, he turned and walked back down the street, kicking out unsuccessfully at an inoffensive-looking mongrel that slunk across his path.

Using the angle irons as levers they managed to prise the wheels from the mud. They then used the irons as runners to get the gun rolling again. Ropes were reaffixed and the cannon could now be pulled from the front and pushed from behind, with a strong man on each wheel to heave them at that point and keep the object moving. The two strongest men were the Turk and the gunner. They kept looking across the gun at each other with respectful glances as first one, then the other, managed to shoulder the wheel out of a potentially difficult rut. Gradually, yard by yard, the cannon began to travel along the post road. There was something near to five miles of ground to cover before it was in its proper place and ready to begin shelling the Russians. It was going to be a long, hard day.

The odyssey of the gun began to attract attention as they fought it forward over the impossible terrain. Cavalry men came out to watch, smoking their pipes, then taking them out of their mouths and pointing with the stems, while offering unwanted advice. Foot soldiers lounged with their hands in their pockets, often reeling off an anecdote about some heavy load they, or their fathers, or their fathers' fathers, had once hauled over similar impossible ground. They too had advice to offer and were not inclined to keep it to themselves, even when the gunner told them to stuff it in their pipes and smoke it.

Everyone thought the weapon was too much like an oriental parade to win a war with, but if it had to be taken from here to there, why they had something to say about it.

'You want to watch that carronade don't careen over to one side,' one soldier advised them, 'and crush the life out of one on you. I seen a gun keel over once and squash a horse flat as a beggar's purse.' There were murmurs of approval at the delivery of this homily. The soldier was encouraged to continue, but not by the haulers of the gun. 'Nasty mess it made. I mind the horse had a rider at the time. He got his boot stuck in the muzzle of the gun. They had to cut un out with a razor. Good pair of boots too. An' the horse weren't bad, when it had a body to fix its four legs and a head to, so to speak. But arter it had been fell on, its chest popped like a ripe cherry under a soldier's boot. Not much use for nothing but the glue factory, arter that.'

Anecdotal warnings were delivered by an ever-increasing audience along the route. During his leisure time between breaths, Wynter told such advisers where they might go to visit the Devil, and when they got there to stay on.

Gwilliams said, 'We could do with Jason's fire-breathing bulls now, eh, sergeant? To pull this beast along?'

One particular patch of the road was a quagmire. At that point the men had not the strength to continue, even though a drummer boy from the 47th had brought them tea, courtesy of the drum major. They sat and drank the tea right there in the cold mud, being covered from head to foot in mire anyway. A staff officer, a colonel, passed by on his horse and told them they were doing sterling work. Their fame was spreading throughout the whole of the army. Even some Frenchmen came to watch from the *Sapeur du Genie* bringing with them stick loaves and bottles of wine, to make a picnic of the affair. To Crossman's consternation the goose girl arrived and waved to him shyly. He felt it discourteous not to return the wave, which had his men looking at him rather curiously.

'Just one of my students,' said Crossman, through gritted teeth.

'Woll,' said Yorwarth through his wooden mouth-cage, 'oof thoss a somple oof stoo-ent, I woll ee a teesher oomorrow.'

'Not of the English language, I hope,' replied Crossman, drily.

After a rest they continued to urge the gun forward, using threats against its ironwork and oaths regarding its parentage, as well as employing brute force. When they came to the Col, where the ground rose steeply, the gun began to get its own back. They would force it two yards forward, only to have it slip back three. Wynter was sent for some blocks, to ram under the backs of the wheels, to stop it rolling back. He returned before the half-hour, clearly drunk.

'How can you get in such a state in just twenty minutes?' asked Crossman. 'It won't get you out of this, you know.'

'Don't care,' grinned the almost legless lance-corporal. 'Don't care a-tall.' He then made the mistake of putting his bare hands on the barrel of the gun, having removed his mittens to drink, and yelled when he could not free them. They were stuck to the freezing scales of the dragon's back. The others were now heaving the gun up the slope and dragging him along with it. He pulled at his hands and screamed with the pain this brought him.

'Don't tear them off,' warned Gwilliams. 'You'll take the skin from your hands.'

'Oh, Christ. Help me.'

'Not if you blaspheme,' said a seaman. 'If you take Jesus' name in vain, the only help you'll get is from the Devil himself.'

'I don't care who does it. My palms hurt bad.'

So far as Wynter was concerned, it was indeed the Devil who came to his eventual rescue.

Ali took out a hunting knife. 'All right, I get them off.'

'You keep away from me, you heathen,' yelled Wynter. 'Sergeant, he's going to chop my hands off.'

One of the interested watchers produced a lantern, which was lit, then Ali warmed the blade of his weapon on the flame. He then began to prise Wynter's hands from the metal, forcing the blunt edge of the blade between the skin and iron. First he got one off, and then the other, and once they were free he clipped Wynter's ear with a practised hand and told him not to play child games and to do his work. Wynter was mortally afraid of Ali, having witnessed the Turk slitting the throats of the sleeping enemy. He grumbled at the treatment, but no more than that. A dark look from Ali silenced even that small voice of protest.

Two Tartars with a wagon were persuaded to hitch their horses to the gun to help haul it up the slope. Once at the top it was then pushed and pulled to the bottom on the other side. Halfway down the gun decided to try to beat its handlers to the bottom. Everyone let go except one of the seamen, who remained hanging on to the large piece of ordnance, which then proceeded to wrench his arm from its socket. He gave a loud scream and fell to the ground clutching his dislocated shoulder. His arm was at a horrible-looking right-angle to his body, pointing, as it were, behind him as if at some Nemesis creeping up to stab him in the back.

'I'll fix him,' said Gwilliams, pushing the others aside as they crowded round the unfortunate seaman, saying helpful things like, 'Does it hurt?'

'Out of the way,' ordered the bone-man barber.

Gwilliams took the screaming seaman's arm, put his foot somewhere in the region of his neck, and gave the wayward limb a practised twist. Everyone heard the *click* as the ball found its socket. The patient had gone deathly quiet now and stared straight ahead. He was sitting up. Gwilliams took him firmly by the shoulders and began to massage him with large strong hands. Then he ordered the man to lie flat on the ground. Once the seaman was prone, Gwilliams walked up and down his back, pressing here and there with the balls of his feet, until at last he allowed the man to get to his feet again.

'How do you feel?' Gwilliams asked.

The seaman flexed his bad arm, shook his head in wonderment, and said, 'I feel grand. Grand. Not a twinge.'

'Well now,' said the gunner looking at Gwilliams with admiration, 'ain't that somethin'? I never saw nothin' like that before. Where did you learn such stuff?'

'From the Red Indians,' remarked Gwilliams. 'They know all about bones. I can fix a bone, soon as look at it.'

'I'll wager you can.'

Crossman slapped Gwilliams on the back. 'Well done. I heard you were good at these things. Now we've all seen it. But, matey,' he said to the gunner NCO, 'I think we had better put your man on light duties for the rest of the trip.'

The gunner agreed.

They hauled again. Finally the emplacement was in sight. A hoarse cheer went up from both the men of the navy and Crossman's crew. Idle watchers fell away, now that there was no more sport to be had in baiting the haulers. Battered and bruised the two sets of men dragged the gun the last few yards and set it in place.

'Now,' said the gunner to Crossman and his crew, 'you shall be allowed to witness what she can do.'

He laid the gun himself, then his men went through the usual procedures prior to firing, loading the piece with a round shot. When all was ready the portfire was applied. There was a tremendous explosion, louder than was required of a normal gun of the size. Several pieces of metal went flying towards the Russian defences, only one of which was the cannon ball. When the smoke had cleared the seamen were shocked to see that the dragon had lost its jaws. The lower mandible had hit the ground at great force and had gone spinning away into a gulley. The upper jaw had flown high and wide and had come down clanging amongst some rocks where a British picquet post was enjoying a quiet afternoon.

'You've blown his bloody top off,' said Wynter aghast. 'Poor beggar's got nothin' to put his hat on now.' He felt the injury almost as if it were himself who had lost puffed cheeks and iron teeth. In the last hour or two he had become attached to the dragon. It was like watching the head of a pet dog explode before his eyes.

'Oi!' came a distant yell from that spot. 'Are you firin' at *us*?'

'Sorry, lads,' called back the gunner. 'Our gun lost its muzzle.'

The cannon itself looked a sorry mess now, flared and jagged.

'We could get someone to cut off the end of the barrel,' suggested a seaman. Like most of the others, he was loath to admit they had hauled the gun all that way for nothing.

'It'd be too short,' sighed the gunner.

'It might not be . . .'

Crossman and the other rangers left the navy men arguing over the usefulness, or otherwise, of the Chinese cannon. When it came to gloominess there was no one quite like a half-deaf gunner for despondency. His ears ringing for most of his life, his head as thick as a dull cooking pot, the gunner lived in a world of his own. In battle he was expected to stand still in a place of loud noises and kicking iron – or run for his life. There was no in-between. He could not march resolutely forward, or fight a steady retreat back to another position. He remained with great metal balls falling on and around him or he fled the enflamed wrath of those whom he had attempted to blast to pieces from a safe distance. It took a special kind of stolid dependency to be a gunner and a rather stoical if dismal philosophy on life. The rangers were pleased to have left such individuals behind and they made their way back to Kadikoi, their spirits lifting with every step of the journey.

When they got back Crossman found a message from Colonel Hawke awaiting him. He went to the colonel and found him in a relatively jovial mood.

'Well now, at least we know who you are, at last, sergeant. Mystery veil lifted.'

Crossman's heart sank. 'My father's been to see you?'

'Yes, we had a good talk. He had already been to the 88th to see your regimental colonel, who referred him to me. I was rather on the listening side at first, you understand, but after his demands had been stated I had my say too. You won't be surprised when you learn he wanted me to send you back on the next ship going home. Said your presence here embarrassed him and compromised his position as major in a noble regiment. I pointed out that so far as the army was concerned, we only had his word that you were his son, that you were of age and could speak for yourself, and that he could no more demand your return to England, or any other country, than he could request the abdication of our dear monarch, bless her heart.'

'I imagine his response was a fit of apoplexy.'

'You could say that. When that did not work he appealed to my common decency. I'm not sure what he meant by that. I was obliged to ask him whether he intended me to be decent to you, decent to him, or decent to the army. After another explosion I was then forced to remind him that so far as I knew majors could not demand anything of colonels, especially majors using language fit only for merchant seamen who preferred to be pressed rather than sent to a penal colony. He saw the wisdom in apology, asked who was my superior, and left. I imagine you have heard the last of him for a while, since the name I gave him belongs to a senior member of the government.'

Crossman groaned. 'I'm sorry about all this, sir. I had hoped I could get through the war without him knowing. He's due to retire and I imagine this will be his last campaign. It's unfortunate that it should happen now.'

Hawke shrugged. 'I must admit I was taken aback, almost rocked on my heels for a while, but I rallied, dear boy. I rallied. Now, I have a fox hunt for you, which will get you out of his hair for a while.'

'Do I have to take the lieutenant on this one?'

A cloud passed over the colonel's face for a moment.

'No, you don't have to. Do you resent Lieutenant Pirce-Smith so much?'

'No, not resent, exactly. I think he's probably a fine officer. He'll make a good leader of saboteurs one day, I haven't any doubt. But, understandably, he finds it difficult to accept someone junior to him giving the orders. I would be the same. Send me out into the field with a corporal who was more experienced than me, with authority over me, and I should resent it highly.'

Hawke looked relieved. 'I'm glad you think we can make something of him. I actually have faith in the man. He's the son of a good friend, you understand. Now, your mission. Come over here, to the map. You see this section of the Russian defences, here? Between the Malakoff and the Redan? Our old friend the ingenious engineer Todleben has built a crane, a giant crane, which does the work of a hundred men in half the time. That's possibly a hyperbole, but you get my meaning? By day we knock down the defences, by night he puts 'em up again, using this wood-and-iron monster worthy of Isambard Kingdom Brunel.'

'I think I understand where this is leading.'

'No doubt. You must destroy the monster, of course, and bring me its metaphorical head.'

'I shall do my best, sir.'

'Of course you will. Now, you expect to take your whole *peloton* with you?'

'I would like to leave Peterson and Yorwarth behind. Their injuries are too recent.'

'That will only leave you with, let's see, the Turk, Wynter and Gwilliams. Will that be enough?'

'It's the kind of fox hunt which will work better with a small number, colonel. When we're behind enemy lines I like a small group I can keep under my eye. We also attract less attention that way.'

'Good, good. And don't worry about your father. I believe we will see his retirement sooner rather than later. Oh, don't look like that, I shan't do anything drastic. Just a word or two in the right ear. You'll be free to work, with him back in England.'

'Scotland.'

'Wherever. You look dubious, sergeant. I can understand why, but you see, in my opinion, majors of regiments of foot are odd items. We struggle to find a use for them, though many are fine soldiers and do good work. It's the rank and position which keeps them odd. They have no real function in a regiment and are best when used for their personal talents. I often think the army would be better promoting straight from captain to colonel. Keep it in the Cs so to speak.' This was a joke and the colonel paused for a reaction, which Crossman failed to give. The colonel gave a little sigh and continued. 'You on the other hand are extremely useful to us. Given a choice between the two of you, the usefulness wins out. So, clear your mind of any doubt. Do your job and one day we'll see what can be done about some sort of reward. Oh, and in the meantime, keep on that Enticknap thing, when you can.'

'Yes, sir.'

On the way back Crossman remembered he was supposed to be taking school. He went immediately to the chapel, to find a thin, earnest-looking sergeant standing before a thoroughly-bored-looking class. The sergeant looked up as he walked in. 'You're late,' said the sergeant. 'We're up to m-n-o-p-q.'

'I'm late, but not for sitting out there. I was the one who taught them while you were lying sick.'

The schoolmaster-sergeant frowned and removed a pair of wire spectacles to polish the lenses on a piece of felt. 'Well, I have to say sergeant, you didn't do a very good job of it. They haven't advanced in numbers or letters a single jot.'

'Sorry about that. But I think they've learned about some other things. For instance . . .'

'In my classroom, the basics come first. Once they have their numbers and their alphabets under their belts, they can look to more worldly matters.'

Crossman gave up and waved to the class. 'Goodbye, class.'

'Goodbye sergeant,' they chorused, mournfully.

The goose girl with her hennaed hair watched him leave with doe eyes. Crossman wondered how long she would stay after she realized he had gone for good. Then again, she might fall in love with the perfectly presentable schoolmaster-sergeant, who after all might appear as a Greek god to a young maiden whose would-be lovers were rustic brutes with large heads and hands, large necks and feet, and few social graces. Then again, was he putting his own values in her head? Perhaps what she wanted in the end was a strong country lad with no nonsense about him?

Who could tell?

6

Peterson and Yorwarth were to remain at Kadikoi. Peterson was not too concerned by this, but Yorwarth complained bitterly in a voice severely hampered by the cage on his face. He did not see the sense in convalescence, he told Crossman. He didn't use his jaws to shoot and he didn't use them to walk. Crossman told him that an injury of that kind took it out of a man, made him weak for a while. Yorwarth still complained. Crossman was adamant.

'Best you stay behind on this one.'

The seventeen-year-old finally gave in. Remain he would. But he wanted the splints off before they left on the mission.

'Gi' me 'at, ser'unt.'

It was the night before Crossman, Gwilliams, Ali and Wynter left on the fox hunt that Yorwarth had his strange splint removed. They began with a celebration, and Gwilliams paraphrasing the seventeenth-century poet Richard Lovelace, 'Wires do not a prison make, nor wooden bars a cage,' then they all had a tot of rum, toasted Yorwarth's jaws, and removed the impedimenta from his face. Strangely there were some white streaks in his baby beard where the wooden splints had been pressing too hard. He stared at these in the mirror, then decided to shave immediately, to examine the damage more closely. Gwilliams did the service for him, then whipped off the hot towel, though he still had his back to his audience.

'Speak!' they all said, Wynter pouring some more rum into the mugs.

'Let's hear your voice,' Gwilliams ordered. 'The real voice, not that mooning note we've had to put up with for the past week or two.'

'Listen you bunch o' pelicans,' said Yorwarth spinning round to face them, 'have you saved me any of that rum? A man could die of thirst here.'

They began cheering. It was not quite the same voice as before, but it was near enough. Gradually, however, the sound of cheering died in their throats. One by one, as they stared into his unshaven face, they realized what the splints had done to him. Each in his time turned away from Yorwarth, embarrassed for the young Australian private. Only Crossman and Wynter remained staring and their expressions were so serious Yorwarth instantly became worried. There *was* something untoward about his mouth. He worked his jaws and found he could not make his teeth meet.

'What is it?' he asked. 'Give me a glass.'

Once he had a mirror in his hand, he studied his jaws. The lower jaw, the mandible, was skewed. It jutted off to the right, while the upper jaw went perhaps slightly left. The effect was grotesque. It appeared as if some strong man had gripped Yorwarth by the top of the head with one hand, by the lower jaw with the other, and simply twisted in opposite directions. When he moved his mouth, one side of his face was chewing to the right, while the other went to the left.

'You've bent my jaws, you bastard!' he cried at Gwilliams. 'How am I going to eat with a mouth runnin' two different ways?'

'It wasn't me,' replied the American, indignant. 'It was the damn accident. In fact I think I put it righter than it was.'

'Perhaps,' suggested Major Lovelace, coming down the stairs and attaching himself to the end of the ceremony, 'you ought to visit the regimental surgeon. He'll no doubt straighten it for you.'

'How will he do that, sir?' cried Yorwarth.

'Well, he'll have to break it and reset it.'

Yorwarth gave a howl. 'I don't want my jaws broke again. It hurt bad enough the first time.' He stared at himself in the mirror again, his expression one of horror. 'Dust and dung, Gwilliams, you've slanted me in two directions. I look like a kangaroo sideswiped with a Fiji-man's club. What am I going to tell my mother? What about my drinking pals? They'll hoot me out of the door. Aw, Christ and Bethlehem.'

'Don't blaspheme,' said a shocked Peterson from her bed. 'You might be going to your maker before this war's over. Maybe they'll work their way back to where they were before. The cage has only been fresh removed. Maybe it'll be all right before the morning.'

But Yorwarth was not to be consoled. And he definitely blamed Gwilliams for the deformity. He said if he wanted to be disfigured he'd have gone into the canteen, got drunk, and got into a fight. That would have been honourable, he said. But to turn it out of shape with a bloody face cage, well that was plain stupid.

It was lucky for Gwilliams that he was on a fox hunt the next morning. He crept out without waking Yorwarth, still indignant that he was being held to blame for the misshapen jaws. Outside, the tattered remains of the morning mists were drifting away. He joined the end of the file of four men, the Turk leading. They went up past the British Left Attack and slipped down into Careenage Ravine, the walls of which were white with hoar frost where even the smallest ray of sunlight failed to reach. Stones cracked and rattled under their feet. They trod as quietly as they could, knowing that sounds carried a long way out on the Heights, but there were so many loose rocks they could not avoid making some noise. Strapped to each man's thighs and waist was a quantity of gunpower, which would be used by Ali to make the bombs.

It had been dewy above the ravine, the mists coming in from the warmer sea leaving droplets of water on their furs. Now they were in the colder regions of shadowland however, those same droplets froze on the soft hairs of their coats and hats. Before long each man looked as if he were encrusted with jewels that sparkled in the early morning light. They followed the ravine in the greyness almost to Careenage Bay, where Crossman was told he would meet a guide, who would take them through the

Russian lines. Crossman did not like trusting anyone outside his circle, even though Lovelace vouched for them, but in this case he had no choice.

Their man was not there when they arrived at the appointed spot, a tor shaped like a dog on its hind legs. This tardiness did not add to Crossman's confidence in the Greek, whose name he had been informed was a doubtful sounding "Diodotus". He had been born in Cyprus and had been taken to live on Lesbos when he was ten. His father had been a maker of sandals and his mother a sewer of sails for fishermen's boats. These, and a few other scraps of personal history, had been given to Crossman to confirm the man's identity when they eventually met.

The group waited for two hours and then a young man came down the slope to their right. The scree slid away before him, making his descent both hazardous and swift. He almost fell the last few feet and landed in front of them. He was a handsome creature with an unblemished skin and thick wavy black hair, which hung down his back. His grey eyes looked amazingly healthy and clear as he beheld them all with a wondrous expression of well-being on his face. A fresh, clean smell accompanied him, as if he had just stepped out of a bath. On his back a thick white sheepskin coat bulked out his obviously slim form. In his hand he carried a goatherd's staff and there was a small goatherd's cap on his head.

'Sergeant Crossman?' said the youth. 'Which is he? I am Diodotus of Lesbos.'

'You are a small boy,' replied Ali at once, without waiting for Crossman to answer. He trusted no one with a Greek name, especially an Adonis fresh from a wood nymph's bower. Then, contradicting himself, 'Only girls come from Lesbos.'

'You are not the sergeant. You are a Turk. We Greeks and Turks do not like each other. Tell me which is the sergeant.'

Crossman stepped forward. 'I'm Crossman. Before we go any further I have to satisfy myself as to who you are.' Various questions were then asked of the youth, which he answered in a calm sweet voice, adding at the end that he bore no personal malice towards Turks, but his father would expect him to show his disdain for them. 'In fact, I am very fond of the Turkish Sufi, Celaleddin Rumi. I have read the *Mathnawi*, which he wrote in 1248. Listen, *Do the camel-bells say "Let's rendezvouz here Thursday evening?" Of course not. They justle together all the while, chattering to each other as the camel plods on.* This is very good poetry.'

Ali glowered at this idiot boy who brazenly told him he held Turks in contempt. Crossman however stood between him and the Greek, and asked the lad to lead them through the Russian defences. Diodotus said he would do so, but Ali could not resist telling him that he had a pistol pointed at the youth and the slightest indication of treachery would force him to squeeze the trigger. Diodotus shrugged and smiled, then led off towards a narrow natural passageway that snaked from the ravine towards the defences which were now in view.

The passageway eventually turned into a tunnel, which might once have been an old sewer or drain, but was now dry and half-clogged with earth and debris. They made slow progress through this brick-walled tunnel, as they had to remove branches, weed and detritus as they went. For much of the way they were working in darkness, but finally they came through to a rusted iron grille at the other end.

'You didn't come this way,' said Crossman. 'No one has been through here in years.'

'No,' replied the Greek. 'I am a trusted citizen of Sebastopol. I go where I please. You, on the other hand, need to be hidden. Now, here is the most dangerous part of the journey. If we are seen leaving this tunnel whoever it is will know we have come from outside Sebastopol. Once we get into the streets however, all will be well. There are many foreigners here, many stranded merchant seamen. If we are stopped I shall tell them you are mariners who asked to be shown about the city.'

'Wouldn't we know the city by now?'

'Not necessarily. There are small craft that slip in from time to time, in shallow-bottomed boats. Skiffs and feluccas. They run the blockade and skip through, as a dragonfly might avoid a pond of frogs. You must be the crew of a felucca. You understand me? If you are caught, I shall run away of course. I have no wish to be hanged or shot by the Russians. Some of the Russians are my good friends.' He shrugged. 'I do what I must for money to live, but I will not die for you, Englishmen.'

'I told you he was not to be trusted,' growled Ali. 'See, he speaks of treachery and giving us to his Russian friends.'

Diodotus lifted his head. 'I would not betray you, Turk. I merely say if all was lost, I would try to escape. You cannot deny me that.'

'No,' Crossman agreed. 'That's your right.'

Diodotus went to the grille and looked first one way, then the other, satisfying himself that no one was about. Then he struck the grille on one corner with his goatherd's staff and the whole fell forward onto soft mud. The British and the Turk left the tunnel quickly. They found themselves in a narrow street with windowless walls on both sides. Hurrying along this street, following the Greek, they reached a small corner house. Here they were ushered inside by the youth. They found themselves in a kitchen where a young woman was stirring something which smelled strongly of cheese.

'My friend,' explained the Greek youth airily. 'She speaks no English.'

The brown-eyed girl, very pretty with high cheekbones making a heart-shaped face, smiled at them innocently.

'We stay here until the evening comes,' explained their host. 'You will eat some food, yes? There is no pork in the pot,' he added in an aside to Ali. 'I will not poison you with the pig meat.'

'Better not,' grunted Ali, 'or next thing I eat is your liver.'

'This is all right, ain't it?' said Wynter, settling on some rugs on the floor. 'Not half bad. You got any cards, Gwilliams?'

'Dice,' came the reply.

Wynter looked disappointed. 'Never mind. I don't like dice much.'

'That's 'cause you can't read the numbers,' said Gwilliams.

'Could be. Or could be I just don't like dice.'

Before Crossman made himself comfortable, he removed the packs of gunpowder that were strapped to his legs and waist, and advised the others to do the same.

'That fire is hot,' he said, pointing to the range on which the woman was cooking. 'It's only got to spit a spark at you.'

Wynter had his packs off in double-quick time. They were gathered up by the Greek who took them into a cooler room.

Crossman settled down to wait until nightfall, when he intended going out alone with Diodotus to inspect the crane.

'They tried to shoot it,' said the Greek youth. 'Your long guns tried but failed. There is not much to hit above the wall. Only the long jib, like the beak of some giant bird. At that distance it is like trying to hit a flagpole. So here you are now, to blow it up, yes? Ah, my friend has made the food. You will dine with me? You will be our guests. She is a very good cook, you know. And there is no pork. No pork, whatsoever. Not shellfish even. Nothing to harm the soul of a Turkish soldier. Eat, please. It is our pleasure. We wish you to enjoy the benefits of our hospitality. Greek hospitality.'

Until the last two words had been spoken, Ali had been preparing himself for a feast. Once Diodotus had uttered them, however, he leaned back, spurning the bowl that was proffered. The girl placed it down beside him and nodded significantly. Wynter wolfed through his bowlful and then asked if he could have Ali's. Ali said he could not. He might yet eat the contents of the bowl, when he had come to a state of peace within himself. The girl seemed to understand this and smiled. Ali smiled back at her. His antipathy towards male Greeks, it was well known, did not extend to the females of the nation. Ali saw no compromise in this. Women were legitimate prizes of any conquering warrior race. They did not dilute the blood. Only when a male Greek went with a Turkish woman were the offspring considered to be dubious human beings.

When nightfall came, Diodotus and Crossman went out into the streets. The young Greek boy seemed a little over-excited, but Crossman put that down to his inexperience in such matters. The world of cloak and dagger did not suit every man. There were those whose hearts raced and whose brains were full of electricity when they were on missions.

'If we are stopped,' said Diodotus, 'you must leave the talking to me. I speak Russian.'

'So do I,' said Crossman. 'Enough to get by.'

'Oh?' The boy looked disappointed. He appeared to want to be essential to Crossman in some way. 'Still, my Russian is very, very good. I expect yours has been learned from prisoners.'

Crossman did not contradict him.

The nearer they came to the outer defences, the more people there were around. Crossman hunched inside his coat. The Greek seemed oblivious of the Russians who went by. True, no one accosted them, but still there was always the chance that one would. There were people here who had met him. Colonel Todleben, the crane's builder, for one. Crossman had been caught inside Sebastopol and tortured once already. He had managed to kill his tormentor, later, on the field of battle, but he never wanted to be taken again. There were terrible memories of those weeks of torture that his brain had managed to bury. He recalled his recovery in the gentle hands of Lavinia Durham, coupled with the even gentler but more possessive fingers of the opiate, laudanum, and even some hours of his imprisonment, but the actual sessions when the pain was induced were buried too deeply.

Finally they reached the area where the crane was in use. It was an ingenious affair on wide wooden wheels that seemed not to sink into the ground, although the pressure on them must have been severe. Oxen were standing by, ready to draw the crane to another spot, should it be necessary to do so. Men swarmed over the ground around the crane, assisting its handler in attaching great blocks and bales that were lifted and dropped into place along the wall. Occasionally a shell came whistling overhead and everyone ducked as it exploded, or a round shot flew and landed, but for the most part the crane was able to work without pause, rebuilding any breaches in the defences that ringed the city. Bastions and trenchworks were being reinforced along the city's perimeter. Artillery batteries were being moved to new protected positions. Crossman could see a complicated trench system running between the Malakoff and Little Redan. The Russians were well and truly defensively organized.

There was danger out there from the enemy. Light was needed to handle the crane and such light, especially backlight, meant exposure to sharpshooters. Even as Crossman watched, a shot zipped through the night and took a careless sailor who had raised half his torso above the wall right in the back. The victim fell forward into the arms of a comrade. Others crowded round for a few moments, then left him when an officer barked an order. The wounded sailor – Crossman could see by his eyes he was close to death – was carried past the spot where the sergeant stood. It was difficult not to feel anger towards the shooter (who for all the world might have been Peterson if she had recovered enough to join with Captain Goodlake's sharpshooters, as was her wont during mission lulls) on the 'other side' of the wall. Crossman had to shake himself, mentally, and remind himself that the soldier who had made the shot was a comrade not a foe, was on his side. The Guards' officer who organised such night raids, with hawk-eyed riflemen handpicked from various regiments, was not indeed his enemy.

'Have you seen enough?' whispered the Greek. 'We should get back to the others.'

Crossman had not finished studying the crane. Where to place the charge? Any amount of gunpowder in the wrong place would explode uselessly without damaging the device. A small charge, in the right place, should be enough to cripple it forever. Well, at least for a few days, perhaps weeks, giving the British and French enough time to blast the defences and weaken them to the point where an attack might be possible. Crossman knew the French were raring to have a go. Champing at the bit. Give them a hole and they would do their damnedest to go through it. Their army was in much better health than the British. Their numbers were greater and their men in finer fettle. They slept in huts, were well supplied, and their state of well-being was superior to that of the British. Crossman wanted to give the French that gap to go through. Perhaps it might be the hole in the dam through which the flood would pour and drown Sebastopol.

'All right,' he said in German, there being some men standing quite close and it being dangerous to use English, 'I'm ready to go back to the others. Let's go before they eat and drink everything in your house.'

'Eh?' uttered the Greek. Crossman realized the other man did not speak German. He should have used Russian. However, one of three workmen just relieved of their shift had heard what he'd said, and suddenly the tiredness left the man's face. He looked interested.

'Others?' said one of the Russian soldiers, also in German. 'You are having a party?'

'No. There's no party. Not really.'

The men came over to him. They were dressed for work in old clothes, but were wearing fatigue caps denoting the 26th Regiment. One was quite elderly, with grey hair and a grey moustache decorating his lined face, but the other two were young men and they looked eager. The same one who had spoken before now continued to press his case.

'You mentioned food and drink. Come on, share with us. We won't tell anyone else.' The soldier turned and spoke to his two companions in Russian and they nodded eagerly.

Crossman had a dilemma. If he stood and argued with these men he was going to attract attention to himself and Diodotus. While he was confident enough on the periphery of Sebastopol society, for there was a great variety of citizens and nationalities in this cosmopolitan city, he knew he did not warrant close inspection. If some Russian officer came over and wanted to know what was going on, then started asking awkward questions, Crossman once again might end up in a Sebastopol prison.

'Oh, come on then,' he said, jovially. 'But I hope you won't be disappointed.'

The soldier who had spoken in German rubbed his hands together in anticipation and jabbered to his companions. Crossman set out with Diodotus by his side. The two had exchanged significant looks and Crossman thought he recognized an expression of 'leave it to me' in the Greek. He was quite prepared to do this because he himself was at a perfect loss. Obviously they could not take the three soldiers back to the house, but at the same time Crossman saw great difficulty in killing them. There were three of them for a start. It is no easy task to kill three men one after another, without at least one of them escaping. Aside from the practical considerations, killing a man on the battlefield, even at close quarters, was not the same as killing a man who was walking by your side, chattering away about trivial social matters, in the streets of a civilized town. The latter actually felt like murder. Crossman knew there were men who could do such things: he believed Lovelace would have little hesitation. Ali would certainly do it, if he felt he had to, and Ali was no cowardly backstabber. And both would quite rightly justify their actions by saying that anyone who jeopardized their life, the lives of their men and the success of their mission, whether knowingly or not, had unfortunately forfeited the right to live. Crossman could not bend his mind to such logic.

Quite suddenly, as these thoughts still churned inside Crossman's head, they turned a corner and his worst fears were realized. They had come face to face with a Russian officer, who seemed inclined to stop and stare at them through his spectacles. He was a young man, a second-lieutenant, and his face bore a serious expression.

The three Russians halted and saluted, since this young officer was clearly not going to let the party pass without a word.

'My Greek friend,' said the officer, speaking to Diodotus. 'Where are you going in such a hurry?'

Diodotus stepped forward and took the officer's hand to shake it, though the lieutenant did not seem inclined to offer it in the first place.

'How good to see you, Leo. How very good to see you.'

'I asked you a question,' said the officer. He turned to stare, first at Crossman, then at the other men. 'Where are you and your companions racing away to? Is the city under attack? Do you know something?'

Crossman could tell the officer was half-joking, so he said in his not-very-good Russian, 'The city is always under attack, sir. Why just a few moments ago, when we were working on the walls, a man was killed before my very eyes. Shot through the heart.'

'No, no,' said one of the soldiers, 'the ball hit him in the head.'

'And who are you?' asked the officer of Crossman. 'Are you a merchant sailor?'

The officer looked an intelligent man. Crossman did not want to say yes and then get into conversation with him over matters of the sea, which would – if the officer knew anything about it himself – expose the sergeant's ignorance. So, putting on an indignant expression, he said, 'I was tutor to some children here, teaching German, until this damn war started. Now I can't get home to my wife and children. I have to do gruelling manual work,' he showed the lieutenant his palms, 'which is ruining the skin on my hands . . .'

Diodotus suddenly interrupted with, 'I myself was a prince in my last life and God neglected to change my skin.'

Suddenly, with this extraordinary remark, all attention was on the Greek.

'How so, my friend?' asked the officer, his eyes lighting up a little. 'Tell us more. Is this to be the subject of one of your epic Greek poems? Please explain.'

'Why,' replied Diodotus with an expansive gesture, 'I can't wear anything next to my skin but silk, or I break out in a rash. I have these beautiful manners which no one taught me, for my mother was a washerwoman and my father a drunk. You can see I have princely looks – the face of an angel, the body of a god. I sleep like a lamb on satin sheets, but toss and turn on rough cotton. It seems obvious to me that I was once a prince whom God is tormenting by leaving me in my old skin.'

The lieutenant laughed. 'You must have done something very bad in your last life, to return as you are now.'

'But then,' continued Diodotus, 'you must admit my poetry is so very princely. It sings. It is mellifluous.'

The officer laughed again. 'It's not bad – not bad. Well, then, where are you off to?'

'A party, sir,' blurted out one of the soldiers. 'These gentlemen kindly asked us along.'

There was a tutting sound from the lieutenant. 'My Greek friend, what are you doing, collecting rough fellows like these? Are you dredging the slums for material for those dreary stories you've been writing? Shame on you. Stick to poetry. Your prose is mundane. Men,' he said to the soldiers, 'you are being used. He will write down every word you say in his little blue notebook and it will re-emerge from the mouth of one of his sordid characters – people of the streets, people of the soil. This man is a writer you know. Good at verse, but horrible at prose. Take my advice and leave him to his devices. If you don't, your grandchildren will recognize your earthy phrases in one of his self-published works and die of embarrassment for you.'

With that, the officer nodded curtly to Crossman, took his leave of Diodotus, and continued on his way.

'What was all that about?' asked the elderly soldier. 'You are really taking our words and putting them down in some book?'

'If you're worried at all, you can go on your way now,' said Diodotus. 'I have no argument with that.'

'No,' said one of the younger men, 'we'll stick with you.'

Diodotus turned and continued walking. Crossman fell in beside him. 'Who was that second-lieutenant?' he asked. The Greek looked behind him. The three soldiers had fallen back a bit. He felt able to talk, quietly.

'That was Lieutenant Leo Tolstoy. Like me, he writes, only I'm better at it than him, though he won't admit it. We show each other our work.' He looked up at Crossman. 'One day you will be proud to mention my name to your family. *I knew him*, you will say. What, the great author, Diodotus? they will exclaim in wonder. You knew him? As a friend? Yes, you will reply, he was one of my greatest companions. We fought together during the Russian war. Then you will probably brag to them that you gave me my best inspirations, that your suggestions had appeared in my works. You will point to a shelf containing a long line of my books. There, you will say, that one entitled *The Sebastopol Incident*. I gave him the plot for that book.

'But you will be lying, of course. All men lie about such things. It is the nature of the beast. To be close to a genius and not to be part of that genius is impossible to bear. You will make things up, out of the ether, and I shall forgive you for it, because by that time we will be writing to each other once every few months. You will be praising my latest tome, and I shall be dispensing literary wisdom to you. You shall be my representative in London, arguing for more and more money from the publishers, as my books sell on the streets of your capital city like hot pies. You and I, my friend, will be as rich as Croesus one day.'

Crossman laughed at the Greek's flight of fancy and then said, 'Until then, we have a more pressing problem.'

'Ah, yes. The soldiers. Down here.' Diodotus suddenly swung sharply down some cellar steps which led to a door with peeling red paint. He knocked on it briskly and when it was opened the sounds of revelry came from within. The three soldiers peered over the Greek's shoulder, seeing in the tobacco fug inside men drinking, girls dancing. 'The party,' cried Diodotus with a shy little smile at Crossman. 'In you go, soldier boys.'

'Here,' said a woman in Polish, 'have you been invited?'

Diodotus ignored her. Pushing his way past her jutting breasts he led the way into the room. Once they were all in, she shrugged and closed the door, going back to sit on the lap of a naval man. He laughed and bumped her up and down, before taking a long swig at a pot of something. The room was extremely hot, and crammed with bodies. Soon the three soldiers had melted into the melee. They were no longer interested in Crossman and Diodotus. They had found their party.

'Shall we leave?' asked Crossman, urging Diodotus towards the exit.

The Greek was beaming, looking around him, nodding at acquaintances. 'What's the hurry? Relax. Enjoy yourself. No one here is worried about saboteurs.'

Crossman winced. 'Are you mad? Keep your tongue.'

Diodotus made a Mediterranean gesture with his chin. 'I would be mad to rush away from here to be with your smelly Turk, now wouldn't I? They're probably all asleep back there. Let's enjoy ourselves for a bit. Oh, there's Lucinda,' he smiled and waved at a buxom young woman with dark hair and flashing eyes. 'I won't be long.' Diodotus forced his way through the mass of bodies to the woman and they disappeared a couple of minutes later into a side-room. Crossman was left feeling foolishly sober amongst a drunken mob of revellers. He took off his coat and hat, knowing he would be close to swooning if it he kept them on in such an atmosphere. Someone took them from his hands and put them on a pile near the doorway. Before long he found he had a cup of vodka in his hand. He swallowed some of the harsh vodka: it numbed his tongue and the lining of his cheeks with its rawness.

Crossman managed to deflect any attempt to engage him in a long conversation. People there were not much interested in talking anyway. They were more concerned with getting drunk. He noticed that his three soldiers were very soon inebriated. One of them was yelling to someone in the far corner of the room. The elderly member of the trio had sat himself down in a corner with a bottle and was drinking steadily. There was a look of mournful gratification on his face: the expression of someone who finds deep satisfaction in being miserable.

'What time is it?' a breathless woman asked the melancholy man, after she had finished dancing on a small table for the benefit of a dozen men.

He took out a battered pocket watch. 'February,' he replied, after looking at it for a very long time. 'Time I went home to Irkutsk.'

The woman flounced away, or would have, if there had not been so many people in her way. She was slightly overweight, probably voluptuous in the eyes of many men, and she had bright red lips. She caught Crossman's eye as she squeezed past him and said in French, 'My, you're a tall one.'

'It's in my family.'

She put her hands on her hips. 'Now how did I know you speak French? It must be in your eyes. Let me look in there. Yes! I see it. French blood.'

Crossman thought not, but who knew all the names of his ancestors in full? One has four grandparents, eight great-grandparents, sixteen great-great-grandparents, and so on, doubling up forever. One had one's name, and the name of one's mother locked away somewhere, but as to all the others, one would have to delve very deeply indeed. It was doubtful any man on earth knew all the names that made him who he was and where he came from. There was definitely Celt and Saxon there, and possibly Norman French, perhaps a touch of Norwegian or Dane, but as to a link with modern France, why that was a matter of conjecture.

'Cat got your tongue?'

'I was just wondering about my French blood. I don't know where it might be.'

'Perhaps it's gone to swell the organ of amour?' He felt her touch his thigh and instinctively jerked away from her. She smiled, then gave him a throaty laugh. 'Don't looked so shocked. I'm a gypsy. We gypsy women are expected to be lewd, didn't you know?'

'I wasn't shocked,' he said, defensively. 'I'm not naive.'

'Not a little. Never mind.' She took him by the hand. 'Come and sit with me. We needn't do anything. Sometimes I just like to be with a gentleman and hear his voice. You have such sweet voices, you gentlemen. Are you an officer in the army? You're not a navy man, not with that skin. You can always tell navy men by the red veins in their faces. They get weathered, by salt, sea and storms, and their skin cracks. Look at that fellow's nose over there! He's a sailor. You can tell.'

Crossman was suddenly glad that he had not pretended to be a sailor, either with the lieutenant they had met or with this woman. It was always best to stay with something one knew well. He talked with the woman for a while, learned that she had been abandoned by her husband, a 'barbarous man from the Caucasian mountains' in Sebastopol when he had fled along with other refugees, just before the siege began. Now she was living on her wits, she said, like many others. Did he think Sebastopol would fall before the spring? He replied he did not know, but there were strong defences around the city. It seemed as if it might hold out forever.

'Ah, but those Frenchmen outside the walls,' she replied. 'They will be desperate to get in to reach me.' She gave another one of her lusty laughs and slapped his knee, as if he had said something risqué.

He liked her. He liked her open manner and powerful voice. She was not one of your faint-hearted lavender-loving females who swooned at the slightest opportunity. She looked as if she took life by the throat and wrung every drop out of it. Even now she was smoking a clay pipe. For some reason this made her more attractive to Crossman, who would have found the act slightly repulsive in someone like Mrs Durham.

'Where are you from?' he asked.

She shrugged. 'I'm an Abkhazian, or was. Now, I belong everywhere and nowhere. I am a child of the Black Sea. The sea will always look after its own, you know. I never starve. I never have to sleep in the gutter. The Black Sea is my father and mother. So long as I never go away from its shores, I shall live a long and happy life.'

'Happy? In Sebastopol?'

'Oh yes, this war is none of my making. I don't have anything to do with it. I simply move around inside the walls it creates and bide my time. This war will be over one day – all wars have to end – and I shall still be here.'

'You seem certain of that.'

She smiled broadly. 'I am. I endure.'

'I wish I was so confident of my own future.'

'You should have faith in yourself. I have faith in two beings, God and myself. Both of us know I will survive this war. I shall grow to be an old lady in some mountain village, perhaps in Georgia, or Turkey. All the other old women will talk about me because I shall refuse to wear black and sit working with a crochet needle all day long on some rickety wooden chair outside my hovel. Instead I shall leer at the men who pass by my door, invite them to my bed, and laugh when they scuttle away, their faces white with worry. I shall wear scarlet and keep my hair dark with range blacking. I shouldn't be surprised if they try me as a witch and finally drown me in one of the five rivers that serve the Black Sea. The Danube I think, or the Kuban. One of those two would be a good grave.'

He laughed. 'You are an extraordinary woman.'

She looked deeply into his eyes. 'You *are* a gentleman. The way you look at me, I know you like me. Not many men look at me at all. They simply grab, take what they can get, and leave me without knowing even what I am, let alone who I am. Yet you gather me in with your eyes. That is very flattering, to be treated like a person. A real person. Are you in trouble with the law?'

He was alarmed by these words. 'No, why should you think that?'

'Because, though you are here with me, and you look at me and talk with me, your eyes continually flick towards that door over there. Who do you think will come out of it? You're nervous. Not many people would notice, but I notice.'

'Yes,' he confessed. 'There are men I would rather not meet. My friend has gone into that room with a woman. I would like him to finish so that we can leave this place. If you're still curious, I must tell you I sell contraband goods. I smuggle them in, past the army, who would of course confiscate them if they found them, and sell them on the black market. Does that disgust you?'

She shrugged and took a long pull of her pipe. 'Not really. People have to look after themselves in times like these. But I think you're lying, anyway. You're more anxious than the crime warrants. And all you would need to do would be to give the army their cut. No, you are concerned about being caught for a worse crime than that, I think.'

Out of the corner of his eye Crossman was relieved to see Diodotus forcing his way through the crowd towards him. The Greek was doing up the buckle of his belt.

'You're a clever woman. I must go now,' he said to her. 'I hope you're right about surviving. And you are correct about my liking you. You've been a breath of fresh air to me.'

'So nice of you to say so,' she said, giving him a last smile.

Diodotus collected him and the pair of them went out into the street.

'What was that whore saying?' asked the Greek youth. 'Did you go with her? I hope not. They say she has the pox.'

'Shut your damn mouth,' growled Crossman, angry. 'What the hell were you doing, going into that room? I ought to give you a thrashing for putting me in danger like that.'

Diodotus looked hurt. 'I meant no harm.'

They hurried through the streets. A cold damp heavy air had settled on the city. The cobbled streets were slick underfoot and they had to tread carefully. There were few people about, but when they rounded one corner, where the mist was swirling in the darkness, two men appeared with a lantern at the far end of the street. In the artificial light Crossman could see they both carried sticks. Around their right arms each had a white ribbon. Diodotus grabbed Crossman by the arm and pulled him along in a direction away from these two characters of the night.

'What is it?' hissed Crossman.

'Vigilantes. Self-appointed police. There's been a lot of looting in the city, as you can imagine. Some of the citizens have formed themselves into a force to patrol the streets.'

'Have they any official status?'

'Not as such. But if they suspect you of anything, they'll beat you senseless with their cudgels, then drag you before the army. The army lets them get on with it.'

Crossman quickened his step, following the Greek down a side alley. It was a good job the youth knew the city well. He himself was lost and he had studied street maps for hours on end. The sound of their boots on the cobbles echoed as they went.

Finally they came to a place Crossman recognized. There was the house! Diodotus knocked on the door, then entered. Crossman followed, right behind him. A quick look behind revealed that they had lost their pursuers, for the lantern was nowhere to be seen.

They shut the door quickly. Inside, the room was dimly lit. Amazingly, everyone was still awake. Perhaps they had been anxious about Crossman and Diodotus. Gwilliams was still eating. He had cheese crumbs all down his red beard.

Just as Crossman was about to address them, the door burst open and the two vigilantes strode inside.

With little to separate them, both Gwilliams and Ali drew pistols from their belts and fired. The sound of the two shots came almost as one: a deafening noise in the confined space. Unfortunately they had both aimed at the same man, who fell with a groan, two rounds in his chest. Before his body had hit the stone floor his companion was outside, running along the dark street, yelling. Gwilliams moved quickly to the doorway, took careful aim, and shot the running figure in the back. The vigilante stopped, walked a few unsteady paces forward, dropped his cudgel, then fell down beside it.

'Quickly,' cried Crossman to Wynter, 'help me drag him in.'

The two of them rushed out and grabbed the body. The man was stone dead, the shot having entered the nape of his neck and taken away half his face. They lugged him back to the doorway, flung him inside, then closed the door behind them. For a while they simply listened, in case there was any reaction to the sound of the shots. There was none. It seemed the good citizens of Sebastopol did not want to get involved. Better to roll over, go to sleep, and find out what had occurred from the gossip mongers when the morning came around.

'You've really done it now, Ginger!' Wynter accused Gwilliams. 'That's what comes of havin' no army trainin'. Panicked, you did. We could have knocked 'em on the head and no one would be the wiser. Instead you have to go and blast away with your bloody cannon.'

'Be quiet, Wynter,' said Crossman. 'What's done is done.'

'At least I acted,' growled Gwilliams, still with a piece of uneaten bread sticking out of the side of his mouth. He finally swallowed the food. 'And Ali. It was instinctive. Who the Hell are they, anyways?'

Wynter again. 'Oh, that's nice. Shoot anyone who comes through the door, eh?'

'Vigilantes,' said Diodotus. He was visibly shaking. 'I never saw anything like that before in my life. We must get rid of the bodies. Then we must go to another house. Katra . . .' He said something in another language to the girl, explaining to the others, 'I asked her to get sheets.'

The girl, who seemed the least perturbed in a room full of agitated people, left and returned with two old velvet curtains. The bodies of the vigilantes were rolled in these, then Wynter and Crossman took one, Ali and Gwilliams the other. Diodotus led the way. They went out into the streets again, a very nervous group. The dock was not far away. Diodotus led them down to the waterfront to where some small craft were moored. Satisfying himself that there was no one around he called to the others and they came out of the shadows. The dead men were then rather unceremoniously unrolled on the edge of the dock and into the water. The group then left, slipping back into the streets.

'That bugger was heavy,' complained Wynter. 'I've got blood all down me trousers.'

'We must go to a new house. I will get Katra,' Diodotus said. He ran off leaving them on the steps of a church. They waited, anxiously.

Crossman wondered whether the youth would ever return. Perhaps he had found the whole episode so unsettling he had decided to abandon them? However, he did return with Katra and began to lead them to another part of the city. They passed through a squalid-looking area where one or two hunched people were sleeping in doorways. Here the streets were full of rubbish and murky foul-smelling water trickled down cobbled slopes. Finally they came to a flimsy-looking shack on the edge of what appeared to be a fishing community to the north of the city. There was a rusty lock on the door which, when Diodotus pulled on it, opened without a key. It had been left closed but not locked. Inside there was a dirt floor with sacking spread about. It was not nearly as comfortable as the house.

'I'll catch my death in 'ere,' said Wynter. 'By buggery, it smells too. What's that stink?'

'Fish,' replied Ali. 'Good smell.'

'For you, maybe. Not for me. I don't mind the smell of horses and such, but rotten fish . . . I hate rotten fish. Look, there's damn scales over everythin'. It's where the fishwives gut the fish, ain't it? That's what we've bin brought to.'

'Only rarely used,' said Diodotus. 'The boats go out only occasionally, when they can.'

Crossman asked, 'Can you be traced to the other house? In the morning people are going to start talking. They'll find the bodies in the harbour.'

'The house belongs to a sailor. He's not here in Sebastopol. He was at sea when the war started and of course he hasn't returned. I think we shall be safe, me and Katra. When shall we blow up the crane? We must do it soon. All the time you are here you are in danger, I think.'

'You think the killings will start a search of the city?' asked Crossman.

'Those two men? No, I don't think so. They'll ask a few questions, but a murder in this city is not unusual. These are strange times. They'll think looters did it.' Diodotus gave another little shudder. 'I never saw anything like it. One minute, standing there, the next, dead.'

'That's how easy it is,' said Gwilliams, cleaning his pistol simply by feel in the dark. 'It don't take but a minute to snuff a man out. Twenty, thirty years those men hung on to their lives, then *bang, bang*, it's over. Can we get some sleep, sergeant? I'm pooped.'

Crossman thought that they should rest. He put Wynter on guard by the glassless window. The rest of them, including Katra and Diodotus, lay down on the fishy sacks and tried to get some sleep. Crossman remained awake for a good two hours, but finally drifted away, just before Gwilliams was due to take over from Wynter on sentry duty. He dreamed some unpleasant dreams. In one he was digging in a deep ditch that constantly filled with water and threatened to overwhelm him. When he woke, it was raining, and large drips were coming through the roof and falling on his face. He wiped his cheeks on his sleeve, then rolled over, to find himself looking into Gwilliams' magnificent beard. With a start he sat up and surveyed the interior of the shack. In the morning light he could see that there was no sentry. Gwilliams had obviously not been woken. Wynter was nowhere to be seen.

Crossman jumped to his feet, his toe catching Gwilliams accidentally on the shoulder. The American opened his eyes. 'What is it? My shift?'

Crossman didn't reply. He went to the window and stared out. Wynter was nowhere to be seen. What the Hell was the lance-corporal playing at? Where was he? Why hadn't he woken Gwilliams?

'Wynter's not here,' Crossman said. 'Didn't he wake you?'

'Nope. Or I would have taken over from him,' replied Gwilliams.

Crossman opened the door and ventured cautiously outside. Their shack was in among forty or fifty others. Most had little metal chimneys with conical cowlings. From some of these chimneys white smoke or steam was issuing. Crossman could smell cooking. Looking west he could see they were not far from a beach of sorts, which was covered in piles of shells. He went back inside and woke Diodotus.

'What's that smell?' he asked the Greek.

Diototus, still muzzy looking with sleep, sniffed hard. 'That? That is shellfish. They are boiling the shellfish.'

'I thought you said they'd stopped fishing.'

'Not stopped completely. And they don't need to go out very far to set their lobster and crab pots, or collect the shellfish.'

'What time do they start cooking? Wynter is missing. Do you think he might have gone to one of those shacks to try to get some freshly-cooked crab or whelks?' Crossman looked at his pocket watch. 'Four hours ago. It would have been about three o'clock in the morning.'

Diodotus shook his head. 'They don't start cooking at that time. Is the soldier gone, then? Maybe he deserted? Maybe he didn't like that we killed those two men?'

'Wynter couldn't care less about those two men. I'm sure he hasn't deserted.'

Diodotus said, 'He seemed unhappy.'

'Oh,' replied Crossman, going to the window again in the vain hopes of seeing Wynter outside, 'he complains a lot, but he's not the type to desert, especially here. If he was going to run he'd do it in the countryside. Damn the man. Why does nothing ever go to plan?'

Gwilliams said, 'It wouldn't be a proper war if it did.'

Diodotus then argued, 'We must not go looking for this man. We must carry on without him and hope he is not caught and tortured. There's no time and a search party would arouse suspicion. We must explode the great crane tonight, then you must leave the city.'

'We'll blow up the crane when I say,' growled Crossman. 'I haven't yet considered how we're going to lay the charge without being discovered. There're always people around that machine. It's not going to be easy. Ali,' he said to the Turk, who was now awake and chewing on a leathery piece of dried beef, 'can you make two packed charges now? I'd like to have them ready to use. Long fuses. We can cut them shorter if necessary.'

'I make, sergeant.'

'Katra, can you go out looking for the soldier?'

Diodotus translated Crossman's words for her and she nodded in affirmation. He was very impressed with her calmness. The women he met in this war seemed far more capable than many of the men. She pulled a shawl around her shoulders and slipped out of the doorway. Someone called to her in that dialect which Crossman did not understand as she walked past another shack. She answered, briefly, without pausing in her stride. Soon she had disappeared into the streets and buildings of the city proper.

'What am I to do?' asked Diodotus.

'Can you get us some food?' asked Crossman. 'And water? We still have to eat.'

The Greek left and returned later in the morning with bread and meat. By noon Katra was still not back. Crossman tried to keep his mind occupied but it was difficult. Like most men of action, especially when in enemy territory, he found nothing harder than sitting around waiting for the hours to pass. The fishing hut was cramped, damp and very, very cold. Every so often one of the *peloton* would stand and thump his chest with his arms to beat the chill out of his torso.

Periods like this always brought to Crossman's mind the times when his father had taken him and James hunting deer. Their father would leave them during the final stalking, promising to return for them when he had located the stag. The two boys would sit down in the dew-wet heather by a burn, or in a copse of trees, and wait, and wait, and wait, until, hours later, when they were shivering in their clothes and the light was fading from the sky, their father's gillie would find them and take them home. Their father, they knew, would completely forget about them once he had the scent of the hunt. It was the gillie, Alistair McCleod, who would remember and take a different path home to pick them up. 'Ye've got tae remember,' he used to say to them, 'that yer fether gets so excited when he sees the quarry, it drives everything else out of his heid.' Oh, they knew that all right. But what kind of excuse was it for leaving two bairns damp and cold for hours on end? None at all, as far as the young Alexander was concerned. The man was a selfish, boorish oaf, interested only in satisfying his own pleasures. Once he reached sixteen or thereabouts, Alexander said so, and tried to draw James in on his side, but his brother was much too afraid to join him in the enemy camp. Major Kirk roared, spat fire and finally struck his youngest son, and Alexander had to weather the whole storm alone. He did not blame James for that. It was a good thing, he thought now, that James had returned to Britain from the Crimea. Otherwise their father would be sending him as an emissary now, to remind Crossman of his duties to him as a son. This would have greatly embarrassed James and would have put Crossman deeply on the defensive. Crossman could handle the old man, but he couldn't handle his brother, whom he loved and admired for many things, notwithstanding his subservience to his father's will.

Evening came. Crossman went to the window of the hut to see Katra returning. She was weaving through the lobster fishermen, who sat repairing their wicker pots. He could see by her face that she had not found Wynter. Well, the man was on his own now. They couldn't spend any more time looking for someone who might be in a Russian prison, or dead. It was probably better if Wynter was dead. The Russians did not like spies and saboteurs any more than anyone else did. Dissemblers were loathed and despised by all and giving them pain was one way of satisfying that hatred. Crossman was sure that if he had caught a man responsible for the deaths of many relations and friends, he too might lose his civilized self for a time.

As he stared through the window at the murky sky above the even murkier sea, something caught his eye. Incredibly, there was Wynter, strolling along arm-in-arm with another man, for all the world as if he were out on a Sunday jaunt. Crossman watched as the two men, the other clearly from some tropical region by the shade of his skin, laughed and joked with one another. They came between the huts and finally entered the room just after Katra came in and began blurting out her tale of woe to Diodotus, who was translating it very badly. She stopped in mid-stream as Wynter entered, followed by his companion.

'What?' cried Wynter, clearly delighted to be the centre of attention. 'Ain't you pleased to see me?'

'God's breath, Wynter,' Crossman said in a seething tone, 'where in the Devil have you been?'

'God and the Devil, all in one,' quipped Wynter. 'That ain't like you, sergeant, turnin' out profanities. I've bin waiting for my friend here, Joseph Bako. He's a blackie, from Zanzibar. Got caught in Sebastopol when the back door was shut, so to speak. We was mates workin' the barges five years back, on the canals, when I took some time to travel and see the world one summer. Joseph here's a sailor, so to speak.' Joseph, who had not stopped smiling, nodded furiously. 'He was working on a grain ship, now at the bottom of the harbour out there. Scuttled by the Ruskis. I seen him go by this mornin' and ran after him. Sorry to say, sergeant, 'cause I can see you're working up a temper, that I lost him in the streets. So what I did was, I waited till he came back again. Hid away in some ruins of a house, guessing he was on his way to work and so would be back. Sure enough, there comes Joseph, large as life, walkin' back down the same street, but by now it's evening. It weren't my fault, sergeant. I was doing things for the better, but they turned out worse. An' that's the whole truth of it. Sorry to be a bother.'

He sounded so contrite that Crossman almost burst out laughing. He might well have done that had he not been so angry with the soldier. He started to give Wynter a lecture about not leaving sentry duty without informing someone, about how they could all have woken up at the point of a bayonet, but finally his fury fizzled out. Joseph Bako had lost his smile now and was looking nervously at Wynter as if he expected him to be shot for desertion. Crossman turned his attention to the other man.

'So, Joseph Bako, you're from Zanzibar?'

The smile came back. 'Yes, sir, from there all right. A sailor, sir. Sometimes on the English ships. That's what I do.'

'You realize we are British soldiers, caught inside the walls of an enemy city.'

'Of course, sir. Yes. Harry has explained this.'

'Don't call me sir, call me sergeant. It's more comfortable for both of us. You will not give us away, then, Bako?'

'Sir, sergeant,' said the other man, 'I am like you. I am not on the side of the Russians. I have worked on English ships. Except for one or two times, like the last time on this Russian grain ship. It was unfortunate.'

Crossman said, 'I don't see any reason why you should be loyal to the British, any more than the Russians. However, I can see that friendship means a great deal to you. I would be happier if you had chosen someone more worthy of such a noble feeling than Wynter here . . .'

'Oh, sergeant!' cried Wynter in a hurt voice.

'. . . however, contrary to the popular saying, we don't choose our friends any more than we choose our relations. The thing is, what are you going to do about us now?'

'Why,' replied Bako, his grin broadening, 'help you of course!'

Wynter chipped in, excitement filling his voice. 'You see, sergeant, here's the plum. Joseph here works on buildin' the defences, near the crane. He could place a charge for us, if we told him what to do. You'd do that, wouldn't you, Joseph?'

'Yes, Harry, I would. You and I, we have drunk beer together, in the famous Swan Inn, outside Manchester. In Zanzibar, if you drink beer with someone, he is your friend for life.'

'In that case, Harry here must have a thousand and one strangers who call him friend,' said Gwilliams, sarcastically.

'There's no need for that,' Wynter said. 'Well, what about it, sergeant? He could be useful to us, our Joseph, couldn't he? Save us gettin' our arses shot off.'

'That's all very well, but what happens to Joseph after he blows the crane up? If they catch him, or even suspect he's responsible, they'll execute him. Joseph, you have no responsibility here. I want you to understand that you could forfeit your life. And forget all this about drinking beer with Wynter. I'm sure amongst your own people this is an important thing, but in our culture it means nothing. Harry Wynter would not help you, were the circumstances reversed, I can assure you of that. You could wait a lifetime on a street corner and Harry Wynter would not appear.'

'Oh, sergeant,' cried Wynter again, 'you can't know that.'

'I am almost certain of it.'

'Harry is my friend,' said Bako. 'We have drunk beer together. I will do it for Harry, but I will also do it for Queen Victoria.'

'You drank beer with her too?' said Gwilliams, in that sarcastic rasping voice of his.

'If you do help us,' said Crossman, 'and I won't deny we need someone who can get close to the crane, then I'll try to see you are rewarded. I can't promise anything, but I'll try. Would you want to come with us, when we leave the city? Once outside you can go anywhere. I'll see you get passage on a British ship. I'm sure I can promise that service for you.'

'I think it would be better if I came with you. The Russians pay me nothing for my work. I would like to be back on the ships. I miss my home island of Zanzibar. I would like to go back there soon, to see my family.'

'In that case,' Crossman extended his hand to take and shake that of Joseph Bako, 'we accept your offer. Thank you.'

They were all rather cramped inside the fishing hut and Katra and Diodotus suggested that since it was now dark they could go outside and use one of the fishermen's braziers to light a fire. This they did, collecting driftwood on the shoreline for fuel. Soon they were sitting around a glowing fire, much like other fishermen along the sea strand. Diodotus said it was unlikely that vigilantes or the army would venture into the shanty village at night, for they were not well liked amongst the local people.

They had brought war to a region which had been prosperous until the siege began. Of course they blamed foreign armies like the Turkish, the French and the British too, but they knew that the Russian Army could have taken the fight elsewhere and didn't. Instead they chose to use Sebastopol as their fortress and brought untold misery down upon its inhabitants.

Crossman sat with Bako and explained, by means of drawings in the sand, where he would like the two charges to be placed.

'If this spar can be broken, the whole machine will crash to the ground,' said the sergeant, pointing with a piece of driftwood. 'Hopefully the dead weight of the fall will be enough to smash the rest of it. If luck is with us it'll take a gun embrasure or two with it. Our guns can open up on this particular weak area in the wall and before they can repair it, the French will make an assault and breach the Russian defences.'

'War is very simple, isn't it?' said Bako, impressed by Crossman's straightforward explanations. 'Perhaps I shall stay here after all. If the French come tomorrow, then it will all be over before the clocks begin striking noon.'

'Don't hold your breath,' growled Gwilliams.

'Gwilliams is right,' said Crossman. 'Plans like this often sound as if nothing can go wrong. In truth, something always goes wrong. Many things go wrong. It's amazing how such simple actions get entangled in all sorts of problems, almost as if the problems were there beforehand, waiting like nets to catch the unwary planners in their folds. The war will certainly not be over by noon tomorrow. You had best come with us, as we planned, and then you'll be sure of escape.'

'Or not,' interrupted Diodotus. 'I shall try to lead you out safely, but there's always the chance of being seen. You could all end up shot.'

'Us,' said Wynter, 'and you.'

'Not me. I was once taken to a fortune teller by my mother. He said I would live until I was eighty. My life is charmed. I am doomed to witness the destruction of all about me, while I endure. Now, sergeant, Katra is leaving us. She is going to her mother on the far side of the city. It is best she stays with her until this is all over. Don't you agree?'

'Of course. Please thank her for her help.'

Katra left a short time later. Wynter said, once she had gone, 'Why don't we just let Joseph get on with it? We could stay here and wait for him. No need to go with him, is there?'

'Never drink beer with Wynter,' said Gwilliams, 'or you'll get the friend you deserve.'

'I'm just tryin' to be practical.'

Crossman said, 'We have to go with him, to make sure the job is done. Ali, are the charges ready?'

'Ready, sergeant.' The two charges had been cleverly packed inside two fascines by the Turk, who had seen that most of the workers on the city's defences were carrying gabions and fascines from one place to the next. A gabion, being full of stones, would have been too heavy, but the bundles of sticks could be carried by one strong man on his shoulders. There would hopefully be no suspicion attached to a worker entering the site with a brace of these on his back, since they had to be brought in somehow. Admittedly, pointed out Crossman, they would normally be part of a load taken in by ox cart, but fascines often fell off the backs of carts.

'I think this will work,' he told Bako. 'Now, Joseph Bako, Ali will show you how to set the charges. Once you have lit the fuses, leave the site immediately. Do you understand? We'll be waiting for you in the street.'

7

Crossman's idea was that his men should create a diversion near the site in order to give Bako some time and space to place the charges on the crane and ignite the fuses. For this purpose he had Ali fashion further, smaller, charges. He gave one to each of his men. To Bako he gave a portfire and told him to hide it from the eyes of his masters.

'I want these to go off precisely at midnight on the last stroke of the clock,' he told his men.

'Which clock?' asked Wynter, quite reasonably, since there were a number of church and tower clocks, and they were not accurate enough to all chime at the same time.

'There's a Catholic church near to the site – St Sebastian's. We'll take our cue from that. It's the first one that strikes. It'll add to the confusion when the others start striking a little later. Hopefully we'll be able to divert the guards and labourers, giving Bako enough time to do his job without being observed.'

'I'll do it fine, sergeant,' said Bako, 'just you wait and see. Don't leave without me though! You know, you promised.'

'I'll keep my word, don't worry about that. Diodotus, what about you? You said you're staying, but will you be all right?'

The young Greek smiled, worries and fears fleeing his face like rats abandoning a ship.

'Yes. I will be fine.'

They rested throughout the day and left the fishing hut when the clocks struck eleven. All were heartily glad to be leaving their damp hideout. Soon they were back in the streets. There was no mist but an icy cold had descended upon the city. It gripped the inhabitants with iron fingers and those who could had added another layer of clothing. Crossman's group had no more clothing to put on, but the excitement of the fox hunt was enough to warm them for the time being. Diodotus was especially eager and kept up a fast flow of talk, his words rushing out almost on top of one another, which irritated the ever calm and pragmatic Bashi-Bazouk, Yusuf Ali.

'You Greeks,' he muttered. 'No wonder you make such bad fighters – you always talk so quick. Yak, yak, yak.'

'Oh yes,' said Diodotus, 'that's the reason we beat you in all those ancient battles – Marathon, Thermopylae, Salamis.'

'What's he talking about?' growled Ali to Crossman.

'The wars between the Greeks and Persians,' replied the sergeant.

'I am Turk, no Persian,' snarled Ali. 'Why he tell me about such wars, eh?'

'Turks, Persians, all the same,' replied Diodotus, airily. 'Always trying to defeat the Greeks and always getting beaten themselves.'

'Thermopylae,' Gwilliams felt he had to point out, 'was not a Greek victory. Four thousand Greeks fell in that battle, and Xerxes and his army walked over their bodies to invade Greece.'

'Three hundred,' argued Diodotus, stoutly. 'There were three hundred Spartan Greeks and they held the pass.'

Here Gwilliams began to get testy. 'No – in the end they failed to hold the pass and were stomped on. That's the truth. There weren't just Spartans there. There was Thespians and Thebans, and Greeks from other city-states too. A whole bunch of 'em. Thousands. Course, there was a million Asians and Africans facing 'em, but that there Leonidas and his three hundred Spartans can't claim the whole show for themselves. That's just a big story.'

'What do you know?' replied Diodotus, nettled. 'You come from the other side of the world. It's not your history.'

'It damn well is,' replied Gwilliams. 'Yes, sir. My ancestors are from right here, alongside your ancestors. It's my damn history too.'

'Thespians?' chipped in Wynter. 'Ain't they actors? What was actors doing, fighting for the Greeks?'

Crossman let them have rein. Discussions like this helped take their minds off the mission, it was true, but he was never one to advocate honing a thing mentally. That sort of exercise led to stale thinking, whereas this sort of debate would liven them up, with lots of lies, truths and half-truths being thrust into the argument with as much spleen as a man might thrust at a hated enemy with his sword. When they reached the more populated areas of the city, where there would be people in the streets, he would stop the debate. It was then that they could start thinking about what they had to do. Time enough then for the final mental preparations.

Crossman's heart was beating at a brisk pace. It was ever thus just before an action. He no more liked killing than the next man, and he certainly was not yet ready to die, but duty had to be done and the idea of a running street battle – for that was what it might come to – sent his pulses racing. There was not much he could do but accept his own feelings. In fact he had been disturbed to find that there was a certain amount of pleasure which accompanied the fear induced by battle. Certainly during the Battle of Inkerman he had felt, at odd times, exalted. In fact his senses were assailed by several emotions, before, during and after action. There would be fear and exultation, and attached to these would be guilt and despair. Each had its moment, or merged with another, or was the result of another. In truth, Crossman felt a tumult of emotions, all affecting each other, all whirling and swirling within. If he tried to read any sense or reason into it all, he would certainly go mad.

Once they reached St Sebastian's church, Crossman said, 'Right. Split up. You know what you have to do. We'll meet back here immediately. Diodotus, you will remain on the steps and wait for us, before leading us out.'

'I understand, sergeant.'

Crossman himself wanted to observe the crane, when and if it came down. He made his way to the crane site, where it had already been working away, repairing the defences that had been battered by allied guns all that day. Once the crane had been destroyed, there would be concentrated fire on the walls between the Malakoff and the Redan, all next day. Then the following dawn the French would attack, take the Mamelon, then proceed onward to the weakened defences of the Malakoff. The British would likewise overrun the Quarries, then attack the Redan itself.

Hawke had suggested that Crossman and his men might want to remain in the city and wait for that attack, which it was thought could be nothing but successful. Once the French were in, the British would follow, and Sebastopol would be in the hands of the allies. Crossman could then walk out of Sebastopol unmolested, if he so desired. He chose not to accept this idea. Attacks were prone to postponement, even cancellation. He felt he might wait longer than expected and then again perhaps the French might never come at all.

There were hundreds of men working hard by lamp-light. The giant crane, its support timbers creaking, was lifting and lowering blocks of stone, and nets full of gabions and fascines, and spars, and other such heavy materials. Crossman looked for his old enemy Colonel Todleben, with whom he had once fought a duel – and lost. He had a scar which was a testament to this sword fight. The great engineer was much admired by Crossman, who had been forced into the duel by duty rather than any personal reason. Crossman couldn't help but feel that if the British Army had owned a Todleben, the walls of Sebastopol would have been down quicker than the walls of Jericho after a bugle call. The colonel, however, was nowhere to be seen and Crossman was quite relieved. Todleben seemed to have a sixth sense for disasters.

Crossman, hidden in the shadows of a building heavily ornamented in flamboyant Gothic architecture, did see Bako though, working along with others by the wall. Just before midnight Bako put down his tools and walked towards the water butt which stood near the oxen enclosure. He took a drink of water from the tub then reached down behind an animal trough and came up with two fascines. He placed one on each shoulder, and began to stroll back towards the spot where he had been working.

Then the worst possible thing happened. Someone stopped Bako and spoke to him. Crossman could not tell whether the speaker was a supervisor or simply a workman. A discussion took place, during which Crossman agonized. What was going on? Had they been discovered? To Crossman's great consternation Bako lowered the fascines to the ground. The two objects would be heavy, but perhaps the man who had accosted him was demanding to inspect them? No, no, Bako was gesturing with his hands, the fascines leaning against his legs. Surely it was just a normal discussion between acquaintances? Then again, maybe it was treachery? Perhaps Crossman and his men were being betrayed? The Russians would pay Bako for such information and there was no telling how well Wynter knew Bako in any case. It was possible that Bako actually hated Wynter. A lot of men did hate Wynter. He was not the sort of man who endeared himself to others. There were those who would jump on Wynter's grave and experience only a feeling of immense satisfaction. However, finally Bako heaved the fascines back onto his shoulders, broke away, and continued his stroll towards the crane.

Crossman's heart was beating fast. He looked at his watch. It said midnight. Where were the chimes from that damn clock? He waited for more agonizing moments which seemed to stretch into forever. Still the chimes did not come. Were they stuck in the throat of the church? Then they came, one after another, dropping heavily on the town. Immediately the chimes of St Sebastian stopped, other clocks began sounding the midnight hour. Then, at last, the first diversionary explosion, followed by another, then another, all in quick succession.

Out on the defences the consternation was evident. Soldiers began running, others appearing from various guard posts. All eyes were turned towards the city. 'Now,' whispered Crossman, as some soldiers rushed past him, their boots crashing on the cobbled streets. 'Now, Bako.'

Indeed, almost as if he had heard the sergeant, the man from Zanzibar quickly placed the fascines in the crook of the two angled joints pointed out by Crossman in his sand sketch. Then Bako calmly went to the nearest battery and lit the portfire from the battery's linstock. The gunners were all staring at the soldiers running through the city streets. Bako walked back to the crane, lit the fuses of the two charges, and then threw away the portfire. He crossed the site and met with Crossman in the shadows.

He said, 'It's done . . .'

Before the words were out of his mouth one charge, then the other, went up. It was an impressive brace of explosions. Crossman felt as if both sides of his head had been struck by planks when the thunderous sound hit his eardrums. At the same time he witnessed the visual destruction of Todleben's magnificent engine. Whole chunks of oak, two feet thick, went flying through the air. Iron bolts whizzed, somersaulting over the heads of stupefied workers. A metal plate, as large as a garden gate, flew edgeways into the building under which the two men were standing, shearing a Gothic gargoyle from its base and sending it crashing to the ground, where it shattered into a dozen stone pieces. Now that two of the most important joints on the crane had been blasted to matchwood, the crane's main support beams were left under enormous pressure. First one cracked, then snapped under the full weight of the mighty machine, which had been in the process of conveying a huge block of stone from one position to another. A second followed. Finally, the towering mass lurched, then came crashing down onto a stone wall. Bricks and dust filled the air. Men screamed as blocks of granite toppled from the heights and fell onto a wooden platform with dull thumps. Several occupants of the platform were catapulted into the air off the ends of broken planks. From high above, the stone block being carried by the crane's arm dropped vertically onto an ox cart, crushing it and killing the poor beast of burden that had toiled in its traces.

Several lamps had been extinguished. Dust filled the air in choking clouds, providing opaque screens. No one seemed to know what was happening. Voices cried out, 'Are we under attack?' On those defences which were intact, sentries began firing out into the night. Within the compound, firing also began. A soldier discharged his weapon into some shadows. Whether he had panicked, or not, or had been carrying out some order, or simply thought he had spotted the perpetrators of the crime was unclear, but what followed was dangerous chaos. More men began shooting, at everything and nothing, until officers were screaming at them to cease firing. Even after relative order had been restored there were bullets whining from remote corners of the defences, fired by soldiers still confused, possibly believing they were under threat from something within the folds of the night. The result was several wounded workers and soldiers, hit by friendly fire, writhing on the ground and calling for assistance. Crossman noted that one or two at least remained unmoving, in awkward positions, more than likely dead.

The great crane was lying in a heap of rubble, many of its oaken limbs broken or twisted. Splinters and chunks of timber lay everywhere about, having fallen like rain upon the site. The machine looked irreparable. It was like some giant bird that had been brought low and was now lying with all its bones broken and its beak snapped. A sad sight to Crossman, whose heart soared at the sight of a magnificent feat of engineering. It was a death, no matter the creature had no life in the first place.

Stalking round the debris of what used to be a wonder of the Crimean peninsula, weeping, screaming at the top of his voice, 'Assassins! Assassins!' was the controller of the crane, once a very important man in the city of Sebastopol, now reduced to the status of just another unemployed worker. His grief was real. Without his machine he was no better than any other man who carried a gabion or fascine on his back.

'Come, quickly,' said Crossman to Bako. 'We must get to St Sebastian's.'

The pair hurried through streets now thick with soldiers and civilians, all milling around, staring at the compound where the crane had stood.

'What's happening?' asked one, in Russian, as Crossman passed. 'Has a magazine gone up?'

'No, the walls have fallen down,' he replied. 'We are exposed to attack.'

The man who had asked the question looked worried. He began to spread the rumour amongst his neighbours. Even before Crossman had left the end of the street they were hurrying away to their houses to collect their most precious possessions. If the rumour took hold strongly enough, the whole city would be up and out of bed, running through the streets, crying havoc. That could only benefit Crossman and his *peloton*. Such rumours had been known to win and lose wars.

The other four were waiting on the steps of the Catholic church. Wynter looked agitated. So did Diodotus. Collecting them, Crossman asked Diodotus to take the lead.

'Get us out of here,' he said to the Greek. 'It's done, finished. A remarkable success.'

Wynter gave a half-hearted cheer, then seeing that he was attracting attention to himself, shut up.

Diodotus took the front and they slipped through the throng. They wound their way through alleys and sidestreets, until they came to the tunnel where they had first entered.

'I'll take you through,' said Diodotus, lighting some dark lanterns he had left at the entrance. There was suppressed excitement in his voice. Crossman guessed this had been the young Greek's first taste of real action. He was in high spirits: that state of false euphoria induced by physical combat. It would not last long, Crossman knew, for it would be followed by all those other emotions, one after the other, until the Greek would be a confused mass of nerves.

Once on the other side of the tunnel they were confronted by the black gullies of the Heights. Ali took over now, ready to lead the party through the maze. Crossman turned for one last word with Diodotus. They could just about see each other's faces in the light from the winter stars.

'Many thanks,' he said, 'you helped to make our fox hunt a great success.'

'It was my very good pleasure,' smiled the handsome youth. 'I shall be able to tell my grandchildren I fought with Fancy Jack Crossman.'

'Oh, you know my nickname?'

'You can't hide romantic things like that, not from Greeks who were once princes. In my next life I shall be Czar of Russia and will remember it was you who won the war for the British and French. I shall be lenient when they catch you and sentence you to hang.' He laughed in that boyish way of his. 'Then again, in your next life perhaps you will be another Gengkis Khan, and threaten my borders with your wild hordes.'

He then did an extraordinary thing. He threw his arms around Crossman and gave him a hug.

'Goodbye my friend,' he said. 'After the war . . .'

'After the war we shall drink retsina together and talk of old times,' said Crossman, knowing the youth wanted some sign of comradeship from him. 'Now go. Katra will be waiting for your return. She'll be worried.'

Diodotus turned quickly. In doing so he somehow lost his grasp of the dark lantern. It crashed to the ground, flaring, illuminating him and Crossman. Crossman instinctively slipped away, into the gully, as shouts went up from the Russian defences facing the Heights. Diodotus stood, momentarily confused.

'Get out of the light!' called Crossman, as the oil on the ground continued to burn. 'Get out . . .'

His sentence was cut short by the sound of several shots. Diodotus staggered backwards, clutching his throat. He then spun round, giving Crossman a hurt look, and fell to the ground. Crossman crawled over to him and found him dead. A ball had gone through his neck, smashing through his spine. Shots continued to whine from stones and rocks near to the body. Crossman left him and finally joined the others.

'What happened?' asked Wynter.

'They got him,' replied Crossman. 'He dropped his lamp and they opened fire.'

'Dead?' asked Gwilliams.

'Yes.'

Ali grunted. 'It is a shame. He was just a boy. A Greek boy, but a boy just the same. Too soft, but never mind. It is great waste.'

'Yes,' replied Crossman. 'Yes it is.'

And that was that. They would speak of it no more in sad, solemn tones. Many dead companions were already occupying positions within their minds. There was only so much room within one soul for the stone memories of dead friends. They had, after all, known the Greek youth but a short time, and younger boys than he had littered the battlefields of Alma, Balaclava and Inkerman. Younger boys than he were dying that very moment, in the trenches, of a sharpshooter's bullet, or one of those ugly diseases which took men in war, or of exposure to the elements. Death was an everyday occurrence. If you knew someone, it was different of course, but they had all witnessed horrific deaths of friends they had known since they were five years of age, back in their own villages and towns.

Still, Crossman, like Ali, thought it a great shame. The boy might have been a great poet one day. Certainly that officer, what was his name? Yes. Lieutenant Tolstoy. Certainly he had thought that Diodotus was destined to become a poet, or why would he have bothered to court the youth? Such an intellectual as Tolstoy appeared to be would not have wasted his time on someone without talent. Here in the Crimea they were losing the flower of several nations, most of them farm hands and peasants, but who was to say that such men would not have risen to greatness in one field or another? There was much talk of a thing called science, back in Britain, which seemed to be overtaking philosophy and physics, or perhaps included them. Crossman was not sure. But the word seemed to have lost its old meaning, of pure *knowledge* and was in the process of gathering a new one, encompassing many disciplines, from collecting minerals to cutting open frogs and studying butterflies. It seemed to Crossman that many labourers, in the meadows or woods, in the mines, knew more about such things of *science* than did learned men in the universities. Who was to say that such individuals of the lower classes would not rise on the back of this science and become great men in a new world?

Getting back through their own picquets was not an easy task, but they did it by stealth rather than words. Having been out for so long, watchwords had changed and it was dangerous to call out. Once back behind the lines they trudged to the hovel. Joseph Bako was shown a place where he could lay down his weary head, and they all slept for nearly sixteen hours.

When Crossman woke, Lovelace was there, shaving. When he wasn't growing a beard for a mission, the major seemed to be forever shaving. He saw Crossman stir in his mirror and turned to speak.

'Awake at last! Good fox hunt?'

'Successful for once,' said Crossman. 'Have the French attacked yet?'

Lovelace frowned and wiped the foam from his face with a towel.

'No. No, there's been no attack. Our friend General Canrobert wants to plan the attack for June.'

'June?' Crossman was astonished. 'By June they'll have defences a mile high. I thought we did this so that an attack could take place at once?'

Lovelace seemed embarrassed. 'That was the intention. That was indeed our suggestion. But you know how these things go. And generals are fickle beings at times. One moment they say they will attack, the next they are cautious and unwilling. Our own people, Colonel Hawke and others, are *very* happy with the results of your raid. I only wish we had troops enough to storm through the breach ourselves and take advantage of your good work, but with sickness and other things . . .'

'June,' repeated Crossman, once more astonished by the high command. 'I thought by June we would all be at home, basking in a British summer. June. I can't believe it. We lost a man out there. The Greek, Diodotus. He was shot through the throat at the very last moment.'

'I'm sorry.'

'It does seem so damn futile, sir. It really does.'

'I know. My sympathies are with you. I wonder our French ally Bob-can't still remains commander-in-chief of the French forces. He seems too cautious by half. But there it is. Oh, and by the way, another friend of yours has popped up again. Corporal Reece? It seems he and his deserters – he's gathered a new lot in by the way – are preying on shipping now. The coast around here is notorious in the winter, treacherous in storms, and Reece and his gang keep a vigilant eye open for craft who get into difficulties. When a ship's in distress, and put out in boats with what they can save from the cargo, Reece is there on the beach waiting to relieve them of it. The sailors are usually exhausted with pulling their boat through the water and can't put up much of a fight. It's piracy from the safe haven of the shore. Reece doesn't even have to put to sea.'

'Will I get another crack at him?'

'Not for the moment, but I'll see what I can do later. Colonel Hawke wants to give him a little more rope.'

Crossman didn't understand this tactic.

'Why? What good will that serve?'

'The more success Reece has, the more the deserters in the surrounding hills flock to him. He has about twenty men now. It might reach to forty. Even French and Turks are joining him. Once we have them all together we can reel in the nets. Better to get them all at once than having to scour the hills for individuals, wouldn't you say?'

'It makes sense I suppose.'

'In the meantime, you can relax, sergeant. Enjoy what remains of the winter.'

'If I relax too much, I'll find myself in some school or other, teaching needlework.'

Lovelace laughed as he adjusted his uniform.

'Stay out of the way, is my advice. Play a few hands of cards with your men. Get into some deep philosophical discussions with Jarrard. There'll be more fighting to do soon enough. Oh, and by the way, your father has been ordered home. Something to do with carrying some important dispatches to England.'

Crossman brightened at this news. 'He has?'

'Yes, but I'm sorry to have to tell you he's refused the commission and remains here. He's sold out and is now a civilian. One of the Travelling Gentlemen, I suppose you'd have to say.'

'What?'

'I knew that would make you unhappy, which is why I left it until last, and halfway out of the door. Goodbye.'

'Wait, sir. What's he doing?'

Lovelace turned as he went down the stairs.

'Doing? I think he's painting. At least, that's what he seems to be doing. Spends all his time in a great fur coat, in front of canvas and easel, painting. He looks like a great Russian bear with a brush in its paw. Don't ask me what the subject is, because I haven't gone that close. Landscapes I suppose, since there's no other subject in front of him. It is said he's an avid student of John Constable, who did that thing with the broken cart stuck in the middle of a pond. What a cart was doing in a pond I have no idea.'

'I think it's meant to be a ford.'

'Well, why doesn't the chap make it look like a ford then. Looks like a pond to me. Well, good luck.' With that Lovelace went bounding down the stairs and out of the hovel.

*

Gradually, winter began to ease away from the landscape as they moved into April. Spring did not exactly fall upon the land with joyous heart, but it did creep across it with green feet. The men in the trenches were still cold at night, still drenched, still mud-splattered and miserable, but there was a promise in the wind of better times to come. Cannons still roared, musketry still rolled, but hope was in the air.

Bako had gone, taken by ship to Constantinople. Wynter had seen him off, along with an incredulous Peterson.

'You always said you didn't like darkies, Wynter. I was always sad about that, since they are people just the same.'

'Darkies, yes, but this is Joseph,' replied the indignant Wynter. 'Joseph is my pal.'

'Somehow,' replied Peterson, shaking her head, 'that makes it worse. Don't ask me why I think it, 'cause I don't know.'

'You just don't like *me*.'

'Well, there is something in that, I will agree.'

Yorwarth's jaw was still out of alignment. He was the butt of jokes now, up and down the Crimean peninsula. A surgeon had promised to 'crack' it for him and reset it, but Yorwarth needed to get his courage up a little more before accepting his kind offer. In the meantime he was getting used to speaking with a strange tilt to his words. They seemed to come out of his mouth sideways, yet were perfectly understandable in the common sense. In fact, Yorwarth was beginning to enjoy being a celebrity. There was one part of him that wanted to remain lopsided: someone had suggested he might get a job in a circus freak show if he kept his crooked jaw. 'Good money to be earned there,' said Wynter, sagely. 'Wouldn't be hasty, if I was you.' Hasty he was not. He was basking, if not in praise, in being the centre of attention. Even the photographer, Mr Fenton, had shown an interest.

And it was not only photographers, with their newfangled devices which ordinary folk thought closer to magic than to the new discipline called science, who were drawn to Yorwarth's malformed visage. No, there were others interested in Yorwarth. Just as amputees gathered at El Madi's coffee stall in the sutlers' bazaar, drifting together almost unconsciously to form a kind of club, the exclusive membership of which was unenvied by those with four limbs and a working head, so there were those with wrongly-set bones who gathered at the feet of Yorwarth. It started with a soldier who simply walked in off the street: a man whose left arm had been broken close to the shoulder and, because he had been ignored by overworked surgeons, had been forced to let it set so that it was the wrong way round. That is, the inner part of his arm, his palm, the inside of his elbow, all faced *outwards*. At the top, where the break had been, the skin was twisted like a rope. The unfortunate victim had difficulty in grasping anything with two hands. In fact, he could not, unless it were something light and easy to manage.

'I just came in to lour,' he said to Yorwarth. 'Yon fowlk tell't me thee had a kedge like a mawkin an' I came to lour.'

It transpired that the soldier came from Suffolk and his speech was so splattered with dialect words only East Anglians could understand him. A 'mawkin' turned out to be a scarecrow. The soldier wanted to know whether Yorwarth's aberration affected his ability to do everyday ordinary tasks, like eating, because he, the soldier, could not do his duties now. It was impossible for him to pick up a musket, load, aim or fire. Until the surgeons got around to resetting his limb, he was on light duties.

Other poor creatures came in at odd times after that. Men with feet on backwards. Men with scapulas sticking up like angel's wings out of their backs. One man had three ribs that had been broken, had exited through his chest, and had subsequently knitted together with their partners to form exposed hoops of white bone. They all took the pilgrimage from whatever part of the Crimea they resided in to meet with the latest victim of wrongly-set fractures. It was as if they were suddenly joined in mind and spirit, were brothers-of-the-bone.

'What a bunch of mishaps,' cried Wynter. 'They give me the creeps, Yorry. Don't you go invitin' 'em here. It's enough to turn a sane man, watching that lot drag themselves in and start droolin' over your cot.'

Yorwarth could not turn them away, though, once they had made the journey to his bedside. They continued to arrive until finally Crossman put a stop to it. There was a danger that the special nature of their duties would be compromised with outsiders lounging around the hovel.

One morning Crossman woke and looked out of the hovel window to see his father walking down towards Balaclava Harbour. Crossman dressed hurriedly – no great feat since he was halfway there already – and followed in his father's wake. Could it be that the old man was finally embarking for Britain? It would be good to get him gone. Crossman felt he could not go anywhere for fear of running into him. Yet, having taken the muddy track down to the waterside, he found his father had merely set up his easel and was finishing a painting he had obviously started at some other time. It was of the ships at anchor.

The hustle and bustle of humanity in this part of the peninsula was considerable. There were sailors, soldiers, and civilians, some carrying goods, some merely out for the air, all milling around, dodging each other, working derricks and ropes and pulleys. It was pleasant confusion. One could almost imagine oneself back in Portsmouth. Within this great heaving mass of people, Crossman had been able to sneak up behind his father and look over his shoulder without being noticed. He found himself staring in astonishment at what appeared to him, though he was no student of art, a brilliant painting. His father had captured movement as well as form on that stretch of canvas. Crossman now remembered something about his father's hero, John Constable. It seemed that particular painter had eased himself away from the static, motionless styles of previous centuries and concentrated on showing how the wind swayed and bent the twigs, branches and boughs of trees. Saplings bent further than thicker stems of wood, and those thicker stems less than boughs. Clouds had the appearance of boating, as they did in the real world, across the heavens. The sum of such consideration was that the painting came alive. Figures seemed to be doing things, not just standing there, stiff and posed. Vehicles, ships, wind-blown objects, were actually moving on the landscape.

Crossman saw that his father was adding the finishing touches to a ship leaving the harbour with all its sails billowing, its hull leaning on waves that battered its bows, its flags fluttering in the breeze. He even recognized the ship. It was the *Surprise*, a rather elderly craft. Crossman was amazed at how his father had caught the graceful motion of the vessel with just the right strokes of the brush, with a delicate smearing of the paint. Even the sunlight on the water seemed to be dancing to a particular tune of nature. How had he done that? How could he do that? He was a boorish oaf. How had such a man with such an ugly disposition managed to create something so beautiful, so courageously vital, so animated it enchanted.

At that moment his father turned and looked up at him, pausing in mid-stroke. Crossman was suddenly aware that he must have given an audible gasp of awe. Major Kirk frowned, went that purply-red colour which often preceded a bout of rage, and glared with baleful eyes at his son.

'What the Hell do you want, sir? Sneakin' up on a man like that? Come to stab me in the back, eh, you scamp?'

'Nothing of the sort, Father,' protested Crossman. 'I was merely admiring your painting.'

The old man turned and looked at his work.

'Didn't know I was an artist, did you, sir?' The redness left his complexion and he went almost dreamy for a few moments. 'Not just a military sketcher, but a proper painter, eh? It's the one thing that helps me relax. Calms me. People seem to like 'em, too. I have a running hind hanging in the palace, believe it or not. Running through the heather and gorse of a Scottish hillside. Painted it one morning in Canlish Glen, just the other side of Ben Law. The dew . . .' He suddenly seemed to realize to whom he was speaking and stiffened. 'But that's no concern of yours. I suggest you get on your way, *sergeant*. Surely you have duties to perform? Why aren't you up on the line, sir? I understand you dawdle in that place yonder, kicking your heels all day. Are you a coward, sir? My own son a coward? Even if he is a chance-child, he carries my blood and he should carry it with pride.'

Crossman bristled. 'I am not a coward, Father. I have special duties.'

'What, like a cook, or a surgeon's mate?'

'Not like either of those gentlemen.' Despite the fact that they were in the regiment to help the sick and wounded, surgeons were regarded as lowly creatures by their fellow officers. Most fighting officers held such creatures in contempt. It therefore followed that the surgeon's staff was held to be even less worthy. They carried buckets of gore and severed limbs to the body part dumps, where the seagulls and rats grew fat. His father was insulting him in the grossest fashion, as they were buffeted by a crew just flushed from a ship and on their way up to the sutlers' bazaar. Crossman felt a need to justify himself. 'I – I am sent out on missions, amongst the enemy. There is in fact a price on my head. Put there by the Cossacks.'

Even before it was out of his mouth, Crossman felt like biting off his tongue. It was not done, to brag in such a way. His father was of the old school who believed you did something and let other people talk about it. You didn't parade your virtues, even in front of family. That was brash and vulgar. One could ravish a maid in the pantry. That was not coarse, so long as one was not discovered in the act. But to fly the boasting flag, why that was contemptible. He saw his father grimace in distaste and knew he had to leave the old man to his painting.

'Go home, Father,' he said, in a low voice. 'I know you think I've lost my dignity, but yours went with the wind. You hang on here as if you believe you're making a point. What you're actually doing is making yourself look foolish.'

There was no greater sin than looking foolish.

'How dare you!'

Crossman let his father have the last word. He walked away from him, forcing a passage through the many bodies on the quays. His heart was beating fast after this second encounter with the old man. Luckily those around him were too busy to notice how heated the exchanges had been. It would not do to let word get back to Colonel Hawke that Crossman had sought out the old man, for that was how it seemed. And was that so very far from the truth? Perhaps he had been waiting for this chance to have another hot discussion with his father. How stubborn his father was: and how unforgivable. How could you pardon a man who showed no remorse for the wrongs he had done to you and your mother? Not a glimmer of contrition had passed over the face of his father. *Chance-child* his father had called him. How base and humiliating! Even *love-child* would have been better than that. But there had been no love in the union. It had not formed part of the seduction. Simply lust on his father's side and helplessness on his mother's. It was a cruel man who took a powerless woman and then left her to die in a world where morals were fashioned of iron.

Crossman arrived back at the hovel in a miserable state. Peterson immediately tried to engage him in a conversation about her shoulder, telling him she was now fully recovered.

'Yes, yes,' he said, shortly. 'Fine. Don't bother me now.'

He went up the stairs and to his room.

Peterson was a veteran soldier with a soldier's rough ways and cynical tongue, but she was also a woman. She saw that Crossman was agitated and part of her instantly wanted to reach out to him, discover the problem, and offer solace. She was not the type of woman who would offer her breast as a pillow to a man, then stroke the head that lay there, but she still wanted to listen, to sympathize, to heal. Thus she followed Crossman upstairs, while Wynter snored on his cot, Gwilliams continued to darn his socks and Yorwarth wrote a letter home.

'Sergeant?' she said, peering into the room. 'Can I say something?'

Crossman was lying on his own cot. Shielding his eyes from the light at the window. 'What is it?' he said.

'You seem – upset, sergeant.'

'I am a little unhappy, yes.'

'Is it something we've done wrong – the *peloton*?'

He gave a short ironic laugh. 'I wish it were.' For a minute or two he fell silent again, then he felt inclined to talk. 'No, it's my father. You know my father is here in the Crimea, Peterson? No, of course you didn't. Well, he was a major in the 93rd, but now he's sold out. In order to annoy me he remains here, as a civilian.'

'That annoys you, sergeant?'

'My father and I hate each other.'

Peterson sucked in her breath. She had never particularly got on with her own parents, a Rutland couple who had a smallholding out in the deep countryside. They had raised her to marry a neighbouring young yokel with seed for brains and a face like a frog. Not that the face had bothered her much, she had not been a pretty girl herself. And the fact that he had been a simple boy, who just happened to inherit a pig farm, could not be held against him either. It was the idea of marriage itself that had frightened her. When she had refused to accept the idea of being wed to this dolt, her parents had bombarded her with recriminations, threats, and various other verbal missiles. Her father had even tried beating her, but she had soon put a stop to that, he being frail and she being wiry and strong at the time. So, wearing her father's clothes, she had tried her hand at being a cabinet maker and when the men had forced her out of that job she had joined the next regiment that passed through Rutland.

So, Peterson was not overfond of her own next of kin, but she would never have used the word *hate*. The fact that Crossman had used it horrified her. If he had said he despised the Holy Trinity it could not have shocked her more.

'Maybe you just have a difference of opinion?' she suggested, quietly. 'All folk don't think alike.'

Crossman remained silent and she got the feeling that her statement had been so pathetically empty for him they did not even warrant a reply. Then suddenly, he groaned, and said, 'Oh my God.' Clearly he was very distressed.

She knelt by his cot. 'Sergeant?'

'I'm sorry, Peterson. This is not the way you should see your leader.'

'Leaders are human too. We're all weak in different ways.'

'That's true. I never realized how weak I am. It's a terrible thing to hate one's father. A terrible thing. I see it tear my mother – my stepmother – I see it tear her in two. I can't understand how such a lovely, gentle lady could have married an oaf like him. She has such a sweet soul, Peterson. You have no idea what she has to put up with. Yet she did marry him. Was he so very different as a young man? I can't think it. People don't change that much. Dashing, I suppose. Looking at his portrait he was a handsome devil, even if the painter lied a little. He rode to hounds magnificently. He was a horseman to the core. I suppose a young woman would be taken with such things. She couldn't have known him, not properly. I don't believe she *knew* him at all. She could not have found out what he was really like until she had lived with him. People don't, do they? They're so stiff and formal with each other during the courtship, with chaperones present and their every move watched and monitored. How can you possibly get to know someone in those circumstances? No wonder men and women often marry their cousins, whom they've known from the nursery, rather than strangers. It's not just that their cousins are available to them. They marry them because they have a certain insight to their dispositions, their spirits, their inner selves. One can't marry one's brother or sister, so the next best thing is a cousin.'

'Sergeant!' reproved Peterson. 'Incest isn't a nice subject.'

'I'm sorry, I forgot I was talking to a woman.'

During the course of this conversation, Peterson had somehow taken Crossman's hand in her own. While he talked she was holding his hand tightly, a sort of comfort and encouragement for him to get it all off his chest. It was almost an unconscious gesture, the holding of hands, but now they had become aware of it. He realized that she had rough, coarse skin – not the hands of a gentle maid – and she was chagrined to find that his skin, though chapped and hardened by the Crimean war, was basically silkier than her own. The hands of a gentleman put to common work later in life. He had never chopped wood as a child, never washed clothes in crude soapy water with a pumice stone, never hacked at nettles with a sickle or dug thorny thistles from ditches, never done a thousand things that Peterson had done as ordinary everyday chores during her growing-up. They both became embarrassed, aware of their different stations in life, and the hands were dropped almost simultaneously.

'Perhaps your father will soon get tired of baiting you, sergeant,' she suggested, after a suitable silence. 'Perhaps he'll go home.'

'I would like to think so.' The tender moment had passed. Peterson's mothering instinct was hidden again. She was back to being a soldier, sympathizing with one of her comrades.

Downstairs there was some kind of commotion going on. Wynter's voice could be heard raised in excitement. Someone played softly on a bugle: a haunting tune that in any other atmosphere might have forced a silence on war and had even the enemy looking into their own souls. This was followed by a few rasping notes on the instrument, some cries and jeers, and the sound of heavy boots taking the stairs two at a time.

Peterson leapt to her feet just as Wynter entered the room. There was a split second when a shadow of suspicion crossed Wynter's face, then the excitement came back, and he cried, 'Sergeant? Peterson? I'm learnin' to play the bugle! Lance-Corporal Mainwaring, down the stairs, he said not many people can blow a bugle first time. Well, I did. It seemed to come natural. Like I've got music in my blood. I might be a trumpeter one day, if I practise hard, like Mainwaring says.' He put the battered instrument to his lips, his cheeks puffed, his eyes bulged, his nostrils flared. To Crossman's horror he then sent out a note that would have indeed been enough to awaken the dead in the morning. It blasted through the room like a warning from an archangel that the world was about to come to an end. It brought water to Crossman's eyes. He sat bolt upright on his cot.

'You do that just once more,' he told Wynter, 'and I'll have you strapped to the wheel and flogged before you have time to inhale again.'

The triumph went out of Wynter's expression, to be replaced by a hurt look. He turned to Peterson for some kind words. She, after all, was a woman, and would appreciate music more than a man like the sergeant.

'You don't need to blow out your cheeks like that,' advised Peterson, unimpressed by the blare. 'In fact it's better you don't. The sound comes from the lips, not from the lungs.'

'What do you know about playing the bugle?' cried Wynter, now thoroughly miffed.

She snatched it out of his hand, wiped the mouthpiece carefully, and then gave a passable rendition of 'Greensleeves'.

'Huh!' said Wynter, taking it back. 'You would, wouldn't you? You always take it away from me, whatever. I find I'm good at somethin' and you take it away from me. That's typical, that is. A man can't find somethin' in his soul that's his own. You always have to spoil it. Well Mainwaring says I've got the stuff, and if I practise . . .'

'If you practise here, Wynter, I'll have you shot from the mouth of a cannon.'

'But sergeant – I need a hobby,' replied Wynter, stubbornly, seeing his fun evaporate before his eyes.

'Take up embroidery.'

Wynter stamped from the room. Peterson watched him go, hoping he had not seen her kneeling by the sergeant's cot. It had all been perfectly innocent, but the circumstances looked strange. Strange enough to feed Wynter's imagination. Hopefully he had seen nothing, or if he had it had been too swift for him to be sure of anything.

'I think you had better join the others, Peterson,' said Crossman, standing up. 'Make sure that Lance-Corporal Mainwaring takes his instrument of torture with him when he leaves.'

'Yes, sergeant.' She went to the head of the stairs.

'Oh, and Peterson?'

'Yes, sergeant?'

'Thank you – for the – the comfort.' He added dryly. 'There's not much that can be done for a tortured spirit like mine, but the thought is very much appreciated.'

Her broad, plain face broke into a smile. 'You're welcome, sergeant. And don't worry, I know we're back to being soldiers again. That's one thing we can both rely on, isn't it?'

'Yes, it is.'

Another blast from the bugle, followed by Wynter's denial and denunciation. 'That wasn't me, sergeant. It was Gwilliams.'

'Get that thing out of here!' roared Crossman, with more vehemence than he actually felt.

There was a scuffling sound from below, then the long and steady moaning and groaning from a Wynter whose toy had been taken away. Once things had settled again, Crossman was aware that the street outside was full of people. Another ship had arrived from England, carrying a large number of passengers by the sound of it. Spring had arrived. The Travelling Gentlemen and camp followers, having wintered in Britain, would be coming back in their droves. It was most peculiar how war attracted quite ordinary people. Was it the sound of the guns? The idea of death being in the air? On the one hand, Crossman could see the fascination of deadly weapons, loud explosions, men in colourful, dashing uniforms going about the serious business of war. On the other, he found the idea of trekking around the world's killing grounds ghoulish and bloodthirsty. There were not only men, but some women too. Women like Lavinia Durham, who seemed to delight as much in the patterns of battle as they would in the pattern of a quilt or wallpaper. As soon as fighting started, anywhere, Lavinia would be on her horse seeking the best spot to view it all from. It was true she expressed horror and pity for the wounded and dead, and she did her nursing best once it was all over, but still, she was there, at the centre, her eyes locked to the bloody scene.

At that very moment, Crossman heard her voice, calling up at the window.

'Alexander? Sorry, Jack? Are you there?'

He went to the glassless window and opened the shutters. Looking down he saw her face beaming up at him. She was dressed in a thin outdoor coat which revealed her figure and, he admitted to himself, she looked adorable. Her white teeth gleamed in the weak sun. Her cheeks were rosy. (Had she been deliberately pinching them?) Beneath the Russian fur hat, her complexion was flawless, like soft ivory that gleamed its pale beauty to the world. Her coat was trimmed at the hem and sleeves with a fur that matched the hat. Furs suited her. She was a wild animal within that demure-looking body. *Inside her is a leopard*, he thought, *which only comes out when* . . . He checked himself, mentally. These old stirrings were not good for him. She was forbidden fruit.

'Mrs Durham,' he replied, trying to sound bored, 'what is you want?'

'Don't use that tone of voice with me, sergeant. You know you find me irresistibly attractive. I can see it in your eyes.'

He gritted his teeth. How did they always know what you were thinking?

'I would still like to know what you're doing, calling up at my window,' he said, aware that there were other people passing by, some of them curious as to the nature of this conversation between a beautiful woman and a man in shirtsleeves at his bedroom window. 'This is not genteel behaviour for the wife of a captain, Mrs Durham.'

Her voice remained light and airy. 'I've come to invite you to dinner, sir, if you please.'

'Dinner?' He frowned. 'I can't dine with you, Lavinia. I'm from the ranks. A sergeant can't dine with an officer and his lady. That's written in stone.'

'Oh, stuff and nonsense. Anyway, it's just his lady. Bertie won't be there. He won't even know about it.'

'Then I *definitely* can't come.'

'Of course you can. You're just being stubborn. Look, there's someone I want you to meet.'

'Who?'

'A lady like myself, only much prettier.'

He smiled in spite of himself. 'No one is prettier than you, Lavinia, and you know it.'

She smiled back. 'Thank you, sir. Not even goose girls with false red hair?'

'Especially goose girls. Who is this person? Why are you always trying to matchmake? I'm perfectly happy, you know.' Several people had paused to listen now and Crossman was becoming acutely embarrassed by the conversation. 'Stay there a moment, I'll come down.'

Grabbing his coatee from the nail on which it hung he descended the stairs and, ignoring Wynter's questions, went outside. He found Lavinia around the side of the dwelling.

'This is very dangerous,' he said to her. 'I have no desire to be stripped of my rank and flogged, thank you very much.'

'Bertie wouldn't do that to you. Not if I told him not to. Now,' her voice became excited, 'you are to come to a place on the wharf, a little blue-and-white cottage. I think you know it.'

He did know it. It had been the residence of the Balaclava Harbour Marine Superintendent before the British had taken it over. Since then it had been in various hands, mostly those wearing generals' gloves. He was not sure who currently resided at that address, but he was fairly certain that the occupant would far outrank him. He did not relish the idea of dining at a house where the party might at any moment be interrupted by some earl or lord whose doting aide was at least of field officer rank. Such a dinner could not be enjoyed in peace, no matter how good the repast. Visions of firing squads were not completely out of the question.

'I know it, but I'm not going there.'

'Oh, don't be so stuffy. General Enticknap has given me the use of it for the next twenty-four hours and he promises he won't come anywhere near it during that time.'

The hairs on the back of Crossman's neck stood on end.

'General Enticknap?'

'Yes, he's a nice old stick and he indulges me from time to time. Not that he receives any favours, you understand. He just likes pretty women to flatter him. I do that quite well, I think. It's in my kind nature to pass complimentary remarks to grizzled old men. "My, how straight and tall you look in that uniform, General Enticknap. Your wife must be a very proud lady."' She then put on a growling tone to simulate the general's voice. '"Wife, ma'am? Don't have such a creature." "Oh, surely? How could such a handsome man escape? I don't believe it." "True, ma'am, I assure you! Now, my dear, what was it you wanted to see me about?"'

'Lavinia, you are incorrigible.'

'I know, it's an attractive feature in a married lady, isn't it? It wouldn't do if I was still a young chit, but I'm not. I can get away with practically anything but murder, now that I have a husband.'

'I can't eat at General Enticknap's house.'

'Yes, of course you can. I won't take no for an answer. I must have you married, or at least engaged, before you leave the Crimea. Once you get back to Britain you'll be spoiled for choice and in the end, like any man, you'll make the wrong one for the wrong reasons. I want you settled with someone I know, so that I shan't be too jealous. It's easier for me if I do the choosing. For you know, Alexander, I am still wildly in love with you.' Her eyes flashed fire for a moment. 'I hate the thought of *anyone* else having you, but the die is cast and I must learn to accept that one day you will belong to another. I would hate it to be a beautiful stranger. A haughty beautiful stranger who doesn't know what was once between us.'

'Really, Lavinia . . .' he began, but she cut him short.

'No, I know what I'm talking about. I dream about that woman. I see her walk by on your arm and she gives me nothing but a contemptuous glance. She has a thousand faces, but none of them is known to me. I have to make her one of my friends, someone I trust and know to have fine, delicate feelings, so that I shall not be hurt too badly.'

'Lavinia, you can't dictate to me over my future wife. That's monstrous, no matter what has passed between us. I will not marry to satisfy you or your so-called jealous feelings.'

'Of course not. But you won't mind if I keep bringing you together with my friends, will you? Just in the hope that you'll do the sensible thing and fall in love with one of them under my approving eye? I promise they will all be exceedingly beautiful. There will be no freckles or spots, no dark complexions, no red hair. Especially no ghastly red hair. They will all have wonderfully patient dispositions, or they would not be friends of mine and put up with me. They will be tender, not given to bursts of hot temper, not spendthrifts. They will be thoughtful, attendant to your every need – in fact I shall only choose the most perfect ladies to parade before you.'

'Lavinia, I am at a loss . . .'

'Eight o'clock this evening. Do not be late.'

With that she was gone, tripping out into the muddy street, vanishing amongst the throng.

Crossman spent the rest of the day fuming. How could Lavinia put him in such a bind? If he went to the dinner he would stand the chance of being discovered by someone in authority. If he did not, he knew she would come seeking him out and demand an explanation. Either way he was going to be embarrassed beyond measure. He probably should not go. Yet – yet he was a man, for all that, as the poet said. He was intrigued by this liaison. All his good common sense told him to lie low for twenty-four hours. Go and visit the regiment on the line. Go somewhere Mrs Durham could not reach him. Yet – yet . . . No, surely it was ludicrous. What should he wear to meet this unknown woman? His sergeant's uniform – worn, holed and threadbare as it was, the colour drained out of it by summer suns and winter rains? He might borrow some civilian clothes from someone. Lovelace? But what if he were caught? It would be far worse to be found out of uniform, in the presence of two ladies. At least if he had his uniform on he might leap up and pretend to be serving them dessert or something, should the door burst open and an officer march in slapping his right thigh with a marshal's baton.

Yet, when the time came, he found himself strolling down the road towards Balaclava Harbour, wearing his tattered sergeant's uniform. All was not lost. If his courage deserted him at the eleventh hour he could walk on, go somewhere else, without having to return to the hovel to put Lovelace's civilian clothes back where he might have found them.

Now, here he was before the door. He raised the knocker. Lowered it quietly. Raised it again and hammered hard. The door opened.

'Goodness, Alexander, don't knock the house down,' said a fragrant-smelling Lavinia.

He breathed in the perfumed air as if he were drinking water after a being lost in the desert. 'Ah, yes. Sorry. Bit nervous. No idea why. Nothing in it, of course.'

'Now you're speaking like Bertie speaks, in those short stuttering sentences, just as he does with his sporting chums. There's no need to be nervous. We're all friends here.' She opened the door wider and he saw that there were candles in silver holders on a table with a white cloth and silver cutlery. Crystal glasses twinkled in the flickering light. There was a log fire in the fireplace which burned merrily. An upright piano stood against the far wall. It too had candles burning in its fixed holders. The whole scene was very cosy. Too cosy by half, for Crossman's liking. He now wished he had chosen the other option or was out on a fox hunt with his men.

'Well, come on in. Don't stand there like a post.'

Crossman glanced along the wharf. There were people about, strolling or walking with more purpose along the stone flags. Lamps had been lit. Many of these were hanging from masts or stays on ships in the harbour. They glimmered as men moved under and around them, doing the various tasks required of seamen aboard ships at anchor. He had no idea what those duties were, but they looked inviting. How he wished he had some knot to tie or sail to sew in the light of one of those lanterns. Why had he not joined the navy, instead of the army? There were few women in the navy. No, that wasn't altogether true. While in the harbour there would be women on board the ships. Mostly women selling things like craftware, food, rat traps, drink, their bodies. You could not escape women, no matter which of the two services you joined. Women found you out, wherever you went.

'What are you dreaming about?' cried an impatient Lavinia. 'Do come in, Alexander.'

Forage cap in hand, he stepped into the parlour. A woman was seated in a chair on the other side of the fire, the side previously hidden from his view. She had her hands in her lap and she looked up at him when he entered. She had dark hair, dark eyes, and an engaging smile. For a few moments he did not recognize her. Then her identity hit him with such a force it almost drove the wind out of his speech.

'Cousin Jane?' he croaked, utterly taken aback.

She rose to her feet. 'Alexander, how lovely to see you.' She crossed the room and kissed his bearded cheek. 'Oh,' she stepped back, seemingly distressed, 'how thin you are. Are you well, Alexander?'

'Quite well,' he replied, firmly, to put her mind at rest. 'Never felt better.'

'There are so many victims here. Of the cholera. Of dysentery. I thought you might be ill. But now I see your eyes have a healthy look to them and I'm not so worried after all. It's simply your weight. I suppose everyone loses a little here. The diet is very plain.'

'I'm fine. And you? How do you fare?'

'I'm also very well, thank you.' She gave a little laugh. 'I could not have said that two or three days ago. I was a ghastly green colour. Seasickness, you know. I'm no sailor, I'm afraid. I was ill almost the whole voyage. Sea voyages are supposed to be health-giving, aren't they? Mine was a nightmare.'

'I heard there were storms. Even good sailors have problems when the waves are crashing over the decks.'

'It's kind of you to make excuses for me, but I tell you, sir, if I were to be punted gently down the River Cam, I should be ill.'

A little cough from behind him reminded Crossman that he and his cousin Jane were not alone.

'Lavinia,' he said, turning to face her, his face as bright as a harvest moon. 'You should have told me it was Jane. I feel I protested a little.'

'Oh, no, not you,' said Lavinia. 'Come, let us sit at the table. Ring that little silver bell by your plate, would you Alexander? It will alert the kitchen that we are ready for the first course. Once we have something on our plates we can talk more comfortably. There's wine there, by your elbow, if you would be so kind . . .?'

'Whose crockery is this?' asked Crossman, picking up the crystal wine glass that stood by his place.

'General Enticknap has kindly allowed us to use his finery,' replied Lavinia.

'So,' Jane said, once they had been served and were eating, the waiter not even flickering an eyebrow at the guest in a tattered sergeant's uniform, 'you are a soldier now?'

'I am indeed a soldier. You may wonder why I joined the ranks under an assumed name, but I'm not going to tell you. It's – it's family business.'

'But Alexander, I *am* family. Almost.'

'Not close enough, I'm afraid, Cousin Jane. In fact I would have difficulty in telling my own brother. I think Lavinia knows more than is good for her, since she nursed me through a fever during which I believe I talked my head off about many private matters. I am here, as a sergeant in the 88th Foot, and that's as far as I'm prepared to go with the subject.'

'As you wish. I shall have to ask Lavinia what she knows.'

'Oh,' he cried, his knife and fork in the air. 'That's not ethical.'

'Of course it is,' replied Lavinia. 'We ladies are already at a great disadvantage when it comes to dealing with men. We must have all the ammunition we can obtain. There are no secrets between us. Are there, Jane dear?'

8

The three friends ate their meal and drank their wine, enjoying each other's company as they had in more peaceful times at home. They toasted each other and those bygone days with enthusiasm. In spite of his fear that they would be interrupted by an enraged General Enticknap, Crossman was thoroughly enjoying himself. He had brought with him his long Turkish chibouque and was looking forward to a good smoke after the meal, Lavinia having given him a gift of tobacco. That, combined with the promise of good coffee, brought him closer to heaven.

Lavinia brought up the subject of the Sardinian Bersaglieri and their distinctive headdress, with its black cock feathers.

'They look so *dashing*, Jane. And their undress cap is red with a pretty blue corded tassel. From a distance it looks a little like a Turkish fez. They are so gallant, the Sardinians. I had one sweep off his broad-brimmed hat to me the other day and tell me that he believed summer had arrived. When I asked why, he said I had opened the door to it with my smile.'

None of this impressed Fancy Jack Crossman, who thought the sweeping off of hats had gone out with cavaliers.

'So, Cousin Jane, what are you doing here?' Crossman asked. 'You are surely not going to stay?'

'I've come to see first-hand what I read about in *The Times*. Mr Russell is a very good writer, of course, but one could not believe that conditions are as terrible as he says they are. I applied to

Miss Nightingale for a position as a nurse, but was turned away. I've decided to help in any way I can.'

'Turned away?' cried Crossman in astonishment. 'Were you not suitable? I should have thought that Miss Nightingale would have been grateful to have you?'

'She thought I lacked nursing experience. I told her that I had been taught certain medical techniques by you as a child, such as to spit on a knee-graze and rub it in, but she felt that wasn't enough.'

'Now you're making fun of me.'

Jane smiled. 'Yes, of course I am, but you're so easy, Alexander. Isn't he, Lavinia? No, the reason I wasn't suitable, *I suspect*, is because I have tendency to put forward my own ideas. Miss Nightingale is definitely a woman who does not like to be crossed. I believe she felt I should cross her at times with my own thoughts on various subjects.'

'That I can understand.'

'So, in fact, I decided to come and see what I could do on my own account. I understand there's a Mrs Seacole here, the daughter of a Scottish officer? If she is able to do it on her own, then surely I'm just as able.'

Lavinia now broke in with, 'Oh, come, we are all just a little too serious. Jane, will you play for us?' Lavinia gestured towards the upright piano. 'It's not much of an instrument, but there's not enough room in here for a grand piano. General Enticknap likes ladies to play for him. I do sometimes. But you are so much more musical than I am, Jane. You have a delicate touch.'

'Stuff and nonsense, but I don't mind playing.'

They all retired to the piano and Jane began with a rollicking tune that belied her 'delicate touch' while the other two sang the lyrics. Lavinia had a passable singing voice: one of which she and her mother were not ashamed. Crossman had great difficulty in holding a tune. While he could move a Greek god to tears with the low notes, his high notes tended to waver and threaten to crack. Still, they all made a brave attempt to stay the course together and the servants in the kitchen hummed along with them, they being more concerned with the joy that flowed forth, rather than any lack of musical accomplishment.

After the third song, Crossman went to the table and took a

drink of water, knocking over a crystal-glass jug in the process. It crashed to the floor and shattered. He turned in horror to Lavinia. 'Please tell me that did not belong to General Enticknap.'

'Oh, but it did,' replied Lavinia, looking as distressed as he felt. 'I think it was an heirloom or something, left to him by his great-grandmother. I believe it had been given to her by an Austrian princess.'

'Oh, my God,' he murmured. 'I'm so sorry, Lavinia.'

'Well, Sergeant Fancy Jack Crossman, you'll just have to explain it to the general in the best way you can.'

A chill went through him. 'I – I can't possibly do that.'

Lavinia's face was hard. 'The accident was your fault. You must take the responsibility.'

Crossman squirmed inside his uniform. 'No, really, you can see it's impossible. I can't, for more reasons than you could imagine. Please, Lavinia. You must be sensible.'

She burst out laughing as a servant came in with a brush and dustpan to sweep up the pieces. 'He *is* easy, isn't he, Jane? Of course I shall explain it all to the general. It isn't an heirloom, so far as I know, and I shall offer to pay for the damage. Now, I have to organize things in the kitchen. Jane, would you mind entertaining Alexander?' Significant looks passed between the two women. Jane went a little pink and looked about to protest, but in the end she simply nodded and sat down again at the table. Crossman went back to his own seat, relieved that he did not have to face an irate general. Lavinia left the room with the servant.

Now that they were alone, Crossman studied Jane a little more closely in the candlelight. Such light was often flattering to young ladies, but he could see that Jane had grown into a beautiful woman. Her dark hair and eyes contrasted with her pale complexion and Crossman felt she radiated that loveliness that Byron had spoken of in his poem *She walks in beauty, like the night*. In fact he spoke the words in his thoughts, *all that's best of dark and bright*, seeing how well they fitted his cousin. Jane, in her turn, allowed herself to be studied for a few minutes, before feeling she should interrupt this evident flow of thoughts.

'Cousin Alexander.'

'Eh, what? Oh, sorry, Jane. We – we have seen so few lovely ladies here in the Crimea. You must forgive me for staring. It's like having a fresh breeze blow in from an English meadow, or a Scottish hillside. I am so sorry if I appear rude.'

'Don't apologize. I do understand. And I'm flattered. But tell me, why do they call you Fancy Jack? It makes you sound like some sort of romantic highwayman.'

'Oh, *that*,' he was dismissive. 'It's to do with being a gentleman in the ranks, nothing more.'

With those remarks out of the way, Crossman suddenly felt awkward in the presence of his cousin. She *was* like some delicate thing blown in from distant shores. And he was not quite prepared for dealing with such a situation. He struggled for something to say, and found himself at a loss. What did one talk to young women about? At first he tried to focus on a local event which could affect the whole war.

'Have you seen our siege railway? The engineers, along with our sappers, are progressing magnificently.'

'The one from Balaclava to the front? Yes, I noticed it today. Such muddy conditions they have to work in.'

'Yes indeed, very muddy.'

'*Extremely* muddy.'

They fell silent again.

Well, that seemed to wrap up that particular subject.

Then he remembered that he and Jarrard had been talking about clocks the other day, following his abortive attempt with the electric clock in the school room. He wondered if Jane were interested in horology. He guessed she would not be up to discussing the enormous potential possibilities of steam-driven sea vessels, or the latest agricultural machine for the furtherance of the management of land. But time and clocks were surely feminine as well as masculine subjects?

'My friend Rupert and I were discussing the electric clock the other day,' he said, tapping the table absently with a silver spoon. 'You recall the one invented by my namesake, Alexander Bain?'

'Oh, really. No, I wasn't aware of Mr Bain's achievement,' Jane replied.

He leaned forward sensing, he thought, some enthusiasm in her reply. 'Well, you really ought to be, Jane. I mean it's a tremendous leap forward in the world of inventions. Clocks have been with us for centuries now, of course. The Romans had water and candle clocks, and I'm sure they were not the first. I suppose there have been three major developments in the centuries between. The invention of the escapement by a Chinese gentleman called Hing, in 725. This was followed by the spiral spring, which Christian Huygens, the Dutchman, gave us in 1675. Then of course there's the chronometer . . .'

He had said the last word in such hushed tones Jane felt he must be speaking of some religious artefact, perhaps a clock that fitted a communion cup and assisted the sacraments, or a special pocket watch with which a vicar timed his Evensong sermon. But no, she was wrong, she learned in the next few minutes, for chronometers were used by the navy in order to determine whereabouts they might be on a world of water. Were they then instruments of navigation? Well yes, they were, but they were also time pieces, very precise measurers of time in fact. And going back, she asked, what indeed was an *escapement*? He told her as best he could, for he could see she was having a little difficulty with some of the terms he was using.

'The most commonly used escapement, essential to any clock, was invented by the Frenchman, Perron, in 1798. It consists of an arrangement of toothed wheels and an anchor.'

At this point, Jane suddenly excused herself, saying she had just remembered something of great importance she had to tell Lavinia. She swept away and into the kitchen. It was with relief that she leaned against the kitchen wall and recovered her battered senses. Lavinia was there and raised her eyebrows in expectation.

'Well?' whispered her friend. 'What has he been talking about?'

'Escapement!' said Jane, her hands fluttering.

Lavinia was horrified. 'Escaping? From here? He isn't going to desert?' she cried.

'No, no,' smiled Jane. 'You don't understand. Neither do I, really. An escapement is something to do with a clock. Apparently it controls the transfer of energy from the device to the hands and provides the oscillator with energy which compensates for that lost through friction.'

'What?'

'I'm sorry, Lavinia dear, I can't repeat it. I'm amazed I managed to get it all out the first time.'

'He's been talking about *clocks*?'

'I'm afraid so. I'm sorry, Lavinia. I'm not equal to his intellect. Even were he to show an interest in me, which I'm not at all sure I'm capable of responding to at the moment – I'm not sure I actually *want* to respond in fact – I would not be able to talk with him. My chatter about what to purchase for an evening meal and whether a particular shade of green suited me would not satisfy his yearning for intelligent conversation. I would be a great disappointment to him, I'm certain of that. I agreed to come to this supper because I wanted to see Alexander – see how he had changed and what sort of man he had grown into – but I do not want to be matched with anyone at the present. You know I am soiled goods, in any case. If Alexander were to learn that I had been jilted . . .'

'If he learned that, he would take the next ship home to England and challenge that blackguard to a duel!'

'I am sure he would not. I must face it, now that Peter has run off with that Austrian – well, *lady* – and left me bereft, my previous suitors have not exactly been flocking back to console me. I am a pariah, Lavinia, and I'm sure Alexander would have nothing to do with me if he knew of the business. Why should he attach himself to one so recently involved in a scandal, and set the tongues wagging against his judgement? Not many would, you know. I shall have to put up with elderly, crusty men leering at me and giving me knowing looks, until my youth fades and they are no longer impressed.'

'It was not your fault,' cried Lavinia, furiously. 'That *awful* man was responsible and I hope someone shoots him very soon. Besides, Alexander did the very same thing to me, you know. At the time I wanted someone to shoot him, too.'

'It was quite different with you and Alexander. You had an implied agreement which no one else knew about, and from what you've told me, it was not cast in stone. With Peter and I, well the announcement was made public, as you know. Alexander only missed reading about it because he was here in the Crimea. I am now officially a fallen woman, Lavinia, to be abused by every dowager from London to Brighton.' Jane smiled. 'I wouldn't want to drag Alexander into all that. It wouldn't be fair.'

'Stuff and nonsense. If you think that would worry Alexander, you don't know him very well, even if he is your pretend cousin. I don't think he'd care a jot about any scandal. Good heavens, Jane, how could he? He's a sergeant in the army, going under an assumed name. *His* scandal would eclipse any that you might find yourself embroiled in.'

In order that her argument could not be refuted, Lavinia left her friend and went back into the parlour.

'What's this I hear?' she hissed severely to Crossman, who had just lit the chibouque.

He took the pipe out of his mouth and said, 'What?'

'You've been talking about clocks!'

He shrugged. 'Yes. Yes, I have. Cousin Jane expressed an interest.'

'No she did not. You simply thundered ahead. What did you expect, that she would be enthralled? I expected you to make love to her.'

'Well – well, I'm sorry, I can't do such things to order. Jane is my cousin. Can't I talk with my cousin without being expected to roll out romantic drivel? Listen!' He pointed to the door. A bugle was playing somewhere in the evening. 'Beating the retreat. I ought to get back. I may be missed . . .'

Lavinia's expression told him he was not going to escape that easily. However, there was a knock on the door. It opened without being answered and a head poked round. To Crossman's horror it was the head of Lavinia's husband, Captain Durham.

'Oh, hello Bertie. Come on in. You've met Alexander, of course? Son of Major Kirk of the 93rd Foot?'

Bertie, chubby and benign-looking, drifted into the room.

'Hello old chap,' he said, extending a hand, purposely not seeing the sergeant's uniform. 'Very glad to see you.'

Crossman jumped from the chair, grabbing his pipe with his left hand, and shaking hands with the right. 'I was just leaving,' he said, quickly.

'Not on my account, I hope,' said Durham. 'Didn't mean to intrude. Just thought I'd let you know that we're about to begin a bombardment. A big one. Tomorrow morning. Thought the ladies ought to know. Be a bit loud I'm afraid. Over 500 guns are going to open up at once. Should be quite a noise, even back here.'

Jane came into the room and Lavinia repeated what her husband Bertie had told them, while Crossman stood awkwardly to attention, fiddling with the hot bowl of his chibouque. He desperatately wanted to leave the cottage, but his feet felt as if they were made of plumbum. So he simply remained, silent and stiff, by the hearth.

Jane said, 'It seems I've arrived at an exciting moment.'

'Indeed it does,' replied Bertie. 'Well, my dear, I'm off. Quartermaster's duties and all that. Also Duty Officer. I'll be back for breakfast, my dear. Goodbye, er, Kirk.'

Crossman did not correct him. 'Goodbye.'

Once he had gone, Crossman made his excuses and said he would be going too. 'Thanks so much for a wonderful evening,' he said to Lavinia. 'Jane, I hope you won't stay in this mud hole for long. You deserve to be back in England, to enjoy the spring.'

At the door, he whispered to Lavinia, 'What was all that about? Why didn't Captain Durham say something?'

'My dear Alex,' she replied, a slim hand on his shoulder, 'you are the son of a baronet. Bertie is the son of a merchant. You forget he was once a sergeant too, when he began his army career.'

'A baronet is nothing.'

'To you, perhaps.'

'But I'm not a baronet. My father is. Nothing to do with me.'

'Like myself, you are gentry, Alexander. Bertie, bless his heart, is impressed by high society. You might ask why, since we both know that high society is infested by more rats than the Thames embankment, but I've never managed to disabuse Bertie of his illusions. He thinks that those born with a silver spoon have silver souls. He believes us to be higher creatures than the rest of the population. Poor Bertie. He aspires, you know, to becoming one of us, not knowing really that he would be taking a step backwards.'

'I shouldn't worry, he'll never get there.'

'Of course not. Birth is the only door. Once you've missed the entrance you can never find it again. They won't let you. And once you've stepped outside, as I have by marrying a man beneath my station, the door is locked behind you.'

'Nonsense. You have dukes and earls asking you to dine.'

She shook her head and gave him a wistful smile. 'Only here, Alex, on campaign. In England they would never do it. Their wives and mothers wouldn't let them. Can you see them letting Bertie into their houses? My father did warn me, of course, but I knew better. If Papa had been a younger man, he might have set himself against the match, but elderly widowers have trouble in resisting determined daughters. And to tell you the truth, I don't mind that much. Bertie's father isn't poor. I shall never want for money. And when Bertie finally leaves the army we'll settle for a nice house in Devonshire, or Dorset, and I shall have a flower garden and be the lady of the village. In any case, I wouldn't have Bertie subjected to the tongues, you know.'

Crossman said, 'Bertie is better off being Bertie.'

'So I've told him, but there you are. He yearns for the impossible. Of course, marrying me was an enormous leap forward for him, but the chasm grows ever wider. Quartermasters, be they commissioned officers or not, stand no better chance than merchants of being accepted. They don't know the passwords, the gestures, the nuances. Poor, poor Bertie.'

'Poor, poor us.'

'Quite. Now, did you like her? Your grown-up cousin?'

'Of course I liked her,' replied Crossman. 'I've always liked her.'

'No, I mean did you *like* her.'

'Lavinia, that's for me to keep in here,' said Crossman, tapping his chest. 'It's no business of yours.'

With that he turned and marched out into the night. Lavinia turned also, closing the door as she did so. 'Jane, my dear, he is besotted with you.'

'Oh, Lavinia,' scolded Jane. 'Please!'

'No, no, he is, I assure you. I can tell. Now, what shall we do? General Enticknap will be back soon. A game of whist to pass the time? You shall own up to breaking the crystal-glass jug, of course. We can't tell him we entertained a sergeant, even if he is the son of a baronet. General Enticknap is not so gullible or easily impressed as Bertie, since I believe there's an earl in that family. And I can't say *I* did it. He might be very annoyed and I'd never get the use of the cottage again. No, it will have be you I'm afraid, Jane. You'd better practise being dreadfully sorry. Widen your eyes, let them go a little moist and have your lips tremble a little as if you expect the wrath of God to descend upon your bowed head. That ought to weaken him. He's only a man, after all.'

Jane protested, but was firmly overruled.

Crossman woke next morning to the thunderous roar of the guns. Bertie had been right. There was a major bombardment in progress. When the Russian guns replied, some 1,000 of them, the whole peninsula seemed to rattle and shake. For the next ten days the bombardment did not cease. Hundreds of thousands of rounds were used. They fell in droves on both sides. The allied troops were fairly well protected by their trenches, but the Russian infantry, often exposed, had dreadful casualties. Some reports said that over six thousand Russian soldiers met their death from that bombardment alone. By day Sebastopol's defences were battered and beaten, by night they were raised again. French attacks were promised, but their commander-in-chief kept calling them off at the last minute, having received counter instructions from his emperor in Paris. It was a frustrating and deadly time, with iron balls raining from the sky, and no real advantage being taken by either side.

Early in May, in the calm that followed a heavy barrage, Crossman took Jane to see some amateur theatricals put on by the Zouaves. The proceeds of the performance would benefit the French prisoners of the Russians. The play had just begun, with some soldiers mincing onto the stage dressed as women. Their faces rouged and wearing wigs of dyed fur, they began squeaking in high voices. Jane protested.

'Ladies do not speak like that!'

'Hush,' replied Crossman, 'French ladies might.'

'I know several French ladies and they do not squeak like mice. And what does that creature in the red wig think he's doing with his skirts? Oh dear, this is rather risqué, Alexander. Petticoats on show?'

'Should I take you home, do you think?'

'Certainly not. I've seen petticoats before. I sometimes wear them myself.'

The conversation might have grown even more dangerous if at that moment there hadn't come the sound of firing. Almost immediately the French soldiers in the audience abandoned their seats and scattered in various directions, it being an open-air performance. The Travelling Gentlemen were the next to leave, hurrying to get a good view of any fighting from the nearest high point. Ladies were assisted from the area by their husbands and gentlemen friends. One of the actors shouted that the Quarantine Cemetery was being attacked by a large Russian force.

'We'd better get you home,' said Crossman, taking a longing look towards the area where the musket balls were flying. 'Back to safety in case they break through.'

'Surely, if they break through,' reasoned Jane, 'nowhere will be particularly safe?'

'Well, that's true of course.'

Bugles and drums were sounding now. The French were rallying.

'Look, Alexander, please leave me to make my own way. I can see you are itching to assist the French . . .' An officer of the *Chasseurs d'Afrique* went striding by, presumably looking for his mount. Some of the horses loosely tethered outside the 'theatre' had been scattered in the rush of exiting patrons, and were now cantering around riderless.

'No, I can't possibly do that.'

She agreed. 'No, I suppose you can't. I'm sorry to be so tiresome. If you hurry me back, you still might have time to return to the action.'

'Not really my place, anyhow. If I had been here alone, or with my men, I should have joined in. But the moment has passed. The French look as though they have the thing in hand. Better we get you home.'

'Home is several thousand miles away,' she said, smiling.

'Yes, so it is. Well, back to wherever.'

All the way back the musketry rolled. The wind was from the west and so the sound of Russian bugles could be heard the whole time. Crossman told Jane that another bugle sound was that of his own Light Division, sounding 'turn out'. Flashes from the muzzles of distant guns lit up the sky, followed by more crackling broken fire from muskets. Then cheers, from one side or the other.

'Shouldn't you be with your battalion?' Jane asked. 'Won't they miss you at roll call, or something?'

'I'm not exactly with the battalion. I'm on special duties.'

'Oh. So long as you won't get into trouble.'

'No, I won't get into trouble.'

He took her back to where Lavinia was waiting. The two women then went off to the hospital, to see if casualties were coming in. Crossman went back to the front, to witness the action. He found to his relief that the French had held the attack and were driving the Russians back. On returning to Kadikoi there was a message for him. He was to report to Colonel Hawke immediately.

Hawke was as usual at his makeshift desk and he gestured Crossman into the room.

'We've got an expedition coming up, sergeant. Kertch. You know the area from your own raid with the canoes, do you not?'

Crossman remembered it well. They had lost Clancy on that little trip. Drowned. It had not been the most favourable of his fox hunts. Getting there had been Hell and getting home had been worse. He hoped the colonel wasn't going to ask him to canoe all the way there again. If so, there might be a few desertions from the *peloton*.

'How will we get there, sir?'

The colonel looked up. 'Get there? With the Highland Brigade of course. Oh, you misunderstand me. This is not a fox hunt. I just want you there to assist the landing parties, should they need it, and report back to me on how things go.'

Crossman suddenly became more interested. 'So this is a large expedition?'

'Oh yes.' The colonel leaned back in his chair and lit a cheroot.

As he puffed the smoke Crossman inhaled deeply. Hawke noticed this and offered Crossman one of his smokes. Crossman took it eagerly and soon the pair of them were creating quite a comfortable fug in the small room. 'So,' continued Hawke, 'apart from the French forces, numbering about 3,000 in all, and the Turks, there'll be the Highland Brigade – 42nd, 71st and 93rd. Marines of course. Left Wing of the Rifles. W Field Battery and some sappers and miners from 11th Company. You'll go as a separate detachment of pioneers. You won't have to do anything of course, except observe.'

Crossman wasn't so sure about this. His experience had been that once his commanding officer was out of sight, other officers felt obliged to order him and his men to do as they jolly well felt fitting. Should the sergeant argue they would put him in his place with amazing swiftness, telling him if he wished to disobey the direct order of a commissioned officer he might think about how demotion and fifty lashes might feel. There was not a lot of weight to having one's own colonel if he was not in the field with you. Still, Crossman was not averse to work, if it was necessary.

'And the object of the expedition?'

'To capture the towns of Kertch and Yenikale, thus commanding the Straits of Kertch and cutting off the Russian supply route through the Sea of Azov!' cried the colonel in delight, thumping his desk top and causing the rickety structure to collapse at one corner. He ignored this minor catastrophe and beamed at Crossman, who also felt a surge of happiness. 'At last, sergeant! Some real action. Sieges are the very Devil. You sit on your arses and rot for months, years on end. This is a grand action. Well, not so very grand, I suppose, small in the context of other expeditions, but by God we need it badly. We need a victory of some sort. Alma is growing very thin. We have to give ourselves a box to stand on.'

'I agree, sir. I totally agree. Who's commanding the expedition? The French I suppose, since they're putting up the most men?'

'Not at all, not at all,' chortled Hawke. 'Canrobert has expressedly requested that Sir George Brown be in overall command. Can you warrant that? General D'Autemarre, leading the

French, is furious of course. His own commander-in-chief recommending a British general, but there you have it, D'Autemarre must eat humble pie for the moment.'

'How many ships?'

'Oh, I should think above 600. Not so petty, eh? Not so small when you talk of those numbers.'

They beamed at each other again, puffing on the cheroots.

Crossman left the colonel and went to see his men.

'We're off on a sea voyage,' he told them. 'To Kertch.'

Wynter's mouth dropped open. 'We're not goin' *there* again, are we? Blood and guts, Kertch nearly had me the first time.'

'Boats?' cried Peterson, not usually one to whine. 'Does it mean boats?'

'Ships. Yes, I'm afraid so. I know you get seasick, Peterson, but this one will be worth it, I assure you.'

'Last time I went on a ship,' Wynter complained, 'I got a big chunk of wood stuck in me.'

Gwilliams looked up. 'See here, Wynter. It's time I run up and down your spine for you. It'll help your bones knit properly. That's why you're always so miserable, is my guess. Your bones don't fit you. They're all out of their sockets and joints. We got to get them to lock back in again, then you'll be a happy man. Indians taught me that. If a man's bones is out of kilter he's bound to be a miserable cur. And that's what you are, Wynter, a miserable cur. Look at me! I'm dying to sail on a ship.'

'Ha, we've seen what *you* can do with bones, Gwilliams. Look at Yorwarth's bloody jaws.'

'Gwilliams,' said Crossman, something occurring to him for the first time, 'I'm not sure you can come on this one. It's a military expedition. Army and navy. There'll be French and Turkish forces there too. Officially you're a civilian barber.'

'And bone-man. Yeah, but look, sergeant, if I'm good enough to come with this bunch, I'm good enough to come anywhere.'

'I'll do what I can,' said Crossman, doubtfully, 'if you really want to come. It might mean a full-blooded battle. In fact it most certainly will. You should be prepared for that.'

'Hell, I've bin in the army too.'

Crossman agreed that this was true. 'What about you, Yorwarth? You've not said anything.'

'Not *straight* anyway,' murmured Wynter. 'It always comes out crooked.' Then he laughed at his own attempt at humour.

Yorwarth replied that he would be happy to go anywhere that Wynter went, just to be on the spot when Wynter had his head blown off.

The last was Ali, who did not deign to speak. He would of course go anywhere the sergeant went, since they were fast friends. Crossman did not even ask the Turk if he was going. He knew Ali would be insulted at such a question.

'Right then,' said Crossman. 'Get your kit packed.'

'Shouldn't take long,' grunted Wynter, 'since we ain't got none.'

Rupert Jarrard came to see Crossman later that evening. They talked by candlelight. 'I'm coming on the expedition,' said the correspondent, 'along with Russell and others. Fenton the photographer's going as well. It should be quite a party.'

Crossman was pleased about that. Jarrard was always good company. He suddenly realized something which had just come to mind. 'I've been meaning to ask you, Rupert, if you would like to meet my cousin Jane, who's foolishly visiting the war.'

Jarrard's eyes glinted. 'Met her. Mrs Durham introduced us yesterday. A very attractive woman. Unmarried, I believe.'

The way he said it sent a jolt of annoyance through Crossman, which he realized with a sudden shock was jealousy. Why should he be so protective of Jane? Surely he would be happy for Rupert and his cousin to find some common ground? Yet, no, he was not, he admitted to himself. He put this down to the fact that he knew nothing about Rupert and women. For all Crossman knew, Rupert could be a philanderer. Crossman did not want his cousin falling in love with a libertine, certainly. No decent watchful male relative could sanction such a thing.

Jarrard was the sort of man most women seemed to find attractive. Broad shoulders, longish curly locks, lithe, clear-cut features. Yes, Crossman was sure Jane would admire Rupert's looks. As to his character, why, the American spoke with a soft burr, was exceedingly polite and charming to females, though he obviously had a roughness to his spirit from his days on the frontier. He could be very tough too. Crossman had seen the civility in Rupert change at a moment's notice when he came up against rudeness or an imagined insult. Jarrard's face would turn to granite and his eyes to ice, and he would put down such offence with a firmness that the perpetrator knew he would be wise not to arouse in the future. Apologies had almost always been forthcoming. Where they had not, they had been extracted by forceful means at six o'clock of a cold and frosty morning, on a patch of ground somewhere out of sight of the authorities.

'Oh,' replied Crossman, coldly. 'Yes, she is unmarried, though that situation may very well change in the future.'

'I hope it will,' agreed Jarrard, not catching the change of mood in his British friend. 'She's not the sort of lady I would expect to become an old maid.'

'No, she is not. I imagine she will be wed to some fine nobleman, and he will be lucky to get her. She's much sought after amongst the *ton*, back home. I shouldn't be surprised if she's got a lord or earl dangling after her right at this moment.'

'She didn't give that impression, Jack. In fact she said to me directly that she had been unlucky in love.'

Crossman's eyes bugged. 'You spoke to her that intimately?' He was a little more than put out that he had spent a whole evening with Jane and had learned nothing of the sort. 'That's coming it a bit fast, Rupert. I mean, the two of you are almost complete strangers.'

'Just happened to come out. I think I said she looked perfectly lovely, and she demurred of course, as a lady would, but I saw that my compliment had pleased her. Then she asked if my wife was accompanying me on my European travels, and I said I had no wife, and what with one thing leading to another, I eventually learned that she was unmarried but had recently been let down badly by a man. No, wait, I tell a lie, Jack, it was Mrs Durham who told me that. Yes, it was she who said your cousin had been "crossed in love" as she put it. I tell you what, Jack, I'm surprised you haven't called the fellow out. If she was *my* cousin, he would be eating dirt by now.'

Crossman's mind was reeling. How was it that Rupert could talk in such familiar and confidential ways to Lavinia and Jane, and he, Jack, could only converse about clocks? It was grossly unfair. It made him feel like some country-bred dolt. Well, he *was* country-bred, but he didn't feel he was a dolt. Not under normal circumstances. And here was this fellow Jarrard, a foreigner, a stranger, an itinerant, able to draw such secrets out of Jane within a few moments of engaging her in conversation. And what about this love *affaire* of his cousin? What was it all about? It was all a bit thick.

'Was she – engaged to some fellow?'

Jarrard looked stern. 'You didn't know? Yes, some rat back in London, I understand. Jilted her. Married another woman. A foreigner.'

The wind went completely out of Crossman for a moment, but when he was able to fill his lungs again, he said, 'I assure you, Rupert, if I had known about this oaf . . . Well, I'm here in the Crimea at the moment, so I couldn't do anything immediately. But something *will* be done. Something will definitely be done.'

'She has no brother and her father is elderly, so it has to be you, Jack.'

'You found that out too?' cried Crossman, miserably. 'Did she tell you her whole life story in ten seconds?'

'Oh, it wasn't ten seconds, Jack. We spent the whole day out riding together. She's a fine horsewoman, by the way. I expect you know that.'

Crossman let out a strangled cry, like that of some animal caught in a trap, startling his friend into jumping off the cot he had been sitting on.

'Are you all right, Jack?' He looked into the glass he was holding in his hand. 'Is it the wine? I agree it's not top drawer.'

Crossman calmed himself. It was difficult but not impossible.

'No – no – I'm fine. The wine's fine. Look, we both have to rest, Rupert, before the expedition. We may not be on the same ship together, but I'm sure we'll meet up sometime in the next few days. I'll look out for you.'

'And I for you,' replied Jarrard, warmly, taking his hand and shaking it vigorously. 'Good luck, Jack. I'm sure you'll fight like a maniac. Keep your head down.'

'I will. I will,' said the bemused Crossman. 'I'm glad you're coming.'

And indeed he was, since it would keep the correspondent out of Jane's way for the period that Crossman was absent.

The following day Crossman and his men boarded the *Arrow* commanded by a Lieutenant Jolliffe. The flotilla set sail and headed out to sea. At first it seemed they were going the wrong way and Crossman wondered if the planned destination had changed, but on speaking with one of the crew it seemed this was probably to fool the Russians. Later, the ship changed course again and they were heading towards Kertch. Peterson, her wound now healed, gave way to her weak stomach. She spent much of the time hanging over the rail, knowing by experience that if she went below she would be ten times worse. Wynter jeered at her, but it was not above six hours at sea that he joined her and regretted his hasty words.

Crossman was rather glad that Jarrard was not on the same ship with him, there being an awkwardness between them at the moment. However, when dusk fell and the flotilla moved silently on through the grey seas, he rather missed his friend. He wanted to chat to him about the new electric telegraph cable that had been laid. Now the Emperor Napoleon, in Paris, could send and receive messages to and from the war front in a matter of minutes. It was a miraculous device. Quite incredible. Crossman was so excited about it he tried to speak with Gwilliams, but while the North American was a classics scholar he had no interest in new inventions. Crossman was left musing to himself, staring up at the sails of the ship, wondering if there would ever be such a message system that spanned the globe. It seemed impossible, but many things previously thought impossible had come into being in this wonderful century of rapid progress.

Even while Crossman was marvelling at the stupendous leap that telegraphy, combined with the code invented by the American Samuel Finley Breese Morse, had made to the world of communications a message had arrived on General Canrobert's desk from an interfering French emperor. Within hours the flotilla had been recalled and the British ships crawled back to Kamiesh Bay under furious captains. The British and French troops were bewildered. Why had they turned back? Surely they had been in striking distance of their target. It seemed another of those mad decisions thrown up by this mad war.

Peterson staggered ashore, grateful to be on dry land again after five futile days at sea. 'I never want to go on another boat as long as I live,' she announced, 'unless it's to go home to England.' She might have got her wish if Colonel Hawke had followed through with his idea to chase Corporal Reece up and down the coast. But before he issued his orders Crossman and his men were on their way to Kertch once more. General Canrobert had resigned. General Pélissier was now commander-in-chief of the French forces and he was not so inclined to take notice of telegraph messages from someone as far away as Paris, be that someone emperor of France or no. General Pélissier ordered the flotilla to sail again. In the sea fog, Peterson cursed all French people, generals and emperors, fishwives and onion sellers, and said she hoped their livers would rot. She rarely forgave.

Along with 3,500 British troops, 7,000 French, 5,000 Turkish, and an odd number of Sardinians, Crossman and his men landed on a beach near Kertch during a long evening. There was some sporadic firing from some Black Sea Cossack vedettes, who retired immediately after there was return fire. Shore batteries opened up and were answered by the guns from various allied ships. Crossman noticed a battle taking place between a British gunboat and some Russian vessels, even as he trudged up the sea strand, and the fog of war began drifting over the landscape.

'Keep together,' he said to his men, as they fell in behind the Highland Brigade. 'Just follow where I go.'

The march took them through meadowland – similar to the downs of Sussex and Hampshire – which was studded with small stone houses owned by Tartars. There was some fighting going on around these dwellings, minor skirmishes it seemed, and a little while later Crossman learned that looting and pillaging was taking place. Allied soldiers were running amuck, despite orders to the contrary, and the houses of civilians were being ransacked and, in some cases, destroyed. Jars of olive oil, poultry, livestock, religious obects, nothing was safe or sacred. Wanton destruction as well as stealing was taking place and the whole scene left a bad taste in Crossman's mouth. While he knew there would always be an element of low life in any army, it was to be hoped that looting did not become a widespread and commonplace act. It seemed that here on this expedition, it had. Officers had lost control of small breakaway groups of soldiers and the civilian population was at their mercy.

After an initial stand, the Russians retreated, leaving the battle-expectant allies to walk into Kertch unopposed. The Cossacks were little better than the looters, setting fire to haystacks and farmhouses as they went. The Tartars were caught between the two forces. Massive explosions shook the ground as the Russians blew up their own magazines. The air was full of acrid smoke. In the background was the constant gabble of Tartar homesteaders pleading with French, British and Turkish soldiers to be left unharmed and their wives and children to be spared.

Crossman and the *peloton* had been left by a salt lake which had been a resting place for dozens of different birds until the landing. Now, the mighty explosions from the Russian magazines, the sound of cannon and howitzer, of mortar and musket, had driven them to the skies. They circled about the lake, flying erratically, no doubt thinking that Hell had opened up. There was a jetty going out into the lake, with two small craft moored to it, which Crossman's 'pioneers' had been ordered to destroy. As they were laying the charges a woman came from behind a patch of reeds and begged them to leave the boats undamaged. It seemed they belonged to her husband and son, who fished in the lake. In the end Crossman could see no gain to the allies in destroying any of it and he left the jetty intact as well.

'What a mess,' said Gwilliams, disgustedly. 'Who's in charge here? Why don't some general come an' put a bit of order into the scene?'

Allied soldiers were running, grabbing, running on again. Not far away a French corporal was setting fire to a chicken coop. Near him were two British soldiers, one of whom took a long pull from an earthenware jug, only to gasp and spit out a mouthful of fluid. 'Oil,' he cried, smashing the jug on the rocky ground. 'Damned cookin' oil.' In the distance a gang of Turks had dragged a mattress from a hovel and were in the process of tearing it apart, possibly in the hope of finding some hidden treasure, but also because their blood was hot and they were acting out of frenzy rather than reason. Still more Turkish soldiers were ripping through fishing nets, hung out to dry, with their bayonets. They were laughing like children.

Ali shrugged, as if to say, 'This is life,' and spat on the ground.

Wynter said, 'Spoils of war, sergeant. You can't deny 'em. When soldiers have had such a bad winter as we've had, why, they're entitled to a bit of compensation from the enemy. If I see somethin' laying around, not doing anything, why, I shall have it just like that.'

'Those houses don't belong to the enemy,' Peterson said. 'They're civilians.'

Yorwarth said, 'No such thing as civilians in a war. I'll wager those Tartars give the Russians all the help they need. I'm with Wynter on this one. You got to take one side or the other.'

'I don't like looting at any time,' said Crossman, firmly. 'If I catch any man stealing, I'll see to it that they're flogged. You hear that, Wynter?'

'Lord Wellington didn't like it either,' Peterson came in again, always reluctant to let an issue hang. 'He would never have it. I mean, think about someone going into *your* village, in England, just taking all your grandmother's things and wrecking the house. It don't bear thinking of, does it? Imagine your village church ransacked. Good Christian people don't do that sort of thing. It doesn't make it any better here, just because they're foreign. Lord Wellington would have said so.'

'What do you know Lord Wellington would have said?' snarled Wynter, as usual feeling he was under attack. 'Anyways, Lord Wellington didn't need to take stuff. He was a rich man. It's all right for lords who have everythin' they want in life. Some of us have to scrape by, don't we? Some of us could do with a ham or a jug of cider, if it's goin' free.'

'Wellington was one of your English gods,' muttered Gwilliams, then added a strange contradiction, 'but he weren't no angel neither.'

'No, but he didn't like looting. You could be shot for looting, in Wellington's time,' Peterson said, dogmatically, as if Gwilliams were hotly arguing the point. 'Look at them! They should be in Bedlam that lot. They've gone staring mad. Ripping up mattresses! Sergeant,' her voice had an alarming note to it, 'watch out! Over there!'

A man with a musket came from behind a blazing hayrick. He fired determinedly into the *peloton* as they stood gawping at him. Luckily the musket ball was spent after fifty yards and dropped with a *plop* into a compost heap ten yards to the right of Gwilliams, the outermost man. The Tartar farmer who had fired the weapon now ran off, leaving his ancient firelock smoking on the ground. When it was recovered by Ali, they discovered it had been fired so many times the bore was not far off that belonging to a small cannon and the ball must have rolled round and round inside it like a marble in a drain pipe before being thrown out of the muzzle. Ali shook the musket and it rattled heavily, its parts being so worn and loose they hardly remained together. Studying the worm-eaten, worn stock, the Turk said the user had been lucky it did not blow up in his face. He finally threw it into the salt lake, putting it out of harm's way.

When Crossman's *peloton* entered the town, later in the evening, he heard that even the museum had been plundered. Ancient Greek artefacts had been stolen, or smashed. This museum had housed one of the finest collections of Hellenistic art in the region. The looters had even employed *droschkies* and *arabas* to haul their plunder away.

'What for?' he asked, shaking his head. 'Do they even know what they were stealing? What would a soldier want with a vase decorated with the portrait of a Greek god, or the bust of an Athenian general?'

No one could answer him. There had been a specific order to respect private property, yet this had been ignored by many soldiers of all armies, though Crossman liked to think that the British were not as bad as the Turks and French, but then the thefts and destruction had not been confined to the latter alone. There were British soldiers, perhaps even British officers, amongst the looters. When he was able to dismiss the columns of black smoke from his mind, and the chaos and turmoil that usually succeeds the sacking of a city, Crossman was able to appreciate the beautiful architecture of the place and the superiority of its position on the shores of the Black Sea. The public buildings were expansive and elegant, and the formal gardens and parks well tended. There were good views of the sea, even from the little stone house where they stayed the night. Inside, the house had clean white walls, which Crossman ordered the men not to deface. There were mats on the floors and pictures on the walls.

The *peloton* stayed at the house for some time. Their services were in demand during this period, mostly for destroying enemy forts and defences of no use to the allies. They were also used as manpower, along with the line regiments, to shift huge quantities of stores left by the Russians: grain, flour, oil. Some of these stores were set alight. Ships and guns were captured, though many were destroyed both by the allies and by the Russians themselves. It seemed the two sides had tried to outdo one another in their barbaric efforts to destroy Russian property. An invasion by the Visigoths or Vandals could not have left a worse mark.

When they were on board ship again, sailing back to Balaclava, Peterson remarked that she did not know what was worse: a battle where men and horses were blown to bits, or an attack on a town where the houses were gutted and fire used to raze property to the ground. Both types of warfare had their ugly faces. 'When I was young,' she said, 'I used to think that at least war cleaned out the old and made way for the new. Burn down a town and build a fresh clean one in its place. But it's not like that. Things don't burn all the way down. Some buildings are left standing, especially the ugly stone ones. What you get is a hotch-potch, not a clean start.' Then she was sick over the side and out of any subsequent conversation.

Crossman reported his observations to Colonel Hawke, including the plundering of civilian and public houses.

'So, the whole show was a success, eh? Good, good. That'll make some of Raglan's favourites sit up. I understand a lot of those sycophants were against the expedition. Well, they'll have to swallow their words now, won't they?' He rubbed his hands together, then looked up into Crossman's eyes. 'Yes, yes, of course, the looting. Most unfortunate. Any soldier caught looting should be severely punished. Still, that's to do with the regiments' commanders. Only they can judge the conditions under which the attack took place and whether the men overstepped the mark. What's important is that the attack was a success.'

Crossman realized that the colonel was one of those who had pressed Raglan to go ahead. He would obviously be the subject of good reports for having advocated that the expeditionary force be sent to Kertch. He asked Crossman if he had heard of any blot on the attack at all, for it all seemed too good to be true.

'None that I know of, sir. In fact I was told that not a single allied soldier was killed in the fighting, though there was one accidental casualty of which I'm not sure. Oh, there was one incident. The 10th Hussars . . .' Hawke leaned forward, alarm on his features. Surely this was not going to be another Balaclava on a small scale? 'The 10th attacked, or were attacked by, some Cossacks. I was employed on leading a party of officers into the hills at the time. You'll remember that I once made an escape from Kertch along that stretch of the country and I was asked to point out the main routes to and from the town. We were on a hillside when we observed the 10th running into several squadrons of Don Cossacks. One or two of the 10th were taken prisoner.'

'They weren't decimated?' said Hawke, quickly.

'No, no, nothing like that. It was a minor skirmish, with the 10th getting slightly tangled and receiving the worst of it.'

Hawke leaned back again, relieved. 'Oh, that's all right then.'

Yes, thought Crossman, that's all right. Only a few light cavalry troopers rotting in some Russian prison. That's quite all right. But then he managed to see the thing through the colonel's eyes, and realized he, Crossman, was being churlish. The colonel had to retain the broad view and his relief was justified. If such an action, with the loss of no lives, could shorten the war then it was for the good of all concerned that it had taken place. With the Russian supply lines cut, Sebastopol would fall that much sooner. Sebastopol *had* to fall, even Crossman was sure of that, and when the city was taken perhaps there would be even more chaos and confusion. The taking of Yenikale and Kertch was a small preparation for the overrunning of the much larger city. Lessons had been learned very cheaply and the allies had to be grateful for that.

'Now,' said Hawke, 'I want you to sit in that chair in the corner. We've got a visitor coming. Before he arrives I want to say it was well done of you to gather all that information on General Enticknap. Very well done. We've got him well and truly in the bag, so to speak. This is one fox that won't get away. He's coming to see me now.'

Crossman's skin crawled in alarm. 'What am I needed here for, sir?'

'Oh,' Hawke shuffled some papers on his desk, clearly nervous, 'as a sort of witness. Just in case things turn nasty, sergeant. I've sent for two marines as well. They won't come in unless I call them.'

'Sir,' replied Crossman, 'I really don't . . .' But before he had time to finish the sentence, a tall man entered. He was indeed a general and Crossman did not need to guess what his name was. Crossman stood up and saluted. Hawke did the same. Then Hawke waved Crossman back down into his seat again, and resumed his own. The general stood in front of the makeshift desk looking puzzled.

'Colonel Hawke, is it?' he said, crisply. 'What is all this? Since when do colonels ask generals to see them?' He glanced to the side at Crossman, trying to lose himself in the corner shadows. 'What is all this?' repeated the general, clearly uncertain of himself. 'Who's this sergeant? Connaught Rangers? That's Colonel Shirley's battalion, isn't it?

Crossman came to attention. 'Yes, sir. 88th.' He could stand this no longer. 'You'll be wanting to speak with the general alone, sir,' he said to Hawke. 'I'll wait outside.'

'You'll wait in here,' ordered Hawke.

But Crossman shook his head and marched out of the room. When he got outside the building there were two armed marines posted one either side of the door. They stared at Crossman, who shrugged and stepped away from them, to wait beneath the window. Soon after he had left the voices inside began as a murmur, raised in volume gradually, until the two officers within were shouting at one another. One of the marines grinned at Crossman, and said, 'Argy-bargy?' Crossman did not deign to answer. He looked away into the distance, feeling extremely uncomfortable. The voices inside began to subside, until Crossman could recognize only the tone of Colonel Hawke. After a very long speech, during which there were only grunts from the general, Enticknap emerged from the building looking very shaken. His face was an ashen colour and there were veins standing out on his temple. He stopped and turned, to stare at Crossman.

'Damn sneak,' he said, as if Crossman were a schoolboy who

had snitched on him to the headmaster. 'What do you mean by spying on me, sergeant?' His voice filled with contempt and loathing. 'That's a foul profession, you've found yourself. Spying on your own people.'

'Special duties, sir,' muttered Crossman, into his beard. The two marines were staring at him, no doubt wondering about this soldier with a 'foul profession'. He cleared his throat. 'No choice in the matter.'

'Huh!' The general stalked away.

Hawke yelled for Crossman, who went back in again now.

'Dismiss those marines for me, Sergeant Crossman,' Hawke snapped, 'then come back inside.'

Crossman went outside. 'You're not needed.'

'Well, there's a how d'ye do,' one of them said, while the other, who had spoken not a word the whole time, simply shrugged and slapped his comrade on the shoulder, indicating they should be on their way. They ambled off, trailing their weapons and falling into a deep conversation. The one who had remained silent until now turned and gave Crossman a half-wave, before nodding at something his companion was saying.

Crossman reluctantly entered the room again, but instead of finding Hawke in a temper, as he expected, he found the colonel exultant. 'Ha! He's on his way home.' Then, remembering Crossman had disobeyed a direct order, he wagged a pencil at him. 'Not a pleasant task, I admit. But he was guilty of corruption, you know. Next time you disobey my orders, sergeant, I'll take those stripes. Understand me?'

'I'm sorry, sir. I just couldn't stomach it.'

'Couldn't stomach it? What? You think I *enjoyed* it? Totally necessary, sergeant. I'd rather charge the Redan than go through that again, though. Slippery snake he was. Offered me a bribe. Oh, not outright, but I can recognize a bribe when I hear it. Anyway, we're shot of him.'

'Are you sure, sir? He looked pretty angry to me.'

'Angry, yes, but he doesn't want a scandal. A court martial would ruin him for life, and he knows it.'

'You really think Lord Raglan would agree to the court martial of one of his favourite generals?'

'No, but when I lay all the evidence before him, he'll make

damn sure Enticknap doesn't remain in the Crimea, believe me. He'll despise you, for bringing the thing to my attention, but I shall say I knew nothing about it until you placed the matter in my hands today. That's what I told Enticknap. I said one of your men had overheard conversations and you had followed them up. Sorry, sergeant, but someone's got to take the blame. Well, that's it then. Business over with.'

Business over with. Not for Crossman though. He had two more encounters within the next day or so, in which the business reared its ugly head again. One was when his father accosted him on the waterfront at Balaclava Harbour.

'Heard about you. Nasty, rascally business. I'm talking about Enticknap. There can't be two sergeants in the 88th who do that filthy work. Didn't like Enticknap, but one doesn't slink around digging dirt.'

'It wasn't my idea, Father. I was ordered to.'

'Pah! If I ordered you to steal the queen's washing, would ye do it, boy?'

'No.'

'There you are then.'

How his father had got to the core of the truth, Crossman did not know. He doubted Enticknap wanted such information spread about the landscape, so it wouldn't have been him. Hawke too would have been close mouthed about the affair. The whole enterprise relied on everyone keeping things to themselves. Crossman sat on his bed for an hour, thinking things over, then sent for Gwilliams.

'Did you give a Major Kirk some information, Gwilliams?' he asked, sternly. 'About General Enticknap?'

'Major Kirk?' replied Gwilliams, in his gruff North American drawl. 'Yeah. That was me.'

Crossman was astonished at his audacity. 'Why did you do that?'

'He paid me,' came the blunt reply. 'While I was shaving him he said he'd seen me with you. He asked me if I was one of your men and I said I was. Then he wanted to know what you got up to, and offered to pay me.' Gwilliams jingled coins in his trouser pocket. 'I told him about Enticknap. Hell, he won't do nothin' with it.'

'You're sure of that?' seethed Crossman.

'I'm willin' to bet he won't do nothin' with it.'

'He's already done so. Well, so I've got a viper in my nest, have I? What am I to do with you, Gwilliams? I can't trust you.'

'Nope. Ain't that a bitch?' said Gwilliams, grinning. 'Look, sergeant, that was dirty work and you know it. It weren't nothin' to do with military secrets, nor to do with this war. That was one officer getting rid of another one. Well, I made a bit of money on the side. It's a one-off thing. Won't happen again.'

With that he left the room, leaving Crossman rather deflated.

The second time 'that business' surfaced again was when Crossman met with a rather less well informed Jane and Lavinia.

Lavinia said, 'Alexander. Have you heard about General Enticknap? It seems he's got to go back to England. Something to do with a domestic crisis. It's just too bad, isn't it? Just when we had a nice rendezvous.'

'Sorry?'

'The cottage, Alex. The cottage. It'll go to someone else now. Heaven knows who that will be. I'm not sure I'll be able to influence them. Oh, it is just too bad.'

Crossman agreed that it was and after exchanging polite enquiries with Jane, he went on his way. Jarrard came to see him later, to try to pump him. 'I know you know something about this, Jack. Let me have it.'

'Nothing in it, Rupert. I don't know the man.'

'Yes, you do. I heard Hawke and Enticknap had a fight. Now the general's suddenly called back home? It stinks of undercover stuff, Jack. You're the undercover man. Tell me what you know.'

'I know nothing, Rupert. Please.'

'All right, but I shall ask Jane about it, when I see her. I'm sure you tell her things you don't tell me.'

'That's a bit stiff, Rupert. Squeezing my cousin.'

'I know, we're a wicked bunch, us newspaper men.'

9

The captain of the ketch-rigged sailing barge said his name was Od Freir. He was a Norwegian. The Norwegians, like the British, were a seafaring nation and as such their sailors fetched up in the most unlikely corners of the world. So long as there was a sea that connected with other seas and oceans, then there would be a Norwegian somewhere within hailing distance. The sailing barge normally plied its trade in the Sea of Marmara and along the Golden Horn to the Bosphorus and the Black Sea, but lately there had been better pickings carrying cargo for the allied armies around the Crimean peninsula. Now the craft had been hired for a specific task and its blond-haired captain – a Viking if ever Crossman saw one – was due to make a great deal of money carrying passengers instead.

'These damn-blast calm seas,' growled Freir, who was polishing a brass swivel-gun set in the front of his unlovely but sturdy craft. 'Yust when you want a big blow, they go all soapy on you.'

Crossman didn't know whether he actually meant 'soapy' or had mispronounced a word like 'soppy' but he let it go.

'Where are we now?' he asked.

'In Hell!' cried a voice from the hold, where his *peloton* was crouched in the dampness, their weapons between their knees. 'In bloody Hell, that's where we are.'

Crossman was dressed in a navy shirt and Nankeen trousers, a close-fitting woollen hat on his head. He looked every inch the sailor. His men were out of sight in the darkness of a barge whose last cargo had been salt-fish and pickled herrings. Crossman knew it stank down in the hold, that the boat was leaking and his men were sitting in bilge-water up to their hips, and that one of them at least had been sick over most of the others. He knew this but could do little to relieve their condition. What was more he knew that this situation might last for hours: until there was a squall at least.

Both Freir and Crossman ignored the plaintive call from below.

Freir said, 'We are one half-mile from the coast. See, those small lights over there on the cliffs? That is houses. Look, we do no good here. Come to my cabin aft. We smoke a pipe and drink some rum.'

'I'd like some rum, please,' cried the same voice, which Crossman knew belonged to Wynter. 'Send some rum down 'ere.'

'Have you got enough for them?'

'I haff plenty.'

The men were given tots, which Crossman refused to increase, knowing that Wynter or Yorwarth would abuse the privilege and get drunk if they possibly could. This was not a time to become inebriated. In a matter of hours they would have to attack the beach and he wanted them all sober. As for himself, he enjoyed the same sized tot, while Freir had a tankard which held about five times more than everyone else. '. . . but of course, I am used to it, since it is my rum.'

With the lamp swinging back and forth across the table which was bolted to the floor between them, Crossman sipped his drink and talked with the Norwegian. 'So,' he said, 'what takes a Norwegian from his home shores into the Black Sea?'

'It's better than the fishing.'

'Is it?'

'Anything is better than the fishing. As a yunk man I worked at the fishing.' Freir held up a hand and revealed that he had two fingers missing. 'Those had the hooks in them. Big hooks, like this,' he curled the forefinger of his other hand over. 'If you get one in, it splits the bone. Better to chop it off straight aways. Always the master of the boat haff a meat cleafer ready by his hand to chop off a finger. Not a good life, the fishing. Too cold, always. And high seas, like this.' He used his hands to indicate rough waters with giant waves. 'Better to come down to warmer waters.'

'These are not particularly warm waters, not all the year round.'

'Ah, this is special journey, for now, while you fight the war. But I am usually in the Med. Or the Marmara and Bosphorus. Not in here, in the Black Sea. And after the spring, the waters is good and warm. Now for a while I run from Samsun or Trabzon to Balaclava. Or even from Burgas. I bring candles, blankets, oil, things like this. Some for the French, some for the British. Some for the people of Crimea. Seven days ago I climb up the Chufut Kale, above Bakhchiserai, to the Karaim people's old synagogue there. No more Jews, but other people live there now. They buy from me barrels of whale oil for their lamps.'

'Yes, I know that place. Near Mangup,' replied Crossman. 'There's a sort of plateau there with ruins of watch towers, broken walls and arches that hang over the grasslands. Quite an eerie area. I know the settlement you're speaking of.'

'That's the place. Many ghosts there. Old peoples, from before civilization. Scythians, Cimmerians.'

While they were talking there was a creaking from the barge. Freir jumped up and went to adjust the sails. When he came back he said, 'The wind is getting oop.'

'How can you handle this vessel all by yourself?' said Crossman, as the Norwegian settled himself again. 'What about when we hit a squall or a storm? Surely you need some help then?'

'No, I am quick,' smiled the clean-shaven captain, brown teeth stark against his white skin. 'I yump from sail to sail. I am like the monkey. Very fit. Very strong.' He crooked his arm to show a bulging muscle through the woollen jumper he wore. 'Ah, listen!' He held up a finger. 'Yes, she is definitely getting oop. Soon we will have some white waves and my little boat will bob like a cork. We will find these bad men of yours when the dark comes later.'

'Sergeant!' someone yelled from the hold. 'Peterson's bin sick again!'

'You'll just have to put up with it,' he yelled back. Then to Freir, 'I'm sorry, some of my men hate the water. They get sick standing on the beach.'

The Norwegian shrugged. 'It happens, eh? I get sick in one of those new chuff-chuffs.'

'A steam train?'

'Yes. I do not like the smell from the smoke. It sends my brain giddy. And so fast! They fly along the iron rails. I do not think the human body is meant to go so fast.'

'Oh, surely? I find the train exciting.'

'Each man to his own. See,' the boat lurched, 'here we have the beginnings of the stormy weather. Let's go oop and look. Always at this time of year we do not haff to wait long for bigger waves.'

Indeed, the sea was getting rougher, and darker, and ghost-like shadows were chasing each other in the hollows of the swell. There were heavy gusts of wind sweeping across the water in patches, rippling the surface, while here and there the waves broke into white sprays. In the distance an even darker shoreline was merging into the sky. Crossman was told to get his oilskins on. Those below decks were not given the choice, since there was not enough sea clothing to cover them all. They would get cold, it was true, but not as cold as those on deck. And everyone would get wet, oils or no oils. That seemed to be a fact of sea life.

The gloomy aspect of the sea and land was reflected in Crossman's spirit. His task here seemed only remotely possible. They had to limp along the coast, pretending to be in trouble, yet actually searching it bay by bay. Freir maintained it was an easy exercise, but then the longer they were out the more money the Norwegian was earning. It did not matter to the boat's captain if they were out there for weeks on end, forever searching for their prey. Od Freir would happily tell Crossman anything to keep the enterprise alive.

Now the rain came, sweeping in from the east. It hit the canvas sails with a steady patter that swiftly became a drumming. The fresh water rolled off the curving canvas and flowed down into the hold in a steady stream. Freir told the occupants of the hold that they would have to work the pumps harder or he would have to put the hatch on and consign them to darkness and bad air. They cursed him. He cursed them back in a Viking tongue. Some of them went to the buckets, to keep up with the water that was now coming in from both below and above. Crossman knew his men had never been so miserable. 'Just thank the lord you're not in the navy,' he told them, trying to cheer them up. 'Remember, this has got to end any day now. If you were on board ship it would last two years or more.'

'Thank you, sergeant, for those comforting words,' yelled Gwilliams, 'but I would no more serve in the British Navy than I would in the Chinese Imperial Guard.'

'You might be pressed, sometime.'

'Not me. That's all stopped now, and you know it, sergeant.'

'Has it?' said Crossman, innocently. 'Well, then, where are we going to get our sailors from now?'

'I hear tell the gentry are going to supply them,' replied the wry Gwilliams. 'They will send their younger sons to the admiralty to be used as deck-fodder for the navy, and good riddance I say.'

Crossman had to smile at that one. But he did not smile for long. Freir, despite his earlier claims that he could handle the craft all on his own, began to yell at him to pull this sheet, or grab that halyard, or 'take the damn tiller if you can't do anything else, soldier-man.' Indeed, Crossman had no idea of the terms the captain was using, and when he had the tiller in his hand, the boat seemed to have a mind of its own, yawing this way and that, as Crossman over-corrected the steering, and in the end it was Ali, called up from below, who was given that task while Crossman was back to being yelled at and cursed, and told to 'reef' one of the sails – a verb which had escaped his vocabulary so far.

Soon the barge, which had seemed a reasonably large vessel while the sea had remained calm, now appeared tiny and liable to be swallowed by any of the waves that seemed to be coming at it from every direction. However, once Freir had all the trappings of the sailing barge the way he wanted them, he once again turned into a reasonable human being and even laughed at Crossman's attempt to make a bowline, the final result of which was a flapping sail and whipping sheet, that lashed the sergeant across the face before he got it under control again.

'Everything all right now,' Freir yelled at Crossman. 'We rush, rush, until I haff the sails in the best way, then I can work her easy.'

Spray hissed across the deck, soaking Crossman and running in rivulets from his head to his boots. One particularly heavy wave shouldered the craft, almost turning her over, had it not been for Freir's skill in using the rudder to take them out of trouble. Crossman had always understood that you steered into the wave, parting it, thus avoiding being broached, but these waves seemed to change direction without warning, so that the steersman had to be constantly on the alert, accepting each stretch of sea as new territory, and fully aware that betrayal lurked behind every other mound of rolling water and each treacherous gust of wind. It seemed every second that they were doomed to drown, yet somehow the boat stayed afloat. Freir, the god of this wooden bark, now glowed with casual confidence, calling the soldiers babies and saying it would make men of them.

The storm continued to worsen and soon Crossman began to feel that the sailing barge would *really* be in trouble. They wouldn't have to fake it. So many British ships had gone down in the Black Sea, since the war had started, it wasn't difficult to visualize this small craft sinking below the waves with all hands on board. It was only three o'clock in the afternoon, but it was as dark as midnight. If they got into difficulties there was no one around to help them. They were on a lonely and perilous part of the coast: that indeed had been the idea.

It was in this area that Reece and his gang operated, preying on small craft just like this one. They rode along the cliffs, sometimes plundering farmhouses, always on the lookout for vessels in difficulty, struggling to find a safe harbour close to the shore. They would wait until a cutter was launched, with a landing party, and attack them as they battled through the surf to the beach. Whatever was in the cutter, or any landing craft, would fall into their possession. A land expedition against the renegade always failed, his lookouts being sharp and his mounts being swift. He had to be lured into a trap of his own making.

The sailing barge had only a rowing boat, which would take up to about four or five men. It had been Lovelace's idea that they find a smallish vessel, hire it, and use it as a decoy. To

Crossman the whole enterprise seemed fraught with problems, but Lovelace had insisted it would work. So here they were, on a tossing ocean, trying to tempt land pirates. They had already limped into three wide bays, two small coves, and up to a long windswept stretch of beach covered in white driftwood and seaweed, without any success. Crossman always felt there would be long odds on coming up against Morgan Reece and his crew of deserters.

'Is that a light I see, up there on the cliffs?' yelled Crossman, through the spray, as another large wave struck their bows. 'Freir, look!'

The captain did indeed look and cried that he had seen it.

'Nothing to do about it,' the Norwegian said. 'We can't launch the row boat in this filthy weather. It would be swamped bad a short time. Better to wait until the blow dies a little, eh?'

'If you say so. I don't want to risk my men.'

'I don't want to risk my boat.'

So they continued to grapple with the storm, until there were breaks in the cloud above and light showed through. The sea became less mountainous and more like the Sussex Downs in aspect. While the light was still too poor for anyone on the coast to witness what was happening in detail aboard the barge, Freir raised a tattered mainsail in place of the good one, let fall the smaller of the two masts as if it had broken and began to limp into the nearest bay with a sideways motion in order to make it look as if the rudder had gone and there was difficulty in steering. When they were close, the rowing boat was launched with seasick soldiers crouched in the bottom, once again awash with water. There was not one amongst them who would not have emigrated to the middle of a wide continent at that moment, given the choice. Of seascapes and waves they had seen enough.

Crossman and Ali did the rowing, they being the only two visible to anyone on the sands. Excitement stirred in Crossman's breast as two figures appeared from behind some rocks, just as the rowing boat was tackling the heavy surf. 'Ready men,' he whispered. 'Bayonets first, until you can use your dry powder.' They had not loaded their muskets for the very reason that the powder would be wet and useless before they reached the shore. So they intended a quick charge, hoping to have the opportunity to load their weapons with powder now wrapped in waterproof pouches.

Crossman and Ali had swords lying beside them in the boat. When the underside of the rowing boat scraped the sands of the beach both men grabbed those swords and leapt out on the strand. They were quickly followed by Wynter, Peterson, Yorwarth and Gwilliams. Every man jack of them was yelling blue murder, as they charged towards the two figures who were between the rocky cliff and the boat. At first those silhouettes of men turned to run but, no doubt seeing it was a hopeless flight, turned once again and armed themselves with pistols. A ball whined past Crossman's ear. There was a misfire from the other man's pistol and Crossman was vaguely aware in the excitement of the charge that this person had dropped his weapon when it fizzed and flared in his hand.

The charging soldiers were almost on the two men when the unarmed man fell to his knees and yelled for mercy. Crossman faltered, as did Ali, but the others were past them with glinting bayonets. Wynter, white-eyed, raised his rifle to pierce the kneeling man. Crossman yelled hoarsely, 'STOP!' But Wynter was too far gone to pull back. Gwilliams, to his right, struck Wynter's rifle a blow with his own. This swift action diverted the point of the bayonet into the victim's shoulder. It had been aimed at the heart. He was a fortunate man. He fell backwards with a scream in his throat, at the same time wrenching at the blade that appeared to be stuck in his scapula.

Wynter, furious with Gwilliams, let go of his weapon and struck out with his fist. Gwilliams punched him back, solidly, on the jaw. Crossman jumped between them. During this melee the second stranger was desperately trying to reload his pistol. Ali knocked it casually from his hand and the man dropped to his knees. The two of them begged for their lives in the local language of the Tartars, the wounded one having at last freed himself from the rifle bayonet. He was staunching a flow from his shoulder with the palm of one hand and waving the other one, pleading over and over again for his life and the life of his friend.

'Bloody bastard!' yelled Wynter at Gwilliams. 'That hurt, that did.'

'You think yours didn't!' Gwilliams shouted back.

'All right, all right, let it rest,' said Crossman. 'Calm yourselves, both of you.'

He knew the fear and excitement of a bayonet charge, possibly into a hail of bullets from hidden weapons behind a belt of rocks, had raised the blood-heat of his men to a dangerous level. In such a charge a soldier's emotions spiral out of control and into a state of frenzy. Crossman's own emotions had been running high too, but the realization that these were not British or French deserters had penetrated and he had been able to stop the charge. Stop it all but for Wynter of course, but fortunately Gwilliams had gathered his wits quickly enough to intervene. He would have to thank Gwilliams later for that, as now was not the time, with heated feelings still simmering in overwrought breasts.

'The important thing is these men are not British or French deserters. Gwilliams was only trying to stop you from killing an innocent man by mistake, Wynter.'

Wynter typically responded with, 'How do we know they're innocent, then, eh? Answer me that, sergeant.'

'Shut up. The point is, they're not Reece's deserters. We're lucky we didn't kill both of them.'

'They're lucky, you mean,' replied Peterson, quietly. She was just glad to be on dry land again. Her head was still swimming and the ground still felt as if it were rolling under her feet, but she was feeling a great deal more like the Peterson she knew and cared for.

Yorwarth added his own two-penn'orth now, with a few choice words about bayonet charges and their worth.

The two prisoners stared up with open mouths at this man who was speaking in this evil-sounding language. What was wrong with the speaker's face? Was it falling into two pieces? One part of it went one way, one the other. What a strange experience they were having on this beach, almost as if it were all a horrible dream, a nightmare. First to be attacked by demons out of the waves. Then for those demons to fight amongst themselves. Now having to witness the surreal vision of the Devil's harbinger, delivering his message in the dark tones of the

Underworld's creatures. Had the pair of them entered some forbidden zone?

Ali made a pad for the wounded man's shoulder and bandaged it tightly. He advised the man to get it seen to quickly, before gangrene set in. Should he keep it clean, Ali said, there was no reason why the young Tartar should not live a long and happy life. The two victims themselves asked Ali why he was running with *rakshasas* and *jinn*? He seemed an ordinary man, they said. He was not wild-eyed and wild-haired like those cacodemons pacing up and down the sands, screaming at one another in voices from Hell. Why would a good and normal man want to keep such company? Ali shrugged and shook his great head sadly. It was his lot in life, he told the two Tartars. He had been bewitched and beguiled by the tall demon with the black hair and now must serve as his slave for the rest of his life, the Turk explained. Would they pray for his soul? We will, we will, came the reply, and God have mercy on your mother's son.

'Well, that was a fine set-to,' said Yorwarth, as they boarded the sailing barge again. 'Did you see the way they looked at me? If looks could kill I'd be deader than a redback stuck to the sole of a boot. What had I done to them? It was Wynter who stuck him, not me.'

'I was first there, that's the only reason,' argued Wynter. 'I can't help it if I run faster than you lot.'

They went back down into the hold, grumbling like mad. Peterson was particularly upset at having to continue the fox hunt. Freir then took the boat on patrol again, sailing up and down the long stretch of bleak coastline, his unwilling passengers hoping against hope that they would eventually attract the attention of Reece and his gang. Crossman went back to musing on life, studying the star patterns and wondering about Cousin Jane's sudden appearance in the Crimea.

Four muskets appeared over the gunwales of the rowing boat and a fierce volley took the deserters by surprise. One man fell with a smoking hole in his chest. Another spun backwards, his arm shattered. There was a shout amongst them for reinforcements from the cliffs behind. By the time this cry for help was even registering amongst those already hurrying down the cliff paths, a second round of shots ripped into them, this time a ragged fusillade. Pistols were taking their toll too in the competent hands of a sergeant and his Turkish aide. When the reinforcements, some fourteen men, began running across the sands towards the scene of the fighting, bodies were scattered over the area and blood was flowing into the shingle.

If they thought their superior numbers were enough to rescue their fallen comrades, they were wrong, for any fool could tell they were running into the same trap. They were completely exposed, no matter how many of them came to the aid of the fallen. The attackers in the boat had all the advantages, even to the point where if they themselves were put in danger all they had to do was put to sea and row back out to the sailing barge.

The barge itself had miraculously ceased dragging itself like a wounded butterfly across the bay and now had its bows pointed towards the beach. A round shot landed amongst the deserters, sending pebbles and dirt flying into their faces. This was followed by a puff of smoke and finally the sound of the shot which echoed across the bay. Someone in that barge was using a gun to put their already beleaguered lives in even greater peril. Three of them turned back immediately, running for the cliff path which they had descended. One of these was shot in the back by Morgan Reece, but the other two escaped his wrath.

Those in the boat jumped out now and dragged their vessel a few yards up onto the sea strand. They were using it as a shield and remained behind it, firing steadily at the exposed deserters. There was nowhere for the latter to hide. They were on a deep wide beach with no rocks or any kind of cover. Some were firing from the prone position. Others had gone down on one knee. But the relentless fire from behind the thick, clinker-built rowing boat was thinning their numbers by the minute. They were caught in a blistering storm of bullets from the six soldiers safely ensconced behind their barrier. Finally, the ketch-rigged sailing barge moved in closer to the shore and Freir began to use grapeshot to spray the enemy. Eventually the deserters began to raise their hands, seeing their position as hopeless and helpless.

'Move away from your weapons,' cried Crossman. 'Any man who moves to touch his weapon will be shot.'

One man had refused to drop his carbine. Crossman recognized him instantly. Morgan Reece was not going to be taken alive. 'You're coming with me, you treacherous bastard!' he yelled at Crossman, at the same time raising his weapon. Crossman pointed his Tranter at the big man, but the revolver merely clicked on an empty chamber. At that same moment there was a deafening blast in Crossman's ear, which made him stagger to the side. He cupped his ringing ear in his hand and watched as Morgan Reece crumpled to the sand, a furious look on his face. The renegade remained where he was, clearly dead with a hole in his chest, though by his expression he still seemed about to remonstrate with Crossman.

'Thank you, Ali,' said Crossman, his head still ringing. 'Appreciated.'

'No trouble, sergeant.' It was the Turk who had taken Reece's life. One of his several single-shot pistols was still smoking in his hand.

'The rest of you men, don't get any ideas,' cried a jumpy Wynter. 'I'll kill any man who looks at his musket!'

There were six deserters left unwounded. Two of them, Crossman discovered, were French soldiers. The rest were from the Army of the East. They were led away to the barge and chained together. A more miserable-looking set of individuals you would not find, now that their anger had gone and had been replaced by despair. Besides these there were two more seriously wounded and one walking wounded.

Crossman was secretly glad that Reece had died in the fight. He would not have liked to see him hang, despite the fact that Reece was a murderer. There was something about Reece's posture and defiant attitude that went against the indignity of hanging. The rest would certainly hang or, if they were lucky, go before a firing squad. For this reason Crossman and his men could not look them in the eye, and did not wish to speak to them except to ask if they wanted food and drink. In a way there was shame involved. They were dragging a group of their own towards the certainty of the gallows. It left a bad taste in the mouth and filled the captors with guilt. Yes, thieves and killers were being brought to justice, but now that they had been stripped of their status as warriors, they looked pathetically young and sorry. They looked like the boys and men you might see in a tavern back in England, drinking ale, smiling a greeting and winking at the serving girl. It felt very bad to be taking such men back to dangle on the end of a hemp rope. It was pointless telling them they might have a chance, that their defence might bring up mitigating circumstances to excuse them of their behaviour. They were going to be executed, and that was certain.

After the prisoners had been made to carry their own dead to the barge and lay them in the hold, one of them asked Crossman if he would write to his brother.

'What will I say?'

'Tell him it wasn't my intent, to become what I am. Things seemed to conspire to make it so. I am guilty and I shall hang, but tell him there was remorse in me for what I did. Tell him I'm sorry for it and that when he sees my name posted up in the parish church as a coward and a murderer, please to take it down before my mother comes to it.'

'Do you live in a village.'

'Aye, a small place in Devon.'

'Then won't that be difficult? People will talk. She will hear of it, anyway. You can't hide anything in small villages.'

'So long as she don't see my name up there,' said the youth, with moist eyes. 'It would kill her. No one will tell her out of respect for my father and her grief. My father was liked very well, before he got caught in the threshing machine and was killed in his prime.' The young man hung his head. 'He would have been so shameful of his son and what I've come to. It's a bad day, for my bad name will be on the family forever. My brother will be feared to go to market, in case someone gives him a look. He has a bad temper on him and does things rash, like me. There'll be anger in him against me, but he'll fight any man who thinks wrong of me. Now I think what a terrible thing I've done to them all. Brother, cousins and parents.'

Yorwarth said, harshly, 'You should've thought of that, before you went against queen and country.'

The soldier shook his head. 'A man don't always think before he does. Sometimes it comes of instinct. With me it was a raid at night. The Russ was waiting for us and cut us to bits. There was only me left, running this way and that, in the dark, trying to dodge them bullets. Then, when I run in a straight line, I found myself out in the hills and just kept going . . .'

'It sounds an easy thing to do,' said Peterson, her own eyes moist.

'Pah, you knew what you was doing,' cried Wynter, who was secretly appalled by all this emotion and how it was making him feel. 'You could've gone back straight away and no one would've thought the worse. All of you, you've all got stories, ain't you? You could all blame somethin' else, or someone else. Fact is, you did wrong and you've got to pay for it.'

Out of all the soldiers of the *peloton*, Wynter was the most likely candidate for desertion. He had the right temperament. He had the same attitude as many of the men in chains: a hatred of authority. Deep down he knew this and it scared him silly. There but for the grace of God went Wynter. When he dwelt on the image of hanging, his throat felt as if it were stuffed with sheep's wool and his heart raced off into the unknown. It was a death which he feared more than any other. This atmosphere of black gloom which preceded a hanging, several hangings, made him feel sick to the point of giddiness.

They reached Balaclava and delivered their prisoners into the hands of the authorities. It was a relief to be rid of them. Crossman went to see Colonel Hawke, but found he was away on business. Lovelace was there instead, behind the desk. He looked bored.

'Oh, hello, sergeant. Successful fox hunt?'

'Yes, sir, we got them, at last. It took days and weeks of searching up and down that coast, but we found them in the end. Half of them died in the battle. The others we brought back. Reece was killed.'

'Well done! Hawke will be pleased.'

'I hope so. It's a dirty business.'

Major Lovelace leaned back in his chair. 'It's *all* a dirty business, sergeant, but it's got to be done. Have you heard about Enticknap?'

'No – what?'

'Shot himself.'

Crossman went cold. 'No, I didn't know.'

Lovelace came forward, over the desk, and knitted the fingers of both hands together.

'Yes, funny turn of events. It seems he locked himself in the room of a Tartar's farm and fired two rounds into his own chest. Didn't die straight away. Must have spent all night there, bleeding to death. Horrible business.'

'Shot himself in the chest?' Crossman felt a soft blow of incredulity hit him. 'Surely, if a man is going to shoot himself he puts the bullet where he knows it will kill him instantly – in the brain. A man shoots himself in the head, not in the chest.'

'Well, I must admit it sounds peculiar. However, it seems he was found slumped in a chair, the pistol in his hand, and two rounds in his chest. One went through the right lung, the other grazed the heart.'

'The right lung,' repeated Crossman. 'Was he that bad a shot?'

'He might have been shaking badly. One never knows the state of mind of a suicide, does one? Perhaps he was toying with it for a while and the pistol went off unexpectedly. I've known that happen. Who was that famous general in India, who tried to shoot himself in the head and missed? Was it Clive? I'll wager he was not serious when he raised the pistol to his temple. Men think about it, toy with the idea, even to the point of putting a loaded firearm to their heads, not really intending to go through with it. Sometimes the weapon goes off accidentally, and they find themselves victim of their own melancholy.'

'But the *chest*.'

'Yes, I grant you that. It is a strange business. What other explanation is there?'

'Somebody else shot him and tried to make it look like suicide.'

'You're forgetting the locked door. The key was inside the room.'

Crossman said, 'Was it actually in the lock, or on the floor?'

'Ah, I see your drift. Lock the door from the outside and slide the key under it.'

'Or toss it through a crack in the shutters.'

Lovelace shrugged. 'I don't know where they found the key. It was my understanding that there was nothing suspicious or unusual, at least concerning the whereabouts of the key.' He stared hard at Crossman. 'Is there some definite purpose behind these questions, or are you following an idle train of thought?'

'I don't know. I'm not sure where I'm going either, sir.' Crossman sat down in the spare chair without being invited. He ran his hands over his face and then stared at his senior officer. 'I find this work very harrowing. When we started out it was just blowing up this magazine or spiking that set of guns, but it seems to have become more – more unsavoury.'

'You're worried about the ethics?'

'Not so much that. I know dirty things have to be done in a war. War is a sordid business in itself. Today I returned with a set of prisoners, deserters and murderers. It's fair to say, isn't it, that they'll all be executed? I don't find that very palatable, I'm afraid. I would rather have not had anything to do with it.'

'I seem to remember that Reece and his men hanged a perfectly innocent farmer in his own barn. You are merely acting as policeman here. The court martial bears the responsibility for the punishment, not you. And after the sentence is carried out, which I grant will be death in most cases, any further responsibility will fall into God's hands. You are not the main agent of justice here. You have a small piece of the work: to produce the accused men. It is the court who will decide whether they are guilty and the judges who will sentence them. Finally, God will carry out a more thorough investigation of the whole affair, take into account any remorse or recognition of sins, and decide whether any further punitive measures are required. Yours is the only part in the affair which does not require you to judge your fellow men. You have got off lightly, my friend. You may shrug your shoulders and pass the blame for any harsh or unwarranted sentence on to others. You are merely the delivery boy, the messenger.'

Crossman smiled. 'When you put it that way . . .'

'I merely state the facts.'

They were both silent for a few moments, then Lovelace said, 'Did you ever make that raid for the coats? For your regiment?'

Crossman shook his head. 'Never found the time.'

'No need now, eh? Warmer weather's come.'

'I suppose so. I know I'd rather have been stealing coats than capturing deserters or spying on generals, but then I don't have a great deal to say about what I do. Ah well, I'll bid you good night, sir.'

'No sweet dreams?'

'We should be so lucky.'

Having made his report, Crossman went to see Jane. He learned she was at Enticknap's cottage. He was not pleased to find Jarrard there. The American greeted him heartily and asked after his health. Crossman said tartly that he did very well, thank you.

'Good, then you can join us for a game of whist – Mrs Durham is due shortly, and she will make the fourth.'

'I think I'd rather . . .'

'Oh, do stay,' said Jane, quickly.

Jane was wearing a white dress and seemed gay enough. But her looks belied the merriment in her tone. She looked very tired, with dark shadows around her eyes and her complexion pale, almost wan. If there had not been a lilt to her voice he would have believed she was close to exhaustion. How she contrived to keep herself so clean and bright was remarkable in a place where the mud crept up one's boots and reached one's collar.

Indeed Lavinia Durham arrived next in riding habit and covered in spots of mud. She put her riding crop on the cottage table and said, 'Yes, do stay, Alexander, that is to say, Jack.' She shook her blouse in a most unladylike way. 'That is, if you can forgive me for looking like a hoyden. My horse insisted on going through every puddle from here to the Heights.'

'Oh – very well then. I could do with some relaxation.'

Lavinia Durham went for a wash and came back changed, her hair freshly combed and her face pink.

'I swear Mrs Durham if you were not married to Captain Durham I should ask for your hand right now,' said Jarrard. 'I've never known a woman like you. You take less time than my manservant to get yourself ready. Most ladies I know would have been in that room for a prehistoric age.'

'Oh, you don't believe all that rubbish, do you?'

The men were both mystified. 'What rubbish?' asked Jarrard, thinking she must mean his observations on her sex.

'Prehistoric ages. There's no such thing. Don't you believe in your bible, Mr Jarrard?'

Light showed through Jarrard's cloudy thoughts. 'Some of it, yes. But I don't believe the world began 4,000 years ago at ten o'clock in the morning, as the good bishops will have us believe. Do you?'

To the astonishment of the two men, Lavinia Durham said primly, yes she did. 'I am firmly of that opinion. It is there in black and white, Mr Jarrard, for all to read. These things they call "fossils" have been manufactured in secret on some island in the Pacific and scattered by heretics in places like Lyme Regis. No one will persuade me otherwise. Good Heavens, why, do you think they find the things all in one place? If these fossils of other creatures were indeed from our distant past, why, they would be in your garden, and mine, and in every garden in the kingdom.'

Jane nodded, adding that Lavinia's arguments seemed very sound.

'Well,' said Crossman, 'I had no idea you were so against the new thinking, Lavinia. I can't tell you why we don't find fossils in our back yards, because I don't know why. I'm not a natural historian. And I have a belief in God as strong as the next man. But I see no reason why He couldn't have made creatures thousands of years ago . . .'

'Millions,' corrected Jarrard.

'Millions of years ago, then, though my mind finds such figures hard to contemplate.'

'You don't believe in Adam and Eve then?' asked Jane. 'Fie, sir, you are unromantic.'

Crossman looked helplessly at Jarrard. 'What has romance to do with anything? I swear, Jarrard, I know why I never win an argument with a woman. It's because they shift the battleground from under one's feet without a by-your-leave. One moment the subject is this, then just when one is about to administer the *coup de grâce*, one finds the subject has changed completely. We are not talking about romance, cousin, we are speaking of the validity of the fossilized remains of animals, fish and birds.'

'And you don't find that unromantic?'

'It has *nothing* to do with it. Romance does not come into the picture at all. Good Lord, let's play cards before my mind spins out of my skull. You exasperate me, all you women. I simply can't be doing with it.'

A hand was dealt during which time Crossman's temper was not improved by Jarrard whispering in his ear, 'I swear you would have called me out, if Lavinia Durham had not arrived at the party.'

Crossman made no comment other than to place a card down on the table with a little more force than was actually necessary.

'By the way,' he said, looking up, 'why are we here?'

'Is that a philosophical question?' asked Jarrard. 'Are we back to God and his works?'

'No, I mean, this was General Enticknap's cottage – who owns it now that he's dead?'

The cards fell from Jane's hand and Lavinia went almost as white as the wall behind her. 'Dead?' whispered Lavinia.

Crossman realized he had dropped a stone into a calm pond. 'You hadn't heard,' he said. 'General Enticknap committed suicide. He shot himself . . .'

Jarrard made a noise in his throat which told Crossman that this was news to his American friend too.

Jarrard said, 'What *I* heard was that the good general was being investigated for corruption. Was it to do with that, Jack?'

'I have no idea. Lovelace told me the moment I returned. Enticknap shot himself twice in the chest, in a locked room.'

Jarrard's reaction to this news was much the same as Crossman's – incredulity. While they were talking the ladies left the room and Crossman could hear Lavinia quietly sobbing in another room, and Jane saying, '. . . that sweet, elderly man.' Jarrard said the circumstances sounded highly suspicious and he was going to get to the bottom of it. Finally, the women came back in, Lavinia bearing a tray with drinks.

'I think we need something to fortify us,' said Lavinia, now completely calm and mistress of her emotions once more. 'I must say that was a great shock, Alexander. That was *too* bad of you. I realize, however, that you were not aware that it was news to us.'

'I'm sorry for it, Lavinia. I did think the facts were general knowledge. Please forgive me.'

She kissed him lightly on the cheek. 'Of course I forgive you.

But if you don't mind, I would rather not continue with the subject. I have to have time to absorb the news. I think you've told us all you know, have you not?'

'I have indeed.'

'Then I think we had better not pick at it like vultures. I'm sure many of the gossips will be doing so tonight and I believe his memory deserves better. He was a good friend to me. It is very sad.' Having stated she did not wish to dwell on the subject, Lavinia then went on to speak about it at length, during which time Crossman went through all kinds of agonies of guilt. 'I hope he was not driven to this extreme by persons jealous of his position. I refer to his close friendship with Lord Raglan. There were those, you know, who envied General Enticknap a great deal. Some will stoop to the most unseemly behaviour to get what they want. There were rumours that there was some kind of plot against him. While I dismissed it as idle chatter at the time, I am now beginning to wonder . . .' She continued in this vein for quite a time. There was little response from either of the men or Jane and eventually her clock of fury ran down. Jarrard patted her hand and she rallied with a sigh, to say, 'Let us speak no more of the matter tonight. This is a happy gathering. Alex – that is to say, Jack – has returned to us in good health – look.' Exasperation now followed the other series of emotions. 'This is all most confusing Alexander, this *nom-de-plume* of yours. I don't know why you have to parade around with an assumed name, now that your father is aware of who and what you are. It would save the rest of us tying our tongues in knots, you know.'

'It's not a *nom-de-plume*, Lavinia,' he replied, gently. 'I didn't invent it for the purpose of writing. And it would be difficult to change it back to my real name, even though its original purpose has gone. You may call me Alexander, Rupert will call me Jack, and Jane shall call me Cousin. I promise you I shall respond to all three with equal alacrity. Look on me as all three in one – an Unholy Trinity.'

Lavinia drew in a shocked breath. 'Alex, that is a most improper remark.'

Crossman could not fathom this side of Lavinia Durham, her high moral tone when it came to Christian matters. In all other things she was totally irreverent. In fact, even regarding certain

Christian matters. He knew of at least one of the Ten Commandments she had broken with ease, being the other participant in that breaking. He could not understand it but he did not believe her to be a hypocrite, exactly. It was more a confused set of beliefs, as if her Truths had been collected in a box and the box shaken violently, so that they all became as entangled as fish hooks.

'The answer to an earlier question you asked, Jack,' Jarrard said, now lighting up a cigar, 'is that *I* now rent this little dwelling. You are a guest in my house, Jack. So you had better be on your best behaviour.' He stuck the cigar in the corner of his mouth, his thumbs in his waistcoat pockets, and grinned.

'Unlike you, Mr Jarrard,' said Jane with a mock haughty expression on her face, 'who did not ask permission of the ladies to light up one of those pieces of tarred rope you seem to enjoy smoking.'

Jarrard whipped the cigar from his mouth. 'I do most sincerely apologize. May I smoke?'

'Yes, you may.'

'So,' Crossman continued the conversation, 'we are on American soil?'

'You are, Jack, you are. I was going to tell you earlier, but it slipped my mind. Now that you know, I must insist that we play an American card game instead of this insipid whist thing. Poker. Poker's the game.'

'But I do not know how to play poker,' Jane replied.

'Nor I,' said Lavinia.

'In that case,' replied Jarrard, 'go and fetch your jewellery ladies, and any spare money you might have to hand.'

The pair of women stared at him, mystified.

'He's joking,' said Crossman. 'Poker is a game of chance. You wager on each hand and try to outwit your opponents by pretending to have a winning set of cards. Rupert here practises his poker expression in front of the mirror for hours on end. The idea is to give away nothing. If you have a tic, which I'm glad to say neither of you ladies has . . .'

'I should think not,' interrupted Jane.

'. . . then you will lose your fortunes.'

'Oh,' cried Lavinia, 'I love such games. I have been an actress, you know, in amateur productions. I shall be able to put on a face of stone. I may even curl my lip in contempt, to emulate the expression on the face of the Ozymandias statue. Mr Shelley's poem? There will be no need for me to practise for hours in front of mirrors like Mr Jarrard here.'

In the end, the game of poker was between Lavinia Durham and Rupert Jarrard, with Sergeant Crossman advising Lavinia, and Jane Mulinder simply watching and dropping in a comment now and again. During the game there was a sharp knock on the front door. Crossman whispered, 'Raise him two kingdoms and a republic, while I answer that.'

On opening the door, Crossman was confronted by the vision of Lieutenant Pirce-Smith in full uniform, headdress under his arm. Both men, unnerved, stared at each other in the lamplight with varying degrees of shock and confusion. It was Lavinia who broke the deadlock.

'Oh, Lieutenant Pirce-Smith, do come in.'

The officer automatically stepped inside, but then seemed anxious to leave immediately.

'I'm sorry,' he said, 'I had not realized – a gathering – it would not be right for me to stay – Sergeant Crossman is here.'

'You sound as if Sergeant Crossman is the enemy, lieutenant,' Lavinia said, rising to offer him her hand. 'Surely we are all on the same side?'

'Your servant, ma'am. Ah, thing is – you must be aware – officers and ranks – not allowed to socialize.'

'Yes, I know that, *officially*. But we're all friends here. No one is going to report you to – who is it, Major Lovelace? Why, Alexander even shares a room with Major Lovelace, so even if someone did say something it would all be simply air in the wind, so to speak.'

'Alexander?'

'That is to say, Jack, or to be more proper, Sergeant Crossman.'

Pirce-Smith looked utterly confused. 'I am completely at a loss, ma'am.'

'May I ask what you're doing here, sir?' asked Crossman. 'This is no longer General Enticknap's cottage.'

'Oh,' interrupted Jane, coming forward, 'it's my fault. I invited him. I knew he was in your group, Alexander, and we ran into one another in the Vanity Fair. Lieutenant Pirce-Smith was kind enough to assist me in haggling over the price of a leather purse. I felt sure it would be all right, so I asked the lieutenant if he would like to join us. Of course, I didn't say who the *us* was going to be, but here we all are.' She smiled bewitchingly, at each of the men in turn.

'You *will* stay, lieutenant?' asked Lavinia.

He seemed to grip his headgear more tightly. 'Well . . .'

'Of course he will,' cried Jarrard, placing an arm around the lieutenant's shoulders. 'This is my house, sir. You are welcome. Dismiss from your mind the fact that Sergeant Crossman is here.' Jarrard waved the hand with the cigar in it, expansively. 'Imagine, if you will, that he is somewhere out on the Crimean peninsula, hunting Russians.'

Crossman was thinking that would be very difficult for a man of Pirce-Smith's limited imagination. However, he was surprised when his lieutenant agreed to this compromise. When Crossman tried to speak to him later, though, Pirce-Smith ignored him and Jarrard, fumbling with some cards, said, 'You don't understand the situation, Jack. You are out somewhere on the steppes, while Lieutenant Pirce-Smith is here in this room. He cannot converse with you, nor you with him. The distance in miles is too great.'

'What?'

Pirce-Smith smiled. It seemed that it was he, Crossman, who had a restricted imagination after all. He gritted his teeth and, to the amusement of the two women, he fell in with the game.

'Here is a message on the telegraph, to you, Rupert. Will you please discover from Lieutenant Pirce-Smith where he has been these last few weeks?'

'To Sergeant Crossman,' Jarrard said, looking over the top of his cards. 'Your message received and understood. Stand to while I speak with the third party. Lieutenant, where have you been these last few weeks? I have an enquiry here from Sergeant Crossman, of the 88th Connaught Rangers. Fancy Jack, they call him, on account of the way he wears his socks.'

'You may inform Sergeant Crossman that I have been doing field work with Major Lovelace.'

Crossman was piqued to hear that Pirce-Smith had been out on a fox hunt with Lovelace. Lovelace had never taken *Crossman* out on a mission with just the two of them. It seemed that officers, after all, trusted only each other. Lovelace was grooming Pirce-Smith for higher things, while Crossman was being left behind. How irksome! Right at that moment Crossman wished he *were* out on the steppes, so that the others could not see his face, for he was sure it was registering his jealousy. He turned away in embarrassment and kept his face averted until the conversation amongst the others resumed normalcy. Finally, he stood up and said quietly, 'I can see my presence here is a problem. I do not much like being treated as if I were not in the room. Thank you, Lavinia and Cousin Jane, for your company this evening. Jarrard. I shall see you later? Lieutenant?' He came to attention and saluted Pirce-Smith, then walked to the door, opened it, and went out into the night. The air was cool on his face. Strangely he felt a sense of betrayal from his friends. It was Pirce-Smith who was the outsider, not he, and he did not quite like being the butt of the joke for the evening. He stood for a moment and listened for any laughter in his wake. Hearing none, he began to stride out towards Kadikoi, until he heard a soft call behind him.

'Alexander?'

It was Jane, tripping lightly through the mud. She caught up with him.

'You shouldn't have walked out like that. Everyone is feeling awful about you.'

'Good.'

'Now, that is not like you, to be so petty. The cousin I knew in England would not have been so silly.'

He was beginning to *feel* silly now.

'I'm sorry, Jane. I can't bear that fellow. He stands on the points of his collars all the time.'

'Oh, he's a bore, but there's no harm in him, Alexander. I'm sure he's feeling ghastly about you now.' She giggled. 'You can be a bit stuffy too, sometimes, you know. Remember the clocks? And he's such a young man, under that uniform, trying to do the right thing and not really knowing what that is in a given circumstance. I think he's just a little bit jealous of you.'

'Of me?' Crossman was genuinely surprised.

'Of course. You are so self-assured. You glow with confidence.

You are a man and he knows he is still a boy. The difference in your ranks makes it that much worse for him. Why, as an officer he feels he *should* know more than you, should be better at things than you, should have more experience of making decisions and judgements. Yet he finds that in all these things, he is your inferior. That must be irksome.'

'If it's true, it must.'

'Of course it's true. You are the master and he the apprentice, the novice, yet he feels it should be the other way around. Sometimes he must all but choke under his stock when he sees how you do the right thing with consummate ease, while he has to agonize over such decisions.'

'He doesn't strike me in that way. He seems unwilling to learn and refuses to take advice.'

'Oh, he's taking it, but he must not let you see that he's taking it.'

Crossman sighed. 'I suppose that makes sense, somehow. Jane, may I ask you a very personal question?' He turned to face her and noticed that her skin was shining in the moonlight. Behind them were the ships, bobbing in the harbour, a forest of masts above them. Lamps were swinging in the breeze, shooting beams across the surface of the black water.

'If you must.'

'Why did you come to the Crimea?'

'Because you told me of the flowers, sun and sky, and the deep blue of the waters.'

'You are bamming me! You surely didn't believe all that? It was meant to be light-hearted banter.'

She laughed. 'Yes, I am making fun of you. Alex, after your letter I felt the most irresistible urge to come and see for myself. There was little to keep me in England, and I . . .'

Crossman's face clouded over as he interrupted sharply with, 'What was his name?'

'Who?' she attempted to keep it light, but in vain.

'You know who I mean. Some fellow asked for your hand, didn't he? Then what did he do? Cry off? I can see it in your eyes. No, no, don't weep, Jane. Oh, Lord, I never know what to do with you when you weep. You must tell me his name. I'll seek him out and . . .'

'No, you must not,' she said, drying her tears. 'That would make it worse. He's gone and that's that. Besides I'm not telling you his name and I forbid you to try to discover it. Those were tears of anger, by the way, not of self-pity. Let us speak no more of it. I wish to forget the whole episode. If you want a reason for me being here, it is to help. Despite the description of the Crimea in your letter to me – you made it sound like some Mediterranean paradise – I was aware through the articles in *The Times* that it was no heaven. I was particularly upset by the reports that so many men were dying of disease. I wanted to help and indeed am spending my days here, as well as some of my nights, nursing young soldiers with bewildered eyes. You see the frivolous side of me, I'm afraid, when I take a little time away from it all, but without that I think I should die of heartache.'

He nodded. 'Or of fatigue. Cholera and dysentery have taken their toll – we lost a man a short while ago – a soldier named Kelly. One moment he was laughing and joking with this comrades, three hours later he was dead. A tough man, too. One of your rugged Irishmen, who could out-drink and out-punch any soldier who cared to take him on. He went out like an old man, with withered yellow skin, his breath so shallow it wouldn't have stirred a dead leaf. I believe he was twenty-two years of age.'

'So young.'

'Young – and still, as you say, bewildered.'

She changed the subject. 'I wonder how Lavinia is doing, entertaining those two handsome men? She has so many admirers here. But then she is exceptionally pretty. I wonder you let her get away, Alex.'

'Yes, I did, didn't I? But, you know, for all her loveliness I prefer the company of someone like you.'

She took his arm for a moment. 'Now why is that?'

'Well, you are a little more serious about life than Lavinia Durham. You do not turn everything into merriment. You do not ride Hell for leather looking for a skirmish the moment a cannon goes off. You have an air about you, which is more queenly than coquettish princess. And your beauty is not to be thrown away, my dear. You could stand with the best.'

She laughed again. 'Cousin Alex, you have a way of putting things which lifts my spirit.'

'I hope so.'

She was quiet for a moment, before saying, 'I spoke with your father the other day. In fact I see him most days, of course, he being my pretend uncle. He urged me to go home.'

'We do not agree on much, but I think that is one piece of advice which is very sound.'

'He also told me not to have anything to do with you. I refused of course, which made him cross. In the end he lost his temper with me a little and stormed away. I think he went sea fishing.'

'Sea fishing?'

'It's a new pastime with him.'

'Good Lord. What will he do next? He's the most boorish man I know, yet he still has the ability to astound me. A boor but not a bore.'

'It's a shame Cousin James has gone home. I think he could have helped you with your father.'

'James, bless his heart, is *terrified* of the old man, as am I at times. I think James is better off at home. Father will soon get tired of dogging my footsteps. I expect he'll be on his way home himself soon.'

The sound of boots on stone came out of the night and Yorwarth appeared in the light of a lantern hanging from a storehouse. His jaw was bandaged up, having been rebroken and reset by the surgeons. It must have been painful for him to speak.

'Sergeant? Sorry to disturb you, sergeant.'

'What is it, Yorwarth?'

'Beggin' the sergeant's pardon,' Yorwarth was being overly polite with a lady present, 'but our battalion's going into battle tomorrow, with some other regiments – but all to be led by our own Colonel Horatio Shirley. Some of us will go at the Quarries. Some of us at the trenches and rifle pits. We're to be the Right Attack, I understand, going at the Quarries. That is, a lieutenant has said so – the officer who sent the message. The same lieutenant who asked us to silence the clocktower.'

'Colonel Shirley's in command, but who's our officer, the officer leading the actual attack?'

Yorwarth's brow furrowed. 'Oh, I don't – wait – yes, I do

remember now. I heard it was to be Lieutenant-Colonel Campbell, of the 90th.'

Crossman nodded in approval. 'A good man. A good officer. And the French?'

'They're going to go at the Mamelon.'

'At last,' breathed Crossman, bunching his fist, 'we're going to attack at last. Thank you, Yorwarth. I'll join you and the others in a minute.'

Yorwarth left.

Jane gripped Crossman's arm. 'You don't have to go with them, do you, Alex? I mean, you're on special duties.'

'It's my own regiment, Jane. You heard. The attack is being commanded by my own colonel. The 88th will be leading.'

'But you don't *need* to go,' she insisted.

He peeled her fingers from his sleeve. 'You don't understand, do you? The Rangers are going into battle. I *have* to be with them. Yorwarth has to be with them, even though his jaw is still not yet set. And Peterson. And even Wynter. When that battle is depicted on our colours, in the future, I have to be able to say *I was there*. It is unthinkable that I am here and do not take part in a battle led by my own battalion's commander. Unthinkable.'

'You're right,' she said. 'I really don't understand. But I want you to promise me something.'

'Of course, if it's in my power.'

Her jaw tightened. 'Do not try to be a hero, Alex.'

'Jane, you don't understand why I have to take part in that battle tomorrow, and you certainly don't understand how I shall conduct myself while I am in it. When the air is full of whining pieces of hot metal, the last thing I shall be thinking about is heroic action. Survival is what will be foremost in my mind. There will be the object in front of me, the Quarries, and I shall be running for it, but when I reach it my mind will have flown somewhere else, like a black crow released from a trap, and I shall fall with great relief in a heap and thank my God he has held my hand.'

'You fill me with terror.'

'It's what we're here for, Jane. Nothing else. I don't mean to frighten you. I'm merely trying to say that when the fighting starts I am no giant.' He kissed her cheek. 'But don't worry, I have the utmost confidence in myself. I am getting remarkably quick at dodging cannon balls, and I'm rather too thin to be hit by a musket ball, so there you are. I shall be back to play another game of poker, with you, Lavinia and Rupert before nightfall.'

She placed a slim pale hand on his arm and looked intensely into his face. 'Please, please do that,' she whispered. Then in a normal voice, 'We are no longer children, Alex, which is a pity in some ways. In those days we could express our feelings freely. Any silly thing said then would be forgotten in an hour and we would be friends again. Now we are constrained by adult conventions and mores – and – and other things.'

'Like opening ourselves to wounds.'

'Something like that.'

'I understand,' he replied, tenderly. 'Believe me, I shall do nothing heroic. I have every desire to stay alive, Jane.'

He then escorted her back to the cottage and went in briefly to tell Lieutenant Pirce-Smith of the coming scrap. The lieutenant's reaction to the news was much the same as that of Crossman. If anything he was little more excited. Crossman could see Jane shaking her head. Then he left and went back to the hovel where his men were ready to take a tot with him.

He was eager to know the details.

'Who's going?' he asked. 'How many.'

Peterson, excited, replied, 'Of the 88th? One hundred men, we're told. And another hundred from the 7th Fusiliers along with two hundred from the 49th, but we'll be leading the charge, won't we, sergeant? The 88th will be at the front.'

'They will if Colonel Shirley is the acting general officer, I'm damn sure of that!' Crossman said.

'That's what I thought,' cried Peterson, unable to contain the exhilaration, which was mingled with a large dose of fear. Like the others, she wanted to be there, *had* to be there, but at the same time was dreading the charge. Storming a position, any position, like the Quarries was a frightening prospect. 'That's what I told Wynter, isn't it, Wynter?'

'That's what you told me,' muttered Wynter, somehow managing to look both awed and bored.

'So,' said Crossman, wistfully, as he broke open a bottle. 'Only a hundred of us?'

'And another hundred with the attack on the rifle pits,' Yorwarth explained. 'That's two hundred.'

'Well, we've lost most of the battalion since we left England,' said Crossman, 'so it's not surprising there's so few left, is it? Listen men, you remember when we were out after the deserters. It was winter and the land was barren then. I heard an officer who was out riding today say that the Balaclava valleys are now covered in long grass, and that wild flowers fill the place in great swathes of colour. I want you to remember that. I'll take you there after the battle, and show you something to live for.'

At that moment Major Lovelace entered the room and all went quiet.

'What's this?' he asked, pointing at the bottle. 'A party?'

'We're going into battle tomorrow, sir,' said the still excited Peterson. 'A grand charge!'

Lovelace, dressed in a fur-lined shell-jacket worn over a tweed coat, revolver on one side and field glass on the other, nodded. His face, under his forage cap, was expressionless as he said, 'I wish you all good luck, gentlemen.' Then he left the room and climbed the stairs to his bed.

'Did you hear that?' Wynter said. 'He called us gentlemen.'

Crossman poured the rum into such containers as there were and raised his glass, saying gravely, 'To the 88th!'

'To the 88th!' they cried, and downed the fiery drink in one.

10

On the 6th of June, 1855, just as the clock struck three in the afternoon, over 500 allied guns suddenly exploded into action, filling the air with metal missiles. Around 400 men taken from the Light and 2nd Divisions, commanded by Colonel Shirley of the 88th Connaught Rangers, were waiting in the wings ready to storm an area of diggings which the British called the Quarries. Crossman was there with them, as was Wynter, Yorwarth and Peterson. The Quarries were heavily defended, being an ideal place from which sharpshooters could operate, picking off allied soldiers when they showed themselves above the trenches. Capturing the Quarries would put the allies one step closer to the seizure of Sebastopol.

The hail of metal fell with murderous effect on the Russian positions. Great clouds of sharp-smelling smoke began to billow across no-man's-land, obscuring the vision of the soldiers waiting to charge. Crossman knew that they would not go up until the French had assaulted the Mamelon, which overlooked the Quarries, or any taking of the latter would be futile. With the Mamelon still in Russian hands the Quarries, even if captured, could not be held. Crossman waited in vain for the bombardment to cease, so that the French could attack, but it seemed the gunners had been told to give the Russians a real pounding.

The thunder of the guns continued up until twilight, when the shells could be seen bursting against a reddened sky. Then when darkness came, the guns fell silent, and only the mortars continued to be pumped up into the heavens. Their trajectories could be plainly followed, as the mortar shells left a trail of sparks across the night sky. When they eventually fell to earth, on or over the Russian defences, a brilliant flash accompanied their explosion. It might have been beautiful, if it were not so deadly and high, terrified screams sometimes followed immediately in the wake of an explosion.

After one such blast Crossman could hear a Russian soldier screaming to his comrades that he had been hit – that there was a jagged hole in his chest – and to help him, help him, please help him. The man's terrified yelling continued for quite a while, punctuated by several more mortar explosions, until finally the wounded soldier fell silent.

Curses and oaths came floating across the night from those receiving the shower of deadly metal. These meant little to most British soldiers, but Crossman understood them and in a way he could sympathize with the callers. Hell's rain was falling on them and naturally they believed that it came from those who were in partnership with the Devil. Their priests had told them as much.

'How long are we goin' to wait here?' whispered Wynter, whose legs were shaking. 'Better to get it over and done.'

'The French won't attack in the dark,' replied Crossman. 'I'd settle down for the night. Nothing will happen before dawn.'

'I hate waiting,' grumbled Peterson.

Crossman said, 'There isn't a soldier alive who doesn't, and perhaps some of the dead are not too keen on it. Here, take one of these blankets each. Wrap up warm. You don't want your muscles to stiffen up.'

'So long as we don't get the cramp when we die tomorrow,' said a man next to Wynter. 'Cramp is a painful business.'

Someone brought some hot soup along the line. They sipped it, listening to the clatter and clink of the French not far away. They would have the worst of it. The Russians weren't going to let go of the Mamelon easily. It was too valuable to them. Both positions – the Quarries and the Mamelon – were stepping stones towards the vastly more important Malakoff and the Redan. Once these latter two fell, Sebastopol would fall. It all depended on the French attack now.

'I hear tell there's mines out there,' said the same soldier who had attempted humour with Wynter. 'The ground's bin planted with nice neat rows of *fougasses* – 'cept they're not so neat, really. I had a friend who lost his leg to one of those things. Blew it right up into the air. We all saw it spinning, before it came down boot first and gave a little sideways hop, as if it was tryin' to stand again without the help of the man what owned it.'

'Thank you for that bit o' knowledge,' replied Wynter, sarcastically. 'I'll be able to sleep the better for it.'

'Just thought you ought to know, see. There's dozens of 'em, maybe hundreds. The Russ is quite liberal with his fougasse.'

'You finished?'

The soldier shrugged and turned away to talk to his companion on the other side.

They tried to sleep, but it was virtually impossible. All that Crossman could manage was a doze every now and then. When grey morning came, the guns began again. This time it was not so intense. As the day wore on spectators began to gather on the Heights: civilians, families and other camp followers. Everyone knew, including the Russians, that an attack was about to take place. It merely remained to discover how great. While the Rifle Brigade band played some light music for the entertainment of the spectators and military observers, Crossman and the rest of the stormers were moved forward, into a trench closer to the battleground. To their right four brigades of French soldiers prepared to charge the Mamelon, just over a quarter of a mile from their most forward position. Crossman was amused to see the French soldiers tossing away empty wine bottles, having fortified themselves with their national drink for the coming ordeal.

Peterson was not so impressed. 'Huh!' she said. 'Can't they go into battle without getting drunk?'

Crossman smiled. 'The French do love their wine. It's not really the need for false courage. Even last night they looked as keen as foxes ready to go after prey. They just love the grape, that's all.'

Once again the guns began their loud crashing cacophony with much more earnestness than earlier in the day. Crossman knew this was the prelude to the attack. Sure enough, a quarter of an hour later the guns stopped suddenly and a cheering and yelling came from the French as their colonel jumped from the banquette and ran towards the Mamelon, followed by a horde of scrambling eager blue soldiers.

The bugles and drums sounded as the French swarmed over the ground to the walls of the Mamelon. Their colonel was killed in that first rush. Up and over the walls went the brave French. Not long after, the French flag flapped from the battlements and cheers went through the spectators on the mounts.

Having taken the fortification, some of the Zouaves continued on in a eager rush towards the Malakoff itself.

Damn fools, thought Crossman. They should have dug in. Now they had crazily let their feeling of triumph overwhelm them. Having overrun the Mamelon they had lost their heads and were chasing the retreating Russians to a much stronger, better defended and more fortified position. It was an old mistake. One of the oldest. To believe that because the first obstacle had been surmounted, the second would be just as easy. The Zouaves had let their hearts rule their heads. Flush with the first victory, they thirsted for more, and Crossman shook his head in disappointment for them.

They're all going to die, he told himself.

At the much more heavily-defended Malakoff the over-zealous Zouaves were repulsed with great force, and were now driven back towards the Mamelon. Now the Russians were flush with victory. They had the French on the run. They stormed the Mamelon, retook it from French hands, and drove the blue soldiers back to their own trenches.

'My God,' said Wynter, disgustedly, 'the Frogs held that for a good few seconds, didn't they.'

'Look,' Yorwarth replied, 'there's a counter-attack.'

They watched enthralled as French reserves surged forwards, but they were not permitted spectator status any longer. The order was given to the British to charge the Quarries. 'Come on lads,' said Crossman, a hard lump in his throat, 'time to go . . .' He climbed out of the trench himself and began his stumbling run towards the objective. The air was humming with metal birds which darted through tufts of dry grass and flew singing from stones and rocks. Just in front of him an unfortunate lance-corporal stepped on a fougasse which blew up between his legs.

The man spun, his eyes bugging and he clutched at his genitals, before dropping like a felled tree at the feet of Crossman, where he lay twitching and jerking. Crossman stared appalled at the fellow's distress. Then he felt a hard thump in the back from someone behind him, urging him on, and he stepped over the body.

As he had predicted, when speaking with Jane, the terror welled up within him like hot lava which threatened to smother his reason. His mind was ragged and frayed and he felt he was staggering through a horrible dream. In the flashes and smoke the ground took on a dirty yellow hue, which removed him somehow from reality. He wanted to get out of there, find a cool green spot under a tree, by a stream, and regain his sanity. If he could just have time to collect his wits, gather his senses and calm himself, he felt he could fight with more conviction.

He resisted the urge to turn round with all his strength of will, keeping his feet treading one after the other in a straight line. Blinding lights flickered and zigzagged in his racing brain. The air became hot, and the biting smoke from rifle and gun stung his eyes and took the lining off his mouth. The membranes of his nostrils burned. He was walking through the hazardous sulphur fires of Hell and he knew if he lost his footing he would perish in them, never to rise again.

Crossman suddenly became aware that Wynter had fired his Minié just over his right shoulder. He stopped himself, aimed, and squeezed the trigger. Nothing happened. He realized he must have already fired the weapon somewhere along the charge. It took him twenty seconds to reload, fire again, and once more he ran through the hot air, still filled with bits of singing metal. Around his feet the stones danced, occasionally splitting in two as a musket ball struck them squarely. Once something flicked at his cap, like a lead wasp passing through. On, on he went, time stretching, his body obeying the commands of his brain reluctantly.

Until now, Crossman, like his comrades, had simply been treading in the footsteps of the officers. Those brave souls at the front, some of them mere boys, turned occasionally, waved a sword, and encouraged the rank and file to follow. Crossman now noticed another wave of British soldiers coming in from a different angle. He suddenly realized his group was not assaulting the Quarries directly, from the front, but was the left hook of a pincer movement. In fact they were attacking the flanks of the Mamelon: two equal forces from two sides. In this way they had managed to skirt the very edges of the minefields, losing the minimum of men to the field of fougasses. His heart filled a little, as the Quarries suddenly seemed a reachable objective. He was nearly there! How long had it been? A minute? An hour? An eternity?

With musket balls still zinging through the air, the two groups of attackers stormed the Quarries. They overwhelmed the Russians, rolled on and over them, driving them back. Crossman was exhilarated by a feeling of victory. He began to feel himself invulnerable, invincible. He had survived the charge! Surely then he would survive the day, whatever happened? A great joy washed through him. All the terror left him to be replaced by a rapidly swelling arrogance: a contempt for the weapons of the enemy and for that which issued forth. The words of a hymn came to him clearly: *Immortal, invisible, God only wise.*

He felt like God at that moment, as he and his comrades did exactly what they had severely criticized the French Zouaves for doing just a few minutes before: they continued on, towards the next objective. In their case this was the mighty Redan, which was as strongly fortified as the Malakoff, which those foolish French soldiers had tried to take.

A struck pebble hit him just below the knee and caused him to wince in pain. Just in time, Crossman remembered he was not God. He was not even an angel. He was a mere man, with mortal flesh. The wound was not bad, but it was enough to remind him that he could be killed at any moment. A British officer was shot to death a moment later, just under the walls of the Redan. Seeing this, Crossman sobered. He suddenly asked himself what he was doing out there, when the objective had been the Quarries. Wheeling about he would have returned to the Quarries where he was supposed to be. At that moment he heard the order to lie down and fire on the Redan's embrasures. He did so, alongside many other British soldiers, while from behind him came the sound of a distant cheer and bugles signalling an advance. A second charge was taking place from the British lines.

Of course, he now recalled, *our own reinforcements are coming up behind us. The 62nd are coming.* The 62nd would consolidate the attack. Now the job was to allow them time to do it. Like those lying with him, he continued to pin down the Russian gunners with accurate fire, until finally ordered to retreat back to the Quarries. There they settled in with quiet pride, knowing they had completed their task. Men lay dead or wounded between the Quarries and the allied trenches, some of them Russians, many of them British. Crossman suddenly thought about his own men.

After a quick search, he found Wynter, Peterson and Yorwarth, all intact. They had all made it through. Flushed with success, and pride in themselves and the regiment, they just had time to share a cup of coffee between them, handed to them by a small drummer boy whose expression was a mixture of simple joy and anxiousness to please.

It was not over. The French held the Mamelon. The British held the Quarries. But the Russians were not going to lie down. Their counter-attacks began a short while later. The enemy came on again and fought desperately to regain their lost positions. Now it was the turn of the British in the Quarries to suffer the deadly showers of scalding rain. All night long it fell, pausing only for Russian ground attacks to take place.

In those pauses a many-throated animal rolled across the rough ground as a great grey wave in the half-light. It was a bristling gigantic beast with spines of steel. On either side of this huge shrieking monster were masters with sticks, driving it on, goading it to rush at the defenders of the Quarries. Each time it was driven back, leaving some of its scales lying on the ground. After the great beast had recoiled, and finally retreated back to its lair, those scales once more became men: soldiers from a different army, with different masters. Men who would never again see home.

In the Quarries there were other men, as desperate to hold on to what they had seized as those who tried to regain it. They moved backwards and forwards between utter exhaustion and frantic activity. The night made unimaginable what would have been terrible enough during daylight. Men drifted in and out of madness. Men needed to be frenzied and fever-brained to stay on this side of death. They fired their weapons until the barrels were so hot the powder cooked and burned before it was rammed down. They fired blindly, crazily, until their pouches were empty of cartridges.

And when their ammunition was gone they fought with fists and working tools. They threw rocks and bottles and foul curses into the faces of the enemy. They grappled with them, bit them, punched them, kicked them, drove them back time and time again. Having gained this stronghold, Crossman and his comrades were not going to let it go. They became primitive savages, almost animals, in that long night: snarling and growling, tearing at the clothes and bodies of enemy soldiers in the dark, pulling hair out from its roots, smashing down with rifle butts and boots on flesh and bone. And when they were not fighting they were digging, hot tears of tiredness mingling with the sweat that ran down their dirty faces as they scooped up dirt and stones with their bare hands to plug holes in the defences, listening with one ear, waiting for that screeching and shrieking from the Russians which preceded another assault.

At one relatively quiet point many of the British defenders of the Quarries fell fast asleep from sheer fatigue, dropping where they stood. But then a crucial moment arrived in the battle and a captain and a colonel climbed the makeshift wall together, and urged the men to rise and meet a new enemy attack. They came out of their deep slumber to fire musket and pistol haphazardly into a howling wave of Russians out in the night. Once again they used every resource to hand, especially their voices, with which they damned the enemy and dared them to advance. Light began to crawl up the sky from the east. The day was dawning on these men from the villages, towns, and cities; from the country shires of Great Britain and Ireland; from highlands, lowlands and islands; from valleys and downs; from estuaries and flatlands and wooded vales; from ridges and fells and river banks and marshes and coves.

And when morning finally came these exhausted shadows of what had once been strong bold men were still holding the Quarries.